ZEBEDIAH

ZEBEDIAH

❖

Patrick J. Simons

Copyright © 2013 by Patrick J. Simons.

Library of Congress Control Number: 2013905481
ISBN: Hardcover   978-1-4836-1613-1
              Softcover   978-1-4836-1612-4
              Ebook   978-1-4836-1614-8

All rights reserved. No part of this book may be reproduced or transmitted in any form or by any means, electronic or mechanical, including photocopying, recording, or by any information storage and retrieval system, without permission in writing from the copyright owner.

This is a work of fiction. Names, characters, places and incidents either are the product of the author's imagination or are used fictitiously, and any resemblance to any actual persons, living or dead, events, or locales is entirely coincidental.

Cover illustration by Sharron Looney

This book was printed in the United States of America.

Rev. date: 04/17/2013

To order additional copies of this book, contact:
Xlibris Corporation
1-888-795-4274
www.Xlibris.com
Orders@Xlibris.com
129373

Contents

Chapter One: Childhood 7
Chapter Two: Going To Town 38
Chapter Three: The Cattle Drive 58
Chapter Four: Leaving Home 86
Chapter Five: Bonebright 110
Chapter Six: Bender 127
Chapter Seven: Goodwin 154
Chapter Eight: Nawlins 179
Chapter Nine: "D" 202
Chapter Ten: The Road to Keller 227
Chapter Eleven: Life in Keller 249
Chapter Twelve: The Crucible 266
Chapter Thirteen: Resolution 292

Chapter One

Childhood

Zebediah could not remember with certainty just how long he had been in the jail cell. Was it two nights, or was it three? His time in jail was a pain-wracked, semiconscious web of confusion, made worse by eyes that were nearly swollen shut. The only thing he did remember with any clarity was being awakened by some unseen person and then being urged up and out of the cell. He remembered struggling to see through swollen slits until finally realizing his cell door was standing open. Zebediah remembered being helped out of the cell and just making out the sheriff's unconscious body sprawled in the adjoining cell before the light was extinguished. Was there someone helping him walk? He must have had help. He could not remember. Someone had to have unlocked the door. Did someone give him a ride? He thought that, perhaps, someone had given him a ride. That must have been it. His mind could not stay focused long enough to make sense of anything.

Zebediah now placed one aching foot in front of the other. His body screamed in protest with every trembling step, but on he went. He was leaving behind the nearest thing to a home he had known in a very long time, battered, bruised, and bloodied. It would be daylight soon, and he must find a place to hide. A place well away from the road. A place where he could rest undisturbed. Every shred of his natural optimism had been stripped away one painful layer at a time. Other men might be grateful for the gift of life itself, but the man struggling down the road no longer saw life as a blessing or even desirable.

The birds were beginning their predawn chorus when Zebediah reached a small country crossroad. In the distance on the intersecting road, he could just make out a small bridge spanning a ravine. Zebediah took a careful look around, then began hobbling toward the bridge. When he reached the bridge, Zebediah could find no pathway leading down to the water. He knew, from his years spent on the bum, that this was a good thing. No path meant people did not often visit this place. If he carefully hid his trail, there existed the possibility of shelter. Not the safest of shelters certainly, but far better than being in the open and exposed.

Zebediah painfully eased his way down the rocky incline. There were dense weeds growing between the rough stones piled against the bridge abutment. He took one careful step then paused to rearrange the foliage, and then he took another. When he at last gained the creek bed, he realized the ravine was somewhat deeper than it had appeared from above. Zebediah walked in the water to avoid leaving foot prints. The water was surprisingly cold, and it offered his aching, bloodied feet a bit of relief. Once under the bridge, he was pleased to find the creek bank mostly free of plant growth and sandy. A man could make a decent bed in the sand.

Sinking wearily to the ground, Zebediah resisted the urge to sleep and instead began to strip off his torn and bloody clothing. Once undressed, he eased himself into the cool water and began washing himself. He knew that he had been badly beaten, but not until he saw his reflection did he realize the full extent of his injuries. His eyes were swollen and discolored, and his already prominent lips were nearly twice their normal size. Someone, a doctor maybe, had bandaged the worst of his injuries, but the bandages were now caked with dried blood. He raised his hand and cautiously touched his right ear and felt the sutures. If it had been bandaged, then the bandage was now missing. Zebediah remained sitting in the water for a long time, cleaning his wounds and letting the cool water wash some of the pain away.

The cool water revived Zebediah to a degree, and though he was dreadfully tired, he set about the task of cleaning his clothes. He wished he had a needle and thread so he could at least try and make some repairs. It was daylight now, and the earth was fully alive. Zebediah was startled into motionless silence by the sound of horses and a wagon approaching. The heavy plodding sound of the hooves told Zebediah that draft horses were passing above him and not a sheriff's posse. It was probably just a farmer going about his business. Zebediah sat motionless in the deep, cool shadow of the bridge and did not move until the sounds of the team and wagon had completely vanished. His old survival skills were returning like an animal's instinct to protect its young. Skills he once dared hope he would never again need to employ. A true home, it seemed, was something Zebediah was never destined to know.

Zebediah wished he could lay his clothing in the sun to dry but knew that would be a foolish risk. It didn't look as if many people used this little bridge, but it would only take one person to destroy what remained of his existence. After wringing out his clothes, Zebediah redressed then smoothed out a place in the sand to sleep. Another thing he knew from an earlier life was that the sand would easily brush off once his clothes were dry. Zebediah made himself as comfortable as he could, and slowly, his weariness overcame his pain, and he began slipping in and out of a tormented sleep. His dreams were haunted by the recurring vision of his door bursting open and then being set upon and beaten into unconsciousness.

Suddenly, Zebediah was startled fully awake. During that initial moment, he thought his fitful sleep must have lasted all day, for it was now quite dark. Was it a gunshot that woke him? Were his pursuers at hand? And then, another loud report and Zebediah realized it was not gunfire but thunder, and it was nearer midday than evening. Rain was beginning to fall, and the sky was filled with lightning. In a matter of minutes, the air temperature dropped several degrees. Zebediah began to shiver in his damp clothing. The wind was now blowing very hard, and for a few terrible minutes, it came straight down the ravine, painfully driving the sand into his wounds. Zebediah huddled close to the abutment. He turned his face to the planking and drew his knees up to his chin. Being under a bridge in a thunderstorm was only a little better than being caught in the open. It was not until the wind direction shifted that the bridge gave him any real shelter.

How long he huddled there he could not say, as the storm continued to build.

In a moment of clarity, it occurred to Zebediah that the storm might at least slow down the posse that was sure to be looking for him. He allowed himself the weak hope that the sheriff and his men would simply give him up for dead and go home, though he did not think that likely. When the storm's fury eased at last, Zebediah ventured a careful look up and out of the gully. Right at the edge of the ravine, he saw corn growing and became instantly aware of his hunger. The skies were still very dark, and the storm did not appear to be over. Zebediah carefully tested the rocks on the far side of the abutment and began making his way painfully back up the steep slope.

Looking behind him, Zebediah realized, to his horror, his feet were leaving a blood trail on the rocks. Had the water loosened his scabs? Had he been leaving a blood trail all along and simply not noticed it? His bloody footprints would be easily visible to anyone standing on the bridge. Yet his hunger outweighed his fear and drove him forward. When he was able to peer above the roadway, Zebediah could see no one on the roads in any direction, but he did not trust his eyesight. He cautiously made his way into the corn patch. It was, almost certainly, field corn being grown for animals, but Zebediah knew it could be eaten if it wasn't too mature. He was in no position to be choosy, and he quickly selected a half-dozen ears, taking care not to pick them all in one spot. Zebediah walked a few paces out onto the bridge and tossed the ears of corn to the sand below. The roadway was muddy, and he knew leaving tracks was the worst thing he could do. As he made his retreat, Zebediah smoothed over his footprints and did his best to hide his trail.

He needn't have worried, for he had no more than regained the semishelter of the creek bed when the skies erupted with a new barrage of wind, rain, and lightning. He was at least grateful that any trace of his visit to the cornfield was being washed away. Zebediah set to work, peeling the first ear of corn, and his spirits were not buoyed by what he found. The kernels were beginning to dent, and the corn was well past the point a person would normally find it edible. The burning cinder in his belly drove him to attempt it anyway. Zebediah broke a few kernels loose and put them in his mouth. As carefully as he could, he began slowly grinding the corn between his molars, his painful teeth and jaw protesting every movement. It took Zebediah the better part of an hour to eat the first ear, but he was beginning to feel a bit stronger for it. Then, he made the fearful discovery that the creek was beginning to rise.

He was sitting in the uppermost portion of the sloping ground beneath the bridge, leaning his back against the heavily tarred planking of the abutment. Zebediah judged that the water would have to rise at least three feet before it would drive him out of the ravine. He had no idea how much rain that might take, but this did not appear to be an ordinary storm. Drawing his knees up against his chest, he did his best to stay warm and began eating the second ear of corn. Lightning flashed, and for a moment, the pitch-black sky was as bright as day. Thunder burst in deafening crescendos, and the wind rose to a constant shriek. Huddled beneath the bridge, Zebediah once thought he saw a coyote or, perhaps, a wolf briefly illuminated by lightning flash. Overwhelmed by the misery of the situation, Zebediah found himself struggling against the idea of simply committing himself to the creek and being done with it all.

The storm continued throughout the day and into the night, or at least he thought it did. Zebediah's mind seemed to be pitching back and forth between reality and a demented dreaming state. It was fully dark by the time the howling winds began to abate. It was so dark

Zebediah could not now see the water, but he could hear it inching closer. He stretched out his aching body when he could no longer endure being in a cramp, only to be forced back into a crouch by the need to conserve warmth. At last, Zebediah's weariness overcame the storm and the pain. He slipped back into a fitful sleep, and he began to dream. All through the cold, windy night that might not have been a night, Zebediah drifted in and out of the dream state, lost in time and space, neither fully awake or asleep. As the sounds of the storm receded into the distance, Zebediah found that he was once again a small boy, and his mother was calling.

* * *

"Zebediah! Where you at, boy?"
"I'm here, Mama, I's comin'."
"Bout damn time! Where you been anyway?"
"Jus' out in the yard, playin'."
"Whut the hell you do that fo'? You ain't old enough to be doin' that kinda' stuff by yo'self!"
"I's sorry, Mama."

His mother was a large woman who seemed permanently angry at Zebediah, forever displeased with everything her young son did. She took two quick steps across the room and delivered a powerful slap to the back of Zebediah's head that sent him sprawling. Zebediah did his best not to cry, knowing that crying would only increase her anger. He bit his lip and fought against the tears that would not stop.

"You cryin', boy? Huh?" asked his mother, the pitch of her voice rising with every word. "You wanna cry? I'll damn well give you somethin' to cry about! You jus' shut yo' damn mouth."

Zebediah crawled quickly behind the old stuffed chair and fought against the tears. He stayed hidden until he thought the redness had left his eyes before daring to venture out. Doing his best to act as if nothing had happened, Zebediah approached his mother and asked, as cheerfully as he could, "Whatcha cookin', Mama?"

"Ain't cookin' nothin' for you," said Mayellen haughtily. She continued at the stove a moment before looking down at the puzzled little boy and saying, "You done sassed me, Zebediah, and if you gonna sass, you ain't gonna eat."

Zebediah began to protest that he had not sassed his mother, but she cut him off before the words could pass his lips. "You lookin' for another slap, Zebediah? Huh? Maybe I need to get the strap?"

"I's sorry, Mama."

"Sorry don't feed the chickens," said Mayellen, barely able to contain her anger.

"But I's hungry, Mama."

"Well, you damn sure should a' thought a' that before you sassed yo' mama," said Mayellen, her voice quaking. "You jus' get yo' sorry ass to bed right now, and if I hear a peep outa' you, I gonna beat yo' ass bloody."

Zebediah hurried to the closet where he slept. He took off his overalls and crawled into the mean little pallet that was his bed. His bed, such as it was, had no sheets, no pillow, and no mattress. His rolled-up overalls served as his pillow. He slept on one-half of an old and not-very-clean quilt with the other half pulled over him. Burying his face between the quilt and his trousers, Zebediah sobbed quietly and tried to ignore the burning hunger in his belly. He sobbed until he could sob no more and sleep took him at last. His dreams were the dreams of a small boy who had never known love or kindness. Zebediah thought he must be a very bad boy to constantly displease his mother the way he did. He desperately hoped that one day he would find a way to make her happy so she might love him.

He was startled awake when Mayellen delivered a kick to his pallet. "Git up, boy."

Before the sleepy Zebediah could make sense of what was happening, his mother delivered another harder kick, while tearing the quilt away and yelling, "I said get yo' ass *up!*"

Zebediah stood up and trembled as he pulled his overalls on. "I needs to use the privy, Mama."

"Then git to doin' it, and hurry up with it," barked his mother.

Zebediah hurried to the outhouse, puzzled because it was still dark. His mother never rose before dawn. When he returned to the house, shivering from the predawn chill, he found a bowl of grits waiting for him.

His mother ordered him to "Sit down and git' to eatin'."

His hunger flamed anew, and Zebediah wasted no time attacking the food before him. Zebediah was surprised to find that his mother had given him a bit more than the meager portion he was used to. While he ate, his mother returned and tossed a ragged carpetbag at his feet. "You hurry up and finish eatin', and when yo' done, you put yo' quilt and the rest of yo' stuff in this bag."

Zebediah was puzzled by this order and dared ask, "Why, Mama?"

"You sassin' me again? You lookin' to git yo' ass beat?" Mayellen's ample bosom heaved as if she was out of breath.

Zebediah ate the last bite of breakfast then picked up the carpet bag and retreated to his closet. The quilt was stiff with age, and Zebediah struggled to force it into the bag. He was still struggling with the quilt when Mayellen reappeared yelling, "Good God, boy! What the hell takin' you so long?" Grabbing the bag away from his small hands, Mayellen quickly stuffed the ragged quilt into the bag. "Now git the rest o' yo' stuff."

The rest of Zebediah's stuff consisted of two pairs of underwear and one extra shirt. He had never owned shoes or socks.

"Grab that bag now, boy! We goin'."

"Where we goin', Mama?"

"Never you mind where we goin', you jus git a move on."

Zebediah followed his mother out the door and down the lane. The sun had not yet risen and the air was still cold. Mayellen was striding down the lane, and Zebediah, burdened by the carpetbag, struggled to keep up. When he fell several paces behind his mother, Mayellen turned back to him and said angrily, "Damn it, boy! Hurry yo' ass *up*!"

"I's tryin', Mama," pleaded Zebediah, fighting back tears.

"You's nothin' but worthless, boy! Now I gots to carry yo' damn bag for ya when I already got my own stuff to carry." Mayellen roughly jerked the bag away from Zebediah then resumed her march down the lane. Even after being freed from his heavy load, Zebediah had to, periodically, run a few steps to keep pace with his mother. When they reached the end of the lane, Mayellen abruptly halted. "We gonna wait here for a bit. Willie be a' comin' by wid his mule and wagon soon. He say he leave us if we ain't ready when he git here."

Zebediah wasn't sure who Willie was. He was probably one of his mama's friends that came by the house sometimes. Zebediah thought his mama had a lot of friends. All his mother's friends were men, and they seemed to like her very much. As curious as he was, Zebediah knew better than to ask Mayellen about her visitors. He had done so once and received the worst beating of his life. As Zebediah stood shivering, he saw the sun rising golden in the east. The birds were singing, and mist was rising from the fields. He thought it all very beautiful and was on the verge of saying so when he heard the clip-clop of an approaching mule pulling a creaking old farm wagon.

As the mule and wagon drew closer, the driver called out, "Hey you, Mayellen. How you doin', sugar?" Zebediah did not recognize the driver, but his mother seemed to know him well.

"Hey you, Willie. I's doin' jus' fine, how's about y'all?" said Mayellen in a very different voice than the one she used with Zebediah. What was it they did to make her so happy?

Mayellen climbed onto the seat next to Willie and ordered Zebediah into the back. "You jus' sit yo' ass down and be quiet, boy," said Mayellen sullenly. Then, turning to Willie she said in a much brighter tone, "Willie, I's so grateful fo' you helpin' me out like this. I don't knows how I can ever pay y'all back."

The man named Willie gave the reins a shake and clucked the old mule into motion. As the mule began plodding forward, Willie turned to Mayellen and said with a sly grin, "Oh I's sure you gonna think of somethin', sugar. You always do."

Mayellen laughed loudly and said, "Well, ya never knows, Willie, I jus' might." Mayellen and Willie continued to talk and laugh while Zebediah struggled to make himself comfortable. The wagon was old and near to falling apart. Nail heads protruded from the rotting floorboards, and the metal braces were ragged and rusty. A few faint traces of paint showed the wagon must have been painted green at one time. The wagon carried the faint scent of manure. Zebediah sat on his bag and held on to the side boards as the wagon creaked and wobbled down the road.

They drove mostly in silence, with Willie and his mother occasionally exchanging a few words. Near midday, Willie headed the mule off the road to a grassy area alongside a creek. He unhitched the mule and led it down to the water while Mayellen alit from the wagon seat and opened up the basket she had brought. She withdrew an old tablecloth and spread it on the ground then brought out part of a ham, boiled eggs, bread, and a jar of pickles, spreading the food on the tablecloth. Willie returned with the mule and said, "Well, lookie here. Damn, that look good, Mayellen!"

"You jus' dig right in, Willie, I brought plenty."

Zebediah remained sitting in the wagon box and watched hungrily while Willie and Mayellen ate and laughed. Willie finally said, "Ain't you gonna give yo' boy somethin' Mayellen?"

The smile vanished from Mayellen's face, and she said darkly, "Well, I s'pose I gotta. That boy don't do a lick o' work and he ain't been nothin' but trouble since the day he was borned. You! Zebediah! Get on down here, and don't you go makin' a pig o' yo'self or I gonna whup yo' ass. Willie here been doin' all the work, and he gots to eat." Mayellen turned back to Willie with a warm smile. Willie seemed confused by the way Mayellen spoke to her young son but continued to eat, saying nothing.

Under the malevolent glare of his mother, Zebediah ate a small piece of ham, a boiled egg, and a slice of bread. Willie gave Mayellen a questioning look at the boy's meager meal, which Mayellen ignored. Zebediah was not upset, as this was more food than he was usually given. When they finished their lunch, Willie stood up, stretched, then went behind some trees along the creek to relieve himself. Mayellen glared at Zebediah and said, "Boy, if you needs to go, yo' best be doin' it. We ain't gonna be stoppin' fo' the likes o' you."

Willie was just buttoning his overalls when Zebediah appeared. Willie looked down at Zebediah and said, rather kindly, "You doin' okay, boy?"

"Oh yes, sir, I's doing jus' fine."

"Okay then, I's just kinda' wonderin', what with the way yo' mama been actin' towards ya and all."

"Oh, my mama jus' talk that way sometimes. She don't mean nothin' by it."

"Well, let's git that ole' mule harnessed up and be gittin' on our way, Zeb, we's still got a fair piece to go yet."

The young boy was rather pleased when the older man called him Zeb. No one had ever called him Zeb before. His mother always used his full name, Zebediah, and her voice always had an edge to it. When Willie called him Zeb, it had a friendly tone that brought a smile to Zebediah's face.

Willie showed Zebediah how to get the harness over the mule's back and then position him between the double tree. Quicker than Zebediah would have thought possible, Willie had the wagon rattling down the dusty road again. Mayellen did not seem any too happy about the fatherly attitude Willie had shown her son. They rode on in silence. The only sounds were the steady clip-clop of the mule, the creaking wagon, and springtime in the country. Zebediah thought it was all very pleasant, while Mayellen sat with her arms folded across her chest and her face as cold as stone. She brightened a bit when Willie started singing an old work song, and she joined in where she knew the words. They met few travelers that day, and Willie always pulled the wagon to the side of the road and stopped whenever they encountered a white man.

The sun was hanging low in the west when Mayellen pointed out where to turn off the road. They made their way up a winding lane lined on both sides by the tallest trees Zebediah had ever seen. In the distance, a hoot owl began serenading the night. It was still early spring, and the air was cooling quickly with the setting of the sun. Zebediah was beginning to shiver when the wagon came to a halt in front of a small but neatly kept house. Before the travelers could get down from the wagon, the front door burst open and a large smiling woman hurried out on to the porch, a lantern in her hand. "Mayellen! You made it!" the woman cried. Zebediah did not recognize this woman, who resembled a somewhat older version of his mother.

"Hey you, Mary! It took us all day, but we finally got here, Sis!"

As Mayellen and the lady named Mary ran to greet each other, a tall man wearing patched but clean overalls came out of the house. The man had his thumbs hooked behind the straps of his overalls and had a toothpick in the corner of his mouth. He too was smiling. "Hey, Mayellen. Glad y'all made it in one piece."

Mayellen broke away from hugging the woman named Mary but held on to the lady's hands. She said to the man on the porch, "Hey, Zeke. You seems to be holdin' up pretty good."

"Oh, I cain't complain, I reckon." The man named Zeke had a deep voice that seemed much too large for his slender body. "How's you doin', Mayellen?"

"Oh, I's fine, jus' fine, Zeke. A li'l bit tired of ridin' in a wagon, maybe," Mayellen said with a warm, friendly laugh Zebediah had never heard from her before. "You all, this here's Willie Perkins. He's the neighbor that was kind enough to help me out today. Willie, these folks is my sister Mary and her husband, Zeke."

The man named Zeke joined the other grown-ups in the yard. Zeke extended his hand. "How do, Willie."

"How do, Zeke, pleased to meet ya."

The woman named Mary turned to Zebediah and looked down at him with a beaming smile. "Zebediah! I ain't seen you since you was but a week old! Lordy, jus' look at how you've grown!"

Zebediah had no idea what was expected of him and stood there holding his bag. "Zebediah, this yo' aunt Mary and uncle Zeke. You be a good boy and say hello to 'em," said his mother.

Before Zebediah could utter a word, Aunt Mary scooped him off his feet and wrapped him in her arms. She placed a big, warm kiss on his cheek then sat him back down. "Oh, that's the way I gotta say hi to my only nephew," said the lady named Mary, laughing loudly.

The man called Uncle Zeke was now standing in front of Zebediah with his hand extended. "How do, Zeb, I'm your uncle Zeke."

Zeke took Zebediah's small hand in his large calloused one and shook it gently. It was the first time in his young life that Zebediah had ever shaken a man's hand, and he thought the experience very fine. Trying hard to emulate the adults, he said, "How do, Uncle Zeke, I's pleased to meet ya."

Zeke had a warm, friendly laugh, and he said, "Well, I's pleased to meet you too, Zeb. Be it all right if I call you Zeb?"

"I reckon so," said Zebediah.

Aunt Mary threw her arms up and said, "Oh my word, you all's got to be starvin'. Come on inside and get washed up, supper's ready."

Zeke turned to Willie and said, "Come along, Willie, and I'll show you where to bed down your mule."

After they had attended to Willie's mule, the two men and Zebediah washed their hands in a basin on the screen porch then entered the house. The furniture was old but clean. Everything was clean and neat, unlike the tumbling-down shack Zebediah shared with his mother. The kitchen was filled with the most wonderful smells Zebediah had ever experienced. "Sit down, sit down," said Aunt Mary. She waited for them to take their seats then said, "Now, let us bow our heads and give thanks for this food and for the safe arrival of Mayellen, Willie, and Zebediah." Mary gave a long blessing, and Zebediah found the blessing confusing, never having heard one before. Mayellen never prayed before meals or any other time that he knew of.

"All right, let's git to it," said Uncle Zeke, smiling. Zebediah was astonished by all the food on the table before him. There was fried chicken, potatoes with gravy, sweet peas, and freshly baked biscuits. Aunt Mary poured a large glass of milk and sat it before Zebediah. Zebediah took small portions as things were passed his way.

"Oh my, Zeb, that won't do," said his aunt, laughing. "You's a growin' boy, and you needs to eat mo' than that." Aunt Mary seemed to laugh with her whole body. She placed another drumstick on Zebediah's plate and added a big dollop of mashed potatoes. Zebediah beamed under the glow of Aunt Mary until his mother's icy glare wiped the smile from his face.

"Zebediah, you gonna say thank you?" said Mayellen.

"Yes 'em," said Zebediah. "I do rightly thank you, Aunt Mary."

"Oh goodness, your mo' than welcome, Zeb. Now enjoy your supper."

Zebediah ate like he had never eaten before. This was by far the most food he had ever consumed in one sitting. The food was plentiful and delicious. Zebediah wondered if it was possible that some people always ate like this. Mayellen rarely cooked, and when she did, most of the food went on her plate. Zebediah ate until he was stuffed, and just when he thought he couldn't hold another bite, Aunt Mary returned to the table with an apple pie. Zebediah had never seen an apple pie, much less tasted one. He only knew that it smelled wonderful. Aunt Mary set a generous slice before Zebediah, who, after a tentative first bite, soon found room for it in his groaning belly.

With the meal concluded, Uncle Zeke rose from the table and said, "Zeb, why don't you come with Willie and me out to the porch. We'll sit a spell whilst the womenfolk clean up in here."

When Zebediah stood up, he was so full he had trouble walking. Nevertheless, being invited to join the men after supper made him feel very proud. It had grown much cooler outside, and it was now fully dark. Zeke lit an old candle lantern, then both men produced pipes and filled them. Zebediah sat down in the porch swing, thinking it quite the most amazing thing he had ever seen. He began swinging slowly, being careful not to go too fast and upset his uncle. He was also acutely aware of the heavy load inside his stomach. The two men talked about farming, the things to look for when buying a mule, and what they each thought was the best possible catfish bait. Zebediah heard little of it for, within minutes, he was sound asleep.

The next thing Zebediah knew was being awakened by his mother early the next morning. For the first time in his life, he was waking up in an actual bed. It was the small bed of a child but it had sheets, a nice clean quilt, and a feather pillow. Zebediah was astonished to find his mother sitting on the edge of the bed and holding her hand to his cheek. "Zebediah? Zebediah, wake up. I needs to tell ya somethin'."

"Tell me what, Mama?" Zebediah was sleepy and confused.

"Zebediah, you gonna be stayin' here wid yo' aunt Mary and uncle Zeke for a while." These were the gentlest words she had ever spoken to him. "I's goin' away for a spell, and I won't be able to tend to ya." Zebediah saw the tiniest trace of a tear appear in the corner of his mother's eye.

"You's goin' away, Mama? Where you goin'? You gonna be gone long, Mama?" said Zebediah with rising panic.

"I might be gone awhile, Zebediah. I don't rightly know. Yo' aunt Mary's gonna take real good care of ya though. Prolly way better than what yo' mama ever done, and her Zeke is a good man too, Zebediah. He be a good one to help you git on in life and such." Mayellen's eyes were now glistening, and a tear rolled slowly down her cheek. She bent down and kissed Zebediah on the forehead. "Bye now, Zebediah. Say a li'l prayer fo' yo' mamma if'n you git the chance."

"But, Mama, I wants to go wid you." Zebediah was now fully awake, his eyes wide with fear, his voice pleading.

"Naw, son, you cain't go wid me. You safe here, Zebediah. You gonna have a fine home here wid your aunt and uncle. I gots to be goin' now, Zebediah. Willie, he be a' waitin' fo' me." Mayellen bent forward and kissed Zebediah again, then she rose and left the room without looking back. A minute later, Zebediah heard the wagon moving down the lane. Aunt Mary's house became very still. It was the only time he had ever seen a tear in his mother's eye and the only time he could remember being kissed by her. Zebediah could not know that he would never see his mother again. In time, the mental scars of his early life would begin to heal, and his mother's farewell would dull the pain of her memory.

Zebediah lay back down, and tears soon filled the bewildered little boy's eyes. He buried his face in the pillow and sobbed quietly for a long time until sleep took him again. The next thing he was aware of was Aunt Mary sitting on the edge of the bed, stroking his cheek.

"Hey, you, sleepyhead," Aunt Mary said sweetly. "Y'all gonna sleep all day or what?" Aunt Mary's voice and laughter seemed to be all one thing to Zebediah.

Zebediah rolled over and smiled. "Good mornin', Aunt Mary." Then the smile quickly fled his face. "My mama done gone."

"I know, Zeb. I know, honey, but don't you worry none. There's just somethin' yo' mama has got to take care of, but you gonna be safe here wid us. Hey," Mary said brightly, "Zeke wanna know if you can help him wid the milkin' and the rest of the chores?"

Zebediah had a puzzled look on his face. "I ain't never done any milkin' before, Aunt Mary."

"Well shoot! It's high time you was learnin' then. If'n you gonna live here on the farm, then you gotta earn yo' keep." There was nothing of his mother's harsh and threatening tone in Mary's voice. Her voice was filled with laughter, and Zebediah knew she was joking with him. "Come on then, let's be gittin' yer britches on. The day's a' wastin'."

Zebediah dressed then followed his aunt into the kitchen, where he found Uncle Zeke sitting at the table, drinking coffee. "Good mornin' to ya, Zeb. Y'all didn't last too long in the porch swing last night." Zeke's voice was deeper and calmer than Mary's, but it carried its own gentle laughter. "Let's head on out to the barn and git ole' Bossy milked while Aunt Mary fixes us some breakfast." Zebediah followed Zeke to the screen porch, and his uncle showed Zebediah where the sparkling-clean pail was kept, sitting upside down on a towel. Zeke handed Zebediah the bucket and said, "I think maybe you jus' might be the guy I been needin' round here to help me wid the chores, Zeb."

He followed his uncle out to the barn, feeling very important. Zeke's barn was small and unpainted and not nearly as grand as some he'd seen on his journey the day before. Zebediah looked around the inside of the barn and saw his uncle's tools hanging neatly on the wall inside the door. Zeke took the pail from Zebediah and hung it on a hook extending from the wall. "Well, Zeb, the first thing we gotta do is git ole' Bossy in the barn."

"How we do that, Uncle Zeke?"

"Oh, that be the easy part, Zeb. Ole' Bossy's gonna be plenty ready to be milked. Come along, I'll show you how we do it." Zeke took an old coffee can from a peg on the wall and lifted the lid from a wooden barrel in the corner. "All you gotta do to get ole' Bossy to come in the barn is scoop up a can full of these here oats and dump 'em in her feed box." Zeke filled the can and handed it to Zebediah. "Now you jus' bring it on over here and pour the oats in this box." The wooden box Zeke pointed out was attached to the end of two boards standing up from the floor. They were wider at the top than at the bottom and all held together in a wooden framework.

Zebediah emptied the oats then looked up to his uncle. "Like so, Uncle Zeke?"

"Jus' like that, Zeb. I do believe you gonna work out jus' fine as my hired man."

Zeke told Zebediah to stand behind him, then he opened a side door and called out, "Hey, Boss, hey, Boss." Soon, a large black-and-white cow made her way into the barn and immediately pushed her head between the boards and began eating the oats. Zeke moved one of the boards to the side and fastened it in place with another short piece of wood on a hinge. Zeke saw the puzzled look on Zebediah's face, and he explained to the boy, "This here be what ya call a stanchion. It don't hurt her none. It just keeps her from movin' around whilst I get the milkin' done." Zeke removed an odd-looking stool from the wall. The stool had only one leg and was shaped like the letter *T*. In one easy motion, Zeke swung the stool under him as he sat down, holding the pail between his knees. He reached under the cow, and foaming milk was soon squirting from the cow's udder.

Zebediah peered over Zeke's shoulder, fascinated by the alternating streams of milk shooting into the pail. "Zeb, one thing you gots to remember is, don't never walk or stand behind the cow. Any cow," he added for emphasis. "You just stand there behind me and you be fine. She's a gentle ole' girl, but you always gotta' be a little careful round livestock. I sho' don't want to see you gettin' hurt." The pail was now half-full, and Zeke switched his grip and began pulling on the two opposite teats. In, what seemed to Zebediah, no time at all, the pail was full to the brim. As smoothly as he had sat down, Zeke regained his feet then turned to Zebediah, handing him the pail. Zebediah stood, wide-eyed at the prospect of carrying the full bucket. Zeke laughed. "Y'all think this too heavy for ya, Zeb?"

"Yes, sir, it prolly is."

"Oh, that's all right, Zeb." Zeke laughed. "I's just joshin' ya some. We'll get you built up though. You be carryin' that full bucket befo' you knows it." Zeke returned the full pail to the hook protruding from the wall then released the cow from the stanchion. "I didn't milk her full dry. We gonna let her calf finish up." Zeke eased the cow back out the side door then released a black-and-white calf from a smaller pen. The calf immediately went about its business of being nursed by its mother. "Well, Zeb, let's go see if Aunt Mary has our breakfast ready." Zeke retrieved the bucket, and together, they walked back to the house. Well before they reached the back door, Zebediah detected more wonderful smells coming from Aunt Mary's kitchen.

"Well, there's the workin' men." Aunt Mary's laughing voice filled the kitchen. "How'd you do milkin' the cow, Zeb?"

Zebediah smiled shyly and said, "Well, Aunt Mary, I didn't do very much. It was Uncle Zeke what did most of it. I jus' help him a little wid feedin' Bossy,"

"Well, that's good Zeb, that's real good. Everybody gotta start somewhere. You don't learn how to be a farmer in a day. Now, you been to the barn, so you wash yo' hands real good, and we'll eat while it's hot. There be hot water in the basin on the porch for ya."

Zeke and Zebediah washed then returned to the kitchen. When they were seated, Aunt Mary said, "We gonna give thanks now, Zebediah. Bow yo' head, please."

He bowed his head while Aunt Mary said a blessing over the food and thanked heaven for Zebediah coming to stay with them and that they were truly blessed to have him there.

"Let's eat it up, Zeb." Uncle Zeke was smiling broadly while he held up his coffee cup for Mary to refill. "After we done eatin', you can help me wid the separatin', Zeb." Responding to Zebediah's puzzled look, Zeke said, "That be how we removes the cream from the milk. We saves the cream, and then on Saturday, we takes it in and sells it at the general store. We drinks all the milk we wants, and what's left over I mix with ground corn for the hogs. We don't waste nothin'."

The whole business of farming was beginning to sound very complicated to Zebediah, but his puzzlement did not last long as Aunt Mary placed two large pancakes covered in syrup on his plate, followed by two thick sausage links. Seeing that Zebediah's eyes were wide with wonder, Mary said, "Zeb, yo looks like you ain't never seen a hotcake befo'."

Zebediah was suddenly feeling very self-conscious and responded shyly, "I ain't seen one before, Aunt Mary."

Zeke and Aunt Mary exchanged glances, and Aunt Mary said, "Well shucks, Zeb, that don't make no never mind. There's lots a' folks that ain't never seen a hotcake. You gonna see plenty of 'em round here though." Zebediah thought that the warmth of Aunt Mary's voice was every bit as wonderful as the smells in her kitchen.

Zebediah tasted a small bite of the pancake and, even after the sizable meal he had eaten the night before, found that he was very hungry again and made short work of all that was on his plate. "I do believe Zeb has takin' a likin' to your cookin', Mary," said Zeke.

"Oh, I aim to fatten him up some, Zeke."

"Well, wid the way he goin' after those hotcakes, it prolly ain't gonna take long." His aunt and uncle laughed together, and feelings he had never experienced swept over Zebediah. The warmth of their laughter brought his mother's departure back into sharp focus.

"Aunt Mary? How long my mama gonna be gone?"

Mary's smile was replaced with a look of infinite kindness. She reached across the table and, squeezing Zebediah's hand, said, "I'll tell you the truth, honey. I don't rightly know. It might be awhile, but don't you to go to frettin', Zeb. Me and Uncle Zeke ain't gonna let nothin' bad happen to ya. We wants ya to know you got a home here with us as long as you want it, Zeb. Fo' as long as you want it," said Aunt Mary, with emphasis on the word *long*. There was a tear forming in the corner of her eye. She sat, smiling and gently squeezing Zebediah's hand for several seconds.

Zeke broke the silence when he set down his coffee cup and said, "Well, Zeb, let's go git the separatin' done." Zebediah followed his uncle to the screen porch and watched as Zeke removed an oilcloth cover from an odd-looking machine. Zeke placed a paper filter inside a metal frame then poured the milk through the filter and into the large metal bowl at top of the machine. He placed a pitcher under one of two spouts protruding from the machine then placed his milk pail under the other. "Well, Zeb, this is how we do it." Zeke began turning a large crank on the side of the machine. The machine began to make a whirring sound, and shortly, both spouts had white liquids coming out of them. Zeke explained to Zebediah that the smaller of the two streams was the cream and the larger was the skimmed milk.

Zebediah thought it quite the most amazing thing he had ever seen. How could you separate cream from milk just by turning a crank? After turning the crank for a few minutes, Zeke smiled and said to Zebediah, "This ain't the most excitin' thing a man can do I reckon. Come on, Zeb, give it a try."

He took the handle of the crank in his hand and was surprised when the crank kept on turning of its own accord. "You don't wanna let it to slow down, Zeb. Keep it a' goin' if ya can." Zebediah felt the crank slowing down and struggled to maintain the speed. He found the crank much harder to turn than he expected. He struggled vainly to keep the separator turning, but little by little, the machine's resistance overcame Zebediah's strength. Zeke reached out and took the crank from him and soon had the machine back up to speed. He laughed and squeezed Zebediah's shoulder with his free hand. "Aw, don't you fret, Zeb. It ain't as easy as it looks, but you gonna get strong. You gonna have this ole' separator hummin' right along befo' you knows it. Aunt Mary usually does the separatin' 'cause most days, after breakfast, I go off down the road to work for Mr. Johnson. We usually real busy this time o' year, but it's kinda' too wet to plant corn today, but if it don't rain, I be headin' over tomorrow fo' sho'."

"Is this yo' farm, Uncle Zeke?"

"Yes sir, Zeb, it is. I got thirty-seven acres, all free 'n' clear. My daddy bought this place over forty years ago, and he got it paid off just before he passed away. I been livin' here all my life. They tells me I was borned in the room where me and Aunt Mary sleeps."

"Is you rich, Uncle Zeke?"

Zeke tossed his head back and slapped his knee, gripped by silent laughter. Zebediah feared he may have upset his uncle, but Zeke was laughing hard. When he regained his composure, he said, "Well, Zeb, I guess you might say I'm rich. In a way I s'pose. I don't have but a little money, but I got my place here. I got enough to eat, I has yo' aunt Mary, and on Sunday afternoons, I go fishin'. There's rich men in this ole' world that ain't near as satisfied as me, Zeb." As Zebediah tried to understand all his uncle was saying, the whir of the separator shifted to a higher pitch. "Well, Zeb, I believe we done got it whipped fo' this mornin'. We git to do it again tonight. We does it twice a day, every day, as long as the cow stays fresh." Zeke shifted the cream spout so it was now emptying into the milk bucket and poured a quart jar of clean water into the bowl then quickly placed the jar back under the spouts. "The water's jus' to git the last of the milk out o' the separator, Zeb. Come on along and I show ya where we keeps the milk and cream."

Zebediah followed Zeke back outside and into a small stone building at the base of the windmill. "We call this the well house, Zeb." Water from the well was flowing into a cement trough running the length of the structure. Zeke removed the top of a silver-colored can, sitting mostly submerged in the water, and poured the fresh cream into it, then he poured the milk into another can. "The col' water from the well keeps the cream, milk, 'n' butter an' such cool and fresh until we ready to take it to town. 'Bout once a week, Aunt Mary churns up some o' the cream and makes our butter. She be a' showin' you how she do that one day soon, and maybe you kin help her some."

Zebediah followed his uncle back to the house, where Zeke showed him how the separator came apart. "Aunt Mary gonna wash these parts up along wid the rest of the dishes. You gotta keep everything real clean around milk, or it kin make ya awful sick." Zebediah spent the rest of the morning following Zeke around as he tended to the chores. Zeke spent some time sharpening the blade on his plow so it would be ready when he got to his own planting. They forked hay for Zeke's mules and shoveled corn to the sow and the shoats. They went to the hen house, and Zebediah had his first experience gathering eggs. "Aunt Mary usually gathers the eggs, but on the days I don't work fo' Mr. Johnson, I take care of it. We eat all the eggs we want, and we sell the extras along wid the cream. Our cream and eggs buys us a lotta' the stuff we cain't grow."

The morning flew by, and before Zebediah knew it, Aunt Mary was calling them for dinner. Mary again said a blessing over the food and again thanked heaven for Zebediah coming to stay with them. Zebediah was becoming giddy with all the food he had been eating. They ate pork chops, boiled potatoes, and early sweet peas from the garden. Then, wonder of wonders, another slice of apple pie. The anxiety Zebediah felt over his mother's departure was fading rapidly. As they ate, Zeke said to Mary, "I'm gonna git the rest of the garden spaded up this afternoon." He turned to Zebediah and added, "We got the peas and taters in the ground, but it'll soon be time for everything to go in." Zeke cocked his head and turned to Zebediah with a sly smile. "You any good at spadin' up gardens, Zeb?"

By now, Zebediah was catching on to his uncle's good humor and responded, "Well, I can sure help ya if'n I can, but I prolly gonna be too little again." Zeke and Mary laughed, and Zebediah instinctively knew it was laughter born of love.

"Well, maybe you jus' the right size to help out, 'cause bustin' up the clods is somethin' that's got to be done. I think maybe you jus' the man fo' the job. Me and my brothers always helped our daddy out bustin' clods when it came time to make up the garden. We always had a lotta' fun doin' it too."

Zebediah wasn't sure what "busting up clods" meant, but if Uncle Zeke said it was fun, then he was ready to try. They rose from the table. Zeke stretched out his lanky frame and said to Zebediah, "I likes to close my eyes fo' a little bit after dinner, Zeb. Seems to help me git along better in the afternoon. You welcome to lay down too if'n ya wants to." Zeke retired to their bedroom, and Zebediah wandered back into the kitchen where Aunt Mary was busy with the dishes.

"You lookin' sleepy, Zeb, why don't ya go ahead and lay down for a bit. You gonna feel better if ya do. Jus' lay down on the sofa if ya want."

Zebediah's system was overwhelmed by so much food, and he required little encouragement. He lay down on the old sofa, placing one of Aunt Mary's small pillows beneath his head. He didn't think he had been lying there long when his aunt began shaking him gently. "Hey you, Zeb. I thought I prolly better wake you up or you gonna be awake all night. You done slept fo' two hours."

Zebediah could scarcely believe it. He sat up rubbing and blinking his eyes in confusion. "Two hours already?"

Aunt Mary laughed. "Yes, sugar, you sho' did. That's okay, a growin' boy need his rest. Uncle Zeke's been spadin' right along. He prolly bout' ready fo' you to come help with bustin' up the clods."

Zebediah put his hat on and hurried out to the garden. Zeke glanced up from his spading and said with a laugh, "Well, there's my hired man. I was startin' to think you done took the day off and went fishin'."

"Nah, Uncle Zeke, I jus' fell asleep. I's here to help ya now."

"That's okay, Zeb. You jus' in time, really. It works better anyway if I get ahead some on the spadin'. That way we ain't bumpin' into each other." Zeke led Zebediah to the spot where he had begun turning over the soil. "See those clods there, Zeb? Jus' step down on 'em with the side o' yo' foot and break 'em up. They too big for plantin' until they be smoothed out some."

Zeke stepped into the first big clod, and it came apart easily under his boot. "The fields is too muddy yet, but this soil just right fo' makin' garden. Too wet an' you got mud, too dry and you got bricks. Right now them clods bust up easy."

Zebediah tested one clod and then another. The earth was cool beneath his feet and had a clean, wonderful smell. The clods broke up nicely under his weight. It was fun. He pursued his clod busting with enthusiasm, and soon he was nearly caught up with Zeke's spading. Zeke laughed. "You gonna have to slow down some, Zeb, or I'm gonna have to let you do the spadin'." Zebediah did slow down, staying just behind Zeke's rhythmic turning of the earth. When Zeke reached the end of the garden, he went back to where he started and began smoothing the broken clods with a rake. "Seeds don't wanna grow in hard dirt, Zeb. That's why we gotta do all this work makin' up the garden. It be worth it though. This here garden gonna give us a lot to eat befo' the summer's over, an' I like eatin'. How 'bout you, Zeb?"

"Oh yes, sir, Uncle Zeke, I likes to eat."

They paused a minute to look over their work. Zeke pronounced himself satisfied with the way it had turned out, and he said to Zebediah, "Well, Zeb, guess what time it's gettin' to be."

"I don't know, Uncle Zeke."

"Well, it be milkin' time again." Zeke laughed, and Zebediah was quickly realizing that farming involved a lot of work. "You reckon you kin help me again?"

"I sho' do my best."

"I know you will, Zeb. I believe you on the way to bein' the best hired man I ever had around this place."

Zebediah's chest swelled with pride. Here he was, not even a full day into living with his aunt and uncle, and he was already doing important work.

Zeke went to the house and returned with the shining-clean milk pail. "Let's see if you remember what we do next, Zeb."

"First thing we gotta do is feed Bossy some oats from the barrel."

"Yes, sir, you got it. Here, le'mme git this wooden box for ya to stand on. If'n the oats git too far down, then ask me to help ya. I don't need my hired man fallin' in the oat barrel." Everything Zeke and Mary said seemed to carry with it a touch of laughter.

Zebediah scooped up a can of oats and emptied it into the feed box then replaced the can back on its peg. "I think we's ready to be callin' Bossy in now, Uncle Zeke."

"You wanna see if you kin' do it, Zeb? I'll open the door, and you stand behind me and call out, 'Come, Boss, come, Boss.'"

Zeke removed the pin from the hasp holding the door and swung it open. Zebediah bellowed out, *"Come, Boss, come, Boss!"*

His uncle laughed and said, "Well Zeb, I think she heard ya."

The cow came in to her stall, just as she had in the morning, and just like before, Uncle Zeke soon had the pail humming with the squirting milk. The only difference in the evening milking was when a cat walked into the barn and meowed loudly. Zeke looked over his shoulder and said with a grin, "Watch this, Zeb." Zeke turned the cow's teat toward the cat and hit the cat squarely with a stream of milk. Zeke laughed and responded to Zebediah's puzzled expression. "Oh, don't worry, Zeb. I been squirtin' ole' Tom 'bout every day since he was borned and sometimes twice. He'd prolly run off and find himself a new barn if I quit doin' it, an' every barn need a cat or two."

"What fo' does a barn need a cat, Uncle Zeke?"

Zeke nodded in the direction of the oat barrel and said, "You see that oat barrel? Well, without ole' Tom, that barrel would be full o' mice in no time. Ole' Tom keeps 'em cleared out. He deserve a squirt of milk now and then."

Zebediah watched the cat licking the milk from its fur. The cat did not appear to be the least bit unhappy at having been squirted, and Zebediah laughed along with Zeke. They let the cow back out into the yard and then walked back to the house. Uncle Zeke carried the milk pail in one hand and draped the other over Zebediah's shoulder. "It's a lot o' work keepin' up wid a farm Zeb, but that don't mean y'all cain't have a spot o' fun now and then."

Aunt Mary was just putting supper on the table when Zeke and Zebediah reached the house. "Hey, you two, yo' right on time. Supper be on the table when you git washed up." Zeke sat the pail of fresh milk on the counter near the separator and covered it with the clean white towel Zebediah had seen the pail sitting on earlier. They washed up in the warm water Aunt Mary had waiting for them. As they ate, Zebediah noticed two large copper pots steaming on the stove and wondered what they might be for.

Zeke and Mary chatted politely about their respective days, but mostly, they ate in silence. Between bites, Aunt Mary asked Zebediah if he had any fun helping out his uncle, and he replied, "Oh yes, Aunt Mary, I sho' did. I be glad when I's big enough to help him out more."

Mary laughed and said, "Oh, Zeb, don't be in too big a hurry to grow up. You gonna be big soon enough. Zeke, when we done eatin', would you mind gettin' the tub ready?" Mary turned to Zebediah and said, in mock seriousness, "You's gettin' a bath, young man. I don't need any clod-bustin' feet on my clean sheets."

Zebediah's mother had rarely bathed him. Mayellen would occasionally go over his face and neck with a rough cloth, but he mostly just washed himself in cold water. When Zeke returned from removing the oilcloth cover from the tub, Mary emptied one of the pots of hot water into the tub then added some cool water from another pail. "Come here and see if this water be about right fo' ya, Zeb." Zebediah put his hand it the water, and it felt wonderful, just like the water Aunt Mary always had waiting for them to wash their hands in.

"It feel real nice, Aunt Mary."

"I'm gonna leave you to it then. When you get done washin', here's a towel to dry off with, and you can put on this ole' flannel shirt of Zeke's. I cut the sleeves off so you can at least see yo' hands. You can wear it to bed tonight, and I'll git' your clothes washed up." Clean clothing was another thing Zebediah had experienced little of. "When we goes to town on Saturday, we gonna fix you up wid some new clothes and a proper pair of shoes. It ain't a good idea to be goin' barefoot all the time on the farm. Now you do a good job o' washin'. Jus' 'cause we live on a farm, don't mean we gotta go around lookin' like bums."

Zebediah undressed and slipped into the warm water. He took the piece of homemade soap and the washcloth Aunt Mary provided then went to work scrubbing himself. He began with his head and worked his way down to his toes. He saw that the water was now considerably darker than it had been when he first got into the tub. He heard Aunt Mary call from the kitchen, "Yo sho' must be enjoyin' that bath, Zeb. Y'all been in there fo' a half hour. Uncle Zeke gonna need his turn pretty soon." So much had Zebediah been enjoying his bath, he could scarcely believe he had been in the water a half hour. He was standing on the rug next to the tub, drying himself, when Zeke spoke up. Zebediah had been so engrossed in his bath, he had not even noticed the whirring of the separator at the far end of the screen porch.

"Bath sho' feel good after a day's work, don't it, Zeb?"

Zebediah was startled by his uncle's voice and said, "Yes, sir, Uncle Zeke, it sho' does."

Zebediah dressed in Zeke's old shirt. Aunt Mary had cut the sleeves off just right, but he was otherwise swimming in it. Zeke laughed. "You gonna be a while fillin' that shirt out, Zeb." In spite of the awkwardness of the shirt, Zebediah felt very good. He was clean and fed, and there was a real bed with clean sheets waiting for him.

While Zeke was emptying the tub, Zebediah walked into the parlor feeling slightly self-conscious. He needn't have worried as his aunt Mary treated his wearing a man's shirt as the most natural thing in the world. "Come here and sit with me, Zeb. I'll read to ya a bit." Zebediah's mother had never read to him. He wasn't sure his mother even knew how to read. Aunt Mary read a story from a tattered old schoolbook and then a Bible verse. Zebediah enjoyed the reading immensely. When Aunt Mary closed her Bible, she asked, "You about ready to hit the hay, sugar?"

"Pretty soon I reckon." Zebediah paused before continuing. "Aunt Mary, how come you and Uncle Zeke doesn't have any children?"

A sad but kindly look came over Mary. She held her hand against his cheek and said, "Me and Uncle Zeke ain't never been blessed with children, Zeb. We prayed and prayed fo' it, but it never happen. That's jus' one mo' reason we so glad to have you stayin' with us." Aunt Mary gathered Zebediah in her arms and held him tightly. He put his arms around her neck hugged her back. For the first time in his life, Zebediah felt very, very safe.

"Well, come along, young man, it's off to bed for you. Zeke be takin' his bath now, but you kin holler to him and say good night."

"Good night, Uncle Zeke."

From the screen porch, Zeke called back, "Good night to you, Zeb. Now remember, we gotta be up early and get the milkin' done again tomorrow."

"Yes, sir, jus' wake me up and I be ready to help ya."

Aunt Mary escorted Zebediah to the small room where he slept. After getting him settled, she bent down and kissed his forehead. "Good night, sugar. You sleep tight now."

"Good night, Aunt Mary."

Zebediah would have sworn he had only been in bed a matter of minutes when Uncle Zeke gently shook his shoulder. "Hey, Zeb, I cain't be havin' my hired man sleepin' all day."

Zebediah sat up and rubbed his eyes. "It mornin' already?"

"Well, it's almost mornin'," said Zeke. "I'll be goin' to the Johnson's to work today, so we need to get started a li'l bit earlier. Aunt Mary has clean clothes for ya. She washed 'em up and hung 'em by the stove to dry last night." Clean clothes, baths, and plates heaped with food were all new and wonderful things for Zebediah.

Zebediah put on his shirt and overalls and followed Zeke to the barn. The sun had not yet risen, and the predawn light was only enough to see where they were going. All around, countless birds were welcoming the coming dawn. Zeke hung up his pail and struck a match to a battered lantern hanging from the ceiling. He turned to Zebediah and said, "I tried milkin' ole' Bossy in the dark once, Zeb, and I had a awful time wid it. She be mostly black, and she kept disappearin' on me." By now Zebediah was laughing along with Zeke's little jokes. Zebediah filled the feed box with oats then called the cow in for milking. The cat put in another appearance and received another squirt of milk. The cow was put back out, and the milk was delivered to the screen porch for separating.

After breakfast, Zeke put on his hat and kissed Aunt Mary's cheek. Mary handed him a small wicker basket covered with a red-and-white checkered cloth. As Zeke was walking out the door, he paused then turned to Zebediah and said, "You the man o' the house while I'm gone, Zeb. You do what ya can to help Aunt Mary out now."

"Yes, sir, Uncle Zeke, I do my best."

"I knows you will, Zeb. Bye now. I be seein' y'all tonight."

"What that basket be that Uncle Zeke carryin', Aunt Mary?"

"Oh, that's his dinner, honey. He don't eat with the white folk he work fo'."

"Why not, Aunt Mary?"

"That jus' the way it is, Zeb. That jus' the way it is. Mr. Johnson is a decent man though. Zeke's family been working fo' them fo' a long time. They pays him fair, and they never gives him any grief." Looking to change the subject, Aunt Mary asked brightly, "Well, Zeb, let's git the separatin' done."

Zebediah helped where he could and together they separated the milk, saved the cream, and gathered the eggs. He dried dishes then tried managing a broom as Mary went about her housework. They had leftover chicken for their lunch with freshly baked biscuits and honey. After they had eaten, Zebediah took another nap, and when he woke, he was looking up at Aunt Mary's smiling face. "Hey you, sleepyhead." She paused a moment then asked thoughtfully, "Zeb, do ya know your letters yet?"

Zebediah hung his head and said, "No, Aunt Mary, I doesn't know any letters."

"Well, we're gonna fix that, startin' today. Let's go sit at the kitchen table." Mary took out a sheet of paper and began writing the letters of the alphabet with the stub of a pencil. "I ain't had but three years of schoolin' myself, Zeb, but I been practicin' my readin' right along. I reckon I can read pretty good, and I aim to teach you how to read too." Zebediah found the prospect of learning how to read very exciting, and by the time they put the paper away, he had memorized the alphabet. "We gonna spend a little time every afternoon workin' on this, Zeb, and you gonna know how to read in no time at all." Mary busied herself with supper, and Zebediah thumbed through Mary's old schoolbook. As his aunt worked at the stove, she looked over her shoulder and said, "Tomorrow, we'll start talkin' about what all those letters sound like. That's all there be to readin', jus' puttin' sounds together. You gonna find it hard to believe jus' how easy readin' is." Zebediah continued to leaf through the book. He was fascinated by the colorful illustrations and wondered if such places really existed. Mary and Zebediah looked up when they heard the back door close.

Uncle Zeke's overalls and shirt were soiled, and he looked tired. In spite of his weariness, he asked cheerfully, "Well, how did you two make out today?" Zeke planted a kiss on Mary's cheek then helped himself to a long drink of water.

"Oh, we made out jus' fine. We got the chores all done, and me an' Zeb started workin' on learnin' how to read. He done got all his letters memorized already."

"Is that right, Zeb? That's good. That's real good, lemme hear ya say 'em."

Zebediah proudly recited the alphabet for Uncle Zeke.

"Well, I'll be. I'm sho' it took me at least two days to learn 'em, maybe three. You gonna be reading up a storm before we knows it. Well, Zeb, I reckon you know what time it is."

"I s'pose it be milkin' time again."

"I s'pose you be right." Uncle Zeke laughed. "Let's git to it so Aunt Mary don't have to wait supper on us. We has a big day tomorrow."

"What goin' on tomorrow, Uncle Zeke?"

"Why, tomorrow's Saturday and we's goin' to town."

After milking, eating supper, and taking another bath, Zebediah was tucked in bed, eager with anticipation for the upcoming trip to town. He didn't exactly know what "going to town" meant, but if Uncle Zeke was excited about it, then it must surely be a good thing.

Chapter Two

Going To Town

When Zebediah accompanied Zeke to the barn the following morning, things seemed a little less hurried. The sun had fully risen, and Uncle Zeke sounded even more cheerful than usual. Once the chores were completed and breakfast eaten, Zeke went to the pen, harnessed his team of mules, then hitched them to his wagon. Aunt Mary began loading their produce into the wagon box. They loaded the large silver can of fresh cream, a case of eggs, and a bushel basket covered with a tablecloth. Zeke went into the house and returned wearing new overalls and a new shirt. The crumpled old hat he normally wore had been replaced by a crisp straw hat. Aunt Mary changed her clothes as well and now wore a brightly colored dress and a hat.

Zebediah's spirits fell, and he felt out of place, having only his tattered old clothes and no shoes. Sensing the boy's discomfort, Aunt Mary said, "Don't you go to frettin', Zeb. We gonna get you fixed up with some new duds today. You gonna be the best-lookin' boy around when I gets done with ya." Everything Aunt Mary said brought a smile to Zebediah's face.

Zeke's wagon was larger and in much better repair than Willie's, and it was being drawn by two mules instead of one. There was room for Zebediah on the seat between his aunt and uncle. Zeke shook the reins and turned the mules down the lane and toward the road. Once on the road, Zeke's mules fairly pranced along, moving a good deal faster than Willie's tired old beast. After they had been on the road a few minutes, Zeke asked, "You wanna take a turn at drivin' the team, Zeb?" Mary shot Zeke a questioning glance, and Zeke said, "I think he can hold the reins a bit."

Zebediah's eyes were wide with excitement. Zeke put his arm around Zebediah and placed the reins in his hands. Zeke kept his hands close, ready to retrieve them in an instant. After her initial apprehension, Mary smiled at the sheer joy on Zebediah's face. Zebediah's turn at driving the team didn't last long. Zeke again took control. "I see a horse and rider comin' our way, Zeb. Y'all better let me have the reins." When the horseman drew near, Zeke stopped the wagon, and to Zebediah's surprise, the white man on the horse stopped as also.

"Hey, Zeke. Takin' the cream and eggs to town I reckon? Mornin' to you, Mary. When did y'all have a child?" Zebediah had little experience with white people and only had things he had heard from grown-ups to go by. This white man did not seem threatening.

"Mornin' to you, Mr. Johnson, this is our nephew Zebediah. He stayin' wid us for a while," said Mary.

"Oh, I see," said the white man thoughtfully. "This must be Mayellen's boy then?"

So happy had he been in his aunt and uncle's company, Zebediah had thought little about his mother, and now here was a white man who knew who his mother was. Zebediah found this knowledge to be both confusing and upsetting.

"Yes, sir, Mr. Johnson, this is Mayellen's son, Zebediah," said Aunt Mary in a quiet, even voice.

Johnson was quiet for a moment then said, "I expect him comin' to stay with you is probably a good thing then."

"It's a real good thing," said Mary. "We real glad to have him with us."

"Well, I'll be seein' ya," said Johnson. "We be hittin' the corn plantin' real hard next week, Zeke, if it don't rain, and it don't look like it's gonna." The white man turned away from the travelers and nudged his horse into a lope.

Zebediah waited until the rider was well behind them before asking Aunt Mary, "How that man know my mamma, Aunt Mary?"

"Well, Zeb, me and yo' mamma growed up in these parts. Most everybody who been here awhile knows everybody else. Don't fret about it, Zeb. Mr. Johnson knowin' yo' mamma don't mean nothin'. He jus' being neighborly, that's all."

Even though Aunt Mary had words of comfort, Zebediah found the exchange with Mr. Johnson troubling for reasons he could not fathom. Somehow, a white man knowing who his mother was just did not seem right. The wagon rolled on. The day was warm, and the sun was slipping in and out of billowing white clouds. The air teemed with bees, intoxicated by the scent of the countless wildflowers lining the road. Every passing plum thicket was a brilliant cloud of white blossoms. Aunt Mary was enchanted by the passing scene, and her sense of wonder began rubbing off on Zebediah. Troubling thoughts of Mayellen were soon pushed aside by the sheer glory of the day. He put his arm inside his aunt's and lay his head against her arm. Mary smiled down at Zebediah and squeezed his knee.

As they crested a small hill, Uncle Zeke said, "Hey, Zeb, look yonder."

Zebediah sat up straight and peered into the distance. "That be town, Uncle Zeke?"

"That be Parkersburg. Parkersburg is what we usually mean when we say *town*. It's where we does our tradin', mostly. Once in a while, we go over to Clarks, when the fair's goin' on, but it's a bit further, so we mostly always goes to Parkersburg." Uncle Zeke always seemed to be in a good mood, but Zebediah could not help but notice that his uncle brightened at the sight of town.

Aunt Mary chuckled and said to Zebediah, "Uncle Zeke always likes goin' to town, Zeb. It gives him a chance to spend a li'l time shootin' the breeze with his friends. That's how he finds out what's been goin' on hereabouts."

Zeke laughed at his wife's words and said, "I do. I surely do enjoy visitin' with folks a bit. Now don't git me wrong Zeb, I loves livin' on the farm and all, but it be nice to see folks now and then. Zeb, don't let her fool ya, I'm pretty sure your Aunt Mary like to visit some too." They all laughed together as the town drew near. Not that Parkersburg was a big place as towns go, having no more than a thousand people, but Zebediah had little experience with towns, and it was by far the largest place he had ever seen. The closer they came to town, the more wagons and carts they saw making their way into Parkersburg.

"The first thing we gotta do is git the cream and eggs dropped off," said Aunt Mary. "They can spoil on us if we leave 'em out in the heat too long." Zeke pulled up alongside a store located on a corner of the main street. There were a number of carts and wagons gathered there on the side street. Several people called out their greetings to Zeke and Mary. Zeke tied the mules to a rail then picked up the cream can in one arm and the case of eggs under the other. He carried them up to the back door and sat them down on the platform.

A sullen teenaged white boy nodded to Zeke and made a notation in the book he was carrying. "I kin take your eggs right now, but it'll be about a half hour before we can get the cream tested. We're awful busy this morning, I think half the county has come to town. You have your name on the can, I'll just move it to the water tank."

Zeke responded evenly, "Much obliged. Just make out a ticket, and we'll be back fo' some groceries befo' we head home."

When Zeke returned, Mary and Zebediah had alit from the wagon. Zeke said to Mary, "We might as well start by goin' on down to Sampson's and look at some clothes for Zeb." Zeke and Mary escorted Zebediah down the street a short distance and into a door on the side of a brick building. They entered the store and waited until the black clerk, Lester, could wait on them.

Lester Wiggins was a dignified older man, mostly bald with a fringe of white hair. He wore dark trousers and a white shirt with a bow tie. He was a slightly built man who stood very erect. "How do, Zeke and Mary. And who's this young fella' you has with you today?"

"How do, Lester," said Zeke. "This is our nephew Zebediah. He be stayin' with us fo' a while, and we lookin' to fix him up with some clothes and a pair o' shoes. Zeb, kin you shake hands with Mr. Wiggins?" His uncle Zeke evidently thought highly of Lester, and Zebediah felt he must be meeting a very important person.

Zebediah stepped forward and, extending his hand, said, "How do, sir, I's right pleased to meet ya." Zebediah noticed that Lester Wiggins' hand was much softer than Uncle Zeke's.

"And how do to you, young man," said Lester with a smile. Turning his attention to Mary, he said, "Now, what did you have in mind for him, Mary?"

"First thing, I want two pair of overalls. Make sho' they a little long to give him room to grow. We can roll 'em up. I want two everyday shirts and one white shirt. I want four, maybe five, pair o' socks and underwear. Let's start with the socks."

The clerk left and soon returned with a box containing many pairs of socks. "If this is what you have in mind, Mary, he can pick them out himself."

Mary looked at the box and turned over a few pair. "Okay, they'll do fine, Lester. Go ahead, Zeb, you pick out the ones you want."

Zebediah's eyes were wide with wonder. Selecting socks is a major event in the life of a boy who has never owned a pair. He made his selections and looked at Aunt Mary for her approval. "Those be good ones, Zeb, why don't you git one mo' pair while we at it." Zebediah picked out one more pair and was smiling broadly as he handed them to Lester.

Lester produced a measuring tape and said to Zebediah, "Let me git you measured for your overalls and shirts, young man." The clerk measured Zebediah in several places while making notations on a pad of paper. "I'll be right back." While Lester was away, Zebediah looked around the store in wonder. There were many people going up and down the aisles, and never had he seen so many wondrous things. Zebediah was still transfixed by his surroundings when Lester returned with the overalls, shirts, and underwear. "How do these look to ya, Mary?"

"Let me hold 'em up to him." Mary held the overalls up to Zebediah. They were a few inches too long in the legs, but they seemed to be about the right size otherwise. "They'll do fine, Lester, now let me have a look at the shirts." Mary held the shirts up across Zebediah's back. "Hold your arms out, Zeb." Mary checked the length of the sleeves. "Sleeves a little bit long, but he's a growin' boy. They gonna fit him soon enough. Yeah, they gonna do, Lester, now let's see some shoes."

Lester addressed Zebediah and said, "Have a seat on this bench, young man, and pull on a pair of your new socks. Zebediah did as he was asked. The socks felt very soft and wonderful against his feet. Lester produced an odd-looking device and said to Zebediah, "Okay, son, jus' put yo' right foot, right down here." Zebediah gave Lester a puzzled look. "This one be yo' right foot son," said Lester kindly.

Zebediah gave the clerk a shy smile and again did as he was asked. "You looking for an everyday shoe or somethin' a bit nicer, Mary?"

"Lester, you got anything that might kinda' split the difference? Somethin' he kin wear on the farm but we can shine up for Sunday meeting?"

Lester returned shortly with a pair of sturdy brown shoes. The shoes had heavy soles and eyelets up the sides. "I think this might be about what yo' lookin for, Mary. It's a good, solid shoe, and they should shine up nice if he takes care of 'em."

Mary inspected the shoes then looked to Zeke for his opinion. Zeke took the shoe from Mary and looked it over before nodding his approval. Mary said, "You go ahead and try 'em on, Zeb."

Lester used another odd-looking tool to help Zebediah slip his foot into the shoe. Putting on a shoe for the first time in your life can be a strange experience. Mary responded to the look on Zebediah's face. "Oh, they bound to feel odd to ya at first, Zeb, but the main thing is that they ain't pinchin' anywhere. What you think, Lester?"

"Stand up, son, and let me have a feel."

Zebediah stood up, and the shoe felt even stranger. Lester expertly squeezed the shoe in several places, asking, "How that feel right there?

How 'bout here? You feel yo' heel slippin' up and down?" Lester turned to Mary and said, "They gonna give him some room to grow. You can put some paper in the toes if'n it be too much. Mostly, they fit him good side to side. Y'all don't want too much room side to side 'cause that kin cause him blisters. Here, Zebediah, let's put the other one on, and you let me know how it feels to walk in 'em."

Lester laced up the shoes and tied them. Zebediah took a few tentative steps. The shoes were stiff and felt very heavy on his feet. He shot all the adults a quizzical look. Zeke spoke first. "Oh, they bound to feel kinda' funny at first, Zeb, but you gonna get used to it. Shoes need to be broke in some. Ya wears 'em a little bit at a time until they softens up." Zebediah took a few more steps. Wearing shoes was already feeling a little less strange.

"Kin I wears 'em when we leave, Aunt Mary?" Zebediah asked hopefully.

"I don't know why not," said Aunt Mary. "Shoes is for wearin'." Mary turned to Lester and said, "Now if you have a white shirt, the same size as those everyday shirts, we kin settle up with ya, Lester."

The clerk left and returned with the white shirt Mary requested, along with a small black tie draped across it. "I'll jus' throw the tie in if you want it, Mary."

"Well, I reckon if'n a boy gonna look his best, he should prolly ought to have a tie to go with his white shirt. Add up what we owes ya, Lester, and Zeke will git ya taken care of."

Zebediah left the store, proudly marching between his aunt and uncle. Suddenly, a thought occurred to him, and Zebediah looked up at his uncle. "Why fo' do we have to wait in the back while Lester git our stuff, Uncle Zeke? Other folks walkin' round the sto' lookin at stuff fo' themselves."

Zeke put his hand on Zebediah's shoulder and said gently, "We'll talk about that when we git home, Zeb." As they were approaching the wagon, Zebediah was startled by the ringing of a bell. He had never heard a bell ringing before. "What that, Uncle Zeke?"

"Oh, that be the church bell is all," said Zeke, laughing at Zebediah's confusion. "They rings it on Sunday mornin's befo' services and at straight-up noon on the other days."

The last reverberations of the bell were fading as they returned to the wagon. "Up ya go, Zeb," said Zeke. "It's time to go dig into that basket Aunt Mary packed fo' us." Zeke had a wide smile, and Zebediah thought something very good was soon to happen.

"Git up there, mules," said Zeke, giving the reins a shake. They proceeded down the street and turned a corner. They rode on to where the countryside began again. In the distance, Zebediah saw a large number of wagons, carts, and mules gathered around a grove of trees, with a crowd of people milling about. As they drew near the grove, Zebediah heard talk and laughter coming from the people, followed by greetings being called out to Zeke and Mary. The next two hours were some of the most bewildering of Zebediah's young life. He was introduced and presented to more people than he could ever hope to remember. Many expressed having known Mayellen, and all the people he met welcomed him. The contents of Aunt Mary's basket were added to a long table already loaded with food.

Something else quite remarkable happened as well. For the first time in his life, Zebediah had the opportunity to play with other children. Zebediah was very confused and had no idea what was expected of him. Before coming to live with Zeke and Mary, his entire life had consisted of only him and his mother and sometimes his mother's "friends." He found it very odd to be among people his own size. Zebediah was shy and reluctant to join in the games the children were playing. The other boys would have none of it. They gave Zebediah their names, and he gave them his. They took him by the hand and said, "Come on now, Zeb, we's just playing tag. It don't take nothing to learn." Within minutes, Zebediah was running around wildly with a dozen other children. Mary turned to Zeke and said, "That's jus' what he's needin', Zeke. That boy's powerful starved fo' fun."

The games ended when an older man rang a handbell and called everyone to come eat. As the people gathered around the table, the same man asked everyone to bow their heads while he said a blessing. With the blessing complete, Aunt Mary handed Zebediah a plate and said to go down the line and pick up what he wanted but to stay away from the cakes and pies until he ate some good food first. Zebediah ate like he had never eaten before, and when he could hold no more, the table was still heavy with food. Zebediah was nearly dizzy from eating.

As the picnic began to break up, Zeke called for Zebediah. "Come along, Zeb, we needs to get the rest of our tradin' done so we can git back home befo' dark." They climbed back aboard the wagon, and Zeke drove them to a store that smelled much like the oat barrel in the barn. Zeke bought two large burlap bags of oats and a large block of salt. As Zeke was loading his purchases in the wagon, Zebediah asked, "What the salt be for, Uncle Zeke?"

"That be for Bossy, Zeb. Cows needs to have a salt lick around. It helps keep 'em healthy." Once again, Zebediah though the whole business of farming was very complicated.

Their last stop was back at the general store, where they began their day in town. The proprietor had a ticket made up saying what their produce was worth. Mary picked up some canned goods, a length of cloth, and two skeins of yarn. Zeke bought a gallon of coal oil and a box of nails. Zebediah was surprised when Uncle Zeke did not give the man behind the counter any money and, instead, the man returned some coins to Zeke. Once back in the wagon, Zebediah asked, "Why that man give you money, Uncle Zeke?"

"Well, Zeb, that be how ole' Bossy and the chickens earns their keep. Sometimes I owes the sto' a bit, sometimes sto' owe me a bit, but it works out about even in the end. What our animals gives us buys most of what we cain't do for our self." There was a note of pride in Zeke's voice as he explained this to Zebediah.

As the wagon rolled on, back toward the farm, Zebediah's eyes grew heavy, and his head began to bob unsteadily. Aunt Mary put her arm around Zebediah to keep him from falling off the wagon seat, and he was soon sound asleep. Zeke smiled at Mary and said, "I think maybe goin' to town agree wid him."

Mary softly hugged Zebediah and responded, "Yep, I believe so. It's a good thing fo' him to have some other children to play wid. Every child need that. This po' little boy has had way too hard a life, Zeke. Bringin' him to stay wid us prolly the only good thing Mayellen ever done fo' him." A tear glistened in the corner of Mary's eye, and she kissed Zebediah softly on the forehead. Zeke reached out and squeezed his wife's hand.

Zeke halted the mules in front of the barn and hopped to the ground. Mary handed the sleeping Zebediah down to him. They smiled at each other, and Mary said, "We might as well put him to bed. I think he ate enough today to last him fo' a week, and it won't hurt him to miss supper."

Mary took Zebediah from Zeke. "I'll tend to him, you kin see to the team and the milkin'. After I git him settled, I'll carry the groceries in and git some supper ready fo' us." Zeke tied the team to a post outside the barn and went inside to change his clothes. Mary undressed Zebediah and got him into bed.

Zebediah opened his eyes just long enough to say, "I loves you, Aunt Mary."

"Oh, Zebediah, I loves you too. Mo' than you will ever know." Mary's eyes were wet as she bent low to kiss him good night. "Good night, sugar. I'll see ya in the mornin'."

When Zebediah next opened his eyes, it was full daylight, and he immediately wondered why Uncle Zeke had not called him for milking. He jumped out of bed and quickly dressed himself. When he entered the kitchen, he found his aunt and uncle sitting at the table, drinking coffee. "Why you didn't wake me fo' milkin', Uncle Zeke?"

"I didn't wake ya because I don't milk on Sunday mornin's, Zeb. I jus' turn the calf out, and she takes care of the milkin' fo' me. When the calf's done, I'll shoo her back in the pen, and that be it until tonight."

"If'n I could git your Uncle Zeke to listen to me, he wouldn't be milkin' at all on Sundays," said Aunt Mary. "I kin only git him to give it up halfway." Mary spoke with a look of mild exasperation on her face. Zeke gave Zebediah a sly wink.

"Well, Zeb, I got yo' bathwater waitin'." Mary responded to Zebediah's puzzled look. "You was too sound asleep fo' a bath last night, and I was afraid you might drown or somethin'." She laughed. "We'll be leavin' for Sunday meetin' in a bit. You get scrubbed up, and I'll have yo' breakfast waitin' when you're done. Here, Zeb, I washed a pair of your new overalls and yo' white shirt and got 'em ironed for ya last night. When you're done wid yo' bath, put them on."

Zebediah was eager to put on his new clothes and began to hurry through his bath. As if Aunt Mary could read his mind, she called from the kitchen, "You take yo' time and do a good job now, Zeb." Zebediah controlled his urge to hurry and scrubbed himself thoroughly. When he thought Aunt Mary would be satisfied, he dried and dressed himself. First the new underwear, followed by his white shirt, and last, his new overalls. He found himself stepping on the ends of his pant legs and had to pull them up in order to walk. In spite of the awkwardness, he was still beaming with pride when he entered the kitchen.

"Well, jus' look at you!" exclaimed Mary. "I said you was gonna be the best-lookin' boy around, and I was right!" she added proudly.

"You look real nice, Zeb. Come on over here and let me help you with yo' pant legs," said Uncle Zeke. Zeke rolled the pant legs up above Zebediah's feet and asked, "There, how that feel? Better?"

Zebediah marched in a quick circle around the table and said, "Oh yeah, Uncle Zeke, that be a whole lot better."

His aunt and uncle laughed, and Aunt Mary said, "Up to the table, Zeb, hotcakes be ready in a minute."

In spite of the quantity of food Zebediah consumed at the picnic, he hadn't eaten supper and his appetite was strong. He made short work of his hotcakes, biscuits, and a glass of milk, fresh from the pump house.

Zeke rose from the table and said, "I'm gonna shoo the calf back in the pen and get the team ready, then I'll git changed for meetin'."

Aunt Mary turned to Zebediah and said, "Now, honey, you go pick out the socks you wanna wear today, and I'll help ya git your shoes on. When Zeke comes back inside, he can tie yo' tie for ya."

Zebediah felt very proud as he selected a pair of socks from the little chest of drawers in his room. He sat on his bed and pulled the socks on then retrieved his shoes from beneath the bed and returned to the kitchen.

"Here, Zeb, sit in this chair, and I'll help you wid your shoes," said Aunt Mary. Mary helped Zebediah on with his shoes using the same little tool Lester had used the previous day.

"What be that thing you use fo' puttin' on shoes, Aunt Mary?"

"Oh, it's called a shoehorn. It just helps yo' feet slide into yo' shoes. You prolly won't need to use it once the shoes has been broken in some," explained his aunt.

Zebediah took a turn around the table then turned to his aunt. "They already feelin' better than yesterday."

"It won't take long, honey." Mary was interrupted when Zeke came in off the screen porch.

"Well, now! Jus' look at you, Zeb," said Uncle Zeke.

"I'm gonna get ready now," said Aunt Mary, "Zeke, maybe you kin help him wid his tie." Mary handed Zeke the tie, smiled at Zebediah, then walked to her bedroom.

Zeke sat down at the table. "Okay, Zeb. The first thing we gotta do is button up yo' top button then turn yo' collar up." Zeke helped Zebediah with the collar then said, "Okay, now then, Zeb, turn and face away from me 'cause I don't think I can get it tied any other way." Zeke was laughing and said, "Now watch how I do this so you can learn to it fo' yourself."

Zebediah cocked his head down and tried to follow Zeke's fingers as he quickly tied the knot and slipped it up to the collar button. Zeke folded Zebediah's collar down and said, "Turn around now, Zeb, and let me see ya. I do declare, Zeb, you is a right, handsome young man."

Zebediah smiled shyly and said, "I don't think I kin remember how you tied that knot, Uncle Zeke."

"Aw, don't worry about it, Zeb." Zeke laughed. "It might take a time or two, but you'll get the hang of it. Now, kin you go sit in the parlor and stay looking nice while I change my clothes?"

"Yes, sir, Uncle Zeke." Zebediah entered the parlor and sat down on the sofa. He picked up Aunt Mary's schoolbook and practiced identifying the letters until his aunt and uncle reappeared.

Mary said to Zebediah, "Zeb, you looks real nice. You gonna make us real proud this mornin'."

"I guess we ready," said Zeke holding the door open.

They all climbed aboard the wagon, and Zeke guided the mules down the lane. This time, when they reached the road, Zeke turned the mules in the opposite direction of the one they had taken the day before. Zeke said to Zebediah, "We don't have near as far to go today. It don't even take a half hour."

The day had dawned bright and still. The sky was cloudless, and spring was erupting from the earth. As the wagon rolled down the road, Zebediah felt as if he was in the middle of a dream. Zeke turned to Mary and said, "Looks like this might be our first hot day if the breeze don't come up some."

Mary nodded in agreement. "Yes, it could get pretty warm. Reverend will be startin' evening services again pretty soon." She looked down at Zebediah and said, "That's what we do when summer sets in, Zeb. We hold church in the evenings so it's not so hot."

Zebediah nodded as if he understood, but in reality, he had no idea what his aunt was talking about. He had never been to church and was too embarrassed to ask what services were.

Ten minutes later, Zeke turned the mules off the road and into a short lane leading to a small white building. The building had a pointed roof, and above the door, a part of the building rose several feet above the main part of the roof and had its own pointed roof. A number of wagons, carts, and buggies were scattered around the building, and the people gathered around were dressed in their best clothes. Several waved and called out to Zeke and Mary as they approached. Zebediah recognized some of the faces from their trip to town. The older man who had rung the handbell at the picnic now stood by the door of the building, dressed in a long black robe, and was greeting people as they entered. Zebediah found it all very puzzling.

They climbed down from the wagon seat, and Zeke shook hands with a number of the men, and Mary exchanged small hugs with several of the women. Several of the adults remembered Zebediah from the picnic and said hello to him, but Zebediah could not remember the names of any of the grown-ups. Everyone seemed very friendly and voiced no objection to Zebediah's silence. The church bell began to ring, and Zebediah shot a quizzical glance up at Zeke.

Zeke chuckled and said, "Well, Zeb, town ain't the only place wid a church bell. There's lots of 'em around. I prolly should of said that yesterday." Uncle Zeke placed his hand on Zebediah's shoulder, and together with Aunt Mary, they made their way to the front door.

When they reached the man in the long black robe, he said, "Good morning, Zeke and Mary. Is this Mayellen's boy? I heard he was staying with you."

Uncle Zeke said, "Good morning, Reverend. Yes, this is Mayellen's boy, Zebediah. Zeb, can you shake hands with Reverend Williams?"

Zebediah stepped forward and extended his hand. "Good morning, sir. I's right pleased to meet ya."

The minister took Zebediah's hand and smiled kindly. "I'm right pleased to meet you too, Zebediah. I do hope we're gonna see you here real often."

Zeke and Mary ushered Zebediah into the church, and the Reverend Williams turned to greet the next congregant. The church's interior had a high ceiling, unlike any place Zebediah had seen. The room had rows of benches and a waist-high railing that divided a portion of the room from the rest. The area on the other side of the railing was the smaller of the two, and in that area stood a table covered with a white cloth. At each end of the table, a candle burned. Beside each candle stood a vase filled with fresh flowers. Between the vases lay a large opened book. Zebediah looked around the room and tried, without success, to make sense of it all. The room was filled with the soft murmur of voices and rustling paper. The room became very quiet when a lady emerged from a door behind the table then walked to the piano and sat down.

As the lady began to play, all the people in the room rose and began to sing. As they sang, the man in the black robe walked down the aisle. When he reached the table at the front of the room, he closed the large book then picked it up and carried it to a large wooden box with a slanted top. Next, the man in the black robe placed the book on top of the box and opened it again. When the song ended, the man standing behind the box raised his hands and said, "Please be seated." Once the people had taken their seats, the man announced the first reading, whereupon he proceeded to read from the large book. When he had finished reading, Reverend Williams asked the congregation to turn to page eighty-six in their hymnals, and invited everyone to join him in a song of praise.

Zeke and Mary removed books from pockets on the back of the bench in front of them, and the room was filled with the sound of opening books. When the book sounds subsided, the lady at the piano began to play again. Zebediah tried to join in the singing, but he did not know the words. Aunt Mary traced her finger along in the book, but this was of no help because Zebediah had only just begun learning to read. When the song ended, the people took their seats again. Reverend Williams announced the second reading. At its completion, he did not immediately call for more song. Instead, the minister asked for everyone's attention then read some announcements about upcoming events at the church. The women's club was making plans for the spring picnic, and a committee was deciding the best time for the men to gather and do some repair work on the roof. The board of trustees would be holding their monthly meeting after services next week. Evening services would be starting in two weeks.

Not until the announcements were complete did the reverend again call for more singing. The third hymn went off much like the earlier two. When the singing ended, the minister asked the people to be seated then stood quietly behind the wooden box, appearing to gather his thoughts. After a moment, Reverend Williams began his sermon. Zebediah understood little of what was said over the next half hour. Many of the people in the room began answering the reverend, as if to add emphasis to the things he said. When the sermon ended, the minister called for yet another hymn, and again the congregation rose in song. When the song ended, the reverend gave another reading from the large book that he called the benediction. The benediction was followed by a long prayer, where the minister asked for God's blessing in the coming week for all those in attendance and for those members who were unable to be here this morning. When the prayer ended, the lady at the piano began to play again, and the congregation rose as the Reverend Williams returned the large book to the table then walked solemnly down the aisle with his hands folded in front of him.

Zebediah again heard the room fill with the murmur of voices and the shuffling of feet as the people began filing slowly out of the room. The minister greeted all the people as they made their way outside. When Zeke, Mary, and Zebediah reached the front step, Reverend Williams extended his hand and said, "Well, Zebediah, I do hope you enjoyed our service this morning, and we look forward to having you back with us again real soon."

Zebediah could think of nothing to say and simply shook the minister's hand and smiled. The minister soon turned away from Zebediah and his aunt and uncle and began greeting the people behind them. Zeke and Mary chatted with people a bit as they slowly made their way back to the wagon. Once they were on the road back to the farm, Zebediah had the urge to ask what everything in the service had meant, but both Zeke and Mary were very quiet and seemed to be in a faraway place, and he said nothing. The silence remained unbroken until Zeke halted the mules in front of the barn. Zeke turned to Zeb and said, "We'll tie 'em up while we go change clothes, then we'll come back and put 'em up." Zebediah had slept through the last return home and was curious about putting up the team.

Once inside, Zebediah asked, "Aunt Mary, is it gonna be okay if I don't wear my shoes this afternoon? My feet are feelin' powerful hot."

"Oh sho', Zeb, you're still gettin' used to shoes. You just need to start being careful where you step."

Zebediah perked up, suddenly realizing the kitchen was filled with a wonderful smell, and gave his aunt a puzzled look, knowing she had not had time to cook.

"I s'pose yo' wonderin' how I had time to cook." Mary laughed. "Well, come on over here and I'll show ya. Mary opened a door of the cookstove and pointed to a large round iron pot covered with a flat lid. On top of the lid was a heap of ash that had once been coals. "This is what's called a dutch oven, Zeb. It was yo' grandma's, and now it belongs to me. You put yo' food in the pot then scoop some hot coals out of the fire box and put 'em on top. Things cook real slow that way. I got this started when I was makin' breakfast, and now dinner will be ready as soon as you and Zeke are done with the team. Now, you run along and change."

Zebediah hurried to his room and changed out of his new clothes. He pulled on his old shirt and overalls, which did not seem so bad now that Aunt Mary had washed them. Zeke was just emerging from the bedroom when Zebediah returned to the kitchen. "Come on, Zeb, I'll shows ya what we needs to do to put the team away." Back in front the barn, Zeke untied the mules and led the team around to where he parked the wagon. Once the mules were freed of their burden, Zeke led them into the barn. He showed Zebediah how the harnesses came off and how to hang them so the lines did not get tangled. Zeke told Zebediah, "Put two scoops of oats in that bucket, and then I'll show ya what to do with it." Zeke gave the mules a quick brushing then herded them outside to their pen. "Just spread the oats out in this trough, Zeb. The mules need a little extra feed now and then. While you're doin' that, I'll fork some hay over the fence fo' 'em." Once the chores were completed, they rejoined Mary in the kitchen, where roasted chicken, potatoes, and fresh peas were waiting for them. Though he had only been with his aunt and uncle a few days, Zebediah could already feel his body growing stronger. He did not tire as easily, although he would not have protested a nap after the meal.

His drowsiness vanished the instant he heard Mary ask Zeke, "I s'pose you'll be goin' fishin' this afternoon?"

"Well, it's Sunday afternoon, and that's what I do if it ain't rainin', and sometimes even if it is rainin'. What you think, Zeb? Should we go try and catch us a fish or two?" Zeke gave Zebediah a conspiratorial wink.

Zebediah didn't know what he was agreeing to but told Zeke earnestly, "If'n you thinks it's a good idea, Uncle Zeke, then we prolly should."

Zeke and Mary laughed at Zebediah's response, and his uncle said, "Well, sir, I do think it's a good idea. Aunt Mary likes to put her feet up and tend to her knittin' on Sunday afternoons." Zeke gave Zebediah another conspiratorial look and added slyly, "And the truth be tol', Zeb, I think maybe she takes a little nap sometimes when I'm gone fishing."

Aunt Mary laughed then said to Zeke in mock seriousness, "You jus' tend to yo' fishin', Zeke."

When they were done eating, Zeke went to the screen porch and returned with a gallon jug wrapped in burlap. He filled the jug from the kitchen pump then wet down the sacking. "I always brings some drinkin' water, and wettin' down the ole' gunnysacks keeps the water cool. Well, Zeb, let's git to it." Zebediah followed his uncle back to the barn, where Zeke retrieved two long cane poles from nails on the wall. He then picked up a shovel and asked Zebediah to fetch the bucket he had used earlier to feed the mules. His uncle stepped into the cow pen and sank his spade into the soft earth. When he turned the soil over, it was teeming with earthworms. "Whoa, Lordy, would you look at that Zeb! Sometimes it takes two or three scoops befo' I finds worms, but I hit the jackpot on the first try today." Zeke quickly gathered up several of the wiggling worms and dropped them in the bucket along with some of the crumbly dirt.

"Well, Zeb, that's all we need. Let's go catch us a big ole' fish." For some reason, Zebediah was expecting to go somewhere in the wagon again, an idea he realized was silly once he thought about it. They had, after all, just put everything away. Zebediah walked along beside his uncle as he sat off down a path leading away from the house and barn. In some places, the path was narrow, and they had to walk single file. Even where it was narrow, Zebediah could see this path had regular use. After walking less than ten minutes, they came to a large cottonwood tree. They paused, and Zeke looked down at Zebediah as he pointed to the tree and said, "I calls this my 'fishin' tree,' Zeb. I has this one little stretch of the creek runnin' by my place, right in front of this big ole' tree. I don't have but maybe thirty feet o' creek bank, but it's enough room for me to do a little fishin'. I even has a 'fishin' bench,' Zeb."

Zebediah was surprised to see a wooden bench not unlike the ones he had seen in the church. "I nailed this ole' bench together years ago. I slap a coat o' paint on it about once a year, and it hangs together real good. It sho' beats sittin' on the ground." Zebediah sat down beside his uncle and watched as Zeke put two large earthworms on a hook. "You see this cork here, Zeb?" Zeke pointed to a cork with the fishing line tied around it. "That's what we call a bobber. If you see that cork go under the water, that's how you know there's a fish on yo' line." Zeke stepped up to the creek bed and swung the baited hook out over the water. "You see how it's movin' real slow? The water don't move very fast, but when it gets down to that fence there, that's when we pull it out and move it back up stream."

And so the afternoon of fishing began. After they had settled into a peaceful routine, Zeke began to patiently answer Zebediah's questions from the day before. "I don't know why things has to be the way they is, Zeb. White sto's like Sampson's likes our money, but I guess they don't like us much. Lester Wiggins' father was a white man, so they hired him to wait on the colored customers. Mostly, Zeb, we jus' goes about our business and tries to keep away from white folk when we can. Johnson, who I works for, is a decent man. My daddy and his daddy both worked for the Johnson family, and now I do. Been goin' on nearly sixty years, but there ain't been one of us who ever set foot inside their house." Zeke placed his arm around Zebediah and squeezed shoulder. Zeke's face had a sad and faraway look that Zebediah had not seen before.

They sat there in silence, letting the beautiful afternoon flow over them. Suddenly, Zeke was roused from his reverie and stood straight up, shouting, "Whoa, Zeb! You got a fish on yo' line!"

Zebediah looked to the spot where he had last seen his bobber floating. His line was zigzagging through the water of its own accord. "Come on, Zeb, let's git him in. Now don't git in too big a hurry. Jus' lift up the end of yo' pole nice and easy like." Zeke was on his knees behind Zebediah, and together they lifted the tip of the pole. First the cork came out of the water, and then Zebediah saw the blue-green flash of a fish break the surface. Zeke guided Zebediah's hands, and they maneuvered the fish in near the creek bank. When it was very near the edge, Zeke lifted the tip of the pole higher and flipped the fish up on to the grass. Zeke picked up the catfish and skillfully removed the hook from its lip. "Oh, that's a nice one, Zeb. About two pounds. Perfect for fryin' up." Zebediah would never again feel more pride than he felt at that moment there with his uncle by the creek.

* * *

There was another resounding crack of thunder, and Zebediah smelled ozone in the air. He knew the lightning strike had been very close, and he was no longer with his uncle Zeke on that long-ago Sunday afternoon. He was back under a bridge, cold, hungry, and in pain. There was another sharp crack of thunder, and the rain came again in sheets. The air was much cooler now and being driven by a fierce wind. Zebediah drew his knees to his chest and huddled close to the bridge abutment.

Chapter Three

The Cattle Drive

As the storm raged on, Zebediah continued to break off kernels of corn and chew them softly. He could scarcely believe that there had ever been a time when he had been safe, warm, and fed. He knew it had been real, though. His memories of those first few years with Zeke and Mary were like a bright light in the sea of darkness that had become his life. His teeth and jaws hurt terribly. His mouth protested every small bite he was able to soften enough to eat. The cold and wet only made his tortured body ache all the more. In spite of the pain, so great was Zebediah's fatigue, a fitful sleep came at last.

* * *

Zebediah carried the brimming milk pail into the screen porch, sat it down, and carefully covered it with the clean white cloth Aunt Mary always kept there for the purpose. He was now big and strong enough to do most chores on the farm without assistance. He had attended Reverend Williams' small school for three winters and could now read as well as Aunt Mary. He had learned some arithmetic, and this too added to his sense of accomplishment. His aunt and uncle rarely mentioned his mother, and Zebediah just as rarely thought of her. As his memories of Mayellen faded, only her leaving remained clear to him.

He entered the kitchen just as Uncle Zeke was coming in the front door. "Hey, Zeb, Bossy showin' any signs of drying up?"

"I don't think so, Uncle Zeke. Her milk is still runnin' pretty strong."

"That's good. We'll try to keep her fresh fo' at least a couple weeks or so, then we'll let her go dry so she can get ready to make next year's calf." Zeke had his usual long drink of water that marked the end of his work day. Sitting down at the table, Zeke looked at Zebediah and said, "I wants you to know, Zeb, it's a real blessin' to have you take over some of the chores. It makes my day a little bit shorter."

"Uncle Zeke, you and Aunt Mary has been so good to me, I jus' wish there was mo' I could be doin' for ya."

"Oh, don't you worry 'bout that, Zeb. You doin' plenty. Besides, yo' still young, and that's the time o' life to be havin' a bit of fun." Almost everything Uncle Zeke said had a way of making Zebediah feel good.

Aunt Mary had been quietly busy at the stove. She had not been humming a hymn as she often did. As she turned to the table carrying a platter of chicken, her face looked drawn and tired. Mary stopped midway between the table and the stove. Her hand went to her chest, and the platter of chicken crashed to the floor. She teetered on her feet for just a moment, her eyes wide with fear. She struggled to speak, managing only to gasp "Zeke" before collapsing to the floor.

Zeke sat, suspended in time, paralyzed by the sight in front them, then he uttered a guttural scream and shot to where Mary had fallen. "Mary! Mary, speak to me! Speak to me, Mary!" Tears were flowing freely down Zeke's cheeks. "Oh, dear God, Mary, speak to me!" In spite of his pleas, his prayers, and his tears, Mary would never speak again. Zeke cradled Mary's head and sobbed uncontrollably until, at long last, he looked to the stricken Zebediah and said, with surprising calmness, "Zeb, go put a bridal on one o' the mules and ride to git Reverend Williams. Hurry but be careful."

Nothing seemed real to Zebediah as he ran to the barn. Everything he saw and everything he touched seemed foreign. Zebediah was caught up in a terrible dream from which he could not wake. He caught and bridled a mule then climbed aboard and urged the mule into a trot. Once on the road, he managed to get the mule into a gallop. Zebediah was far from being an expert rider, and he put his arms around the mule's neck and held on for dear life. He ignored the discomfort of riding a mule bareback and urged his mount onward until he reached the parsonage. Not bothering to tie the mule, he slid off its back and ran up the steps to the porch. Zebediah pounded on the door and called out at the top of his voice, "Reverend Williams! Reverend Williams!" He was still pounding on the door when the minister and his wife came around the corner of the house looking very alarmed.

"Zebediah?" asked the puzzled minster. "What on earth is the matter?"

Zebediah did not realize that he too was crying until he tried to speak. "It's Aunt Mary. I think she be dead. We needs you to come, Reverend." Zebediah's throat felt constricted, his voice was thick, and he struggled to get the words out.

"There, there, son," the reverend said kindly, putting his arm around Zebediah's shoulder. "You come along and help me git my horse hitched to the buggy. We'll git all this sorted out." Mrs. Williams hurried into the house and soon returned carrying the minister's dark coat and hat.

Mute and numb, Zebediah followed the reverend to his small barn. Together they slipped the harness over the mare then attached the reverend's two-wheel buggy. "Zeb, just tie your mule to the back o' the buggy and ride with me." Zebediah did as he was asked then took his seat next to the minister. Reverend Williams gave the reins a shake and said, "Git up there now, Dolly." The mare loped easily down the lane, and gaining the road, the minister settled her into a trot with the slightest flick of his whip. As distraught as he was, Zebediah could not help but notice how much smoother the buggy rode than the farm wagon, to say nothing of riding a mule bareback. As they made their way back to the farm, Zebediah heard the church bell begin ringing behind them.

Once they were on the main road, the reverend questioned Zebediah for details regarding what had happened to Mary. Zebediah's mind was spinning with emotion, and he could only speak with difficulty. All he could tell the minister for certain was his aunt had clasped her hand to her chest then collapsed to the floor and did not move again. Reverend Williams offered words of comfort, assuring Zebediah that anyone with a heart as pure as Mary's would surely be welcomed into the kingdom of heaven. The kind words did not offend Zebediah, but the minister's words did not seem equal to his unbearable loss.

With the mare at a trot, they reached the farm in half the time it took in Uncle Zeke's wagon. Reverend Williams halted the buggy in front of the house and slipped the lead line around a post. He waited for Zebediah to join him, and together they entered the kitchen. Uncle Zeke was no longer on the floor cradling Mary's head. He was now sitting on a kitchen chair with his face buried in his hands. Zeke did not immediately respond to the presence of Zebediah and the minister. Not until several seconds had passed did he lift his head and speak. Zebediah was again astonished by his uncle's remarkable calmness as he said, "Evenin', Reverend, it's good of you to come so quick. Thank you fo' goin' to fetch him, Zeb."

The reverend knelt beside Mary and held his fingers to her neck. A look of sorrow and compassion crossed the minister's face as he turned and said, "I'm afraid she's gone, Zeke. All we can do now is to pray for her deliverance into the arms of the lord." Reverend Williams drew a small Bible from his inside coat pocket and began to read aloud. He prayed for Mary and assured the Lord that no finer soul would ever come his way. Zebediah bowed his head and tried to find solace in the minister's words. While the reverend spoke, Zeke again buried his face in his hands and wept anew, his strong back convulsing with every sob. The tears were flowing freely down Zebediah's face as well. The house where he had known such happiness was now possessed by an indescribable sorrow.

Reverend Williams stood up and placed his hand on Zeke's shoulder. "Come along, Zeke, let's go to the parlor. My missus rang the church bell right after we left, and others will be coming soon."

Zeke rose to his feet, and after a long look at Mary, he numbly allowed the reverend to guide him into the parlor. Zeke collapsed in his armchair. Suddenly, Zebediah's uncle looked very old and very tired. Zeke's weather-beaten face was streaked with tears; his eyes were red and seemed to be focused on something very far away. "Kin I get you somethin', Zeke?" asked Reverend Williams. "I can make some coffee if you want some."

Zeke continued to stare into space for several seconds before quietly saying, "I'd like a glass of water, if it's not too much trouble."

Reverend Williams turned is head to Zebediah and said, "Zeb, would you mind?"

Zebediah walked back to the kitchen. He took a pitcher down from the cupboard and pumped the handle at the sink until the water was running cold. He filled the pitcher then took glasses from the shelf. Zebediah spent a long moment looking down at his aunt's body. She looked very peaceful, as if she had simply taken a break from her day to lie down and rest a bit. Zebediah prayed fervently that wherever Aunt Mary was, she was indeed at peace. He returned to the parlor and placed the pitcher and glasses on a table. He poured his uncle a glass of water and handed it to him. "Would you like some water, Reverend?"

"Yes, thank you, Zebediah. If you please."

Just as Reverend Williams spoke, Zebediah heard the sound of animals and wagons in the yard. He stepped on to the front porch and recognized members of the congregation. There were more people making their way up the lane. For the next two days, life was a blur. People brought food, cooked meals, and cleaned the house. Men from the church brought lumber and built a coffin for his aunt. Men tended to the milking and other chores. The minister's wife and other ladies prepared Aunt Mary for burial. Then there came the long, slow ride to the church with Zeke and Zebediah driving the wagon bearing Aunt Mary's coffin. Several members of the congregation chose to walk behind the slow-moving wagon. Inside the church, Reverend Williams spoke in glowing terms of his aunt. Hymns were sung and prayers prayed. At last, six men, all friends of Zeke, carried the coffin to the churchyard cemetery, and after a few more prayers, Zebediah's beloved aunt Mary was committed to the earth.

The weeks and months that followed his aunt's passing were not the hardest of Zebediah's life, but they were, by far, the saddest. Mary's sudden death left Zebediah weak with loss, but the effect her passing had on Zeke pained Zebediah nearly as much. Overnight, Zebediah watched a strong, hardworking, decent, and kind man become someone very different. No longer did Zeke approach the business of the farm with the same mixture of dedication and gentle, good humor. Zeke never raised his voice or a hand to Zebediah, and yet Zebediah knew a profound change had come over the man he had come to love.

Although Zebediah was but a boy, he shouldered the work of the farm like a grown man. Throughout that terrible summer, Zebediah kept the corn weeded, and in the autumn, he picked it all. Zeke seemed far away and had little interest in the chores or anything else. Zebediah thought the passing of time should begin easing Zeke's terrible sadness as it had his own. To Zebediah's distress, his uncle's depression only seemed to worsen. Zebediah no longer accompanied his uncle on Sunday afternoons after Zeke expressed his desire for time alone. Although Zebediah never saw his uncle take a drink of liquor, he suspected him of doing so while on his solo fishing trips. Zebediah sometimes did his best to fill in for Zeke at the Johnson farm on those days his uncle did not feel well enough to work. The Reverend Williams visited often and spent hours talking with Zeke. For Zebediah, a life that had once been so wonderful had become a dull routine of hard work and little pleasure.

The first streaks of daylight were breaking across Zebediah's window as he roused himself from slumber. He cocked his head with surprise as he caught the smell of bacon frying. He dressed quickly, and when he entered the kitchen, there was his uncle at the stove.

"Mornin', Zeb, 'bout time yo' draggin' yo'self outa' bed." Zeke laughed. For the first time in a very long time, his uncle sounded like his old self.

Zebediah looked at the mantel clock and saw it was still very early. "Well, Uncle Zeke, this is about the time I gets up every day." Zebediah's chuckle matched his uncle's.

"Oh, I know. I's jus' havin' a bit o' fun with ya. Sit down, Zeb, I have yo' breakfast ready."

Zebediah's heart soared. His uncle seemed, at last, to be emerging from his well of depression. This was the first time since Mary's passing that Zeke had cooked anything.

"I has one more surprise fo' ya, Zeb. I already did the milkin'." Zeke addressed Zebediah with a broad grin and was clearly pleased by the effect his improved mood was having on Zebediah. "If'n you don't mind, I'll leave the separatin' to you, though. I needs to be gittin' over to the Johnson place."

"Oh, that's fine, Uncle Zeke. I don't mind doin' the separatin'."

Uncle Zeke took a sip of coffee then gave Zebediah a more serious look. "Zeb, there's somethin' I need to ask ya about. There's a man by the name o' Hamer who has several head o' fat cattle he needs to walk all the way over to the auction barn at Logan. He asked Johnson if'n he knew anybody he could hire to help out, and Johnson asked me about you. I tol' him I had to talk to you first, but I think you ought to consider doing it. Hamer said he would pay four dollars. That's pretty good money for about three days o' work."

Zebediah was surprised and asked, "I ain't never drove no cows befo', Uncle Zeke, do ya think I kin do it all right?"

"Oh sure. I don't know why not, Zeb. I did plenty of it when I was young. The main thing is to keep 'em from going too fast. Movin' 'em too fast takes some o' the weight off of 'em. This man Hamer is gonna ride horseback behind 'em and you and some other boys will keep 'em from turnin' down the side roads. Mostly ya just walks 'em slow between the fence lines. Ain't really nothin' to it."

"You say he's paying four dollars?" Zebediah had never had a paying job and he had never had more than the few coins his aunt and uncle had given him to spend in town.

"That's what Johnson tol' me. I've seen this man Hamer around, but I cain't say I know him. If Mr. Johnson say it, then it prolly' true though."

"When he plannin' on doin' this Uncle Zeke?"

"Next Monday, if'n he can git' his help lined up. That will git his cattle there in plenty of time fo' the auction sale on Thursday. It should give 'em enough time to drink all the water they wants once they git there."

Zebediah didn't need much time to think about it. Driving cattle seemed like a fine adventure, and the four dollars sounded almost too good to be true. "Why sho', Uncle Zeke. I think it sound like fun."

"Good enough then, Zeb, I'll tell Johnson yo' willin' to do it." Zeke looked at the clock and said, "Well, Zeb, I has to be goin'. I'll see ya tonight."

Zebediah felt as if a terrible burden had been lifted from his shoulders as he went about the remaining chores. Maybe things were on their way to becoming what they once were. Maybe Uncle Zeke might even start thinking about getting married again. There were single ladies who gave him their attention whenever they went to town and church. Zebediah's mind filled with possibilities. When he thought of earning a few dollars, it occurred to him that he might, in time, be able to earn enough money to begin buying the farm from Zeke. The improved atmosphere around the farm continued until Monday, when Zeke drove Zebediah over to the Hamer farm.

The Hamer farm was even more imposing than the Johnson's. The house was large; the outbuildings numerous and well kept. Zeke drove the wagon into the yard, where they were greeted by a stern-looking man standing next to a large gray horse.

"You Zeke? Is this yer boy?"

"Yes, sir," Zeke said evenly. "I'm Zeke, and this is my nephew Zebediah."

Hamer looked directly at Zebediah and, after a moment, said, "He looks like he'll do. I'm Mr. Hamer, Zebediah," said the man, emphasizing the word *mister*. "Daylight's wastin', lets git 'em moving."

Zebediah was quickly introduced to three other boys, all of them near his own age. After receiving their instructions, the four boys took up positions, walking in front of the herd, two on each side of the road. When they reached a crossroad or a lane, it was the boys' responsibility to block access to the side road by holding their arms out and shooing any wandering steers back to the road. The cattle walked at a gentle pace, much slower than a man intent on getting somewhere would walk. The cattleman, Hamer, seemed content with this pace. A short distance behind Hamer, a black man named Billy drove a heavy wagon pulled by a team of draft horses. The wagon was heaped with bags of feed for the cattle and other provisions for the trip. They plodded along through the morning, stopping briefly at midday for dry biscuits and water. As the sun was setting, the herdsmen came upon a man holding open a pasture gate. Hamer called to the boys to get the cattle turned through the gate. Once headed into the pasture, the cattle needed little encouragement. They smelled water and were eager to drink. Billy and the heavy wagon were the last to cross into the pasture. Hamer told the boys to keep the herd together and, if the steers didn't stop, to get them walking in a circle. The man who had been holding the gate open shook hands with Hamer. Zebediah guessed they knew each other.

Hamer rode up and addressed the boys, "Now you all listen up. The steers can't get out of this pasture, but this pasture is a mile square, and I don't want to be spendin' all day tomorrow gettin' them back together. I don't think they'll stray far from the water, but here's how it's gonna work. Billy's gonna fix y'all somethin' to eat, and then y'all gonna eat one at a time. Same goes fo' sleepin'. Three of ya will stay awake while one of ya sleeps. If I find this herd strung all over hell in the mornin', I'll fire the lot of ya, and there ain't gonna be nobody gettin' paid. Do y'all understand what I'm sayin'?" Hamer's piercing nasal voice sounded like death itself.

All the boys quickly responded, "Yes, sir, Mr. Hamer."

As per Hamer's instructions, the three boys on duty kept walking slowly around the herd. Billy unloaded some of the bags of cotton cake and scattered their contents near the water hole. This drew the steers into a tight circle and made the herding job easier. The boys had been warned to keep the steers calm and to avoid spooking them at all costs. By the time the moon had fully risen, most of the steers had bedded down for the night while Zebediah and the other boys continued to walk around them in a slow circle. When it came Zebediah's turn to eat, he was greeted with cornmeal mush. He looked at Billy questioningly, and the cook responded.

"You got some kinda' problem, boy?" There was nothing friendly in Billy's voice.

"No, sir," said Zebediah meekly. He sat down cross-legged on the grass and quickly ate the mush. It was some of the worst food Zebediah had ever tasted, containing neither salt nor sugar. A vision of his mother and her cooking flashed through his mind. The only way he could eat the mush was to down it quickly and avoid tasting it. Zebediah sat and ate his poor meal under the malevolent glare of Billy.

When Zebediah finished eating, he handed the dish to Billy, who growled, "What the hell you handin' that to me fo', boy?" With a flip of his head, Billy said, "Hot water by the fire, wash yer dish so's the next boy kin use it."

"Yes, sir," said Zebediah.

"And don't you be givin' me none o' yo' damn *sir*," barked Billy. "I's Billy. Jus' plain Billy and nothin' else. Now git yo' sorry ass back to the herd, and let somebody else come eat."

Zebediah scoured the dish and spoon then hurried back to the herd. He relieved the boy named Jimmy and took up the slow march around the cattle. The cooling air carried the sweet perfume of springtime mixed with the musk of the cattle. The full moon shed its ghostly light on the sleeping cattle while many confusing thoughts flooded across Zebediah's mind. Hamer was harsh, but he was a white man, and Uncle Zeke taught him to just be polite, no matter what, when dealing with white men, but Billy was a black man. It did not seem right for a black man to be treating other black people the way Billy was treating the boys.

Once Zebediah and the other boys had eaten their mush the following morning, they guided the herd back to the road. None of them had slept more than three hours. They were already tired, and the day was only beginning. Even worse, they all knew there would be at least one full day of droving ahead of this one. Suddenly, driving cattle was no longer a lark. His uncle had always taught Zebediah to approach work with humor and a sense of fun. Zeke had told him more than once, "You'll get jus' as much done, and you'll feel better at the end o' the day." Neither Hamer nor Billy appeared to share Zeke's approach, and the two older men only became more difficult as the day wore on.

It was a warm morning and quickly growing warmer. The air was dead calm, and soon swarms of flies began tormenting both the cattle and the herdsmen. Instead of simply blocking the cattle's path to side roads, the boys were now faced with the task of getting in front of animals that kicked up their heels and tried to escape the flies. The agitation of both the steers and Hamer continued to grow throughout the morning. Zebediah and the others struggled to keep the cattle from running hell-bent down the road, while Hamer kept up a steady stream of abuse from behind. Only Billy, who was now trailing well behind the herd, seemed unperturbed.

By midday, the situation had worsened to the point that Hamer ordered the boys to keep the cattle moving because stopping would only make matters worse. The steers had become very agitated and thirsty, and the four young herdsmen even more so. By mid-afternoon, the situation was growing desperate. The steers were extremely restless, and the boys were nearing exhaustion. At last, Hamer ordered the boys to halt the cattle. He allowed them to go to Billy's wagon one at a time and get a drink. The scowling Billy grudgingly handed them each a few dry biscuits. The halt did not last long, and soon the boys were again struggling to control the steers, which were still being tormented by the flies.

The afternoon felt like an eternity before the herd was, at last, guided into a small pasture seemingly there for the purpose. In spite of the boys' heroic efforts to keep the steers under control, Hamer was nonetheless very angry. "This ain't the damn pen I was hopin' to git to. This is at least two miles short of where we should be." Zebediah and the other boys could not tell if his anger was directed at them or if he was simply angry about falling behind.

The evening meal was identical to the previous days'. Billy's sour attitude appeared to soften slightly as he encouraged the boys to drink all the water they could hold. Then, as if driven by some inner demon, Billy added, "We don't need none of ya sorry asses gittin' sick or dyin' on us, now drink up!"

Zebediah and the other boys took long drinks of water before and after eating their mush. They all returned to the wagon for more water as their shifts ended throughout the night.

The next morning dawned misty and cool. There was a slight northerly breeze, insufficient to blow the fog away. The steers were much calmer on, what the boys hoped, would be the last day of the cattle drive. If the cattle found the weather more to their liking, the four young men did not. The temperature continued falling throughout the day, and the morning mist became a steady drizzle. Both Hamer and Billy donned bright yellow slickers, and their broad hats kept the rain from their faces. The boys did not have rain slickers, and only Zebediah had a hat and shoes. They struggled onward all through the cold, wet day, and even after it was fully dark, Hamer gave no indication of stopping.

Fighting to maintain their footing in the muddy darkness, the boys crested a small rise and were delighted to see lights in the distance. Hamer called out from behind, "Two more miles is all we got to cover." The burst of energy the boys experienced at seeing the lights of town was short-lived. Two miles, as they discovered, is a long way to move cattle, on a cold, dark, rainy night. By the time the steers were, at last, secured in the pens at the auction barn, it was nearing midnight. The boys were cold, wet, and exhausted. Billy arrived in the wagon and again distributed dry biscuits. "Too damn wet fo' a cookin' fire. This is gonna have to do ya."

Neither Hamer nor Billy made any mention as to what the boys were expected to do now that they had reached their destination. After Billy unhitched and fed the horses, he crawled under the tarp covering the wagon bed, and his snores were soon heard. Hamer said nothing to the boys. He simply turned and cantered his horse down the town's main street. He dismounted in front of a hotel, then he stripped the horse of its saddle and carried it inside with him. The four boys milled around, wondering what to do next. Eventually, they decided to burrow into the downwind side of a haystack and try to sleep as best they could.

The four boys were awakened early by the sounds of cattle lowing, people talking, heavy wagons on the move, and a train whistle. As the boys emerged from the hay, they saw Billy making preparations for departure. They hurried to the wagon, only to be greeted by Billy's growl, "What the hell you all lookin' at?"

The boy named Jimmy spoke up, saying, "We was hopin' we could git somethin' to eat, Billy."

"You all is done wid the job, and feedin' yo' sorry asses ain't my lookout."

"But we starvin', Billy."

Billy glowered at the boys and, after what seemed a long time, withdrew a bag of dried biscuits from below the tarp and tossed it down to the boys. "That's all yo' gittin' from me, so jus' be gittin' on yo' way."

Zebediah ventured to ask, "When we gettin' paid, Billy?"

Billy tightened his grip on the whip in his right hand and snarled, "Now how in the god damned hell am I supposed to know that? If'n it was up to me, none of yo' lazy asses would be gittin' a penny." Billy turned back to the horses, and the whip flashed over their backs with a resounding crack. "Get up there!" The huge horses moved into a lope, and the wagon drew quickly away from the bewildered boys.

With nothing else to do, they distributed the biscuits among themselves and ate them. It was poor fare, but their hunger overcame the quality of the food. The boys idled, watching the activity around the auction barn. There were more cattle and hogs than any of the boys had ever seen. About mid-morning, Hamer rode up. Zebediah removed his hat and asked, "We's wonderin' about when we gonna git paid, Mr. Hamer."

"I paid your folks before we left. You need to go take it up with them." The boys stared mutely at Hamer. "What the hell you lookin' at? You best be gittin' the hell on the road home if y'all know what's good for ya."

The four boys stood, their gaze locked on Hamer for a long moment before lowering their eyes and saying in unison, "Yes, sir, Mr. Hamer."

Hamer said nothing. He turned his horse and rode over to the auction barn, dismounted, then disappeared inside.

For several seconds, the boys stood and stared at each other blankly. At last, Zebediah shrugged his shoulders and said, "Well, I guess we might as well do what the man says." They turned toward the road and began walking back the way they came. Unburdened by the demands of a cattle herd, the boys should have been able to walk considerably faster, but fatigue and hunger were taking their toll. They numbly trudged along the road made muddy and uneven by the rain and the passing cattle. As they came to the ridge where they had first seen the lights of Logan, one of the boys pointed and said, "Hey, look yonder. Might that be a colored church?" In the distance they saw a black man tending to the shrubbery outside a church that looked very much like the one where Reverend Williams preached. As the boys approached, the man trimming the bushes lowered his shears and watched intently as the boys made their way up the lane.

When the boys came within earshot, the man raised his hand and called for them to, "State yo' business befo' you come any closer." The boys stopped where they were. The man by the church was clearly ill at ease by the approach of the four boys, whose appearances had become quite rough in the course of their adventure.

Zebediah removed his hat and said, "Good mornin', sir. We was just wonderin' if you might know where we could get somethin' to eat?

We's all powerful tired and hungry, and the man we was workin' fo' didn't pay us fo' helpin' move his cattle."

The man lifted his chin and asked, "Is that what I heard las' night? I thought I heard cattle on the road, but I couldn't see anything because of the rain and all. Come on up here, boys."

The boys approached the man and presented themselves. Zebediah said, "I'm Zebediah, and this here is Jimmy, Tom, and Michael," pointing to each boy in turn.

The man stepped forward and shook hands with each of them. "I'm Reverend Charles Drinkwalter, and this is my church. You boys is lookin' a little rough around the edges." The fear had left the minister's voice. "Come around back to the pump and wash yourselves. I'll get my missus to fix you boys up with somethin' to eat."

The boys took turns pumping water and washing themselves in the cold water. Reverend Drinkwalter entered the house then reappeared shortly with tin cups. "You boys drink yo' fill. This is a good well, and it brings up fine water. My missus is gonna have somethin' ready for ya real soon. Now, do you boys mind tellin' me just what happened to ya?"

Zebediah and the others related the tale of their three difficult days spent working for Hamer and how the black man Billy had been no kinder. Drinkwalter listened carefully, interrupting now and then to ask a question. "You say this man Hamer comes from over near Parkersburg? He promised to pay you then he didn't? He said he paid the money to yo' folks before y'all left? That's odd. That's mighty odd." For the next half hour, the minister patiently heard the boys out.

At one point, Zebediah asked, "Do you think there be any chance of us gettin' paid our money, Reverend?"

Reverend Drinkwalter appeared to think deeply before shaking his head sadly and replying, "Unless he really did pay yo' folks befo' y'all left, then I doubt it, boys, I really do. Mind you, it ain't right. It ain't anywhere close to right, but I wouldn't go gettin' my hopes up."

"So there's nothin' we can do?" asked the boy named Tom.

"Well now, I didn't say there's nothin' we can do," said the minister with a sly smile. "All I said was I don't think you're gonna see your money."

Drinkwalter smiled at the confusion on the boys' faces for a moment before continuing. "Ya see, boys, us ministers mostly all knows one another, and one way or another, we're all connected for miles around. I'll be writing to all the preachers I know around Parkersburg, and any that I don't know will hear from those that I do know. This man Hamer is gonna have a mighty tough time gettin' a black man to work for him in the future, and if this man Billy belongs to a church, and maybe even if he don't, he's gonna get a talkin' to."

The reverend's speech brought smiles to the boys' faces. The minister continued. "Now, I know that ain't gonna put any money in your pockets, but it might keep what happened to y'all from happenin' to somebody else."

The boys nodded their heads approvingly at what Drinkwalter told them. They were standing silently, contemplating the minister's words, when the back door opened and a lady called for them to come and eat. "Come on, boys, let's get y'all fed," said the Reverend Drinkwalter, clasping his hand on Zebediah's shoulder. The reverend directed the boys around the corner of the house to a covered porch where a long table loaded with food awaited them. Not since his aunt's passing had Zebediah tasted anything so wonderful. The minister introduced his wife to the boys, and a pain flashed across Zebediah's heart when he learned that this lady, too, was named Mary.

The boys ate their fill, and while they ate, the Reverend Drinkwalter suggested they take the day and rest up. He invited them to spend the night in his haymow, and in the morning, he would give them a ride at least partway home. "I'd really like to be able to take ya all the way back to yo' folks, but tomorrow's Saturday, and I have to get ready for Sunday services. I kin get ya partway home, though, and still be back in time." Zebediah and the other boys readily accepted the offer.

Reverend Drinkwalter did not ask the boys to do any chores in exchange for his hospitality; they volunteered. He told the boys it was unnecessary, but the boys were insistent. The minister smiled and said, "You boys has had some good upbringin'. I'd like to be able to tell yo' folks they should be proud of ya. I guess, if ya want to, y'all can sweep out my barn. I don't have but the one horse, and the barn doesn't git in too bad a shape, but go ahead."

The boys grabbed brooms and shovels and made short work of the barn. The straw that had been in the horse's stall was carried outside and placed on a pile of soiled straw. Zebediah located clean straw in the mow and put down fresh bedding in the stall. One of the boys spotted a curry brush hanging on the wall and gave the minister's gelding a thorough brushing. When they stepped back into the sunshine, they saw Mary Drinkwalter working in her garden and quickly offered their help. "Well, aren't you just the nicest boys! I never turn down help weedin' the garden." Her laughing voice again filled Zebediah with thoughts of his aunt.

One boy had a hoe, one had a rake, and two of them were on their hands and knees. Together they thoroughly weeded the garden. Zebediah asked the minister's wife if he should scatter the straw they had cleaned from the barn between the rows. That was how Mary and Zeke had taught him to make a garden.

"Is that a good idea?" asked Mrs. Drinkwalter.

"Oh, my aunt and uncle that raised me swears by it," said Zebediah. "They say it keep the weeds down and helps hold the water."

"Well, I'm in favor of anything that means less weeding. If I didn't enjoy eatin' so much, I could probably learn to live without a garden." Mrs. Drinkwalter laughed.

Zebediah and the boys hauled pitchfork after pitchfork of the soiled straw to the garden, and by the time Mrs. Drinkwalter called them for supper, the garden was neatly mulched. Over supper, the minister's wife told the boys, "You've probably figured out by now that I'm not a born country girl. Charles here talked me into it, and I'm still learning about gardens and the like." The minister and his wife exchanged smiles, and she squeezed his hand before continuing in a more serious tone, "I want you boys to know, I'm truly grateful for your help today, and Charles is as well."

Michael spoke up and said, "Ma'am, we's mighty grateful too. We's glad to be able to help y'all out some." The other boys murmured their agreement.

The reverend spoke next, saying, "We should try and get an early start tomorrow, boys. I figure if we leave about sunup, I can take y'all about three hours down the road and still get back in time to prepare for Sunday. I should be able to save you at least a few miles of hoofin' it."

The boys insisted that even that much was unnecessary, but neither the minister nor his wife would hear any argument. Mrs. Drinkwalter assumed a stern look and wagged her finger at the boys, saying, "Now if you're gonna argue with us, I'm not gonna fix ya any breakfast," whereupon both the minister and his wife broke into laughter. The boys gratefully agreed to the ride.

After dinner, the boys insisted that the minister's wife allow them to wash the dishes. Mary Drinkwalter protested weakly then agreed. Mr. and Mrs. Drinkwalter sat at the kitchen table, drinking tea, while Zebediah and the others washed and dried the dishes. While the boys worked, Mrs. Drinkwalter said, "You know, Charles, I think maybe we should just go ahead and adopt these boys." Everyone in the kitchen laughed.

"I think we'd have to see collections go up some before we could afford to keep 'em fed, Mary." The reverend laughed, but the boys felt a twinge that perhaps the minister and his wife could ill afford their generosity.

Seeing the concern on the boys' faces, the reverend quickly added, "Oh, don't you boys fret. Our congregation is made up of generous folk. We set aside money in our budget for this very thing. I'm proud to say, we've never turned a hungry person away from our door and never will as long as I have something to say about it. What we tell the folks we help is, when you get on your feet again one day, just send us a little donation so we can help out another person, and we'll be square."

All four of the boys quickly agreed and assured the minister and his wife that they would be only too happy to repay their kindness if and when they could. After completing the dishes, Zebediah and the others went back to the barn and climbed into the reverend's haymow then made themselves comfortable. After three nights in the open and little sleep, they were all soon dead to the world. It seemed to the boys that they had little more than closed their eyes when they heard Reverend Drinkwalter calling from below.

"Mornin', boys! The missus has hotcakes and bacon ready and waitin' fo' ya."

The four groggy boys stumbled to the pump and washed their hands and faces as smells of breakfast drifted on the predawn air. They greeted Mrs. Drinkwalter and thanked her for breakfast. She thanked them again for helping in the garden. When the boys again offered to do the dishes, they received a firm "No, thank you."

"I do appreciate the offer, boys, I truly do, but Charles really does need to be on his way if he's going to be home in time to prepare for Sunday." Mary Drinkwalter stepped forward and hugged each boy, wished them all well, and told them she would be praying for their safe return to their families.

Reverend Drinkwalter returned to the kitchen dressed in clothing more suited for travel than the pulpit. "Well, men, let's get going." They followed the reverend back to the barn where Drinkwalter explained that they would have to first remove the luggage boot from the back of the buggy. "There's no way five of us will fit on the seat"—the minister chuckled—"but if we take the boot off, two of you can sit in back, and three of us should fit on the seat." The reverend released a springloaded latch on each side of the boot and easily lifted it off. "Nothin' to it," he said. The boys helped harness the gelding and attach the harness to the doubletree.

As they were preparing to drive off, Mary Drinkwalter came running. "Oh my, I almost forgot this." She handed an old canvas bag to one of the boys. "I put together enough food to see ya home. Now you boys be safe and stop by and see us again if you're ever back in these parts."

Zebediah and the other boys thanked Mrs. Drinkwalter for the food and assured her they would indeed visit again if they had the chance. The minister addressed his wife and said, "I'm gonna try and be home by noon, Mary." He then turned his attention to his horse, shook the reins, and called, "Git up there, Buck." The big gelding easily got the buggy moving, but the Reverend Drinkwalter evidently knew his horse quite well and chuckled. "He knows this is more than what he's used to pullin'. It's usually just Mary and me, but he'll do fine." The sun was just clearing the horizon as the party made its way onto the road.

As they settled into the ride, the Reverend Drinkwalter asked each boy in turn to tell him about his life and family. When it came Zebediah's turn, he spoke only of the time he had spent with his aunt and uncle. He told the minister, "I never really knowed my folks. They died when I was real young, and I came to live with my mamma's sister and her husband. They's my real folks." Zebediah felt a twinge of guilt at not having told the minister the whole truth. Although Mayellen had receded into the distance, she continued to reassert herself in Zebediah's mind from time to time. His early childhood had blurred into an unhappy collage of indistinct memories that centered around pain, hunger, and loneliness.

Between the boys' stories, Drinkwalter told them about his own life. He hadn't grown up around Logan but had been born about fifty miles farther west. His father had been a free black man in the days of slavery and had built one of the first black churches in the region. Although he was far from rich, his father had somehow managed to save enough money to send Charles away to a proper seminary. Upon his graduation, Drinkwalter had been only too proud to follow his father into the ministry. It was while he was away at school that he met the daughter of one of his teachers, who was to become his wife. He chuckled as he related funny tales of his wife's transition to country life, which had not always gone smoothly. He would have been honored to take over his father's church, but his father was still active at the time and his congregation too poor and small to afford two clergymen. At the time of his father's passing, Charles and Mary had become well settled in their current church, and his father's pulpit was passed to another man.

When they came to a creek too small to warrant a bridge, the reverend brought the buggy to a halt. He drew his watch from his breast pocket and said, "Well, boys, I think it's about time for me to turn around and head back. Old Buck can have a drink here, so it's gonna work out pretty good." The boys helped the reverend unhitch the horse then led him off the road a short distance to a small pool. The gelding quickly put his nose into the water and drank heavily. "Good boy, Buck, drink your fill. You earned it this mornin'." Reverend Drinkwalter held the lead line loosely and patted Buck on the back. As the horse drank, the boys turned the buggy around and got it pointed in the direction from which they came. The minister's horse was again hitched to the buggy, and after handshakes all around, the Reverend Drinkwalter made his departure.

The boys were refreshed but subdued as they began their walk home. There was little to say as they had all just experienced the same things. The silence was broken by occasional small talk as the boys continued getting to know one another. Zebediah's traveling companions all had similar stories. Their parents were sharecroppers who worked very hard and had very little. They all lived in constant fear of their landlords as well as what some of the poor white people were capable of. He had never given the matter much thought, but Zebediah was beginning to realize that Zeke and Mary were considerably better off than the majority of black people. Until today, it had not occurred to him just how rare it was for a black man to actually own the land he lived on. Zeke's farm was not large enough to completely take his living from it, which was why he worked for the Johnson family, but the house he went home to every night was his own.

They trudged on, pausing at midday to eat some of the food Mary Drinkwalter had packed for them. After a long afternoon of walking, the boys began seeking shelter for the night. It was to be the first of a great many nights Zebediah would spend sleeping under bridges in the years to come. The ground below most bridges, as he learned, is usually free of vegetation because of the deep shadow. Bridges put a roof over your head, and best of all, they get a traveler, who would rather not be seen, completely out of sight. The boys sat on the sand beneath the bridge and ate more of the food, leaving enough for the next day's morning and midday meals. By the next evening, they hoped they would be back with their families.

Zebediah and the others slept well, considering they had no blankets and only a bridge for shelter. The next morning, after eating, as they climbed out of the creek bed and back to the road, they were startled by the sound of a fast-approaching horse. The cattleman Hamer galloped up and demanded, "What the hell are you boys doin' under that bridge?" Hamer did not appear to recognize the young men who had been so recently in his employ.

"We was just spendin' the night, Mr. Hamer," said Zebediah, removing his hat.

Hamer's eyes bored into the boys' until at last he spoke, "You the boys that helped me move cattle?"

"Yes, sir," answered the boys in unison. "We's jus' on our way home."

The horseman continued to stare at the boys for several uneasy seconds before briefly nodding his head in acknowledgment. He then turned his horse and loped away without speaking further. The encounter left the boys badly shaken because, as unpleasant a man as Hamer was, things could have ended much worse had the rider been a complete stranger. Never again would Zebediah emerge from beneath a bridge without first listening carefully then only slowly raising his head above the roadway while looking in all directions. This caution would serve him well in the years to come. The boys walked on in silence. An hour passed before any of them spoke. Jimmy said the man

Hamer was not unlike the man who owned the place his family lived on.

"My pap ain't never had a good word to say about the man, but we cain't seem to quit him neither," said Jimmy with more than a trace of anger. "It jus' ain't right that a man kin work himself half to death year after year and not have a damn thing to show fo' it while white folks lives in nice houses and wear fine clothes." All the boys murmured their agreement. Zebediah spoke a little less forcefully than the others. He was held back by the growing realization that, when compared to these boys, his had been a life of privilege. None of the other boys owned a pair of shoes, or if they did, their shoes weren't for driving cattle. What Zebediah did not tell the others was he was wearing his everyday shoes and had another pair at home.

At midday, the travelers paused beneath another bridge and ate the last of their food. The boy, Michael, said they weren't far from where he would be leaving them. When they had finished eating, they stretched out and rested awhile before continuing on. When they returned to the road this time, it was with great caution. They even invented a game they would play for the rest of their journey. The boys had become spies searching the whereabouts of the rebel troops so they could report back to General Grant. Now, when they saw someone coming, they would get off the road and hide until the other traveler had passed.

The game continued until Michael announced, "Well, boys, this is where I turns off. I sure hopes to see y'all agin real soon." The boys exchanged back slaps and handshakes then waved to Michael as he made his way home. Tom was the next to leave. Zebediah and Jimmy realized that Tom and Michael lived near enough to each other and that they must have surely known each other even though they had never mentioned it.

As Zebediah and Jimmy topped a hill, they could see Parkersburg in the distance. Jimmy said, "Well, Zeb, the next lane is mine. You could prolly stay the night if'n you still has a ways to go."

Zebediah did have a ways to go. He guessed it would be about two more hours of walking before he reached the farm. In spite of his weariness and growing hunger, he thanked Jimmy for the offer of hospitality and said he'd best get on home. "My uncle Zeke gonna be worried about me if'n I don't show up tonight. Besides, I know he needs my help with the chores." Jimmy and Zebediah shook hands and expressed their desire to see each other again soon. Jimmy departed down the lane, and Zebediah continued to the Parkersburg road, where he too made a turn in the direction of home.

In spite of his fatigue, with the end of the trip at hand, Zebediah increased his pace. Once he reached the Parkersburg road, Zebediah estimated he probably had about an hour and a half left based on the time it took to go from the farm to town. He did not, of course, have any way of telling time, but if he had, he would have been pleasantly surprised to find that he covered the remaining distance to the farm in well under an hour. Even after nearly a week of intense effort, missed meals, and little sleep, Zebediah felt light on his feet and broke into a jog as he made the turn into Zeke's lane. Nothing could have prepared him for what he was to find.

As Zebediah neared the house, he was startled to see a number of white people in the yard, one of which was his uncle's employer, Johnson. Zebediah slowed his pace and approached cautiously. The man Johnson was speaking to lazily raised a finger and pointed to Zebediah then said something to Johnson. Johnson turned to Zebediah and said, "Hey, Zeb. I've been wonderin' when you was gonna show up. Zeke said you'd probably be coming today."

"Evenin', Mr. Johnson. What's goin' on?" Zebediah was both puzzled and wary at what he was seeing.

"Zeke's gone, Zeb. He left a couple days after you did," Johnson said kindly.

"Gone? Gone where?" asked the bewildered Zebediah.

"That's the odd part, Zeb. He didn't tell me where he was going. The morning you left on the cattle drive, Zeke came to work like usual, but instead of heading to the field, he asked me if I would be interested in buying his place."

Upon hearing these words, Zebediah felt his insides turn to ice, and it was several seconds before he could weakly respond, "Zeke sol' you the farm?"

The tone of Johnson's voice continued to be kind as he continued to explain, "I tell ya, Zeb, I was just as surprised as you are. I asked him why he wanted to sell, and he never made that very clear. He just asked if I wanted to make him an offer. He said he'd been in one place for too long and it was time to move around some. We bargained for a bit, and when we agreed on a price, we went into town and signed the papers. I brought Zeke back here, and I ain't seen him since."

So deep was Zebediah's state of shock, he could neither move nor speak. After another long pause spent staring mutely at Johnson, Zebediah said weakly, "That's all he said? He wants to move around some?"

"I'm afraid so, Zeb. He gave me this envelope to pass on to you when I saw you," said Johnson, withdrawing an envelope from his pocket. "I don't know what's in it. He didn't say, and I figured it's between you two."

"So this is yo' place now, Mr. Johnson."

"Yes it is, Zeb," said Johnson, evenly.

"Where's I supposed to go?" asked the bewildered Zebediah.

"I'm afraid I can't help you there, Zeb. These folks is movin' into the house. They'll be living here and sharecropping for me. I suppose you might want to go see Reverend Williams. Maybe he would able to help."

"What about my clothes and stuff?" asked Zebediah.

"Zeke gathered your stuff together, and it's in a canvas bag in the barn. I'll show you where it is," said Johnson, motioning for Zebediah to follow.

Not until Zebediah began following Johnson to the barn did he become fully aware of the other white people in the yard. The man Johnson had been talking to was wearing a greasy hat and ragged, soiled overalls. The man had few teeth and had not shaved in some time. His wife and several children were little cleaner. The woman's hair was tied in a messy knot. She wore a badly faded dress, and her face had a weathered and defeated look. The children were thin and poorly clothed. All their vacant eyes bored into Zebediah with undiluted hatred. Here, on the land where he had known unconditional love, he now felt the very opposite. Once inside the barn, Johnson pointed out the bag containing Zebediah's belongings, hanging on the wall.

As Zebediah shouldered the bag, Johnson glanced over his shoulder in the direction of the white family and, when he was sure he was out of earshot, said to Zebediah, "Zeb, I know this has got to be awful tough on you. Zeke's always been a good man, and I don't know what came over him. It's hard findin' good people to sharecrop, and I have no idea how these folks are gonna work out, but, Zeb, I don't think you should waste any time movin' on. You know what these people are capable of."

Zebediah did know. Both through his own experience and from what Zeke and Mary had taught him, Zebediah knew that the larger landowners like Johnson were not nearly as dangerous as the poor whites, who seemed to hate the very existence of black people. Johnson extended his hand to Zebediah. Zebediah had never shaken hands with a white man before but, after a moment's hesitation, took Johnson's hand. "Good luck to you, Zeb. I hope you can find a place to live nearby, and if you can, I'll have work for you."

Zebediah thanked Johnson then turned and walked past the white family, down the lane, and away from the farm. He did not look back. When he reached the road, he made the familiar turn in the direction of the church. Not until he had covered another mile did the combination of hunger, fatigue, and his sudden homelessness hit him with full force. Suddenly Zebediah's feet were very heavy, and he knew he did not have the strength to reach the parsonage this night. A short distance ahead, Zebediah saw a small bridge. A bridge he had crossed hundreds of times going to and from the church. Until this moment, he had never given it any thought, but tonight, it would be his home.

Below the bridge, Zebediah settled into the sand, exhausted and hungry. As he sat, weakly pondering his immediate future, Zebediah remembered the envelope. He unsealed it, wondering what it might contain. The first things he saw were the twenty-one-dollar bills wrapped inside a letter. The tears ran freely down Zebediah's face as he struggled to read his uncle's neat block printing in the fading light.

Zeb,

I don't know if this is the best or the worst thing I ever done. Nobody knows better than you how I've been since your aunt Mary died. I tried, Zeb, I really did, but everywhere I look, I see her face, and a terrible sadness comes over me. I don't want to put the burden of taking care of me onto you. You has your own life to live, and there's better ways to live than taking care of a sad old man. The money ain't much. I wish I could of done better by you, but it should see you for a while. I want you to know, Zeb, no man was ever prouder of his son than I am of you even if I'm not your real pap. I hope you can find it in your heart to forgive me someday.

Uncle Zeke

Zebediah read the letter twice more before dissolving into convulsive sobs. Never, even in the darkest days of his early childhood, had he felt what he felt now. Suddenly, he was all alone. There were Reverend Williams and the congregation, but at this moment, they too felt far away and foreign. He buried his face in his hands and sobbed.

* * *

Not until a resounding clap of thunder woke him did he realize that he was, in fact, under a very different bridge, many miles and a lifetime away from the farm. How long he had been asleep he could not say. His dream may have lasted an hour, or it may have lasted a minute. Zebediah had only the vague sense that he had been slipping in and out of consciousness and that every part of his body was screaming in pain.

Chapter Four

Leaving Home

The rain had stopped, but nothing indicated the storm was over. If anything, the wind's ferocity had increased. The creek below Zebediah had grown to twice its original size, and the distance between the water and the bridge abutment was steadily shrinking. The time when Zebediah had soothed his battered body in the deep shadow of the bridge now seemed as distant as life on the farm. The wind had shifted and was again blowing straight down the gully. Wind-driven sand stung Zebediah's wounds painfully. He could only turn his face to the bridge abutment and shelter himself as best he could. Zebediah broke off a few more kernels of corn and began to slowly chew them. A white-hot pain shot through his jaw that nearly caused him to faint. When the initial pain subsided, he began fishing the particles of corn from his mouth and, along with the corn, a large piece of a molar. His mouth was filling with the warm salty taste of his own blood. Zebediah would have cried, but his body was spent, and he had no tears left. He could only close his eyes and let his mind go blank until the world around him vanished again.

* * *

The morning came sweet and beautiful. It was the kind of morning that, during his years with Zeke and Mary, overwhelmed Zebediah with the sheer joy of living. The earth was surging with life and bathed in the red-gold light of dawn. The air was filled with the scent of sweet clover, the hum of bees, and the song of a thousand birds. On this morning, however, Zebediah felt no joy. His entire being was gripped by nameless, faceless fear. He was more alone than he had ever been, and in his stomach, hunger burned like a dull red coal. Zebediah carefully tasted the creek water. It did not taste as bad as he feared it might, but he knew taste alone did not make it safe to drink. With nothing to do and no place to go, Zebediah sat on the sandy creek bank, staring into the slowly moving water. At last, he picked up his bag and began to make his way to the road.

The jarring experience of his encounter with Hamer as he and the other boys climbed from beneath the bridge was already a part of Zebediah's survival instinct. He climbed halfway up the bank, paused, and listened carefully before raising his head above the roadway. Seeing and hearing nothing alarming, he climbed back to the road, shouldered his bag, and began walking in the direction of Reverend Williams' church. Zebediah had no plan in mind, only vague thoughts of getting something to eat and perhaps some advice as to what he should do next. The morning was warming quickly, and Zebediah was soon perspiring. He had neither water nor anything to carry it in, and Zebediah made a mental note to be on the lookout for a jug or a jar that might serve the purpose.

Three quarters of an hour later, Zebediah turned into the church's lane, and another five minutes found him at the parsonage. He knocked at the front door and, receiving no answer, knocked again. When his second knock went unanswered, Zebediah walked around to the back of the house, but the minister and his wife were not to be found tending their garden either. He looked inside the barn and saw that the reverend's horse and buggy were missing. Zebediah suddenly realized it was Sunday morning and the yard should be filled with people. Zebediah struggled to grasp what was happening. Finally, it dawned on him that today was the spring picnic, and the congregation was miles away and in the direction opposite of that which he had been traveling.

After drinking his fill at the parsonage pump, Zebediah sat down on a tree stump and pondered his situation. He sat in a fog of confusion. Suddenly, he spotted the carrots growing in the reverend's garden. His hunger quickly overcame the shame of stealing from the minister. Zebediah ate several of the young carrots and a handful of radishes. With his hunger temporarily at bay, Zebediah began searching the reverend's barn for something he might carry water in. He spotted an earthenware jug sitting high on a dusty shelf. Suspecting the jug might have once been used for coal oil, he pulled the cork and carefully sniffed the mouth of the jug. To Zebediah's astonishment, he smelled not coal oil but the pungent tang of moonshine liquor.

When the shock of this discovery passed, Zebediah burst into laughter at the thought of the strict and stern tea-totting Reverend Williams keeping a jug of shine hidden in his barn. The humor he found in the jug's discovery quickly led him to wonder what else he didn't know about people. Zebediah shook the jug and saw there was very little left in it. He went to the pump and emptied its remaining contents on the ground then thoroughly washed the jug inside and out before filling it with water. Zebediah considered waiting for the minister's return, but he had the growing sense that this was no longer his place. Zebediah secured the jug inside his bag and hoisted the strap to his shoulder. He took a long last look around. At that moment, Zebediah wanted only to flee and to get far, far away from everything familiar.

Zebediah made his way down the road and away from the life he had known. As he walked along the dusty road, he began to feel strangely better and his spirits began to lift. He was alone to be sure, but he was also free. He had clothing and a bit of money. He had a water jug, and he knew he could always find a place to sleep under a bridge. What fine adventure might be waiting on the road ahead? By late afternoon, Zebediah had entered into totally unfamiliar country. As he made his way along the road, he was overtaken by an old black man driving a mule and wagon. When he drew alongside, the man stopped and, after looking carefully at Zebediah, asked, "You Zeke's boy, ain't ya?"

The man's question startled Zebediah, but then he slowly realized that he had seen this man somewhere before. "Yes, sir. I'm Zebediah. Zeke's my uncle."

"How do, Zebediah, I'm Parsons. Judah Parsons. I go to y'all's church every now and again. I live about the same distance from three different churches, and I likes to spread my business around some." Parsons threw back his head and laughed a nearly toothless laugh. "Kin I give ya a ride, son? I'll be headin' on down this road fo' a ways yet."

Zebediah hesitated, unsure how to respond, when Parsons said encouragingly, "My ole' pap always said, 'A po' ride beats a good walk any day.'" Again the old man tipped his head back and laughed.

Zebediah realized the old man was not a threat, so he joined in the laughter and lifted his bag into the back of the wagon. Parsons shook the reins and got the mule moving. As the old mule and wagon rattled down the road, the memory of the trip he made with his mother and Willie on that long-ago spring day flashed across his mind. Zebediah's memories of Mayellen might have grown indistinct, but when she made her presence felt, it was like being stabbed through the heart with an icicle. Whatever happiness Zebediah felt at being offered a ride was tempered by a confusing tangle of emotions ranging from fear to rage. As they rode on, Parsons began to gently probe Zebediah as to why he was out on the road so far from home. Zebediah told him only that Zeke had sold the farm and retired. With no job and no prospects, Zebediah had decided to travel around some.

Parsons soon gave up trying to question Zebediah, or perhaps he was merely wise enough not to pursue the matter. They traveled mostly in silence for another half hour, then Parsons halted the mule and told Zebediah they had reached his turn off. As Zebediah began climbing down from the wagon, the old man asked, "Son, do ya have anything to eat?"

Zebediah admitted that he did not. "No, sir, I ain't had much all day. Jus' a few carrots."

"Well tarnation, son! Why didn't you say so?" said Parsons. "I ain't got much o' anything else, but I got plenty a' cornmeal and beans. I raises my own beans and gets my own corn ground into meal. Now git back on and come on along, 'tain't but another quarter mile."

Zebediah was weary and hadn't the energy to protest. He climbed back aboard the wagon, and Parsons turned toward a ramshackle cabin. As they pulled up in front of the humble dwelling, Parsons said, "I has me jus' a little dab o' land here. A bit over two acres. It ain't much, but it keeps me fed. I do little jobs fo' folks round here fo' a li'l cash money." They climbed down from the wagon, and even before putting the mule away, Parsons said, "Would you mind hold'n' ole' Jack for a minute, son? I'm gonna go git a fire goin' and put some water on befo' I put the mule up."

As Parsons walked to the cabin, Zebediah observed that the older man had a pronounced limp. From his years spent living in the country, he knew that it was not unusual for older men to suffer infirmities brought about by years of working the fields. As he waited for Parsons to return, Zebediah looked around the yard. The barn was no more than a makeshift roof covering a small part of the mule's pen. Chickens roamed freely, and in the distance, Zebediah heard the grunt of a hog. The essence of Parsons' farm was not significantly different from Zeke and Mary's, just smaller and not nearly as well kept.

Parsons returned from the cabin and said, "I got the fire going, and there's water heatin'. After we get ole' Jack put up, I'll git' to mixin' up some corn bread. I'll make extra 'cuz I knows yo' hungry."

Parsons quickly removed the harness from the mule and hung it rather haphazardly from hooks on the underside of the roof. It appeared to Zebediah that the harness was being left somewhat exposed to the elements and in a place where the mule might chew on it. The old man did not appear concerned. "Come along, son, we'll pull a few turnips for our supper too. The privy's round back over here," said Parsons, pointing to a weather-beaten outhouse.

Zebediah followed Judah Parsons to his garden, which stood in marked contrast to the rest of the farmstead. It was enclosed by a wire-mesh fence to keep the rabbits away, and all the rows were neatly weeded. The spaces between the rows were carefully mulched with a combination of straw and tree leaves. In spite of his limp, Parsons quickly made his way to the far end of the garden and pulled a large handful of small turnips.

"They's a little small yet, but I think the small ones is the best eatin' anyway," said the older man while holding them up for inspection. "The big ones kin git a little woody if ya let 'em go too long." Parsons spoke while he hobbled to the rusty pump in front of the house. "One o' my neighbors helped me pull my well las' fall, and we put new leathers in it. The pump looks a little rough, but she brings up good water." By the third pump, the water was flowing freely, and the old man carefully washed the dirt from the turnips. "Well, come along then, Zeb." Parsons paused then looked back over his shoulder. "Is it all right if I call you Zeb? I shoulda' asked first."

Zebediah smiled and said, "Oh sho', that's what most folks call me. My mamma was about the only one who always called me Zebediah." Zebediah instantly regretted mentioning his mother, but to his relief, Parsons gave no indication of ever having known Mayellen.

"Well, Zeb, it is then, and please call me Judah," said Parsons as he held the door open for Zebediah.

Given the unkempt appearance of the farm yard, Zebediah had not expected the interior of the cabin to look any better. To his surprise, however, the one-room cabin was neat and tidy. An old dresser with a cracked mirror stood next to a single iron-framed bed that sported a brightly colored quilt. A small square kitchen table with two chairs and a padded rocker in front of the fireplace completed the inventory of furniture. Parsons laid the turnips down on the counter and checked the water heating on the stove. He turned to his young guest and asked, "Zeb, could I trouble ya to fetch in a pail o' water fo' me? I used up the las' o' what I had here on the stove."

"Oh yes, sir, Judah, I be glad to." Zebediah picked up the white enameled pail and returned outside to the pump. He hung the pail on the spout and began working the handle. As the pail filled, Zebediah reflected on everything that had happened to him of late. In spite of the hardships, he had a growing sense of his ability to survive. As he returned the pail of water to the cabin, thoughts of the many times he had returned to Aunt Mary's kitchen after milking with Zeke flashed across his mind.

Zebediah returned the water pail to the washstand. "Oh thank ya, Zeb. I appreciates it," said Parsons with a smile.

On the counter, Judah Parsons was busy stirring up batter for corn bread. When satisfied with its consistency, the older man lifted the lid of the kettle and, seeing that the water was now boiling, moved it to a cooler part of the cookstove. Judah Parsons had the quick and precise movements of a man long accustomed to taking care of himself. Parsons held up a small stone bottle and explained, "I has a neighbor, down the road a bit, who's nice enough to bring me a li'l milk every day or two. I used to keep a cow, but it got to be too much work fo' an old man, an' I couldn't afford the feed no mo' anyway. I don't need much milk though. Jus' enough fo' stirrin' up ma corn bread." Parsons firmly seated the cork in the stone bottle and, after carefully wiping it clean, lowered it down inside the water pail. "'Tain't near as good as a pump house, but it's what I has, so I does it this way."

Parsons put the pan of corn bread batter in the oven and, after a look inside the firebox, said to Zeb, "I knows you's hungry, but the corn bread is gonna take a bit to bake. Beans is soft'nin' up real nice, and they should both be ready 'bout the same time. It's a real nice evenin', what say we goes out to the porch and sit fo' a bit?"

"That sound real nice, Judah." Zebediah followed Parsons to the porch, where the older man settled into a battered wooden rocker while pointing his young guest to a weathered kitchen chair. Zebediah took his seat, and they sat in silence while Judah stoked his pipe. The younger man gazed at the countryside, now bathed in pronounced late-day colors and lengthening shadows. Zebediah had always wondered why the evening light made all the colors so beautiful. He was roused from his reverie when Judah Parsons broke the silence.

"I knows jus' how much t'baca to use. When this here pipe is smoked out, corn bread 'n' beans is gonna be ready." He gave Zeb a sly look and added, "I's had a lotta' practice." The old man laughed, and Zebediah could not help but share his host's good humor. Parsons paused a moment then asked in a more serious tone, "What y'all plannin' on doin', Zeb? You headin' fo' any place in particular?"

Zebediah gazed off into the distance for several seconds before answering. "I don't know, Judah. I really don't. I guess I'm jus' gonna head on down the road an' see what I kin find." Zebediah's tone was quiet and tentative. Judah Parsons seemed both kind and friendly, but Zebediah was loath to tell the story of his abandonment. He told the old man nothing that gave any indication of his not knowing Zeke's whereabouts. Zebediah expected that the next time Parsons visited Reverend Williams' church, he would learn the full story of Zeke's departure. By then, he would be far away, and there would be no need for him to relate that painful story himself.

Parsons rocked and puffed his pipe in silence before abruptly tapping its contents against his boot heel. He stood and ground out the last few glowing particles. "I think we's ready to eat, Zeb."

Zebediah followed Parsons back inside the cabin. He savored the aroma of the baking corn bread while Parsons lit a coal oil lamp. Judah used an old towel to protect his hand as he lifted the pan of golden corn bread from the oven. What Zebediah saw before him looked as perfect as anything he had ever seen in Aunt Mary's kitchen.

The old man inspected the pan of corn bread carefully then said, "We'll jus' let that cool a bit befo' we cuts into it." Judah lifted the kettle's lid and probed the contents with a fork. "They's jus' right." Parsons gave Zebediah another sly wink and said, "Like I tol' ya, I's had a lot of practice. I been cookin' pretty much the same meal since Moses was a pup." The old man laughed again. Parsons emptied the contents of the kettle into a strainer then poured the beans into a dish. He looked to Zebediah and said, "I don't know 'bout y'all, Zeb, but plain beans kin git mighty old." The old man gave Zebediah a sly look and winked as he poured a generous dollop of molasses over the beans and stirred it in.

Parsons cut a generous slice of corn bread for Zebediah and asked, "Would you rather have yo' beans on top or beside the bread?"

"On top is how I usually eats 'em," said Zebediah.

"Me too." The old man smiled. When Parsons sat the plates on the table, Zebediah could not help but notice that his share of the meal was by far the larger of the two. Before Zebediah could speak, Parsons raised his hand and said, "You eat up, young fella'. I'm gittin on in years, and I don't need to eat all that much anymore. What I has on my plate is gonna be a big plenty."

Zebediah began to weakly protest, but Parsons simply smiled and began eating. Zebediah was surprised when the old man did not say a blessing before eating, as that had always been the custom at Aunt Mary's table. Sensing Zebediah's puzzlement, Parsons said in a kind voice, "You free to say a blessin' if'n ya want, son. I won't stop ya." He paused a moment and said evenly, "The way I look at it is, Zeb, if'n the Lord as powerful as they say he is, then there ain't much I kin tell him."

Judah Parsons' words shocked Zebediah nearly as much as Zeke's departure. After a moment's confusion, he weakly stammered, "But you's a church goin' man, Judah."

Parsons laughed and said mischievously, "Well, truth be tol', Zeb, I mostly jus' goes for the visitin'. Some weeks, that's the only folks I see." Then in a slightly more serious tone, he added, "I think if people was to tell the truth, Zeb, the visitin' is why a lot of 'em's there."

As the initial shock of Parsons' words passed, Zebediah realized there was truth in the old man's words. He had always been puzzled at how some people could pray and sing hymns on Sunday morning and then behave so poorly the rest of the week.

Judah Parsons continued. "Now, Zeb, don't git me wrong. I ain't about to try and tell you or any other man how they oughta think about things, but if I was to give ya any advice, I'd say jus' try to go through life wid yo' eyes wide open, Zeb. There's plenty o' people out there who's more than willin' to pull the wool over 'em fo' ya, and a lot of 'em are the folks who never miss church."

Again, Zebediah saw wisdom in the old man's words. As he turned to his food, he said a silent blessing as he ate. Zebediah made short work of the simple meal. He could have easily eaten more, but he had no desire to say anything that might offend this kind man who had befriended him. After eating, Parsons washed the few dishes with the remaining hot water. Zebediah offered to do the drying, only to be waved away. "Oh, I don't never dry 'em, Zeb. I jus' lets 'em dry themselves. Seems to work out pretty good too." The old man chuckled.

When the dishes were draining, Parsons turned to Zebediah and said, "Well, Zeb, if'n it wasn't gettin' so dark, I'd git the checkerboard out, but I think I'll jus' have another pipe befo' turnin' in." Parsons turned the lamp down to a flicker then led the way back to the porch where the pair reclaimed their seats. When the old man's pipe was drawing nicely, he said, "Mighty fine evenin', Zeb, mighty fine." It was a fine evening. The moon had just cleared the horizon, and the air was alive with the sounds of night. Countless crickets were chirping, owls were calling, and in the distance, a coyote began serenading the moon.

They sat in silence, but Zebediah sensed his host had questions. If the old man had a certain curiosity about Zebediah's circumstances, it was certainly understandable. Out of a sense of gratitude, Zebediah began relating some of the events that led to his current situation. He began by repeating the same lie he told Reverend Drinkwalter. "I don't really remember my mama. I kin just sort o' see her face. She died when I was real young, and Zeke and Mary took me in. They's my real folks."

Judah Parsons nodded his head. "Now that you mention it, I remembers you comin' to live wid yo' aunt and uncle. Gotta be ten years or mo' now, don't it?"

Zebediah thought for a moment then answered, "Eleven. It was eleven years last month." The good memories of those eleven years far outweighed the bad ones. In fact, Zebediah's only bad memories of his life on the farm were Aunt Mary's passing and Zeke's departure. If the bad memories were few in number, their impact on Zebediah was enormous. More than anything, his time spent with Zeke and Mary taught him to cherish the good things that come into your life because there was no promise of them lasting.

"I remember yo' aunt Mary very well," said Parsons. "She always seemed to brighten up whatever room she was in. She was taken much too soon. That had to be awful hard on ya, son," said the old man gently.

Zebediah had never thought of his aunt in exactly those terms before, but he realized that Judah Parsons had described Mary's effect on people perfectly. "I was ready to go wid her when it first happen, and I think Zeke was too. It was awful hard on him, and I don't think he ever really got over it," said Zebediah quietly. "After Zeke sol' the farm, he say he have jus' enough money to spend the rest of his days sittin' and fishin'." Zebediah had now told Parsons two lies, and though he felt some shame at his lack of honesty, the truth of Zeke's departure was still too raw and painful to discuss.

To Zebediah's relief, Judah Parsons asked no more questions about how he came to be on the road. Instead, the conversation took a surprising turn when Parsons offered up that he too had been on the bum for a few years. The expression "on the bum" was the first of many things Judah Parsons was to teach Zebediah during the time he would spend with him.

"Yes, sir, when I was a young man," Parsons paused and took a puff on his pipe before continuing, "and I don't actually know how old I is, Zeb. I spent a few years jus' travelin' from place to place. I rode freight trains when I could. I think ridin' freights was a lot easier back then 'cuz the trains didn't go near as fast as they do nowadays. A man could easy run up alongside an empty car and hop on. You'd have to be mighty careful tryin' it now, though. Now, riverboat'n', that was the best! If'n you could hire on as a deckhand or a stoker, that was a fine way to travel. Riverboats is about gone now, though," Parsons said with a trace of sadness, "but it's somethin' to think about if'n you was to git the chance. If'n a man's gonna be on the bum, I think it's always best stickin' close to big rivers and railroads."

Judah Parsons quietly puffed his pipe before continuing. "Hell, I knowed this one ole' boy who stole a rowboat in Ohia, and him and me floated all the way down to Nawlins in it. We fished all the way." Parsons slapped his knee and dissolved into laughter at the memory. When he recovered, the old man continued. "Now, Zeb, I cain't really recommend stealin' 'cuz stealin' ain't right fo' sho', but if you gonna be on the bum, you prolly gonna have to do it at one time or other. But, Zeb, don't never go stealin' from po' folks. There ain't no need to steal from the po' 'cuz they likely share what they have if ya jus' ask. No, sir, if you has to steal to survive, then steal from the richest-lookin' place you kin find. Just be damned careful when you do it. After midnight's the best time so's you kin be long gone befo' they know anything's missin'." Parsons puffed his pipe in silence before continuing in a serious tone. "And, Zeb, whatever you do, don't never try stealin' a horse. White folks will lynch a colored man if'n he as much as think about stealin' a horse. It's better to walk to the end of the earth and have yo' feet fall off than to try ridin' there on a horse you stole."

Parsons tapped the bowl of his pipe on the arm of the rocking chair and rose to his feet. "Well, Zeb, it's time fo' this ole' man to be turnin' in. I wish I had a bed to offer ya, but I don't. I do have an extra quilt that I only uses in the winter though. I think if ya fold it over a couple times, it won't be too bad to sleep on."

Zebediah smiled as he said, "Well, Judah, I spent las' night sleepin' under a bridge, so yo' quilt sound pretty good."

Judah Parsons perked up and chuckled as he said, "I see you got that one figured out already. I done slept under a passel o' bridges in my time. They ain't the best roof in the world, but at least they's some kind of a roof, and unless it happens to be a popular spot fo' fishin', you'll most likely be left alone. Just be careful when you go makin' yo' way back to the road."

Zebediah laughed again and said, "Oh, I already learned that one too, Judah. Me and the boys I was with 'bout found ourselves in a bad fix, so's I'm real careful now." Zebediah related the story of his trip home from the cattle drive and the unpleasant encounter with Hamer.

"Oh, I knows of Hamer," said Parsons. "He be a mean one." Parsons cocked his head toward Zebediah and asked, "That man Billy still workin' fo' him?"

Zebediah was startled by the question. "Oh yeah, Billy drove the supply wagon. He sho' ain't the friendliest man I ever met."

"No, he ain't," said the older man. "He damn sure ain't, and I's knowed him all his life." Parsons gave Zebediah a wry look and said, "Billy's my youngest brother. That boy was pure cussedness from the day he was born. He like to drove our poor mamma to distraction with his sassin', and she couldn't never manage to beat it outa' him."

"Billy's yo' brother?" asked Zebediah incredulously.

"He is. I don't but just barely claim him though. I ain't seen him in years. Not since our mamma passed. I think Hamer's the only man he ever work fo'. The one's jus' about as hard to git along wid as the other." The older man looked down at his boots and shook his head with evident disgust. Parsons lifted his head and said, "Funny how things happen, ain't it, Zeb? Seems like a man's always runnin' into somebody that knows somebody that he knows. Well, let's go git that quilt out."

Back inside the cabin, Parsons turned up the lamp. The room was now bathed in a soft amber light that made the humble place feel very warm and inviting. Then, Zebediah's host opened the bottom drawer of the chest and removed a large quilt. Judah Parsons looked up at Zebediah and chuckled as he said, "My mama made this. She and my pap had nine children, and she always said she made her quilts big enough to throw over all of us at the same time. She said it was easier to keep track of us that way." Parsons smiled as he said this, but Zebediah could tell the old man's mind was filled with memories. "My mama and pap been gone a long time now, but I still misses' 'em. My brothers and sisters scattered to the wind, and that dammed ole' Billy's the only one I was ever able to halfway keep track of."

ZEBEDIAH

Lost in thought, the old man gazed at some distant thing for a long moment before suddenly turning his head to Zebediah and saying, "Well, the past is past, and ya cain't do a damn thing about it, Zeb. Things is what they is. I've always tried to spend mo' time lookin' ahead than lookin' behind. I think lookin' ahead kinda' helps keep a man from goin' crazy." Parsons smiled and said, "Jus' listen to me, jabberin' on." Parsons retrieved a broom from beside the stove and said, "Hold the quilt fo' me, would ya, Zeb? Let me give it a good sweep befo' we put it on the floor." Judah gave an area along the wall opposite of his own bed a vigorous sweeping then took the quilt from Zebediah and began spreading it on the floor. Zebediah didn't think the older man actually moved very much dust, for the floor was already quite clean. Such was the size of the quilt, Parsons was able to fold over three layers on the floor and still leave enough for Zebediah to cover himself.

Straightening himself up, the old man said, "Well, 't'ain't the best bed in the world, but 't'ain't the worst neither."

"Oh, it looks a sight better than the bottom side of a bridge." Zebediah laughed.

"Well, I'll leave ya to it then," said Parsons. "Jus' blow out the lamp when yo' ready. Good night, Zeb."

"Good night to you, Judah, and I do wants ya to know I appreciate what you've done fo' me," said Zebediah.

"Oh hell, Zeb, feedin' a man some corn bread 'n' beans 'n' givin' him an ole' quilt to sleep on ain't doin' very much."

"Well, it means a lot to me, Judah. It really does," said Zebediah.

"You welcome, Zeb." Judah Parsons paused a moment then added, "If'n you git' a chance to do someone a good turn one day, jus' think o' me when you do it, and we'll be even up, Zeb."

Zebediah removed his clean overalls from his bag and rolled them up for a pillow. As he settled himself, he reflected on his conversations with Judah Parsons and Reverend Drinkwalter and how similar their advice had been. Zebediah soon heard the old man's snores from across the room, and as his fatigue overtook him, he fell asleep thinking about how much better the world would be if people simply shared what they had and tried to take care of one another instead of spending their lives tryin' to grab all they could and control the folks around them.

The next thing Zebediah was aware of was the smell of coffee; so deep had been his sleep. He opened his eyes and saw through the window that it was full daylight. As Zebediah was dressing, Judah entered from the porch.

"Well, good mornin' to ya, Zeb. You looked like you was plumb wore out, so I just let ya rest. Coffee should be 'bout ready." Parsons shot Zebediah another of his sly looks and continued. "I put just enough t'baca in my pipe to brew a pot o' coffee." The old man chuckled as he lifted the lid of the coffee pot and sniffed the contents. "Yes, sir, I thinks it's ready. Do ya drink coffee, Zeb?"

"Well, I've never had much of it. I guess Zeke and Mary didn't think I was old enough or somethin'."

"I'll pour you a cup. You kin drink it if ya want, I'll let ya make up yo' own mind. Myself, I'd hate to think o' goin' through life without havin' ma coffee in the mornin'." Judah laughed.

Zebediah admitted to himself that the aroma of fresh coffee in the mornings smelled awfully good and that he'd always enjoyed it. "Thank you, Judah, I do believe I would like to have some. It smell real good."

"There ain't a better way to start the day, Zeb. Leastwise, that's how I look at it," said Parsons with a satisfied smile. "A nice cup o' coffee and a pinch o' t'baca in my pipe make the world look pretty good most mornin's. Enjoy yo' coffee, and I'll go see if my old hens laid any eggs las' night," said Parsons as he limped out the door, carrying a small wicker basket.

Zebediah finished dressing and used the privy. When he returned to the cabin, Judah Parsons was busy at the stove, beating eggs and stirring up more corn bread batter. Parsons chuckled as he looked over his shoulder and said, "I'm afraid there ain't a whole lot of variety in my cookin', Zeb."

"You ain't gonna hear me complainin', Judah. I jus' wish there was somethin' I could do to thank ya for what you already done fo' me."

"You don't owe me nothin', son, but I do have a couple little jobs I've been putting off. One of 'em's gittin' up on ma roof and stickin' a few new shakes in so it won't leak no mo'. I ain't no spring chicken, and gittin' up on roofs kinda' scares me some."

"I ain't never fixed no roof before, Judah, but I'll be glad to help y'all out," said Zebediah, pleased that he could do something to repay the old man's kindness.

"Oh, I do truly appreciate that, Zeb. I'm afraid that if I was to fell off the roof, that would prolly be the end o' me. I has some cedar boards I been savin', and after we eat, I'll show ya how to make a shake. I made a heap o' shakes fo' folks over the years. Bein' able to make shakes ain't a bad thing fo' a man to know how to do Zeb. If'n ya knows how to make 'em and put 'em on, you kin almost always find a little work here and there." Judah Parsons dished up a generous slice of corn bread surrounded by what must have been a half-dozen scrambled eggs.

As they began eating their breakfast, Zebediah asked the older man, "You ever been married, Judah?"

The old man laughed at the question, then responded, "I been married twice, but not fo' a long time now. I never seemed to have much luck wid ma wives." Judah chuckled, then continued, "One ran off wid a preacher man after we was married but a year, and the other one jus' ran off. I never did hear what become o' her. Hell, we might still be married fo' all I know." Parsons laughed then paused before continuing in a more reflective tone, "I guess it's all fo' the best. If'n they didn't want to be wid me, then there ain't no use tryin' to force it." Parsons looked directly at Zebediah and said, kindly, "I do hopes you kin find someone to settle with though, Zeb. A good wife kin bring a man a lot o' comfort."

As they finished eating, Zebediah asked, "Will you let me wash the dishes, Judah?"

"No, sir, I won't." Judah Parsons chuckled then added, "I guess I's jus' a little set in ma ways, Zeb. I appreciate you offerin', but I has ma way of doin' things, and it makes me feel kinda' uneasy if I git away from ma habits." The older man suddenly perked up and said, "Hell, I never thought about it, but that jus' might be why I was never able to keep a wife!" Parsons threw his head back and laughed heartily. Zebediah could tell that the older man was not terribly sad over the departure of his wives. "You jus' sit there an' enjoy the rest o' yo' coffee, Zeb. It won't take me but a minute to git the dishes washed. There's mo' coffee there on the stove if ya want some."

While Judah busied himself at the sink, Zebediah poured himself more coffee. He decided that he liked coffee and that he must acquire a coffee pot. It suddenly occurred to him that he had never learned how to make coffee, and he asked Parsons, "Judah? Do you reckon you could teach me how to make coffee?"

The old man laughed and looked back over his shoulder. "Well, Zeb, there ain't much to it, but I kin sure show ya. I mostly only makes it in the mornin', so I guess you gonna have to hang around till tomorrow if ya wants to learn."

Zebediah laughed and said, "Well, I guess if you kin stand havin' me around, I could prolly stay till then."

"Well, Zeb, to tell the truth, I'm enjoyin' havin' a bit o' company. It kin git kinda' lonely here by myself sometimes, but I tries not to think about it too much. Besides, I been thinkin' that if yo' gonna go on the bum, then maybe it might be worth some o' yo' time to let me tell ya about some of the stuff a man should know about bein' on the road. It maybe could save you some trouble on down the line."

"Oh yes, sir, Judah, I'd like hearin' all about it." Zebediah was beginning to realize that the life of a vagabond might not be all that simple.

"There ain't no hurry," said Parsons. "After we git the roof mended, we kin spend all afternoon talking about it." Putting the last dish in the drain rack, he turned to Zebediah and said, "Let's go learn how to make shakes, Zeb."

Zebediah followed Parsons out to his makeshift barn. "See those boards there in the rafters, Zeb? Why don't ya go ahead and fetch one of 'em down. Use this ole' box to stand on if ya cain't reach 'em."

Even stretched out to his tiptoe height, Zebediah could not quite touch the boards. He stood on the box and began shifting one of the boards free. "This board here look about right, Judah?" Zebediah asked.

The old man studied the board with a practiced eye for a moment and said, "Yes, sir, I believe that one gonna do jus' fine, Zeb."

Zebediah wiggled the board free and lowered one end down to Judah. He then worked the other end clear of the rafters and stepped down from the box. Judah took the board in his hands and looked at both sides and sighted down its length. "Yes, sir, this'll do jus' fine."

The older man carried the board around to the back side of the barn's single wall and laid it across a crude bench running the length of the wall. Parsons looked back over his shoulder and said, "Ya really only need three tools for makin' shakes, Zeb. A drawknife, a saw, and a hatchet. And if ya git good wid the drawknife, you kin do without the hatchet." Judah reached below the bench and retrieved a narrow wooden box. "I keeps ma tools in this here box that I hang under the bench. The bench keeps the rain off, and the box closes up good and tight." Parsons sat the box on the far end of the bench and released two hatches. "I made this here toolbox a good many years ago, Zeb. If a man does a job right, he don't have to keep doin' it over."

The box contained a variety of tools, all perfectly clean. "Here's somethin' to remember, Zeb: if ya keeps yer tools in a wooden box and you put a li'l oil on 'em, they'll never rust on ya. I learnt that from ma ole pap. He done a whole lot o' carpenterin' in his life. Me and my brothers divided up his tools when he passed, and this is what I have left of 'em. He taught all us boys how to make shakes and, knowin' how to do that, put food in our bellies mo' than once." Parsons removed a short saw from the box and displayed it to Zebediah, explaining, "This here is what they call a cabinet saw. It has a blade that's shorter and stiffer than most saws, and it's jus' the ticket fo' makin' shakes. Now you watch me make one, and then you kin try yo' hand at it."

Parsons butted the board against a raised ridge that ran along the front side of the bench, leaving about a foot of the board extended past the end. "I uses the end o' the bench to keep me squared up when I saws. Some men use a square and draw a line on the board wid a pencil, but yo kin save a lot o' time by jus' practicin' yo' eye." Parsons eyed the end of the bench and with a few sure stokes cut the board off cleanly. He picked up the piece and placed one end against the raised rib. "Ya always has to make sure you's working with the grain o' the wood when you go to shavin' it down, Zeb." The old man cocked his head toward Zeb and said wryly, "And you'd be surprised at how many people ain't smart enough to figure that one out." Parsons removed the drawknife from the toolbox and began shaving one end of the board. "The main thing is, Zeb, don't try and go too deep. Just practice takin' nice smooth cuts. Once you git the hang of it, it shouldn't take mo' than about eight or ten strokes to git it shaved down." Judah Parsons spoke while he worked, and in less than a minute, one end of the board had been shaved down to a fraction of its original thickness.

"Now this is the easy part, Zeb," said Judah as he held the shingle at the thick end while resting the narrow end on the bench. One deft chop with the hatchet on each side of the shake produced a taper on the sharp end, leaving it about two inches narrower than the thick end. "And there ya have it, Zeb. That's how ya make a shake."

"You make it look pretty easy, Judah," said Zebediah with a smile.

"Well, Zeb, when a man's made as many as I has, it is easy." The older man laughed gently and said, "Okay, young feller, you give it a try."

As Zebediah began adjusting the length of board hanging over the end of the bench, Parsons interrupted and said, "Le'mme show ya a trick, Zeb. Ya really only need to measure the first one, then ya hold that one back." Parsons placed the newly made shake under the board and lined up the ends. He then slid the board back until the shake touched the end of the bench. "There ya go, Zeb, all lined up. Ya always wanta save that first one back and use it fo' sizin' the rest of 'em. Butt that shake up against the bench, then move the board back out the width of the saw blade. You kin make shakes the same size all day long if'n ya do it like that."

Zebediah sawed into the board and managed a reasonably clean cut. Parsons eyed the end and said, "Not bad, Zeb. A little bit crooked, but you'll git better at it. Let's try another one." Zebediah again used the original shake to gauge his next cut, just as Judah had taught him. "Use nice, smooth strokes Zeb. That's what gives ya the best cut." Zebediah proceeded to cut the remainder of the board into lengths. As Parsons gathered up the pieces, he inspected the ends and kept voicing encouragement.

"Now, Zeb, learnin' how to use the drawknife is the tricky part o' makin' shakes," said Parsons. Some fella's use a plane, but the drawknife is a lot faster once you git on to it." Judah Parsons turned to Zebediah and said with a sly smile, "Besides, I ain't got a plane. Like I said befo', jus' don't cut too deep 'cuz you kin wind up ruin'n' the piece yo' workin' on. Befo' you try it, le'mme show ya how to hone the edge. Back when I was makin' a lotta shakes fo' a livin', I'd dress up the edge of the knife every hour or so. It's a lot easier job if ya keep the blade good and sharp."

Parsons withdrew a small wooden box from his toolbox. He opened its lid and displayed the contents to Zebediah. "These is called honin' stones, Zeb. If a man is gonna try makin' a business outa' makin' shakes, then he needs to spend a li'l money and buy a good set o' stones." Parsons removed the cap from a small oil can and placed a few drops on the darkest-colored stone. "Ya always wanna use a li'l oil on yo' stones, Zeb. It keeps 'em clean and makes everything work better. Back in the ole' days, we used whale oil, but you cain't hardly find that no mo'. You start with the coarsest stone, then the middle coarse stone, then the fine stone. Once you git a good edge goin', you kin prolly skip the coarse stone unless you gits a chip in the blade." Zebediah watched as Parsons expertly applied the stones to the drawknife, leaving a razor-sharp edge.

The old man held the drawknife out in front of him and said, "Try to hold it about like this, Zeb. It's better that ya go a li'l too shallow than goin' too deep." He handed the drawknife over to Zebediah and said, "Okay, son, you go on ahead and try it."

Zebediah placed the end of one of the pieces he cut earlier against the raised edge. Trying to imitate Parsons, Zebediah made his first hesitant cut into the cedar, and the blade immediately dug deep. Parsons smiled and said, "That's bound to happen when you're first learnin'. This one's ruint, but go ahead and practice shavin' on the end of it anyway. You bound to spoil a few of 'em when yo' gittin' started."

Zebediah adjusted the knife's angle and tried again, and again the blade dug deeply, though not as deep as before. Parsons said, "Cedar makes the best shakes 'cuz it's real slow to rot. 'T'ain't a hard wood though. It cuts real easy unless it's too wet. That why you don't wanna go too slow wid the blade, Zeb. Goin' too slow is what makes it wanna dig in. Go ahead and put up a new piece and try it again."

By the time Zebediah was on his fourth attempt, the shavings were beginning to come off thin and curly. Following Judah's advice, he learned to rock the blade slightly on each pass so he wasn't trying to cut across the entire width of the board. When he reached the end of the eight original pieces, Zebediah had produced three usable shakes.

"T'ain't bad. 'T'ain't bad at all," said Parsons as he inspected Zebediah's work. "I's seen men go through half a cord o' lumber and not have nothin' but firewood to show fo' it. Some men jus' never git the hang of it, but you gonna do fine if ya keep after it, Zeb. Now, if ya he'p me carry my ole' ladder over to the cabin, I think we have enough shakes to git the roof fixed. At least, I hope we do." Parsons laughed.

Judah Parsons' ladder was leaning against the far end of the barn wall, and when Zebediah went to lift it, he was astonished by its weight. Seeing the surprise on the young man's face, Parsons chuckled and said, "I made her outa' solid oak about thirty-five, forty, years ago and I ain't wore it out yet. Le'mme take one end of it, Zeb." Together they carried the ladder to the front of the cabin and leaned it against the eave. The edge of the roof was barely high enough to warrant using a ladder, and Zebediah could have easily reached the roof by standing on a box, but he understood why a man Parsons' age would not want to go climbing around on a roof.

"Here's why I want ya to use the ladder, Zeb. If a man breaks a bone, he kin find himself in a helluva mess. I seen men die from broken bones that turned to poison on 'em. If yo' gonna go on the bum, you has to be damn careful that ya don't git' yerself into a spot where ya kin git somethin' broke. They ain't many colored doctors around, and a lotta the white doctors won't treat a colored man. So jus' be careful, Zeb. It'll pay off fo' ya in the long run." The old man's words were sincere and encouraging, and Zebediah knew he was speaking from experience.

Parsons stepped back away from the cabin and shielded his eyes from the sun as he studied the roof. Spotting what he was looking for, he pointed out the place he thought the leak was coming from. "Ya see where that ole' shake is split down the middle there, Zeb? I think that one and the ones beside it are prolly what's causin' my leak. Take a hold of the end of it, and try wigglin' it some. It prolly gonna come right out. Jus' feel around some there, and pull out the loose ones. If'n we need mo' shakes, we kin always make some. I think the fo' we have is prolly gonna be enough, though."

Zebediah eased his way over the roof to the place Parsons pointed out, and just as the old man predicted, the shingles he identified came out easily. One by one, Parsons tossed the new shakes up to Zebediah, who wedged their thin edges under the shakes above them, then he tapped them into place with a hammer. Parsons passed Zebediah a few nails with extra large heads and said. "Jus' try and drive these down through the new shakes, Zeb. Ya don't really wanna have nail heads showin' when you do a roof, but unless we wanna tear 'em all off and start over, that's the best we kin do." Zebediah drove the nails home and made his way off the roof. Judah Parsons was clearly pleased by having gotten his roof repaired.

Obviously happy, the old man said, "Zeb, I's gonna stir us up some dinner, and while that's cookin', I'm gonna catch one o' my ole hens and get her into the pot fo' our supper. I think a man prolly oughta celebrate gittin' his roof mended by havin' some chicken an' dumplins', don't you, Zeb?"

"Oh, that sound real good, Judah. I ain't had any chicken an' dumplins' since my aunt Mary passed." Zebediah realized that, for the first time since his aunt's passing, he was able to say her name without being gripped by terrible sorrow. He no longer felt the stinging pain of her loss, only the warm memory of her presence. Though she was no longer among the living, Zebediah's memories of Aunt Mary would bring him comfort for the rest of his life. Zebediah could only pray that his uncle Zeke would one day be able to make his peace with Mary's passing.

Parsons caught and cleaned a chicken and put it into a pot of water. With Zebediah's help, the old man picked a large handful of young onions, then he inserted his hand into a potato hill and pulled out a clutch of new potatoes. Parsons smiled at Zebediah and said, "A few sweet peas and we gonna have us a regular feast, Zeb." Back inside the cabin, Parsons cut up the onions and added them to the water. "I'll put the rest of the fixins' in when it starts gittin' closer to bein' done." Parsons gave Zebediah a conspiratorial look and added, "I think this ole' hen's prolly about as old as I am, and she's gonna need to stew awhile."

After a meal of corn bread and molasses, Parsons said, "Let's go find us a shady spot to sit, Zeb, and I'll tells ya what I knows about bein' on the bum." Back on the porch, Parsons began relating the things to do and not do when on the road. Trains to try "catching out" on and trains to be avoided. Over the next few hours, Zebediah was amazed to learn that there was a whole language of symbols used by traveling men. A squared U shape signified a campsite. An *X* with a closed top and eyes by the side said the campsite was safe. Zebediah learned the signs that alerted travelers to active cops and dangerous towns to be avoided. Judah Parsons drew symbol after symbol in the dirt and quizzed Zebediah repeatedly as to their meanings. The older man would occasionally excuse himself to go check the chicken simmering on the stove. With every trip Parsons made to and from the kitchen, the aromas coming Zebediah's way kept getting better.

Parsons said, "Well, Zeb, I got the dumplin's stirred up, and I added the peas and spuds. She won't be long now." The older man tapped a measure of tobacco into his pipe and said with raised eyebrows, "It's gonna take just this long." Zebediah had by now developed a great respect for Judah Parsons' method of timing.

Their evening meal was indeed the feast Judah promised. Both men were so full that Parsons announced he wasn't going to bother washing the dishes. The old man smiled at Zebediah and said, "That's the thing about bein' an ole' bachelor, Zeb. I kin' pretty much do as I please." Parsons scraped the dishes and poured the remaining hot water over them. "They'll keep till mornin'. How are ya at playin' checkers, Zeb?"

"Oh, I played checkers a lot wid ma uncle Zeke, but I hardly ever beat him, though." Zebediah chuckled. "I think he jus' let me win once in a while so I wouldn't git discouraged."

Parsons got out his checkerboard, and they played well into the evening. They lost track of the number of games either of them won, deciding, eventually, to call it even. They returned to the porch, and the older man enjoyed his pipe as the moon climbed above the horizon and the sounds of a summer night filled the air.

Zebediah departed the following morning after promising to stop and visit if he ever passed that way again. It was never to happen. Over the coming years, Zebediah traveled far and wide. The things Judah Parsons taught him about life on the road proved invaluable, and they helped Zebediah survive until he at last found a home.

Chapter Five

Bonebright

When Charles Bonebright heard the whistle announcing the arrival of the mid-morning train, he left his wife in charge of the store and walked the two blocks to the corner of Main and First. Standing in the shade of a large cottonwood, a half block from the depot, Bonebright anxiously scanned the platform, looking for any unfamiliar face. This was the first Monday of the month, the day his sugar shipment arrived. It would be an easy thing for a revenue agent to realize Bonebright sold far more sugar than his small-town store could possibly account for. The merchant lived in constant fear that his illegal activities would be discovered and he—a family man, business owner, town councilor, and church deacon—would likely be sent to prison and publicly disgraced.

Bonebright was a slight, nervous, rapidly balding man with a thin mustache. The morning was warm and still, and he waited nervously in the shade of the tree until the train was well away from the station. He waited several more minutes before he was satisfied. Bonebright's piercing blue eyes darted back and forth across the platform. He had seen no strangers today, and it appeared that his luck had held again. Bonebright didn't know what he would do if he spotted a revenue agent. Other than running to the livery and saddling his horse, he had no plan of escape. In any event, he could hardly abandon his wife and children. Bonebright mused over his family. They were the reasons he had gotten himself into this awful business in the first place.

Charles Bonebright had married well. A little too well, perhaps, as his wife required a standard of living he could scarcely afford. His daughters were growing up, and the expense of keeping them properly clothed increased with every passing year. His wife was now speaking of the need to take the girls east in order that they might receive a proper education. That the Bonebright daughters would be thrown in with the common children of the town had become quite unthinkable to his wife. Bonebright's constant need of money had driven him deeply into the illicit liquor business. For one week every month, he lived his life as a condemned man whose time was running short.

Bonebright returned to the store and walked on through to the back room. He went out the back door and stood on the small loading platform at the back of the building, glancing nervously up and down the alley as he waited for Childers to arrive. His nervousness only increased when the freighter turned his four-horse team and heavy wagon down the alley. Some unspoken communication passed between the two men. Childers and Bonebright exchanged the tersest of greetings. The freighter began unloading the shipment of sugar into a storage building across the alley from the store. Childers did not need to be told where to unload the sugar; he knew. Bonebright was one of Childers' regular customers, but the sugar shipment always earned the freighter an extra "tip." The "tip" Bonebright gave Childers was only one of his aggravations. The county sheriff had developed the unnerving habit of strolling into the store on "sugar days," tipping his hat to Mrs. Bonebright and casually commenting to Charles on the large quantity of sugar he had seen Harley Childers hauling from the depot that morning. The sheriff, too, left with a "tip."

Sheriff Goodwin did not threaten Bonebright, nor had he ever demanded money of him. In fact, the sheriff had never so much as uttered an unkind word. He didn't need to. Clyde Goodwin's eyes were small, dark, and cold. His disposition had a sour, determined quality, and though his message might be unspoken, its meaning was crystal clear. If Bonebright wanted to avoid trouble with the law, he had best understand on which side his bread was buttered. Bonebright knew it would only take one telegram from Goodwin, and revenue agents would descend upon the town of Keller. If that was to happen, then Charles Bonebright's entire world would come crashing down around his ankles.

If he lived in fear of the revenue agents and Clyde Goodwin, Charles Bonebright feared his wife even more. Her requirements had quickly outgrown the perfectly serviceable rooms above the store, and he now, along with his bank, owned a large house a few blocks away. The strain of the combined mortgages on the house and store were the source of many sleepless nights. Bonebright's illegitimate activities also left him too frightened to attempt renting out the apartment above the store lest his renter get wind of his secrets.

The grocer had a long night ahead of him. He assumed his wife had an idea as to the nature of his nighttime activities, but she never questioned him. Mrs. Bonebright too, had her fears. After supper with his family, Charles kissed his wife and daughters good-bye then excused himself. He walked to the livery stable and, after retrieving his horse, led the gelding to the alley behind his business. Bonebright housed his buggy in the storage building, and once he had it loaded with ten bags of sugar, he hitched his horse. He covered the sugar with a tarp then composed himself to wait. When it was fully dark, he drove slowly and quietly out of town.

Ten bags, or five hundred pounds, was all he would ask of his horse and buggy at one time. Harley Childers' heavy dray and four-horse team could easily handle the entire shipment in a single trip but would be far too conspicuous. Even now, alone in the moonlight, Bonebright was afraid. Could revenue agents be following him at a distance? That's what they would do if they wanted to apprehend the actual makers of the illegal whiskey. All his senses were keenly alert, and a sour ball of acid filled his stomach. Four miles from town, at the end of a long lane, at the crest of a small hill, stood a farmhouse made ghostly by the moonlight. If a lamp burned in the window, he was to enter the lane. If not, he was to keep moving. Tonight, he saw the lamp.

After looking carefully in all directions, Bonebright turned into the lane, but he did not drive to the house. About a hundred yards from the road ran a narrow ravine, all but invisible from the road it paralleled. It was down into this ravine Charles Bonebright turned his horse, and when he was well hidden from the road, he stopped and dismounted. Bonebright lit a small candle lantern and, keeping it near the ground, began walking in a slow circle. When he found the tarp, he left the lantern sitting on the ground then retrieved his horse and led him back to the spot of light. Under the tarp, Bonebright found a quart jar containing ten dollars. He pocketed the money and unloaded five bags of sugar, being careful to place the bags on one half of the tarp so they could be securely covered over with the opposite half. After covering the sugar and throwing some tree limbs over the cache, Bonebright blew out the candle then led his horse back to the lane. When Charles next saw the farmhouse, the lamp in the window was gone.

It was past 2:00 a.m. when Bonebright returned his horse to its stall at the livery. He was exhausted, and there would be at least two more nights like this one before his monthly deliveries were complete. Bonebright had plenty of time to think while out on his nighttime missions. He thought about his family, his church, and his position in the community. What kind of fool would put all that in jeopardy? True, his illegal activities more than doubled his legitimate income, but at what risk? What would happen if he was sent to prison? Perhaps the courts would take those other parts of his life into consideration. What would the other prominent citizens of Keller think? Surely, those men must understand his position. Bonebright resolved to discuss the matter with the Reverend Bender at the next board-of-deacons meeting.

Over the next two nights, Bonebright delivered the remainder of the sugar. As a church deacon, he often regretted his contribution to the illegal-whiskey trade. Bonebright tried hard to dismiss the people who drank moonshine whiskey as being of the lower social order and unlikely to ever confront him in church. Bonebright had his wife and family to consider after all. If his wife required a few more new dresses than the other ladies in Keller, it was only because their position in the community demanded it. His wife's desire to send the girls away to school was sounding more reasonable to him, although she had lately voiced the opinion that she would, of course, need to accompany them. This last idea, he found troubling. Still and all, a man had to protect his family and maintain his place in society.

Charles Bonebright felt a surge of pride anytime he thought of his wife. Emma was easily the most attractive woman in Keller, and he always felt slightly intimidated by his wife's beauty. They had been married eight years, and even now, he could still scarcely believe his good fortune at her having chosen him. If there was anything about Emma that Bonebright had found disappointing, it had been Emma's general indifference to church attendance. He was thrilled that her attitude had changed of late. Now, Emma never feigned a headache to avoid services and had become a regular at the women's Bible study. Charles knew of at least two occasions she had sought spiritual counseling from the new minister Reverend Bender and had done so without any prompting from him. He must remember to speak to the reverend and thank him for the consideration he had shown Emma.

Charles Bonebright became a much happier man once he had completed the monthly sugar deliveries. He generally enjoyed the rest of his life. He chatted with the shoppers and gave excellent service. If an elderly customer needed goods delivered, he did so with never a thought of charging extra. For three weeks a month, Bonebright's life settled into a comfortable routine of tending the store, morning coffee with his friends, and dinner with his wife and daughters. Sundays were a special pleasure for Charles as he strode to the front of the church and took his place alongside the other deacons.

The second Wednesday of each month was the day the Keller town council met. Charles Bonebright and the other council members were proud of the progress their town had made under their guidance. After a lengthy process of first convincing the community and then securing the financing, the town's main street was scheduled to be paved over the coming year. The company to whom the council had let the contract had already begun shipping in the heavy paving bricks that would be laid in the street. A year earlier, the council had been successful in getting eight, gas streetlights installed along Main Street. The council was already giving an eye to converting the gaslights to electricity if and when a steady source of current became available. These were exciting times for the town of Keller. The scent of progress was in the air, and construction of new homes and business made the little town hum with activity.

Most matters coming before the Keller town council were routine and easily dealt with, but on this particular night, things proved to be very different. As council chairman, Bonebright tapped his gavel and brought the meeting to order at precisely 7:00 p.m. The first matter of business was a proposed ordinance that would ban chickens and other fowl from roaming freely within the town limits. The councilmen decided to take no action at the present time but would carry the matter over for further consideration. The second proposal, a measure put forward by Councilman Schmalle, was to increase the salary of the town's maintenance man by two dollars a month. After some considerable discussion, it was agreed to increase his salary by a dollar and a half, subject to review in six months, at which time the salary might be returned to its current level at the council's discretion.

Bonebright read from the agenda and announced "Mr. John Corker has requested that he be allowed to address the council this evening. Mr. Corker, I don't believe I've had the pleasure, I'm Charles Bonebright." Bonebright proceeded to introduce the other members of the council then asked, "What is it you would like to discuss with us, Mr. Corker?"

A tall broad-shouldered man wearing an expensive suit and carrying a leather valise advanced to the podium. "Good evening, gentlemen. As Mr. Bonebright said, my name is John Corker, and I'm from Clinton." Corker had a full head of wavy hair, and his ruddy face was accented by a thick dark mustache. "I shan't take up much of your time, gentlemen. I've come to begin the process of bringing a new business to your community."

The mention of a new business coming to Keller made Bonebright and all the other councilmen perk up and smile broadly. "That's wonderful news," said Bonebright. "We're a progressive community, and we're always on the lookout for new businesses that can help us keep growing."

Councilman Hitchcock asked, "And what would be the nature of your business, Mr. Corker?"

Corker turned to Hitchcock and said, "I've already acquired two lots on First Street and have an option to buy a third. It is my intention, gentlemen, to construct a hotel and saloon on them."

At the mention of the word *saloon*, the council chamber grew very quiet. At last, Bonebright broke the uneasy silence and asked, "You do know, sir, that we are a dry town and have been so since our founding over thirty years ago."

Unperturbed, Corker said, "I am indeed aware of that, gentlemen, as I am also aware of your desire for progress."

Councilman Schmalle arched his eyebrows and asked dryly, "And how, sir, do you suppose the presence of a saloon in our community will make us more progressive?"

Corker had come to the meeting well prepared and answered smoothly, "Your town of Keller is the only 'dry' community along the rail line for fifty miles in either direction. In spite of your progressive attitude, gentlemen, it's also been slowing down your development. For all your good efforts, Keller is lagging behind where it could be. Gentlemen, I am in no way, proposing a lawless, wanton den of inequity where vice is free to flourish. No, my good sirs, not at all," Corker said sharply. "The saloon I propose to build will be adjacent and connected to my hotel. It will also be located—by your leave, gentlemen—within easy walking distance of the depot. I believe, gentlemen, that it will be an addition to your community that travelers will find most attractive."

The councilmen glanced at one another in uncomfortable silence for a long moment. At last Bonebright spoke, "Mr. Corker, we will, of course, require some time to study your proposal in more detail. Although I am in no position to extend any promises, and I am most assuredly not promising anything at this time, I think it likely we can reach an agreement on your hotel." The other council members nodded their heads and murmured their assent. "Your saloon, however, is problematic and quite another matter. As I said earlier, Keller has been a dry community since its founding, and none of our residents has made any effort to change that situation. Additionally, Mr. Corker, I am unsure this council has the authority to grant permission to build a saloon. We must consult with legal council, of course, but in my reading of our charter, this is a matter that may well have to be submitted to a vote of the people."

"Oh, certainly, gentlemen. Understood," said Corker with a broad smile. "I had no expectation of coming away from this meeting with an answer. I am simply looking to get the ball rolling so to speak. I have prepared copies of my proposal for each of you. Everything is spelled out in detail, along with an artist's rendering of the buildings I propose to build." Corker lifted his valise from the floor and placed it on the table beside him. He removed five portfolios and handed one to each council member. Corker then returned to the podium and, with studied ease, closed his valise. He raised his head to the council and said evenly, "I'm prepared to spend a good deal of money in your community, gentlemen. I do hope we can reach an accommodation beneficial to us all. I shan't take up any more of your time. Good night to you, sirs."

Corker bowed ever so slightly to the council, gathered his things, then turned and walked out of the chamber. The council meeting had taken on the ambiance of a funeral as the council members struggled with their thoughts. After several seconds, Bonebright asked those in attendance if there was any further business to be brought before the council. Luther Boggs rose and asked to speak. Boggs was the town gadfly. He never failed to attend a public meeting and could be counted upon to express his vehement disapproval of virtually everything. After being repeatedly rejected by the voters in his attempts to win election to the council, Luther Boggs now devoted his life to making the lives of the serving councilmen as uncomfortable as possible.

With a tone of resignation, Bonebright said, "The chair recognizes Luther Boggs."

Boggs walked directly to the podium. A small, wiry man with steel-gray hair and burning eyes, Boggs stood only a little taller than the podium. What Boggs lacked in stature, he more than made up for with tenacity. One by one, his piercing gaze moved from member to member until it came to rest on Charles Bonebright. "I can hardly believe you would be in favor of building a saloon in Keller, Mr. Bonebright." His words were spat out in an angry, mocking tone. The meaning of Boggs' words was painfully clear to the merchant.

Before Boggs could launch into a full rant, Bonebright interrupted him by saying, "Mr. Corker has only put forward a proposal, Luther. We've yet to act on it in any way, and he's far from being able to build anything."

"Why don't ya just decide the matter right now?" asked Boggs fiercely.

"We have only just heard the proposal, Luther, and we've not had time to either study or discuss it," said Bonebright, struggling trying to maintain control of the discussion.

"Oh, I see," said Boggs mockingly. "In other words, you lot haven't seen the color of the man's money yet. What will it take to buy this council? A box of cigars and a shot of liquor?"

Charles Bonebright brought his gavel down sharply and said, "You're out of order, Luther, and there will be no more of that talk!"

Boggs snickered and then said with exaggerated politeness, "My sincere apologies to you and your fellow councilors, Mr. Bonebright. The last thing I would want to do is upset any of your tender sensibilities." Boggs glared at the red and angry faces of the councilmen one by one then very politely added, "I've no more to say tonight, gentlemen, but rest assured, I'm not done talking. No, sir, not by a long shot." Boggs' parting glare was leveled directly at Bonebright, who felt his insides turn to ice in the face of the small man's malevolence. Boggs knew everything, and he didn't care what happened to anyone.

Largely unnoticed by the others in attendance, Clyde Goodwin sat in the back of the room with his chair tipped against the wall. Goodwin smiled inwardly as he listened to the exchange between Boggs and the council. It was one of his duties as sheriff to serve as the sergeant at arms at all public meetings. Tonight, when it appeared he might be asked to escort Luther Boggs from the building, was the closest he had ever come to actually exercising that duty. Where Boggs saw a cause and the excuse to raise hell, Goodwin saw opportunity. He wasn't sure exactly how the game would play out in the end, but he knew there was always profit to be made in playing both ends against the middle, and Clyde Goodwin had every intention of turning a profit.

Bonebright said, "The secretary will please note the proposal put before this council by Mr. John Corker of Clinton. All councilors in favor of advancing this matter for further consideration, please signify by saying aye. Anyone opposed to advancing this measure, please signify by saying nay. There are no nays. The secretary will please note the matter is put forward for consideration by unanimous vote. Any further business?" asked Bonebright. When he received no reply, he brought down the gavel and announced, "This meeting of the Keller town council is hereby adjourned." The council members said little as they gathered their papers and prepared to leave. A few exchanged raised eyebrow glances as if to say, "What do we do now?" but mostly they simply collected their things and left.

In spite of his weariness, Charles Bonebright did not go directly home. Instead, he walked with his hands clasped behind his back, in a circuitous route around the town, taking a nearly an hour to reach his house. So deep was the merchant in thought, he would have been hard-pressed to remember any detail of his walk. Bonebright entered his home through the kitchen. The silent house informed him that his family was abed. Bonebright made his way quietly to his study and softly closed the door behind him. He lit the gaslight and adjusted its brightness. He paused and listened carefully to see if his arrival had caused his wife to stir. When he heard nothing, Bonebright carefully removed the books that hid the wall safe. The merchant opened the safe and withdrew a pint bottle of moonshine liquor. He drank down a fiery gulp then waited for the initial shock of the whiskey to become a warm blanket covering his body, then he took another drink. Bonebright recorked the bottle and returned it to the safe. He replaced the books then sank wearily into his armchair. His desire for sleep went beyond words, but Charles Bonebright knew sleep would be slow to come this night, if it came at all. Sleep did come though, albeit of the light and fitful variety. Bonebright was startled awake when his wife touched his arm.

Emma Bonebright was clearly alarmed. "Charles? What on earth are you doing? I woke up and you were not in bed, and I became very frightened. Why are you sleeping in your chair?"

"Oh my, I am sorry, darling," said Bonebright. His head was spinning, and his eyes were refusing to focus. "I sat down to relax for a bit after the council meeting, and I must have dozed off. I'm terribly sorry to have frightened you, my dear," said Bonebright, desperately hoping his wife would not detect the liquor on his breath.

"Well, come along then, Charles," said Emma sternly, extending her hand to her husband. "It's late, but you can still get some decent sleep before you have to open the store."

Decent sleep had become both an alien concept and a distant memory to Bonebright. The little sleep he had managed in the armchair had been filled with nightmarish visions of his world in collapse. The haunting specter of losing everything as he withered away in a cold gray prison cell danced before his eyes. He must find a way out of this terrible predicament; he simply must. His mind desperately searched for a solution, but Charles Bonebright could see no good way out. He knew he was losing his ability to think clearly, and the failure to think clearly would lead to mistakes he simply could not afford to make.

Taking his wife's hand, Bonebright rose and followed numbly as she led the way upstairs. He washed his face and cleaned his teeth. The new dental powder he now carried in the store had the taste of mint, and he hoped it would be sufficient to cover the remaining scent of liquor on his breath. He put on his pajamas then joined his wife in bed. The warmth of her presence only magnified the risks he had undertaken and now this new problem. A saloon might well kill off the illegal-whiskey business. Bonebright could only hope that the new businesses in town would increase his legitimate trade enough to compensate for the loss of his illegal income. In his heart, he thought that prospect unlikely. Perhaps he could open an additional business, but what?

A troubled sleep took Bonebright at last and when he awoke, the predawn light was upon his windows. After trying vainly for a bit more sleep, he rose and went in to shave. The face Bonebright saw staring back at him this morning looked considerably older than the face he remembered. He was unpleasantly surprised when he realized that his fringe of dark hair was now flecked with gray. He tried to erase the image from his mind as he finished shaving and made ready for the day. After dressing, he joined his wife in the kitchen. Dinner in the Bonebright household was always taken in the dining room, but breakfast was eaten in the kitchen, often before their young daughters rose. Bonebright ate his breakfast and drank his coffee mechanically, scarcely tasting his food. Emma Bonebright knew something was deeply troubling her husband but asked no questions. He was not the only one concerned about their world collapsing.

Bonebright looked at the kitchen clock and, after donning his coat and hat, kissed his wife good-bye. It was a stunning early summer morning. Perfectly warm without the oppressive heat and humidity that would arrive in a few weeks. The air was windless and alive with birdsong, the good fragrances of the earth, and the sounds of the town going about its early morning business. The doors of the livery were standing open, and Bonebright saw Harley Childers urging his Belgians into motion as the freighter began his daily rounds. From inside the smithy, adjoining the livery, he heard Karl Emmett's hammer ringing at the anvil. As Charles was reaching for his keys, he saw Luther Boggs lounging casually on the bench in front of the store.

Seeing Bonebright approach, Boggs stood, tipped his hat, and said with exaggerated politeness, "Good morning to you, Mr. Bonebright. A truly lovely mornin', ain't it now?" Boggs' words always carried a trace of mockery and malice, but never more so than this morning.

Struggling to maintain his composure, Bonebright responded, "Good morning, Luther. Yes, it is indeed a lovely morning."

Boggs grinned at Bonebright for a long, anxious moment then again, tipping his hat, said, "Good day to you, Charles. I trust you'll have a lovely day."

The intensity of the small man's gaze nearly unnerved Bonebright, but the merchant managed to respond, "And you as well, Luther." Bonebright hoped against hope that his voice did not betray his inner turmoil.

Once inside the store, Bonebright became calmer as he settled into the routine of getting the store open for business. He took off his coat and donned his apron, raised the blinds, and lit the gaslight in the dark back corner. He brought up a fresh block of ice from the ice house in the basement and placed it in the icebox where the dairy products were kept. He unlocked the safe and withdrew the cash drawer and, after carefully counting and recording the amount of money on hand, opened the cash register for the day. He kept back the cash the register would likely require then sat at his desk, preparing a deposit he would take to the bank when it opened at 9:00 a.m. Bonebright loved the feel of money. In the privacy of his office, he would sometimes tenderly caress the bills and coinage with his fingers before putting them in the bank bag.

Bonebright's pleasant interlude with his money was interrupted by the ting-a-ling of the front door opening. He gathered up the cash and returned it to the safe then went to tend to the customer. As a rule, he had few customers this early, and if he did, it would most likely be a working man on his way to his job and in need of tobacco. Bonebright's office was immediately behind the counter, and when he stepped into the store, he was surprised to see not a working man but Cyrus Hitchcock, his fellow councilman and banker.

"Cyrus!" said Bonebright with some surprise. "What brings you in this morning? I don't think I've ever seen you here at this time of day."

"Good morning, Charles, I hope I'm not interfering with your getting the store open." Hitchcock was the very picture of a banker. He was somewhat portly and expensively dressed. The banker had a full head of gray hair with a neatly trimmed mustache and mutton chop sideburns. A heavy gold watch chain was draped across his vest, and Hitchcock was a man never seen in public without his silver-headed walking stick.

"Oh no, Cyrus, not at all. I have things pretty well organized. What brings you in so early?" Bonebright did his best to put up a relaxed front, but his insides were quaking. He could imagine nothing good resulting from the banker paying a visit at this hour.

"Charles, you have a little sign that says you'll be right back, don't you?" asked the banker.

"Yes, Cyrus, I use it now and then when Emma isn't here and I need to run a short errand."

"Would you mind terribly putting it up and locking the door, Charles? I'd like to speak to you privately and without interruption."

"Yes, of course, Cyrus," said Bonebright as he hurried to the front door. He hung the sign in the window and slid the lock closed. When he returned, he found the banker already seated in his office.

Desperately trying to control his nerves, Bonebright asked, "What can I do for you, Cyrus?"

The banker's sad large eyes rested on Bonebright for a moment, then he said, "It's about the meeting last night, Charles. I'm in a genuine quandary as to how we should proceed with this matter. I heard a rumor sometime ago that this Corker fellow was looking to move into Keller, so I got in touch with a banker friend of mine over in Clinton and asked him to check the man out. From what I've been able to learn, Corker's on the up and up. He owns a number of hotels and other businesses."

Bonebright paused and chose his words carefully. "As I said in the meeting last night, Cyrus, I have every reason to think we can reach an accommodation with Mr. Corker on the hotel. Goodness knows the town could use one. I do, of course, have serious moral reservations about building a saloon in our community." Bonebright spoke with a sincerity he did not feel.

The banker lit a cheroot and gazed out the window a moment before turning his eyes back to Bonebright and saying calmly, "Charles, we both know there's a bit more to it than that."

The banker spoke softly and evenly, but the words hit Bonebright like icy water. At last he stammered, "What do you mean, Cyrus?"

Again the banker looked off into space, drew on his cheroot, then said, "We're both men of the world, Charles, and I don't think we need to put too fine a point on it. You know very good and well what I'm talking about."

Bonebright felt himself being crushed under the weight of the banker's gaze, and try as he might, he could not find words to respond. Had it all been so obvious?

"I'm not here to judge you, Charles," said the banker in a kinder more encouraging tone. "A man does what he must to take care of the ones he loves and, to my way of thinking, you've not harmed anyone. If it's of any consolation, Charles, you can be assured that you are not the only citizen who's finding himself in an uncomfortable position this morning."

"Why don't we simply approve the hotel and deny the saloon, Cyrus?"

The banker idly rolled the cheroot between his fingers and appeared to be deep in thought. Hitchcock took his time responding, "I fear it will not be that simple, Charles. Corker is a man of considerable means and great determination. If we deny his saloon, he will likely go around us and take the matter directly to the governor.

He's done similar things in the past and has succeeded every time he's tried. Corker has deep pockets and the ear of many powerful people at the capital. If we try fighting him, we could damn well bankrupt the town and ourselves along with it. I, for one, have no intention of going bankrupt, Charles."

Bonebright was suddenly aware that his head was cradled in his hands and he was no longer looking at the banker. Pulling himself together, he managed to weakly ask, "What do propose we do, Cyrus?"

"I'm not sure yet, Charles, but we have to find a way to work through this in some fashion where no one loses any money and no one goes to jail."

Bonebright visibly winced when the banker mentioned jail.

Sensing Bonebright's deep anxiety, Hitchcock said, "Chin up, Charles. Don't get discouraged. We need to keep our wits about us. We'll find a solution, and the sooner we get to work on it, the better off we'll all be. We have some time, and we're not without resources of our own. The main thing is, we need to be thinking about our options, and that's why I'm here this morning. Nothing's going to happen overnight."

"Thank you, Cyrus. You're right of course. We have to use our heads here."

"That's the spirit, Charles," said the banker, rising to leave. "Oh, before I go, there's one more thing I want to ask you. Charles, is the apartment above the store still vacant?"

"No one's lived there since we moved into the house last year, Cyrus."

"You can reach the apartment from inside the store, can't you?"

"Yes, Cyrus, there are both inside and outside stairways," said Bonebright.

"Charles, there are other prominent citizens with a vested interest in the outcome of this issue, and I was wondering if it might be possible for us to use the apartment, on occasion, as a place to meet and discuss our strategy. If you agree, it would be a place where we can meet without attracting undue attention."

"Yes, of course, Cyrus," said Bonebright gratefully. "Whatever you need, Cyrus. All the furniture is still there."

"That's excellent, Charles," said the banker, shaking Bonebright's hand. "I'll get in touch with you when the time comes. I must let you get back to business."

Bonebright followed the banker to the front door and unlocked it. As he held the door open for Hitchcock, Bonebright saw Luther Boggs across the street, leaning against a light pole with his arms folded across his chest. As the banker emerged from the store, Boggs stood up straight and tipped his derby and bowed to them. If Hitchcock noticed Boggs, he gave no sign of it. Bonebright, on the other hand, felt the little man's malevolent mockery pierce deep into his being. Whatever confidence the banker's parting words may have given Bonebright had now vanished, and the merchant was again gripped by a sense of impending doom.

Badly shaken, Bonebright retreated to his office. For the first time in his life, he had the strong desire for a drink of liquor early in the morning. He sat, staring vacantly at the wall for a long time as he slowly regained his composure and returned his thoughts to the store. The front door jingled again, and the merchant rose and went to take care of the customer. The rest of his morning passed uneventfully. Customers came and went. Goods were purchased and goods were ordered. Emma arrived at ten o'clock as usual. At some point during the day, the thought occurred to Bonebright that he might secure a bottle of whiskey in the apartment upstairs. The only time Emma ever visited the rooms was to take a brief rest during an especially busy day. Yes, he could easily find a place to secret a bottle and thus be prepared for a morning like this.

Chapter Six

Bender

An uncharitable person might be inclined to describe Theresa Bender as "mousey." She was a small nervous woman with quite unremarkable looks. Her general appearance was not enhanced by her thin hair, heavy glasses, and an unfortunate tendency to lisp when agitated. Her father had spent considerable money on elocution lessons in the hope of correcting his only child's difficulty with speech. The lessons had helped but had only been partially successful in correcting the problem, as Theresa was prone to anxiety, and at such times, her lisp became as pronounced as ever.

Her husband, the Reverend Richard Bender, was a study in contrast. Standing well over six feet tall, broad shouldered, and with flowing blonde hair. Reverend Bender's striking physical appearance was complimented by a resonate baritone that penetrated every part of the church when he rose to preach. Bender was admired by the men in his congregation, who saw him as a man's man, and adored by the women, a number of whom thought of him in a very different way. It seemed especially odd to many of the congregants that such a handsome man would have made such an unlikely marriage.

Bender had been, at best, a mediocre student at seminary, and some of his personal habits had been considered shocking by fellow students that knew of them. He was known to have often left campus without permission, to return hours later with the smell of tobacco on his clothing and liquor on his breath. If others thought the ministry an odd choice of profession for a man who clearly had passions other than the church, Bender himself had no such reservations. He knew that pastors of large churches were paid very well and resided in handsome homes provided by their congregations. Even better, in the mind of Richard Bender, was the absence of the hard physical labor to which every other member of his family was condemned. Bender had no difficulty reconciling his lack of any actual faith, with the other rewards the church had to offer.

In their senior year at seminary, students were matched with the calls coming in from the various churches in the synod. The great majority of the churches' extending calls were looking for assistants to aid in the work of larger congregations. All the students knew pastoral assistants were poorly paid and that assistants often spent years in these positions before moving on to lead congregations. Of those congregations seeking men who would serve as full pastors, all but one was small, distant, and isolated. The exception was the town of Keller. The town was of middling size and growing rapidly. Best of all, in Bender's opinion, was the fact that Keller was served by a railroad, which meant he would be able to, occasionally, escape the confines of a small-town ministry.

Nearly to an individual, the seminarians viewed the years spent as assistant pastors to be a part of a natural process of apprenticeship that would eventually find them leading congregations. Richard Bender did not see things that way at all. The thought of spending years working for a farmhand's wage filled him with revulsion, and he set his sights on the position at Keller. Unfortunately for Bender, there were two major obstacles standing in his way. First, there was the matter of his middling grades. Such a plum assignment would, almost certainly, go to one of the honor graduates if they chose to pursue it. Secondly, although the church itself did not require its pastors to be married, individual congregations often did put forward such a requirement, and this was the case with the church at Keller.

Being single, with no prospect of marriage on the horizon, and in the middle of the pack academically would have deterred most men, but Richard Bender was not most men. Bender had been vaguely aware of the bishop's daughter for some time. She was a shy, unbecoming young woman who resided deep within her father's shadow. Richard had occasionally observed her going to and from the bishop's manse, market basket in hand, but mostly he saw her in chapel. Theresa Miller was an unassuming small presence who sometimes played piano if the regular pianist was unavailable. On the occasions when she played in chapel, Richard, along with everyone else in attendance, could see the strain on the young woman's face. Although she played very well, the experience of playing in public was clearly something she found trying.

On a Sunday morning, ten weeks ahead of graduation, Richard Bender sat in chapel. He sang the hymns mechanically and said amen at the appropriate times, though he was otherwise paying little attention. Though only minimally engaged in the service, his eye came to rest on the bishop's daughter, who was today seated at the piano. Like a bolt from the heavens, he felt the stars align. Bender resolved that he would begin, that very afternoon, to court Theresa Miller. What Richard Bender lacked in scholarly zeal was more than compensated for by self-confidence. Sunday afternoons, when families were at home, was the time deemed appropriate for the seminarians to call on their prospective mates. Dressed in his best suit, Richard Bender knocked on Bishop Miller's door, hat in hand, at precisely 2:00 p.m.

It was Theresa herself who answered the door and, after her initial surprise, asked the caller, "I assume you are looking for my father, Mister . . ." She paused and tried to think of the visitor's name but could not.

"Bender, Ms. Miller. Richard Bender, and yes, I would like to speak to your father, but only to secure his permission that I might call on you."

"Call on me?" said Theresa with an audible gasp.

"Yes, of course, Ms. Miller, might I speak to your father?" asked Bender brightly.

Viably stunned, Theresa paused before responding, "Please wait here in the foyer while I go and speak with my father, Mr. Bender. He's resting in his study. I shall only be a moment." Though trying desperately to suppress it, her voice betrayed a trace of the dreaded lisp. As he waited for Theresa's return, Bender eyed the richly furnished interior of the bishop's residence. Though other seminarians had been invited to dine with the bishop, he had not, as that privilege was extended only to the very best students. Those honored with an invitation to the bishop's house were the men the church already had its eye on as future candidates for high office. Richard Bender had taken the initiative to secure his own invitation to the bishop's home.

A few minutes later, Theresa Miller returned and said, "Please come with me, Mr. Bender, my father will see you in the study." She led him down a hallway, to the door of her father's study, and said, "Please go on in, Mr. Bender, he is expecting you."

"Thank you, Ms. Miller," said Bender, bowing to her slightly.

Theresa did not respond but merely gave Bender a small smile before returning to the parlor. Though he had been told to go right in, Bender knocked anyway.

From within, the bishop's familiar voice called. "Please come in, Mr. Bender."

When Bender entered the room, he found the bishop seated behind his desk. The older man rose and extended his hand to Richard and said, "Good afternoon, Mr. Bender. Please sit down." When seated, the bishop eyed Bender carefully before speaking. "I must say, I'm rather surprised by your appearance here this afternoon, Mr. Bender." There was no trace of either suspicion or surprise in the bishop's voice, only a perfectly level statement of fact. Bender knew he was facing his first test and that his hand must be carefully played.

"I've come to ask your permission to call on your daughter, sir," said Bender in his best "from the pulpit" voice.

It would have taken an excellent poker player to read anything in the bishop's face as he looked at Bender. There was no trace of emotion—good, bad, or indifferent. He simply eyed Bender coolly for a few seconds, a waiting period that grew increasingly uncomfortable for Bender. At last the bishop said, "So Theresa tells me. And what, Mr. Bender, prompted this move on your part?"

If Richard Bender had ever entertained the idea that the bishop might be something of a fool, those thoughts had now vanished like chaff in the wind. Bender chose his words carefully. "It was in chapel this morning, sir. Until this morning, I had never fully appreciated just how beautifully your daughter plays the piano. It suddenly struck me that I must make her acquaintance."

"I see," said the bishop. "Yes, she does play beautifully, doesn't she? She's often played in church before, Mr. Bender, yet you only noticed it today? That's really quite remarkable."

"Sir, what I experienced this morning was not unlike the feeling I had when God called me to the ministry," said Bender with all the earnest humility he could muster.

The bishop eyed Bender coolly for more uncomfortable seconds before responding with a barely discernible laugh. "Very well then, Mr. Bender. Theresa says she's willing to see you. This is all very much up to her. Need I explain what's expected of you, Mr. Bender?"

"No, sir. I am a gentleman, sir, and my intentions are honorable," said Bender in the most serious tone he could manage.

The bishop stood and, extending his hand to Bender, said, "Good day to you then, Mr. Bender, I'll leave it up to you young people to get acquainted." Again the bishop's words bore the faintest trace of cynicism.

While the bishop's spoken words were saying one thing, the man's overall demeanor was sending a very different message to Richard Bender. The message that went unspoken, in the handshake that lasted a second longer than it should have, said, "I don't believe a word you're saying, young man, and you'll try playing me for a fool at your peril."

Bender shook the bishop's hand and thanked him. He breathed a sigh of relief as he closed the door behind him and went to make his acquaintance with Theresa. He had passed the first test. When he reentered the parlor, he found the bishop's daughter seated in front of a window, working on a needlepoint. Theresa was so engrossed in her work that she only noticed his return when he spoke. "Good afternoon, Ms. Miller, your father has graciously allowed me to call on you."

Theresa was slightly startled by the sound of his voice and stared at him blankly through her thick glasses for a moment. Regaining her composure, she sat her work aside and said, "I must say, I am really quite surprised by your visit, Mr. Bender."

"Richard. Please call me Richard, Ms. Miller," said Bender in a voice he hoped was both warm and reassuring.

"Very well, Richard," said Theresa with a small smile. "What on earth prompted you to pay me a call?"

Bender did not fail to notice that she did not invite him to use her first name. "It was during services this morning, Ms. Miller. I had, of course, heard you play before, but this morning I was suddenly taken by just how beautifully you play, and I resolved, then and there, to make your acquaintance." Bender held his hat in his hand and smiled broadly at Theresa.

She eyed him skeptically for a few seconds then said, "Please sit down, Richard. May I get you something to drink? Tea or perhaps some lemonade?"

"Oh, lemonade would be wonderful," said Bender. "I've not had any in quite some time."

"I made some for Father after church, let me fetch it from the icebox." Theresa rose, and Bender did as well. "Oh, please be seated, Richard, you needn't be jumping up every time I do," she said with a small smile. "I'll only be a moment."

Theresa Miller disappeared into the kitchen and returned a few minutes later with a tray bearing a pitcher of lemonade, glasses, and a plate of cookies. "I thought you might like some cookies, Mr. Bender, I baked them yesterday. They're Father's favorite, oatmeal and raisin." She sat the tray on a table then filled their glasses then presented his to him along with the cookies. She returned to her chair and, upon sitting, placed her hands in her lap and looked at Bender with a curious expression. "So, Richard, tell me about yourself."

Bender smiled earnestly and said, "Mine is not a very interesting story I'm afraid, Ms. Miller. I'm just a farm boy dressed up and come to town. My father, my brothers, and most all of my extended family are farmers. It's a life I felt destined to lead myself as I very much loved life on the farm. It was only when the Lord's call became impossible to ignore that I gave up one dream to pursue another."

"Do you feel that you have been truly called, Richard?"

"Oh, very much so, Ms. Miller. Right up until the day I began seminary, I was scarcely able to see myself being anything but a farmer, but once I was here, I knew I had made the right choice."

"Farming, too, is a noble calling, Richard," she said evenly, as if not quite believing him.

"Oh, it is! Indeed it is!" said Bender quickly. "There is great nobility to be found among those who earn their living from the land. I would think, being the daughter of a bishop, you would understand, better than most people, just how strong the Lord's call can be."

"That is, of course, true, Richard. However, I've lived most of my life in and around this seminary, and I know from experience that there have been many who believed they had heard the call, only to find their senses had deceived them."

Bender was quickly realizing that Theresa Miller's social awkwardness was not to be confused with a lack of intelligence. After only this brief meeting, he had become acutely aware that he must exercise even more caution than he originally thought. The bishop was no fool, and neither, evidently, was his daughter.

Hoping to steer the conversation in another direction, Bender asked. "And you, Ms. Miller? What is the story of your life?"

Theresa Miller appeared to be assessing Bender's sincerity and regarded him calmly for a moment before beginning. "There has been no great excitement in my life either, Richard. My great regret is never having known my mother. She died giving me life. My father never remarried, although many in the church and in our family encouraged him to do so. He always maintained that he had had but two great loves in his life—my mother and the church."

"It must have been terribly difficult for you, Ms. Miller."

Theresa did not respond as Bender had anticipated and said, "I regret never having met my mother, but it's hard to miss someone that you never knew. I did not have a mother in the conventional sense, but I did not grow up without love, Richard. I'm sure you know Mrs. Pemberton? The church's regular pianist?"

"Oh yes, of course," said Richard. "She also teaches music at the seminary."

"Yes, and she does so very well. Martha was my father's housekeeper and my governess while I was growing up. It was only after I was of age to tend to Father's house that she took up teaching. She is my mother in every way that matters," said Theresa as if issuing a mild challenge to Bender.

"Is she the one who taught you to play piano?" asked Richard.

"Yes, she taught me the piano and much more," said Theresa wistfully. "Most of my education was acquired through tutors, and she was the one who, along with my father, oversaw that process. When I went away to school, I found that I had been very well prepared. I have her, and my father of course, to thank for that," said Theresa evenly.

"If I may ask, to where did you go away to school, Ms. Miller?"

"Boston. The church maintains a finishing school there for the daughters of clergymen. I was there for two years before returning home." There was not a trace of boastful pride in Theresa's voice. She spoke evenly and directly. Theresa Miller was sending Bender the tacit message that she amounted to more than her physical appearance might indicate. Their conversation continued back and forth in a similar vein until Theresa glanced at the grandfather clock and said, "My goodness, Richard, it's four o'clock. I had no idea," she said with a smile and a small laugh. "I'm afraid you must excuse me now, Richard. It's time I began preparing dinner."

Bender and Theresa both rose, and she escorted him to the door. Before leaving, Richard bowed slightly to her and extended his hand, unsure how she might respond.

She accepted his hand and returned a ladylike handshake. "Good day to you, Richard. Your visit has been surprising, but not unpleasant." She spoke with a good humor that did not, however, reveal very much.

"And a very good day to you, Ms. Miller," said Richard, letting the handshake linger a moment. "Might I be allowed to call you Theresa?"

She gracefully withdrew her hand and eyed him carefully before responding. "We shall see, Richard. We shall see."

"Might I call on you again, Ms. Miller?" asked Bender hopefully.

Again Theresa paused before speaking. "I suppose you may, Richard, but please do me the courtesy of sending a note first and then waiting for my response. The campus message system works very well."

"Oh yes, of course, Ms. Miller. I was perhaps rather too bold in coming to your home unannounced," replied Bender earnestly.

"You've conducted yourself as a gentleman, Richard, and you spoke to my farther, as is proper. I think your boldness may be overlooked." Theresa's words carried a trace of coyness that Bender had not expected.

Bender again bowed slightly to Theresa. "Good day, Ms. Miller. It's been an enjoyable afternoon, and it is my fond hope you will allow me to call again."

"Good day, Richard," said Theresa without further comment.

Bender turned and walked away in the direction of the campus. Theresa watched until he reached the sidewalk then returned inside and closed the door. She went to the kitchen and began preparing the evening meal. Her mind was in the throes of conflicting emotions. While she was still rather suspicious of Bender's motives, a small seed had taken root. Dare she allow herself to think this handsome young man might actually be interested in her? If he wasn't interested, then what game might he be playing? Her initial impulse was to seek her father's counsel but, after a moment's reflection, decided against it. Although Theresa Miller loved and trusted her father, an inner voice was telling her that his may not be the best advice in this situation. The bishop could always be counted upon to err on the side of protecting her. It was clear to Theresa that this situation was hers and hers alone to deal with.

To Theresa's surprise and relief, the bishop asked no questions regarding Richard Bender's visit as they ate. Sunday supper was, by her father's choice, a simple affair taken in the kitchen. It was his preferred way to end what could often be a trying day. Again, at supper, she was briefly tempted to ask the bishop for his opinion of Bender but again quickly dismissed the thought. It was too early to be asking for anyone's advice. After all, who knew if he would even call again? "I'm being ridiculous," she thought. "I'm thinking like a silly little girl who should know better. I doubt I'll ever see him again. But then again . . ." Her thoughts trailed off. Before today, the only young men to ever call on Theresa Miller had been the shyest and most awkward of the seminarians. Country boys who struggled to converse and could only stare down at their feet, never meeting her eye. Young men who Theresa knew would fail miserably as clergymen, and she was perfectly willing to spend her life as a spinster rather than venture down that unhappy road.

Bender returned to his dormitory with his own set of problems to work through. He was relieved to find his room deserted, as he had no desire to discuss his day with his roommate, Cavendish. With a bit of luck, the subject would never come up. Leo Cavendish was a decent enough chap most of the time, but Bender did not trust him with secrets. His roommate was a true believer with few, if any, uncertainties on all things moral. Should Cavendish get the slightest inkling of the game Bender was playing, he could be counted upon to shout it from the rooftops, and the first rooftop would be that of the bishop. Most of the seminarians had learned to take Cavendish's moral certitude with a grain of salt, although they all distrusted him to a degree. Once Leo became morally certain on any issue, he took on the temperament of an Old Testament prophet, and there was nothing that could dissuade him. The man Bender longed to talk to at the moment was Mickey the bartender, whom he knew would be unavailable on a Sunday evening.

The dining hall was nearly deserted when Bender went in to supper, which was not uncommon for a Sunday evening. Students who lived nearby often went home on weekends. Others took Sunday supper with the families of the girls they were courting, a situation Richard hoped would soon be his own. He lingered over his soup and bread and considered his next move. He mustn't appear overly eager because that might well give the game away, and neither must he stay away too long. He considered his options and decided he would send Theresa a note inviting her to attend midweek vespers with him. He thought she sometimes did this anyway, but his memory was unclear. Upon returning to his room, he wrote a note and dropped it into the campus message box.

Returning to his room after classes the following Tuesday, Bender checked his mailbox and found a note from Theresa awaiting him. He felt strangely happy upon seeing the note. He unsealed the envelope and read the following:

Dear Richard,

I would be pleased to accompany you to vespers on Wednesday evening. Please call for me at 6:30 p.m., and I shall be waiting.

Sincerely,
Theresa Miller

Try as he might, Bender was unable to read anything into the note that might reveal her feelings one way or another. The note was simply short and to the point. Nothing more, nothing less.

Late Wednesday afternoon, Bender dressed carefully. He wanted to be presentable but did not want to look overdressed and thus convey the idea he was trying too hard. Once satisfied with his appearance, he walked to the bishop's residence and rang the bell at precisely six thirty. Theresa greeted him wearing a light-yellow spring dress with a hat and matching handbag. "Good evening, Ms. Miller. Your dress looks like spring itself."

Theresa appeared somewhat bemused by Bender's comment and responded, "Thank you, Richard. That was a lovely thing to say, and I might add your summer blazer and boater make you look very smart as well." Theresa stepped onto the veranda and locked the door behind her. She then smiled at Richard and took his arm. "I think we have time for a bit of a stroll around campus before services, Richard. The campus is so lovely this time of year, with the grass so green and so many flowers blooming."

Thinking quickly, Bender responded, "I was so hoping you would suggest a walk, Ms. Miller, and I couldn't agree more about how beautiful the campus is in spring." The truth be told, Bender had never given the campus much consideration. The seminary had never been a place he viewed as anything more than a temporary stop along the way. He knew the name of his dormitory and the names of the buildings where his classes were held, and little more. Trees, shrubs, and flowers interested him not at all. If he went out for a walk, it was never to stroll around campus. Bender's walks took him out an unlocked side gate and along a roundabout path to one of several saloons he enjoyed visiting in the city. He was always careful to never visit any saloon twice in a row, lest he become recognized. The exception was Mickey's place. Mickey was himself a former seminary student who had chucked the whole business and bought a saloon. Mickey had identified Bender as a seminarian the moment he walked in the door. He also swore that Bender's secret was safe with him, and the two had become fast friends.

Arm in arm, Richard and Theresa strolled around the campus for twenty minutes before arriving at the front door of the chapel. Along the way, Theresa pointed out the individual buildings and when they were built. She knew the history of every building on campus, as well as the life stories of many of the men who had worked and taught in them. She knew where they had come from and to where they had gone after leaving. Some had retired, some had left teaching to return to the pulpit, and still others rested in the small cemetery, tucked away in the southeast corner of the campus. The cemetery was bordered by a low brick wall, and until Theresa mentioned it, Bender had been unaware of the cemetery's existence.

When the couple arrived at the front of the chapel, they found a number of seminarians, faculty members, and their wives milling about the entrance. Some of the young men were accompanied by the girls they were courting. They stood about in small groups, chatting amiably and enjoying the lovely evening. As Richard and Theresa approached, the hum of conversation dropped to a whisper. The seminarians were, to an individual, shocked to see the very handsome Richard Bender escorting the very plain Theresa Miller. Having prepared himself mentally for this moment, Bender handled the situation with aplomb and paid no attention to the people gathered there. Theresa's response was very different. Bender could sense her rising tension, and he reached over and patted the hand that was now tightly gripping his arm. Of those gathered outside the front door, none was more struck by the appearance of the couple than Leo Cavendish.

Richard and Theresa entered the chapel and walked to the front and seated themselves in the bishop's pew. It was quiet inside the church, and the quiet turned to stony silence as the pair made their way to their seats. They were joined a few minutes later by the bishop himself, who emerged from the pastor's entrance behind the pulpit. At the appearance of the bishop, Bender rose, and not a single individual failed to notice the bishop shaking Bender's hand before sitting down alongside the young couple. Those who knew Bender well were suspicious. Those who knew him slightly were surprised. Richard Bender was not someone who blended into a crowd, and even those who had never exchanged a word with him knew who he was and found the situation interesting.

Shortly after the bishop made his appearance, Martha Pemberton entered from the same door and took her seat at the piano. She spent a moment arranging her sheet music then began playing softly. There was something about the midweek evening service that demanded a contemplative quiet, and that something extended to the music as well. There were usually three hymns sung at the vesper service—at the beginning, in the middle, and at the end. No real sermon was delivered at vespers, only a few brief words between the prayers offered up by the rector. Although the bishop presided over the entire synod and the seminary, the church where he often preached was under the administration of the rector.

At the conclusion of the service, the congregants rose and, as custom demanded, waited for the bishop to make his way down the aisle. Theresa was the one they usually saw accompanying her father, but tonight she was on the arm of Richard Bender. They walked out, beside the bishop, in full view of the students and faculty. Again, Richard felt Theresa's hand tighten on his arm, and again he patted her hand gently. She was clearly feeling great stress, and Richard hoped that his reassuring gesture was winning her favor. Bender himself gave no indication that he was even aware of the hundreds of curious eyes upon them. Near the back of the church, sitting on the aisle, Leo Cavendish waited, his eyes boring into Richard Bender with an intensity Richard had never seen. Cavendish was the only one Bender acknowledged in any fashion, giving Leo a small nod and slight smile as they passed. Cavendish did not reciprocate.

Once outside and away from the church, Theresa relaxed her grip on Bender's arm. They walked back to the bishop's residence, mostly in silence. The experience had clearly been difficult for her, and Bender was being careful to say or do nothing that might add to her distress. He had expected to bid her good night at the door, but Theresa surprised him by inviting him to stay for tea.

"Father and I usually have tea after vespers, Richard. You'll join us, won't you?" Theresa gave Richard a smile that expressed her gratitude for the support he had shown through this difficult evening.

Bender realized immediately that the game was suddenly at a critical juncture and quickly responded, "Why, how nice of you to invite me, Ms. Miller. I would be delighted to take tea with you and your father." Richard Bender, in fact, did not care for tea at all and much preferred a cup of strong coffee. This was not, however, a time for honesty.

She smiled at Richard and said, "It's Theresa, Richard. Please call me Theresa."

Bender lowered his head as if he had just been humbled then raised his eyes to her and, smiling warmly, said, "Very well, Theresa it is." Bender knew he had just won another round.

To his surprise, she reached out and squeezed his hand then said, "I must go and put the kettle on. I'll only be a moment. Make yourself comfortable, Richard. We take our tea out here on the veranda on evenings as lovely as this. Father will be along directly."

Bender settled himself in a wicker chair and placed his hat in his lap. He sat with his elbows on the arms of the chair. His fingertips were touching as if gripping a ball with both hands. He gazed, lost in thought, at the tops of the trees that were now silhouetted in the dying purple light. He heard the door open and immediately rose to his feet as the bishop appeared.

"Please be seated, Mr. Bender," said the bishop in the warmest tone Bender had yet heard him use. "Let me light the candle lantern," said the bishop, lifting the glass and striking a match. "A lovely evening, don't you think, Mr. Bender?"

"Oh, indeed it is, sir. Indeed it is," replied Bender, striving for sincerity.

The bishop sat down in the chair opposite Bender and paused before he spoke.

His intelligent, penetrating eyes were again taking stock of the younger man. "You have conducted yourself as a gentleman should tonight, Mr. Bender. If you continue to do so and assure me that your intentions are honorable, we need never speak of it again." The bishop's words were delivered with precision and carried with them an implied challenge.

Bender looked down at his hands thoughtfully before lifting his head and facing the bishop directly and saying, "My intentions are entirely honorable, sir. On that, I give you my word as a gentleman and as a man of God."

The bishop's eyes betrayed a degree of skepticism, and he did not immediately respond to Bender's statement. The bishop focused on Bender for an uncomfortable moment until at last he said, "Very well then, Mr. Bender. I take you at your word."

Richard sensed the bishop may have had more to say, but they were interrupted by Theresa's return. She came bearing a tray containing a teapot, cups, and a plate of small cakes. Upon her arrival, Bender again rose to his feet and offered to take the tray. "Please be seated, Richard, I have a much better chance of spilling things if I attempt to hand them to someone." Her voice carried a certain confident quality Richard had not, as yet, heard from her. Although he knew her to be somewhat awkward, Richard was pleasantly surprised as she sat the tray down with considerable grace. She surprised him again by giving him a sly smile and saying, "You see, Richard, my time spent at finishing school was not a complete waste of father's money."

At her statement, both Richard and the bishop broke into spontaneous laughter. There were smiles all around, and they were in a warm mood as she poured the tea. "I don't know how you take your tea, Richard. Father takes a lump of sugar, while I prefer a squeeze of lemon."

Bender smiled and, addressing them both, said, "I guess it's the country boy in me, but I take neither. I like good, honest tea, hot and on the strong side."

Whereupon the bishop immediately interjected, saying, "Hear, hear, Mr. Bender! I too grew up on the farm, and I always took my tea hot and strong in the mornings. It wasn't until I achieved middle age that I came to enjoy a lump of sugar."

The trio engaged in friendly conversation for the next half hour, then the bishop rose and excused himself. "I'll be bidding you young people good night. It is my habit to retire to my study for a couple hours of reading before turning in. Good night, my dear," said the bishop, bending to kiss the top of his daughter's head. "Good night to you, Mr. Bender," said the older man, extending his hand to Richard.

"Good night to you, sir," said Bender. He remained standing until the bishop had closed the door behind him. He then sat down and fixed his gaze on Theresa. With a somewhat mischievous smile, he asked, "Well, Theresa, I do hope you have found this evening to be as pleasant as I have."

She responded in the same mischievous tone, "Indeed I have, Richard. It was a most pleasant evening."

Richard sat down again and paused before asking in a more serious tone, "Theresa, do you see yourself living your life here at the seminary?"

Theresa did not hesitate and responded, "I certainly see that as one possibility, Richard. I am qualified to take over Mrs. Pemberton's position as music teacher and may do so should she decide to retire. I am without firm plans at this time."

"It's been my observation, Theresa," Bender continued in a serious, measured, tone, "that people, be they male or female, who have grown up in a clerical household tend to be either very much in favor, or very much opposed, to living the clerical life as an adult. There doesn't seem to be much middle ground. Might I be so bold as to ask how you feel?"

It became clear to Bender that Theresa had given considerable thought to this very question, as she quickly responded, "There was a time, in my adolescence, when my answer would have been an unequivocal no to the clerical life, Richard. At that point, I had experienced quite enough of living at a seminary. I saw only too well all the petty politics and bickering that go on away from the eyes of the congregants. However, my father's quiet devotion to his calling has had its effect as well. Working through the small problems of people relating to one another is part of the process. An important part."

"So you are at least open to the prospect of remaining in the clerical life?" asked Bender hopefully.

"I am open to that prospect, and I am also open to the prospect of teaching music," said Theresa evenly. "I intend to make no hasty decision, one way or the other."

Bender remained silent and looked at Theresa. He was feeling himself being moved in a quite unexpected manner. The prospect of developing genuine feelings for this girl was a possibility he had not considered. Genuine affection for Theresa Miller could complicate matters to no end. At last he spoke. "It's getting late, Theresa, I should be going."

"If you feel you must," said Theresa with a wry smile. Bender was not the only one who had felt something stirring inside.

Bender took out his watch and, looking at it, said, "Yes, I must. I've both reading and writing to complete tonight before I sleep." Bender was surprised when she reached across the table and squeezed his hand for the second time that evening.

"Thank you for a lovely evening, Richard," she said with a smile.

"You are most welcome, Theresa. I do hope you will allow me to call again," said Richard hopefully.

She gave Bender a coy smile and said, "I think I might be persuaded to see you again, Richard. Provided, of course, you continue to conduct yourself as a gentleman."

"I am a gentleman—first, last, and always," said Bender smiling broadly. They rose, and he extended his hand, which she accepted easily. He had the sense she would not resist if he embraced her but decided not to chance it. "Good night, Theresa. Pleasant dreams," he said with a smile.

"And to you, Richard. Don't stay up too late attending to your studies. Everyone needs their rest."

After bidding each other good night, Bender returned to his room, which, to his disappointment, he did not find deserted. Upon his entry, Leo Cavendish looked up from his desk and eyed Bender sharply. "I see you were not alone tonight at vespers, Richard." Cavendish's words were terse and challenging.

Bender did not immediately respond but eyed his roommate coolly. "And if I had company, what of it, Leo?"

"It's your choice of companion that I found most curious Richard." Cavendish's words had a tone of incredulity tinged with scorn. "Many people found it curious."

"Oh, really, Leo? How so?" asked Bender, as if genuinely surprised by Cavendish's statement.

"There are any number of girls far prettier than Theresa Miller who would be happy to be seen with you, Richard, and yet you accompany the bishop's daughter to vespers. I find that very strange, as did many others. Very strange indeed," said Cavendish in a judgmental tone.

Bender felt a surge of genuine anger at his roommate's remarks, and he let it show. "I fail to see how it's any concern of yours, one way or another, Leo," Bender said sharply. "And for your information, Leo, tonight was not the first time I've called on Ms. Miller. I'll thank you to keep a civil tongue in your mouth when you speak of her in the future." To his surprise, the normally well-controlled Richard Bender found himself to be slightly trembling as he delivered his remarks with considerable heat.

Leo Cavendish, for all his moral certitude and religious intensity, was roughly half the size of Richard Bender, and the force of his roommate's words had their desired effect. After briefly recoiling under the words and malevolent gaze of Bender, Cavendish quickly softened and said, "You are, of course, quite right, Richard. I had no business making such a remark. I hope you can find a way to forgive me."

Above all else, Richard Bender was a quick-witted opportunist, and he immediately seized control. "Regardless of what others may say about me, Leo, I am first and foremost a man of God. Of course I forgive you." Benders words were delivered quietly and with a humility he did not feel. It had suddenly dawned on him that having some genuine feelings for Theresa Miller could be turned to his advantage when dealing with Leo Cavendish and anyone else who might try getting in his way. "I trust we need never have this conversation again, Leo."

Cavendish rose and crossed the room. He extended his hand to Bender, saying humbly, "Richard, I most sincerely regret my remark about Ms. Miller. And no, we need never have this conversation again."

Bender took Cavendish's hand while simultaneously clapping the smaller man on the shoulder and saying warmly, "Think no more of it, Leo, and do not trouble yourself. All is forgiven." As Cavendish thanked him for his kindness, Bender thought, "Leo, I trust you like the slimy little rat you are, and I do not believe for one second you will keep your nose out of my business. I only hope it doesn't end very badly for you." Bender seated himself at his desk and began reading. His study habits were mechanical. He had trained himself to retain the things the professors wanted while devoting as little actual thought to the business as possible. Bender looked at the wall clock. It was getting late, and he wanted a drink. After a moment's consideration, he reluctantly decided to continue reading.

The coming weeks were filled with activity as graduation approached. Bender managed to submit a highly acceptable senior thesis that boosted his class standing to the top third. Outside school, Bender devoted himself to winning Theresa Miller. The position at Keller was still open, and when the appropriate opportunity presented itself, he managed to tactfully broach the subject with the bishop. Bender was cautiously optimistic when the bishop did not flatly reject the idea. He also took it as an encouraging sign that the bishop had begun addressing him as Richard and no longer gave any indication that he was suspicious of Bender's motives.

Bender's progress with Theresa was even more encouraging. To his surprise, he found that he genuinely enjoyed her company, and that was making the process much easier. He had begun taking Sunday supper with Theresa and the bishop. There were picnics, first in the company of the bishop and then just the two of them. Bender advanced his plan slowly and carefully. There was the first embrace, which was followed by a more ardent embrace a few days later. The first kiss, and then a progression of kisses that grew increasingly passionate. The process culminated when Bender proposed on bended knee and she accepted. Bender presented himself before the bishop and, with Theresa by his side, formally asked her father for his daughter's hand in marriage. The bishop embraced them both and gave his blessing.

A few days after becoming engaged, Bender received a message from the bishop requesting Bender's presence in his office. Bender arrived at the appointed time and found not just the bishop, but several other senior clergymen as well. The bishop did not rise when Bender entered; he simply pointed Bender to a table and chair facing the panel of clergymen. "Please take a seat, Mr. Bender," said the bishop. The bishop addressed the other clergymen and asked, "Are there any of you who do not know Mr. Bender?" There were two men in attendance Bender had never seen before, and they requested introductions. Once the introductions were complete, the bishop addressed Bender and asked, "Do you know why you have been summoned here, Mr. Bender?"

Bender did in fact have a very good idea what this meeting was about but answered humbly, "No, sir, I do not."

"The gentlemen you see before you, Mr. Bender, myself included, represent the synod's selection committee. Although the ministers they choose to engage is a matter entirely up to the individual church, it's rare when a congregation does not seek this committee's approval when engaging a recently graduated student. This is especially true if the student is being considered for a position as a full pastor and not an associate."

"I see," said Bender, trying hard to put forward a humble face and suppress his rising sense of excitement.

The bishop continued. "I believe you have expressed interest in the currently vacant position at Keller? Is this correct, Mr. Bender?"

"Yes, sir. I think the position in Keller would be both interesting and challenging," said Bender.

"We have reviewed your application, Mr. Bender, and have given the matter our conditional approval," said the bishop.

"Oh, thank you, sir," said Bender, revealing more excitement than he had intended.

"Before you thank me, please understand, and in no uncertain terms, Mr. Bender, this is a provisional appointment, and there are conditions that must be met."

"Yes, sir, I will do my best to fulfill my duties," said Bender earnestly.

"Again Mr. Bender, please be aware that it will require more than your best effort," said the bishop soberly. "The conditions I'm going to lay before you will be met fully and without exception. Do you understand what I'm saying, Mr. Bender?"

For the first time since the meeting began, Bender felt genuine trepidation and replied, "Yes, sir."

The bishop and the other members of the committee eyed Bender coolly for a moment before the bishop continued. "Very well then, Mr. Bender, these are the additional requirements you must meet. First, you are to remain here at the seminary for an additional six weeks following graduation. During this time, you will serve as the rector's assistant."

The rector, whose presence on the committee had gone unnoticed by Bender, spoke up. "We shall get to know one another very well in the coming weeks, Mr. Bender." All the members of the committee shared a small laugh. The rector's voice was not threatening and carried a certain good humor that Bender found reassuring.

Following the momentary levity, the bishop tapped his finger on the desktop and regained control of the meeting. He then continued in his most serious tone yet. "In addition to assisting the rector, you will be receiving a series of tutorials under various senior faculty members. Be prepared, Mr. Bender, as you will likely find these tutorials demanding."

Bender's exceptional self-confidence was now being tested, and he replied to the committee in a quiet voice, "Yes, sir. Understood."

"Lastly, Mr. Bender, upon your successful completion of this six-week training period, you will receive your provisional appointment to Keller. The congregation at Keller is currently being served on a rotating basis by pastors from nearby congregations, and they will continue to do so until such time these pastors deem you ready to assume the position on your own." The bishop assumed a very stern countenance and paused before continuing. "Make no mistake, Mr. Bender, you can fail at any point in this process, and failure means your appointment will be revoked."

"Yes, sir," Bender responded quietly.

"Very well then," said the bishop, "Rector Wilson will be contacting you in the very near future. He will be the one overseeing your progress. Take great care not to disappoint him, Mr. Bender." The bishop's voice, though delivered with little emotion, carried the implicit message to Bender. "Young man, you have nearly achieved your goal, but this is not a gift."

"Yes, sir. I have no intention of disappointing the rector or any other member of this committee."

"I wish you success," said the bishop. "You are dismissed, Mr. Bender. Keep a close eye on your mailbox."

Bender took his time walking back to his room. His emotions were a mixture of elation and fear. The prize was at hand. His plan had worked even better than he had dared to hope, but now he had been presented with an unexpected challenge. Bender walked head down, and his hands clasped behind his back for a long time. He only became aware of time passing when he realized it had now grown quite dark. Slowly, his nerves had settled and he regained his focus. The path was clear. He must now apply himself as never before. Bender increased his pace; he had just enough time to eat before the dining hall closed for the evening.

After supper, Bender went for another walk, the last thing he wanted was to deal with Leo Cavendish. Cavendish was still a year from graduation and had recently announced, to Bender's distress, that he would be attending the summer session and thus reduce his class load during his senior year. This was a piece of news Bender did not want as the game reached its climax. The summer sessions were held primarily for the benefit of serving clergymen but were open to others as well. Dealing with Cavendish was an unwanted complication being forced upon him. Bender began preparing himself for whatever trouble Cavendish might cause. Although he did not know what his roommate might do, Bender had no doubt Cavendish would do something.

Leo Cavendish looked up with arched eyebrows as Bender entered the room. "You're late this evening, Richard," said Cavendish in what had become his usual challenging tone.

Seeking to parry Cavendish's thrust, Bender responded mildly, "Oh, I'm sorry to have worried you, Mother. It won't happen again."

Unfazed by Bender's jab, Cavendish retorted, "It's your immortal soul I'm concerned for, Richard."

"Leo, my soul is not yours to worry about! I'll thank you to worry about your own soul, and let me tend to mine!" There was rising heat in Bender's voice, and Cavendish backed off. However, the biggest problem when dealing with Cavendish was that he never backed off completely. Cavendish only made tactical withdrawals before regrouping and launching his next assault.

Bender never told Cavendish that he had received the appointment to Keller, albeit it was a provisional assignment. This, of course, did not prevent Cavendish from finding out about it, which he did within a week. Cavendish always had his ear to the ground and possessed an unnerving ability to ferret out secrets. He was, of course, quite disturbed when he found out about the appointment and wasted no time in expressing his feelings to Bender. "So, Richard, it appears as if your little plan has come together," Cavendish spoke with mocking sarcasm.

This time, Bender did not attempt to finesse Cavendish but walked directly up to his intense roommate and, jabbing the small man in the chest with his forefinger, said hotly, "Leo, I've listened to all I'm going to from you. I'm telling you for the last time, get your nose out of my business and keep it out. If I get assigned to Keller or to darkest Africa, it's no concern of yours one way or the other, and there's not a single thing I need to explain to you."

Towering over Cavendish, Bender glowered down at his roommate, who at last took a step back and said, "Very well, Richard. Very well." Cavendish's voice carried not a trace of remorse and he offered no apology.

As Bender entered into the long days of intense preparation, an uneasy peace settled over the roommates. They exchanged little beyond cursory greetings. Bender's new situation required him to be present in the rector's study early in the morning, followed by tutoring sessions in the afternoons, and then back to the rector's residence in the evenings. Bender was now delivering sermons at some of the sparsely attended week day services. Though not many heard him speak, those who did came away impressed. A glowing Theresa was always present on those mornings he was slated to speak.

When at last Bender emerged from what he had come to call the crucible, he felt a satisfaction he had never known. He had applied himself as never before and had left all those responsible for his training suitably impressed. He found himself alone in his room, on the eve of his wedding, in a curious mood. He was, at the same time, very tired and yet quite pleased with himself. The prize was now so close, he could reach out and touch it. Then, Bender made a rash decision. He decided to pay Mickey one last visit and have a wee celebration with his friend before consigning the seminary to his past.

By the time he arrived at Mickey's door, Bender was in a jovial mood. In spite of his high spirits, he was careful not to overdo, limiting himself to only a few drinks. He had no desire to see the whole plan come undone by presenting himself at the marital altar with a hangover. Thus, he was feeling only a slight glow when he clasped Mickey's hand and bid him farewell.

In spite of his weariness, there was an adrenaline-fueled spring in Bender's step as he walked back to campus. Regardless of the route he took within the city, all his various paths converged at the only bridge near the campus. Bender was halfway across the bridge and whistling softly when Leo Cavendish emerged from the shadows. Cavendish pointed his Bible at Bender and hissed, "I knew it! You've been to a saloon! This whole charade has been nothing but an evil game on your part, Richard! You are a deceitful blackguard and a conniver, Mr. Bender, and I'm not going to let you get away with it!" Cavendish's voice had risen to a shriek. "The bishop is going to know! Everyone is going to know how evil you are!" screamed Cavendish, pointing his Bible at Bender like a pistol, his body quaking with rage.

If Bender's decision to visit Mickey one last time was ill conceived, Cavendish's decision to confront his roommate on a deserted bridge after midnight was much worse. What happened next transpired in less time than it takes to tell the story. More quickly than Cavendish evidently thought possible, Bender caught the small man by the lapels of his jacket and, lifting him completely off the ground, said, "I've come too far to let you queer things for me now, Leo, you son of a bitch, and you're not telling anybody anything." Bender's words were savage, and his face was no more than an inch from Cavendish's. An instant later, Bender slammed Cavendish backwards against the iron framework of the bridge with all his considerable strength. The small man's head snapped back violently against the girder, rendering him instantly unconscious. Without a moment's hesitation, Bender lifted Cavendish and threw him over the railing. It was spring and the river was high. Cavendish may have already been dead when Bender heard the body hit the water twenty feet below, but even had he been fully alert, Leo Cavendish could not swim.

Bender paused, momentarily shocked by what he had just done, yet he regained his composure far faster than he would have ever thought possible. He turned to continue on to the dormitory then caught a glimpse of Cavendish's Bible lying on the walkway. Bender quickly stooped and, in one continuous motion, picked it up and pitched it into the river that it might follow its owner.

Bender returned to the dormitory, bathed, and retired. He slept remarkably well for having just committed a murder. He rose early after only a few hours' sleep and ate breakfast in the dining hall for the last time. He shaved and cleaned his teeth. He packed his bags and dressed carefully in his best suit. At 10:00 a.m., the bishop joined Richard and Theresa in marriage, with the rector and his wife serving as witnesses. A photograph was taken, and after the wedding luncheon, the newly married couple boarded the train for Keller.

* * *

The badly decomposed body of Leo Cavendish was discovered several weeks later, many miles downstream. The body was never identified. Seminary officials and law enforcement contacted Richard Bender in Keller regarding his former roommate's disappearance. Bender explained that he had been extremely busy those last few weeks at seminary and had seen little of Cavendish. Bender added that his roommate had been becoming increasingly withdrawn, and he had begun expressing his doubts about continuing in the ministry.

Chapter Seven

Goodwin

Clyde Goodwin emerged from a deep sleep and reluctantly forced his eyes open. "Good," he thought, "It's still dark." He could sleep a little longer before the old man launched into his daily cursing and abuse. He closed his eyes again and, a moment later, heard the rain. It might be later than he thought, but no matter. He could still doze a little longer. Goodwin rolled over and made himself comfortable. Before drifting off, something compelled him to open his eyes again and, in the dim light, he saw his father sprawled on the floor. Goodwin didn't find this sight particularly alarming, as his father had passed out dead drunk on the floor many times before. It was raining harder now, and the rain was suddenly punctuated by a lightning flash and a sharp crack of thunder. The lightning flash momentarily illuminated the single room, allowing Goodwin a better look at his father, who did not appear to be breathing.

If Clyde Goodwin felt anything at the thought that his father might be dead, it was relief, but mostly, he didn't feel anything. If the miserable old bastard was dead, he could always check later. There was no rush, and it certainly wasn't anything worth getting out of bed over. Goodwin closed his eyes. The sound of the rain on the tar-paper roof had a soothing effect, and he was soon deeply asleep. When he next opened his eyes, the room was filled with a ghostly gray light. The rain had eased, but rolling thunder could still be heard in the distance. He glanced in the direction of his father, who did not appear to have moved. Goodwin rose and dressed. He pulled on his boots and picked up the coffee pot on his way out to the privy.

On his return, Goodwin stopped at the pump and filled the coffee pot. Once back inside the cabin, he stirred the embers in the cook stove and tossed in several pieces of sumac. Sumac doesn't burn long, but it burns hot and is ideal for brewing a pot of coffee. Goodwin ground a handful of beans and dropped the coffee in the water. Taking a deep breath, he walked to where his father lay. He nudged the prostrate man with the toe of his boot. "Pa? Pa, you passed out on the floor again. Why don't ya get up and git in bed?" Dooley Goodwin did not respond to Clyde's nudging. He knelt down and touched his father's face. Dooley's skin was cool, and when Clyde held his fingers in front of his father's nose, he felt no breath. "Well, what do ya know?" Clyde said aloud. "The old son of a bitch is deader than hell."

Goodwin stood up and looked at his father a moment longer. Then he reached down and picked up the whiskey bottle still clutched in the dead man's hand. Amazingly, the bottle was nearly full, which was a very rare thing for Dooley Goodwin. Clyde thought to himself, "He must have just walked in the door and keeled over before he had a chance to get started on the bottle. It's just too damn bad I wasn't awake to see it happen. I would have really enjoyed watchin' him die." Clyde pulled the cork from the bottle then took a hard pull. Such a sizable belt of hard liquor would have left most fifteen-year-old boys coughing and sputtering, but a bystander would have thought young Clyde had just taken a drink of water. He re-corked the bottle and sat it on the table then turned to check on the coffee. It looked and smelled about right, and he moved the pot away from the hottest part of the stove to let the grounds settle. While he waited, Goodwin walked to the cabin's lone window and gazed absently out at the dark day. The rain was easing, and the sky appeared to be growing lighter in the west. "Well, if it clears off, I guess today's gonna be as good as any for leavin'," thought Goodwin.

He filled his father's big enameled tin cup with coffee. The rain had stopped, so Clyde ventured outside. Out away from the cabin,

Goodwin scanned the horizon and thought to himself, "Yes, sir, I do believe it's gonna be clearin' off before long. Those clouds is movin' real fast." Goodwin sipped the coffee, taking care not to burn his lip on the metal cup. It tasted good, and he suddenly wished he had brought the whiskey bottle with him so he could lace the coffee with it. "No worries," he thought, "there's plenty of time. Plenty of time." He sat down on a tree stump and began thinking back over his fifteen years as he continued sipping his coffee.

Looking back at life was not something Clyde ordinarily did, as there was next to nothing about his life he had any desire to remember. On this peculiar morning, however, his memories were stirring of their own accord. Goodwin had only the vaguest recollection of his mother. He wasn't sure how old he had been when she died, but he knew he had been very young. Clyde was the youngest of four boys and even the memories of his two oldest brothers were beginning to fade. Goodwin had the idea that something must have gone very wrong with his birth and that his mother had never fully recovered. An indistinct image of a tired-looking woman with prematurely gray hair was all he had of her. His mother rarely left her bed, and it had been his older brothers who had seen to his needs.

Goodwin remembered his oldest brother telling him that their pa had never been a kindly man, but it was not till their mother died that the old man became truly mean. Dooley Goodwin had divided his life between serving as a lawman and as a cattle thief, crossing that line in both directions several times. He ended his life here on this mostly worthless homestead. One hundred and sixty acres was much too small to make a living on unless a man wanted to break the sod and plant crops. Dooley Goodwin considered himself to be a cattleman, and he had little use for the backbreaking labor of farming. Since filing his claim, Dooley had raised the few cattle his small holding would support and hired himself out as a part-time deputy and other work that came along, provided it didn't involve pushing a plow.

Clyde was not just the youngest boy in the Goodwin family; he was much younger than his brothers. As nearly as he could remember,

Karl, his next older brother, was about eight years older. Jack and Bob were a good deal older than Karl, and Clyde's memories of these brothers were not much clearer than those of his mother. He could vaguely remember the morning his father rose to find Jack and Bob gone, along with two of his best horses. Clyde had a nightmarish vision of Dooley returning from the barn in a rage and how Karl had tried to shield him from their father's fists. The older boys left a note, but Clyde never learned what it said. He only knew that the note took his father's rage to a new level, and not even Karl was able to protect him completely. Karl left home three years after Jack and Bob, and young Clyde was left alone with Dooley. Something seemed to go out of the old man when Karl left, and Dooley only rarely struck Clyde. If he was spared physical abuse, Clyde did not escape his father's tongue, and once, in a drunken rage, Dooley screamed at Clyde, telling his young son that he held him responsible for his mother's death.

Clyde had only been allowed to attend school sporadically, a few weeks here and there. He never attended school for more than two months at a stretch before Dooley decided Clyde was needed at home and pulled him out. Being at school gave Clyde the rare opportunity to be around other children, something that he viewed as a mixed blessing. While it was always a relief to be away from his father, he was confused by the way other kids would try tormenting him. However, unless a boy was a great deal bigger than Clyde, few ever tried picking on him twice. When taunted, his response was immediate and savage. Young Clyde Goodwin found girls to be a complete mystery, and women would never be something he could fully come to grips with. The lessons themselves did spark his interest however, and in spite of his chaotic education, Clyde somehow managed to become a capable reader with a sketchy grasp of numbers.

As he sat thinking about his life, the sun broke through, and for a moment the world looked fresh and clean. The moment passed quickly, and Clyde dumped the dregs of his coffee on the ground. He considered having another cup or, perhaps, another pull on the whiskey bottle but decided instead to begin preparations for leaving. Clyde got out the oversized saddlebags Dooley used when away on extended manhunts. He emptied their contents on the table and selected the things he would keep. It didn't take Goodwin long to pack. His extra clothing amounted to very little. He packed flour, sugar, coffee, and the few canned goods on hand. He kept the tin plate and small cast iron frying pan from his father's kit. He filled the two large canteens at the pump then went to the barn and found the hammer.

Clyde pulled the heavy wooden box out from beneath Dooley's cot. The long oaken box was reinforced with strap iron and secured by two heavy padlocks. He had never been able to find where his father hid the keys, and he was in no mood to look for them now. Dooley's hiding place could be a mile away for all he knew. Clyde brought the hammer down on the first lock with no effect. When additional strikes failed to break open the locks, Clyde said aloud, "This is going to be even harder than I thought." He went back to the barn and rummaged around in his father's tools until he found a large cold chisel. He thought, "If this don't do it, I might have to stash the damn box somewhere until I find something that works."

Goodwin carefully positioned the bit of the chisel against what he thought would be the weakest part of the shackle and, being careful not to hit his own fingers, brought the hammer down with all his strength. He was elated when the shackle shattered. He quickly moved on to the second lock, where the chisel produced the same result. Inside the box, he found the prizes he was looking for. The Winchester carbine and the heavy-caliber Henry rifle, both cleaned and oiled in their scabbards. Neatly coiled alongside the rifles was a gun belt holding his father's .44 Colt revolver, along with several boxes of cartridges for all the weapons. After removing the guns and ammunition, Clyde carefully searched the box and found the money he had always suspected was hidden there. It was only twenty-three dollars, but it was twenty-three dollars more than he had before breaking into the box. He packed all the ammunition in the saddlebags.

Clyde went to the barn and saddled his father's horse. He opened the gate for the brood mare and her foal then slapped the mare on the rump, yelling, "Go on, Buttermilk, git on outa' here! Go find yerself a home somewheres." Buttermilk was the mother of his father's horse, and she had faithfully produced a foal every spring for the past six years. Clyde thought, "She's been a good ole' horse, but she ain't the traveler Sam is, and I sure don't need a damn baby tagging along." He led Sam to the cabin and tied him to the railing, then went inside and returned with the saddlebags and rifles, which he attached to the saddle. He wrapped his blanket inside Dooley's rain slicker and tied it on behind the saddle. Dooley always used the rain slicker as a ground cloth. Clyde hung one canteen on each side of the pommel then untied Sam and led him some distance away from the cabin and tied him securely to a fence post.

Back inside the cabin, Goodwin removed the chimney from the lamp and threw it through the window. He carried the glass lamp base to the barn and emptied its contents over a pile of straw then shattered the base against the anvil. Goodwin struck a match and dropped it on the fuel-soaked straw then turned away from the barn and walked calmly back to the cabin. Once inside, he removed the cap from the two-gallon can that held their extra coal oil. Clyde was pleased to find that it was nearly full. He walked to where his father's body lay and emptied half the oil over Dooley's corpse then distributed the remainder around the room, leaving a trail behind him as he walked out the door for the last time. He took a look around then struck another match. By the time he mounted Sam, the house and barn were both fully engulfed in flame. Goodwin raised his hat then laughed and yelled, "So long, you old son of a bitch! Welcome to hell!"

He had given little consideration to his next move, but Goodwin instinctively turned Sam to the north and into the wind. Their nearest neighbor to the north was a good three miles distant, and with a little luck, they might not even see the smoke. He spurred Sam into an easy gallop, wanting to be well away from the cabin in the event their much-closer neighbors to the south came to investigate. About two miles away from the cabin, Goodwin rode around to the back side of a hill then eased Sam up the incline, halting the horse when he could just see over the ridge. Unfortunately, it was too far away to see if any neighbors had arrived, but the place where he had known such misery had nearly vanished in the flames.

As he watched the fire consume his old life, Goodwin considered his good fortune. It wasn't just being free of Dooley once and for all, but the old bastard had chosen a rainy night to die, thus allowing Clyde to burn the place down with little danger of the fire spreading. Not that Goodwin wouldn't have lit the fire on the hottest, driest day of summer. He would have done so without a second thought, but there was no point in burning out the neighbors if he didn't have to. Goodwin couldn't have cared less about the neighbors either, but he instinctively understood that it was best to avoid unnecessary trouble. As he turned to continue on his way, he saw that the mare and foal had followed him, and they were now standing at the base of the hill, looking up at him. "Damn it, Buttermilk! I done told you to git!" He spurred Sam into a hard gallop, charging straight at the mare. Buttermilk and the foal danced away from Sam, then the mare trotted back toward Goodwin. After repeated attempts to drive the mare away, he realized Buttermilk had no intention of leaving. Clyde sighed heavily then drew the .44. Keeping a close grip on the reins, he rode close to the mare and shot her between the eyes. "You had yer chance, old girl," said Goodwin, shaking his head.

The terrified foal danced away while Goodwin removed the spent cartridge and replaced it with a live round from the gun belt. He holstered the revolver and set a course that he thought would put the most distance between himself and any settler's cabins as the bewildered foal stood by its fallen mother. As far as he knew, there were few houses to the north, and if he wasn't already on the open range, he soon would be. He urged Sam into a canter and, after a half hour, decided he had put enough distance between himself and the fire. Clyde slowed the horse to a walk and let Sam set his own pace. The prairie was exceptionally green, and wildflowers were brilliant and abundant, though Goodwin was scarcely aware of the beauty around him. Goodwin's mind was filled with a contentment born of being forever free of Dooley and his wretched homestead.

An hour later, Goodwin eased his way up a small hill, pausing before he reached the crest. Well to the east, he saw a cabin with a few ramshackle outbuildings. Beyond the cabin to the north, there was nothing but open land. "Just like I thought. I didn't think there was much of anything up here." He turned Sam back down the hill and passed well to the west of the cabin. No one ever taught Goodwin to avoid being outlined against the horizon; he just knew it was a good idea if one didn't want to be seen. He continued at a leisurely pace, allowing Sam to drink when they crossed creeks and to snatch a mouthful of grass when he chose. Later that afternoon, they reached what might be considered either a large creek or a small river, and Goodwin turned Sam straight up stream. He didn't think he was being pursued, but why take a chance? Having Sam's hoof prints disappear for a mile or two in the flowing water would certainly slow down anyone who might be following him.

Goodwin had given little thought to food all through that first glorious day of freedom, but as the sun began approaching the horizon, his stomach told him he should be on the lookout for a campsite. Spotting a sheltered area several yards back from the creek, Goodwin headed Sam in that direction. Once inside the small grove, he unsaddled the horse and replaced the bridle with a halter. He tied Sam securely to a tree, leaving plenty of rope for the horse to graze. Clyde withdrew the carbine from its scabbard and set out on foot. Game was plentiful on the prairie, and if a man went hungry, it was his own damn fault. Easing his way around a plum thicket, Goodwin spotted a covey of prairie chickens. He took careful aim and, with one shot, secured his supper. Goodwin watched the rest of the birds take to the air in a mad rush and resisted the temptation to try a wing shot. He had what he needed, and there was nothing to be gained by wasting ammunition.

He cut a stout piece of green willow and secured the larger end with heavy rocks. After plucking and cleaning the bird in the stream, he impaled the carcass on the pointed end of the pole. Goodwin quickly gathered up an armload of driftwood, and within twenty minutes, the prairie chicken was roasting. While the bird was cooking, it suddenly struck Goodwin that he should have waited until it was fully dark before starting a fire and that the fire he built should have been much smaller. He vowed to never repeat that mistake. Even if he wasn't being pursued, there was never any reason to give your location away if it could be avoided. After ensuring his meal was safe from falling into the coals, Goodwin took the carbine and climbed the nearest hill, getting down and crawling the last few yards to the top. Lying on his belly, he carefully surveyed the countryside to the south for signs of movement and did not return to his campsite until he had assured himself he was not being followed.

For the next several weeks, Goodwin drifted, avoiding both towns and people whenever possible. If he had to enter a town for supplies, he would first find a place to cache the Henry and the revolver, not wanting arouse suspicion as to why a teenaged boy was so heavily armed. He hoped the saddle carbine would draw little attention while not leaving him completely disarmed. Clyde would sometimes survey a town from a distance for a full day before entering at what he thought would be the busiest time. Again, his instincts were telling him that he was more likely to come under suspicion by riding in alone than if he could be part of a crowd. Goodwin never spent a minute longer in a town than he had to and was always cautious to never do or say anything that might arouse curiosity. He thought it unlikely that Dooley's death would be investigated with any vigor, considering his father's history, but Clyde Goodwin was nothing if not cautious.

It would not be accurate to describe Clyde Goodwin as happy during the months he spent roaming the prairie. Goodwin didn't experience happiness in the ordinary sense. Happy and sad were both alien to his nature. He cared not at all for people and cared for his horse only to the extent that he needed Sam for transportation. If he were to wake up one day and have no further need of the horse, he would not hesitate to dispatch Sam with as little emotion as he had the mare. Goodwin did, however, experience a certain sense of well-being that was the product of being free of his father. His long, rambling summer came to an end when he awoke one dark, cold morning to a stinging wind. The leaves had mostly fled the trees, and much of the waterfowl had departed for warmer climates. It occurred to Goodwin that he should have turned Sam southward some weeks ago, but it was too late to worry about that now. He would simply scout out a decent-sized town and get a job of some kind and a warm place to sleep for the winter. Towns were easier to find than they were to avoid.

After the initial icy blast, the weather again turned mild. Goodwin knew that however pleasant indian summer might be, it would not last. He turned Sam eastward and, two days later, crossed a rail line. Staying far enough from the tracks to take cover if necessary, Clyde began following the line on a parallel course. He saw few trains over the next day as he continued north. The low number of trains led Goodwin to conclude that he was probably following a branch line. At last he came to a trestle spanning a rather imposing canyon that must have been a real obstacle for the builders of the line. Goodwin looked down into the canyon and considered riding through it. The walls were steep and studded with trees and rocks. After a few minutes' consideration, he decided to try taking Sam across the trestle on the narrow walkway running alongside the tracks.

Goodwin listened carefully for the sounds of an approaching train then dismounted and put his ear directly on the rail. When he had assured himself there were no trains in the area, he began leading Sam on to the walkway. Sam took a few cautious steps onto the bridge then balked and pulled back strongly. Goodwin tried repeatedly to coax the horse onto the bridge, but Sam adamantly refused. He had nearly decided to make camp for the night and attempt the canyon in the morning when it occurred to Goodwin to try blindfolding the horse. He removed his other shirt from the saddlebag and tied it around Sam's eyes. Then, keeping his left hand inside the bridal where Sam could feel it, Goodwin again tried leading the horse on to the walkway. This time Sam followed. Clyde led the horse slowly and carefully out onto the trestle, speaking softly all the while. By the time he reached the midpoint of the bridge, Goodwin began allowing himself to think he might succeed. Then, disaster struck.

Sam snapped his head back violently, and the blindfold fell from his eyes. Goodwin never knew if an insect of some kind had irritated the horse or if the blindfold simply came untied. Regardless of the cause, the horse reacted in blind panic, rearing back against the reins. As Sam reared, a front hoof caught Goodwin squarely on the jaw, sending him sprawling backward and tearing the reins from his hands. Free from any restraint, Sam was now completely disoriented and mad with fear. After a moment of wild confusion, Sam did the worst thing possible. He wheeled away from Goodwin and leapt over the side. Time seemed to stop during the terrible silence between Sam's leap over the railing and his hitting the water. Goodwin overcame his paralysis and staggered to his feet. In the dying light, he saw Sam's lifeless body being swept rapidly downstream, along with nearly everything he owned.

Goodwin's mind raced. His initial thought was to get off the trestle and begin pursuing Sam downstream. He quickly dismissed this idea as it was now close to full darkness and the horse's body had already disappeared down the swiftly flowing river. Going in search of Sam would have to wait for daylight. Most boys would have been too shocked to move, but Clyde Goodwin was unlike most boys. After a few minutes spent considering his situation, he turned and continued on across the bridge. If he happened across a place to hole up for the night, he would take it; otherwise, he would just keep walking. Goodwin had already consigned Sam and his possessions to the past.

For the next half hour, Goodwin trudged along the tracks. It was growing colder by the minute, and he had yet to spot a place that might afford him shelter. He was becoming very tired when a light emerged in the distance. As he continued along the track, more lights began appearing. "Well, I guess my luck ain't been all bad today," he thought. "It looks like I done found me a town." Goodwin's only sense of time over the past several weeks had been the rising and setting of the sun but now, for the first time since departing the homestead, Clyde wished he knew the time of day. It was nearly winter and darkness fell early, but he had no idea just how late it might actually be. Walking into a town in the dead of night might well get him arrested if the town had a lawman who had managed to stay awake. A night in jail would certainly be preferable to a night spent on the open prairie, but getting locked up would likely result in his being sent on his way the next morning. "No," he thought, "I'll spend the night out here in the open if I have to and check out that town in daylight."

It was growing colder by the minute, and the cold was now being amplified by a stiff northerly wind. The moonless night was very dark, yet in the dim star light, Goodwin was just able to discern the outline of a small bridge a short distance ahead. He hurried to the little bridge and carefully made his way below it. "'Taint much shelter, it's at least stoppin' most of the wind, and it might be enough to keep me from freezing," thought Goodwin. Clyde suddenly wished he had put some of his matches in his pocket instead of keeping them all in the saddlebag. This was another mistake he vowed never to repeat. The creek bed was littered with driftwood and it would have been an easy thing to build a fire. Now he would be forced to suffer the cold, and suffer he did. All through the long, bitter night, Goodwin shivered, and when his shivering grew uncontrollable, he stood up and ran in place until he warmed enough for the tremors to stop. He drew his knees to his chest and huddled close to the bridge. What little sleep he managed that night was measured in minutes.

When the predawn light arrived at last, Goodwin found the ground covered with a thick coat of frost, but mercifully, the winds were now calm. He stood up with difficulty, his body stiff and aching from the cold. He considered waiting awhile longer before entering the town, but the cold and hunger made the decision for him. Before setting off for the town, Goodwin had the presence of mind to remove the gun belt and search out a place to hide the weapon. A teenage boy wearing a Colt .44 on his hip was sure to draw way more attention than he had need of. He found a pocket between the bridge's timbers, where the gun and holster would be safely out of sight and protected from the weather.

Goodwin climbed out of the gully and began walking as briskly as he could in the direction of the town. He hoped his rapid pace might warm his body, but the effort met with only limited success. He was chilled to the bone and weak from hunger. As Clyde staggered along with his hands in his pockets, his stride grew increasingly uneven. Then, it suddenly dawned on Goodwin that he had not lost everything. He still had fifteen dollars hidden in his boots, and that was more than enough to secure him a room and food until he could find work. This sudden realization did much to alleviate his misery and suddenly, he felt a little better. As he neared the outskirts of the town, the sign along the tracks read Keller.

By the time Goodwin reached the town's main street, the day had turned dark and cloudy, and the wind was rising. The little town seemed gripped by a deep, brooding melancholy. Goodwin saw few people stirring as he made his way along the town's main street. He looked about in vain for a store or, better yet, a cafe where he might get a meal. There was no cafe to be seen, only a general store and a few other businesses, none of which appeared to be open. Everything in the little town looked very new. The curious exception being the presence of large trees. Evidently, the town's founders had carved their village out of a grove of large cottonwoods. As Goodwin stood shivering on the boardwalk, he saw four Belgian horses pulling a large freight wagon approaching.

When the teamster drew even with Goodwin, the driver halted the horses and said, "You look about half-froze, son." The freighter spoke in a deep, rumbling voice. The driver had long hair protruding from below a high-crowned, broad-brimmed hat that came down to just above his eyes. The man's face was punctuated by a substantial mustache, and he wore a heavy sheepskin coat and laced-up boots that rose nearly to his knees. The butt end of a ten-gauge shotgun protruded from a scabbard attached to the side of the seat.

Though Goodwin did not feel happiness or humor the way others did, experience had taught him when it was appropriate to laugh. "I reckon I'm a little past half," he said with a practiced chuckle.

The teamster reached below his seat and withdrew a heavy buffalo-robe. He tossed it down to Goodwin and said, "Pull that around ya, son. I keep that with me for when the weather turns cold."

Goodwin needed no encouragement and quickly pulled the robe around him. "I do rightly thank you, Mister. I lost all my stuff tryin' to cross that river outside yer town. Goodwin's my name. Clyde Goodwin."

"Harley Childers," said the teamster. "Where'd you try crossing the river anyway?"

"Out yonder by the railroad trestle."

"Good lord, son, yer lucky ya didn't git kilt," said Childers with alarm. "They built that trestle there because it's the narrowest place for miles, upstream or down. A mile either way and you could have walked across and barely got yer boots wet."

"I wish I'd a' known that," said Goodwin quietly. "I thought about walkin' across the trestle, but high places make me real dizzy, and I start losin' my balance."

"I know that can happen sometimes," said Childers. "Why don't ya climb on up, and I'll drive you over to Ms. Emily's boarding house. You'll be able to get some breakfast and thaw yourself out."

"I do rightly appreciate it, Mr. Childers," said Goodwin as he climbed aboard the freight wagon.

"Harley. Just call me Harley. It makes me nervous anytime somebody calls me mister," said Childers with a smile.

"In that case, I do rightly appreciate it, Harley," said Clyde, returning Childers' smile. Goodwin felt that his luck may have just taken a turn for the better. If he could get warmed up and fed, he could then get to the general store and buy a coat. If the river widened like the driver said, he might yet be able to salvage the guns and saddlebags. It would require hiking back out to the trestle and beyond, but if Sam's body had gotten caught up on a sandbar, it would be worth the walk.

Harley Childers turned the horses around in the middle of the street and got them headed back in the direction from which he'd come. "So what brings you to this neck of the woods, Clyde? I'm sorry, you did say your name was Clyde, didn't ya?"

"Yes, sir, I always go by Clyde. I've been spendin' some time wonderin' around ever since my pa passed on, and I wound up here. I ain't never had any place in mind to travel to."

"I couldn't recommend makin' a life out bummin' around, but it ain't a bad thing fer a young man to do before he settles down. I done it for a while myself. I think it does a man good to git out and see some of the world before he puts down roots," rumbled Childers.

"What brought you to . . ." Clyde paused, trying to remember the name of the town.

"Keller," said Childers. "They named the town for a man by the name of Samuel Keller, who was the first person to file a claim in the county. I don't know if he ever done anything else though," said Childers. The freighter spoke quietly and directly, betraying little. "I guess the folks around here thought that since they had to name the place something, Keller was as good a name as any." Childers offered Goodwin no explanation of how he came to be in Keller.

Childers smiled slightly as he told the story, but Goodwin could not tell if the man helping him was enjoying having a bit of company or not. "Well, here we are," said Childers, halting the team in front of a large two-story-frame house. "I'll go in with ya and introduce you to Ms. Emily."

They climbed down from the wagon, and Childers secured the lead line to the hitching post. "We'll just go on around back," said Childers. "That's where the dining room is." Childers sat off on a graveled walkway leading around the side of the house. When they reached the back door, Childers entered without knocking.

"Harley Childers!" boomed a woman's merry voice from the back of the room. "What in tarnation are you doin' back here? I done fed you once already this morning!" The woman laughed.

The freighter's demeanor changed little, and he said quietly, "I picked up a young feller who could do with some breakfast and some thawin' out. Emily, this here is Clyde Goodwin. Clyde here ran into some bad luck tryin' to cross the river yesterday."

A slightly plump woman of early middle age emerged from the kitchen and advanced across the floor while drying her hands on her apron. "How do you do, young man, I'm Mrs. Kellogg, but after my husband passed away, everybody took to calling me Ms. Emily." She reached out and shook Goodwin's hand. "Oh lordy, son! Your hands are like ice. Come on over here and warm yourself by the stove, and I'll fix you something to eat."

Childers replaced his hat and turned to leave, saying, "Well, young feller, it's been nice meetin' ya. I need to be gittin' those ole' horses on down the road. Good day to you, Emily."

"Good-bye, Harley. And see to it you stay gone this time!" The proprietress laughed. She turned to Clyde, who was holding his outstretched hands over the potbellied stove. "So . . . Clyde, is it?"

"Yes, ma'am. Clyde Goodwin."

"Will bacon and eggs do ya, Clyde, or would you rather have hotcakes?"

"Either one would be fine, ma'am. Fix whatever is easiest for you," said Goodwin.

"Well, aren't you just the nicest young man," said Ms. Emily. Her voice was warm and melodious, and she seemed to fairly radiate good cheer. "Bacon and eggs it is then." She gave Clyde a wry look and said, "I already used up all my hotcake batter, and I really didn't want to stir any more up. Help yourself to a cup of coffee when you're ready." She laughed again and set to work in the kitchen.

As he began warming up, Clyde realized he was still wrapped in the blanket Childers had given him, and he asked Ms. Emily, "Ma'am, I still have Mr. Harley's blanket, and I need to git it back to him."

"Well, that won't be hard," Ms. Emily replied from the kitchen. "Just fold it up, and I'll take it up to his room in a bit."

"Oh," said Goodwin, "I didn't know he lived here."

"Oh sure, Harley was one of my first boarders when I opened up. This was the house my husband and I built when we moved here. After he passed away, I opened the house up to boarders to help make ends meet and to keep myself busy."

"Would you happen to have any rooms available, Ms. Emily?" asked Goodwin.

Ms. Emily paused her work and stepped back into the dining room. "I do have a room. A small one. I can't let you stay for free though, son."

"Oh no, ma'am, that's not what I'm asking. I have a little bit of money that should last me until I kin find a job of some kind."

Ms. Emily eyed Goodwin carefully. For all her good cheer, Goodwin could see Ms. Emily was a businesswoman. After inspecting Goodwin for a moment, she said, "Well then, that's a different matter entirely. The room lets for two dollars a week without meals, three dollars with, and I need to be paid a week in advance. I serve breakfast and supper. You're on your own at noontime. Do you think you can manage that, young man?"

"Yes, ma'am," said Goodwin. "I have enough money to git me by for at least a few weeks, and if I ain't found work by then, I'll clear out."

"Very well then," said Ms. Emily. "I'll show you the room after you've had your breakfast."

Clyde ate the bacon, eggs, and fried potatoes Ms. Emily laid before him with relish, and when he finished eating, he followed her upstairs. The room was small but had a cozy feel, and it looked out over the backyard. It was furnished with a single bed, a dresser, and a small table and a chair. It had its own sink and a closet. Ms. Emily pointed out the bathroom at the end of the hall. It was the first time Clyde Goodwin had ever seen indoor plumbing.

"Clean linens every Friday, Mr. Goodwin, and you can put your own lock on the closet. I respect my boarder's privacy. I just ask that you don't keep anything in there that might burn my house down." Ms. Emily laughed.

Goodwin completely failed to grasp the humor in the landlady's statement, but he was savvy enough to laugh along. "Oh, no need to worry about that, ma'am," said Goodwin. "My folks wouldn't never let me play with fire, so I keep plumb away from it." He paid for a week's rent with meals then left to purchase a winter coat at the general store. When Goodwin arrived at the store, he was greeted by a man not a great deal older than himself. Goodwin appeared to be the first customer of the day.

"Good morning," said Charles Bonebright. "What can I do for you?"

"I'm needing a winter coat," said Goodwin, "something warm but not too expensive."

"Right over here," said Bonebright. "I think these working man's coats might be what you're looking for. They're made of a tough canvas-type material and have a good sheepskin lining. They're not what a man would ordinarily wear to church, but they'll keep you warm enough."

Goodwin tried on the coat and quickly said, "Yes, sir, this'll be fine. Just what I'm looking for."

"Excellent," said Bonebright, "the coat is two dollars and a half, and for another two bits, I'll throw in a pair of wool mittens."

"I expect I better have the mittens," said Goodwin then added, "you wouldn't know of anyone in town who's looking to hire a man, would you, Mister?"

"Bonebright. Charles Bonebright." The shopkeeper parried Goodwin's question and asked, "I don't think I've seen you in the store before, young man."

"Clyde Goodwin, Mr. Bonebright. I just got in to town early this morning. I'm an orphan, and I been traveling around some since my pa died. I've been on the lookout for a place where I might stay put awhile. I lost most of my stuff crossin' the river and need to get outfitted again. I'd be willing to do most any kind of work."

Bonebright eyed Goodwin carefully then said, "Our little town of Keller is an up-and-coming community, and you couldn't do much better for a place to put down roots. I don't need full-time help, but I could use someone on Thursdays when my freight gets delivered, and maybe for a few hours on Saturday afternoons when I'm the busiest."

"I'd be mighty grateful for the chance, Mr. Bonebright. I won't let you down. I've been pulling my own weight pretty much since I was old enough to walk, and I ain't scared of work." Goodwin spoke convincingly, but in truth, Clyde had little more regard for physical labor than had his father.

After another moment eying Goodwin, Bonebright spoke, "Freight comes day after tomorrow. Be here at ten o'clock. The job will last until the work's done. That means unpacking goods and stocking them on the shelves. It varies some, but it'll probably be about five or six hours work. If I like the way you handle yourself, I'll have you back Saturday afternoon. Let's say noon till five. If you work both days, I'll pay two dollars a week. Fair enough?"

"Oh yes, sir, Mr. Bonebright, that sounds more than fair." Though Goodwin felt no emotion, he succeeded in convincing Bonebright of his sincerity and eagerness to work. Before Goodwin paid for the coat and mittens, he remembered to ask the merchant about a padlock. When the transactions were complete, he shook hands with Bonebright and departed with renewed optimism. In just a bit over two hours, he had put a roof over his head and had secured enough work to extend his funds by at least a month. If he could pick up a little more work, he would be set for the winter. The first order of business now was walking back out to the river to see if he could find Sam's body and perhaps salvage the rifles.

With food in his stomach and his warm coat to protect him from the wind, Goodwin was able to travel considerably faster on his return trip to the river. When he reached the trestle, he turned downstream, staying on the top of the canyon and keeping the river in sight. Just as the freighter said, the river began to widen considerably after no more than a twenty-minute walk. Goodwin eased down the side of the canyon and began hiking along the riverbank. A half hour later, he found Sam's lifeless body in shallow water only a few feet from shore. The air had warmed considerably, and Goodwin removed his coat and then his boots. He rolled his trousers up above his knees and waded cautiously into the river. The water was cold but bearable.

The carbine was completely out of the water and appeared to be dry and undamaged. After Goodwin detached the carbine and scabbard, he untied the saddlebags and returned them all to the riverbank. Retrieving the Henry was going to be far more difficult. Sam was a big horse, and he was lying directly on top of the rifle. Even if he could manage to move the horse's carcass, there was the very real possibility of the Henry having been badly damaged or completely ruined. Goodwin tried rolling Sam over by lifting his legs but soon realized the combination of the horse's weight, the soft sand, and flowing water would require far more strength than he possessed. After several fruitless minutes spent wrestling with the horse's dead weight, Goodwin returned to dry land to warm his feet and consider his options.

The morning had grown mild, and when Goodwin lay back on his coat, fatigue quickly overtook him, and he was soon asleep. He didn't know how long he slept, but when he awoke, the sun had disappeared behind the clouds and the wind was rising again. He pulled the coat around himself and scanned the riverbank for anything he might use as a lever. He pulled his boots on and, after searching a few minutes, located a small pine tree that had been nearly felled by a beaver. The beaver had gnawed the trunk down to no more than two inches in diameter. Goodwin had no difficulty breaking the tree off and stripping the limbs. After again removing his boots and rolling up his trousers, Goodwin returned to the river with the pole and waded back to Sam's body. Without the sun, the water now felt much colder, and putting his feet back in the river made him gasp.

He paused a moment before wading out to the horse, letting himself become accustomed to the icy water. The water level seemed higher now and flowing faster. The carcass was now near to floating. Forcing the thick end of the pole under Sam, Goodwin pried up and rolled the horse over much easier than he had thought possible. The dead horse rolled too easy, for now Sam was beginning to drift away. Goodwin slogged after the horse and struggled to remove the scabbard. The leather had grown soft, and gummy in the water and was refusing to yield. Abandoning the scabbard, Goodwin tried unbuckling the cinch and fared no better. Sam's body was now picking up speed, and Clyde struggled with the current. He extended his reach and snatched the Henry from the scabbard, and the act of freeing the heavy rifle caused Goodwin to lose his balance and pitch forward into the water.

Gasping for breath, Goodwin struggled back to the bank with the Henry. At that moment, he had every reason to doubt the wisdom of trying to recover it. Reaching shore, Goodwin immediately wrapped himself in the coat. Slowly, ever so slowly, his teeth stopped chattering and his nerves began to calm. He had little doubt that his new coat had just saved his life. As he waited for the shivering to stop, Goodwin scooted over to where he had dropped the saddlebags. He opened them and found that while one had filled with water, the contents of the other had remained mostly dry. To his astonishment, he found that the pint jar containing his supply of matches had survived the plunge from the bridge, unbroken. Until this moment, he had not dared dream he could be so lucky. With a burst of new energy, Goodwin let the coat fall away and rushed to gather driftwood. Spurred on by the cold, he soon had a fire burning. He undressed and huddled inside his coat as he dried his clothes on a long stick, item by item.

As he waited for his clothes to dry, Goodwin inspected the Henry. The butt end of the stock was badly cracked, but when he sighted down the barrel, it appeared to have survived unbent. The mechanism had partially filled with sand, but Goodwin could not hear the rattle of broken parts when he vigorously shook the rifle. When he got the opportunity, he would disassemble the mechanism and clean it thoroughly. Getting the stock repaired or replaced posed a stiffer challenge. The main thing now was to get the rifles securely hidden until he became familiar with the routine of the boarding house and could get them both secured in his room. When Goodwin was at last able to get dressed, he kicked the remnants of the fire into the river. It was late afternoon, and he still had a long walk ahead of him. He gauged the direction back to Keller and set off on a course directly across the prairie. He hoped he could make it back in time for supper, but if he had to go hungry, it would hardly be the first time. At least he would have the cover of darkness to help him hide the rifles.

By the time Goodwin had cached the rifles under the bridge, there was very little light remaining. He removed the revolver from its hiding place then buckled the gun belt high up around his chest, where it would be hidden by his coat. He threw the saddlebags over his shoulder and hastily made away from the little bridge. It had occurred to Goodwin that having retrieved his saddlebags would provide a good cover story for his daylong absence if anyone asked. With a little bit of luck, no one would ask any questions at all. When he entered Ms. Emily's kitchen, the supper dishes had been cleared away and the landlady was sitting at the table playing cribbage with Harley Childers.

Childers looked up calmly at Goodwin's entrance but said nothing. Ms. Emily piped up, "Well, young man, I was beginnin' to think ya left town already." Ms. Emily's voice carried not a trace of reproach, and she seemed genuinely glad to see him.

"I went out lookin' for my old nag, and I was at least able to save my saddlebags," said Goodwin.

"Too bad about your horse, son," said Childers in his low, rumbling voice.

"You go and run your bags up to your room, Clyde, and I'll get your supper set out. I don't make a habit of holding meals for boarders, but I had a feelin' you might be out lookin' for your stuff."

Goodwin was genuinely surprised and said, "I do thank you kindly, ma'am. I wasn't expecting y'all to do that for me."

"Like I said, I don't make a habit of it, but you did pay for supper, and it's only fair you get to eat it. Now run those bags up to your room and get washed up."

Goodwin climbed the stairs to his room and deposited his coat, saddlebags, and gun belt in the closet then secured the door with the padlock. He opened the faucet and, after a moment, was astonished to find warm water coming out of tap. This was his first experience with running water, and he had no idea that warm water could be achieved any way but heating it on a stove. As Goodwin was washing his hands, he was startled by a sudden hissing sound from across the room. The first image that flashed across his mind was a snake. He wheeled around, instinctively reaching for his sidearm. Goodwin stood frozen, for a long moment but saw nothing. Then the hiss came again, and he realized the sound was coming from the metal coils set against the wall. He carefully put his hand on the metal fixture and found it hot to the touch. "Well tarnation, this must be what keeps the room warm," he said quietly to himself.

When he returned to the kitchen, Goodwin found fried chicken, biscuits, and mashed potatoes with gravy waiting for him. Having never dined on anything but his own cooking and Dooley's sporadic efforts, Clyde thought his supper to be, by far, the best meal he had ever eaten.

As he was finishing his meal, Ms. Emily asked in her laughing voice, "Ya got room left for a slice of pie, Clyde? Harley here has been eying it, and I'm afraid he might get to it if you don't get there first."

Goodwin became self-conscious and said quietly, "Well, I don't rightly know, ma'am. I ain't never had any pie before."

"Never had a piece of pie?" said Ms. Emily before turning to Childers and saying with false severity, "Well, that settles it, Harley. You're just gonna have to dream about pie till the next time I decide to bake one." Mrs. Kellogg paused a moment then turned back to Childers and said, "Unless someone else takes pity on ya."

Childers responded with a low rumbling laugh but did not speak. Ms. Emily sat a generous slice of apple pie before Goodwin and said,

"You enjoy this Clyde but you best keep an eye on Harley because he's not to be trusted around pie and, truth be told, I think he cheats at cribbage about half the time."

Upon hearing this jibe, Childers put his head back and laughed heartily.

"Nah, don't you believe that, Clyde. Harley don't cheat at cards or anything else," the landlady laughed. "I just like keeping him on his toes."

Childers withdrew his watch from his vest, looked at it, and said, "Well, Ms. Emily, we're gonna have to finish this game tomorrow, unless you'd like to just go ahead and concede now." Childers smiled and gave the landlady a sly look.

"Concede to you, Harley Childers? You ain't gonna live long enough to see me concede a cribbage game to the likes of you." Both Childers and Ms. Emily laughed warmly, and it was clear to Goodwin the two were good friends.

After Childers bade them both good night, Goodwin ventured to ask the landlady about the mystery of the hot water. She responded kindly, "Well, Clyde, it's getting to be a common thing these days. Maybe not so much out here on the prairies as it is back east. The boiler in the basement sends steam up through the pipes to the rooms and heats water at the same time. My husband insisted we install it when we built the house. He said he had spent all the time splitting wood he ever needed to. It really ain't as complicated as it might sound. By the way, if it gets too warm in your room, turn the handle at the base of the radiator to the right. That will cut back the amount of steam it lets in. Go the other way with it if gets too cool."

Goodwin thanked Ms. Emily again for having held supper for him then retired to his room. He removed his boots, undressed, then climbed into bed after blowing out the lamp. Before falling into a much-needed sleep, Goodwin resolved to remain where he was for as long as he possibly could. In the days that followed, Goodwin became familiar with the routine of the boarding house and used the occasion of Ms. Emily's midday nap to smuggle the rifles into his room. Alone at night, he carefully disassembled, cleaned, and oiled all the weapons. Once he was satisfied with his work on the Henry, he slowly and quietly worked the mechanism until, at last, he loaded the rifle and tested chambering and ejecting cartridges. Although the mechanism appeared to be functioning properly, it would take the talents of a gunsmith to repair or replace the cracked stock.

In the weeks that followed, Goodwin worked faithfully for Bonebright, and as word of his reliability got around Keller, he found himself working nearly every day at a wide variety of tasks. He occasionally cleaned the livery stable for Karl Emmett, helped Childers deliver coal, and proved himself an able carpenter's helper during the warmer months. He kept busy and made himself respectable. Goodwin was extremely careful to never let on that he was hating every minute of it. As the months turned into years, Goodwin's thoughts began turning to buying a new horse and moving on. Then, he got the chance to serve as a part-time deputy sheriff. Though Clyde Goodwin was not an especially big man, he was tough, fearless, and cool-headed. The citizens of Keller found these to be desirable qualities in a lawman. The part-time job of deputy led to his being appointed and, later, as the community grew, elected county sheriff.

Chapter Eight

Nawlins

Zebediah was suddenly roused from his stupor by a sharp crack of thunder and the smell of ozone. His pain-wracked body was tingling from the lightning strike, and his eyes were still refusing to focus. There was the fresh taste of blood in his mouth, and his jaw ached terribly from the broken tooth. As the endless stormy night wore on, Zebediah's thoughts were becoming ever more confused. Although he felt as if he had been drifting into extended periods of sleep, Zebediah was slowly realizing that his periods of unconsciousness had probably been very brief. Zebediah did not know if he was experiencing sleep or something else. As he huddled against the bridge abutment, Zebediah's physical pain was overshadowed by a sadness he had not felt since the passing of Aunt Mary. The creek was now a torrent and was but a few feet away. Why not just stagger into it and surrender to his fate? Zebediah was on the verge of acting on this impulse when his consciousness vanished again.

* * *

Zebediah jumped from the train well before it entered the city. He was reasonably certain the city in the distance was New Orleans, but this was his first visit to the city. Zebediah dusted himself off and looked around. He began hiking along the tracks, searching for any symbols left behind by traveling men. Several minutes later, he spotted what he was looking for. There, carved into the side of a tree, was an

X with a closed top and an arrow pointing out the direction to a safe campsite. Zebediah knew, however, what was safe for a white traveling man wasn't always safe for a black man. He made his way cautiously in the direction indicated by the arrow. Away from the tracks, the trees and foliage grew increasingly dense. There was, however, a discernible track, and the memory of Zeke's fishing trail flashed across his mind.

After following the path for a few minutes, Zebediah smelled wood smoke and advanced slowly the last few yards to the camp. From deep in the shadows, he scanned the camp and was able to make out a dozen men, several of whom were black. Tired from traveling and much relieved, Zebediah called out, "Travelin' man comin' in," then made his way slowly into view. Experiences, both good and bad, had taught Zebediah the best way of entering what the traveling men called "jungles." Had he seen only white men in the camp, Zebediah would have quietly retreated then moved on in search of a safer place.

The men gathered around the fire looked up. A few grunted their greetings, but mostly, they eyed Zebediah cautiously. Once they deemed him not to be a threat, they returned to their conversations. There was a stew of sorts in a battered pot hanging from large stick near the fire. Zebediah understood that before he would be allowed to partake of it, he must first add something to it. Zebediah opened his bag and withdrew a clutch of potatoes he had liberated from a garden the previous day. He used most of his remaining water to clean the potatoes then cut them up and added them to the pot. The men nodded approvingly and one by one began giving their names. Mostly, they weren't real names but rather the monikers they had given themselves.

"Ridge Runner," said a thin country boy with haunted eyes.

"Deacon," said a grizzled older black man wearing a battered derby.

"Steamer."

"Ramblin' Jack."

And so it went until all the men in the camp had given their names. "Zeb," said Zebediah.

The other men nodded to him, and the man who called himself Deacon spoke, "You added to the pot, Zeb, so he'p yourself. We tries not to take out any mo' then we puts in."

"Yes, sir," said Zebediah as he proceeded to ladle a portion of stew into his tin plate, roughly equal to the potatoes he had added in. "I thank ya all kindly," said Zebediah, sitting down to eat. The other men at the fire murmured their acceptance of Zebediah into the group. After he had eaten, Zebediah began to carefully ease his way into the conversation. When he felt comfortable, Zebediah ventured to ask, "Do any of y'all know where a man might pick up a few days o' work?"

Nearly in unison, several of the men said, "Docks." Deacon added, "There's most always work to be had on the docks. Mighty hard work though. You earns yer money movin' freight. Most men don't stick with it fo' long, that's why they's most always lookin' to hire. I'm too old and wore out for it myself, but a young man like you prolly do all right." Several of the men murmured their agreement.

"Is this here camp close enough to the docks, or should a man be lookin' for somethin' a li'l closer?" asked Zebediah.

"Well, there's more than one set of docks," said Deacon. "The closest one is prolly about a thirty-minute walk, which ain't bad. There's other docks further downriver that's prolly hour or mo' away. As hard as the work is, I'd stay as close to the job as I could. If ya git hired on, you kin bet there's gonna be some other travelin men there. They'll know the campin' spots."

Zebediah thanked Deacon for the advice then, as the sun was setting, retired to his bag and unrolled his blanket. Keeping his possessions with him under the blanket, Zebediah drifted off to sleep. When morning came, some of the men had already "caught out," but Deacon remained. Zebediah and Deacon shared the little food they had, then the older man gave Zebediah directions to the docks. "'Tain't hard to find the docks, Zeb. Jus' keep followin' the tracks you come in on. Befo' long, you'll start seein' heavy wagons and such, movin' on the road. Jus' follow 'em, and you won't have no trouble findin' 'em. You'll likely hear boats blowin' their whistles."

Zebediah packed his belongings and shook Deacon's hand. "I appreciate the advice, Deacon. I might be back tonight, or I might not. I guess we'll see what happens. If I don't make it back, then I hope to see y'all somewhere on down the road."

"Good luck to you, Zeb," said Deacon in his gravelly old voice. "Dock work is mighty hard, but y'all young and strong. You kin manage it."

Zebediah made his way back out of the woods and, keeping with his well-conditioned habit, looked carefully in all directions before emerging from the cover. Once satisfied, he shouldered his bag and began hiking along the rail line, near enough to the tree line to hide himself if necessary. It was still early, not more than an hour past sunrise, and yet the still air was heavy with moisture and the temperature was climbing steadily. As Deacon had predicted, Zebediah soon saw heavy wagons loaded with cotton bales and other goods, streaming in the same direction. He began following the flow of traffic and was soon joined by other people. Some appeared to be local folks going about their daily business, and others Zebediah quickly identified as traveling men.

A few blocks inside the town, a tall, lanky black man emerged from a side street and fell in alongside Zebediah. The man beside him was so similar to Zeke in appearance, Zebediah could not help but do a double take. The man's face, however, was much younger than Zeke's and bore no resemblance to his uncle. Without introducing himself, the man asked, "Headin' fo' the docks?"

"Yeah," said Zebediah, "a fella' tol' me I might find some work there."

"He tol' ya right," said the man. "There was seven boats at the wharves yesterday, and they said two mo' was due in today. Should be plenty o' work fo' at least the next few days."

"Do y'all know who I should talk to about hiring on?" asked Zebediah.

The lanky man laughed softly and said, "You done already talked to him."

The man was several inches taller than Zebediah, and he glanced down at Zeb's puzzled look and grinned. "I be the one y'all needs to talk to. I s'pose you thought you'd be lookin' fo' a white man, didn't ya?"

Not knowing if he should laugh or smile, Zebediah responded evenly, "Well, I guess I prolly did."

"Well, you ain't the first one who made that mistake," said the tall man. "I ain't really the boss, they jus' calls me the straw boss. The man has me give the colored men the eyeball and decide if they has what it takes to work the dock. You think ya got what it takes?"

"I aim to find out," said Zebediah.

"You look plenty strong fo' yo' size. What's yo' name, son?"

"Zebediah. Most everybody jus' call me Zeb."

"Zeb, I'm Pickens, jus' plain Pickens." They came to a tall wooden fence that partitioned off the wharf area. "Jus' follow me, Zeb, I'll show ya where ya need to go. Zebediah followed Pickens along the fence until they came to a door with a sign posted above it reading Colored Workers. Inside the gate stood a small whitewashed building. Pickens knocked on the door, and a man's high-pitched voice called from within. "Come in, Pickens."

Before entering the office, Pickens removed his hat then turned to Zebediah and said quietly, "Take yo' hat off, Zeb." Zebediah removed his hat, and they entered the building. "Mr. Turner, this here's Zebediah. He lookin' fo' work."

A fat bald white man looked up from his desk. His ruddy face was set off by the coldest blue-gray eyes Zebediah had ever seen. A large cigar jutted from the corner of the man's mouth. The man behind the desk did not immediately speak. His cold, dead eyes bored into Zebediah, filling him with fear. At last the man said, in a voice less hostile than his appearance, "He looks strong enough. You ever work on a dock befo', Zebediah?"

"Naw, sir, I ain't," said Zebediah, "but I's done plenty o' hard work. On the farm and such."

"You gonna think farmin' is plumb easy compared to workin' a dock, but I'll give ya a try. The work is a day at a time as I need the labor. It's a dollar a day, and fo' the first week, ten cents of yo' pay goes to Pickens fo' findin' ya."

"Thank ya, sir," said Zebediah. "I appreciates it."

The man behind the desk drew heavily on his cigar and, after discharging a heavy cloud of smoke, looked directly at Zebediah and said, "We'll see how much you appreciate it after movin' twenty tons of cotton. Go ahead and git him squared away, Pickens."

"Yes, sir, Mr. Turner," said Pickens. "Come on along, Zeb."

Away the office and out of earshot, Perkins said quietly, "Ole' man Turner ain't half as scary as he looks, but I wouldn't go crossin' him. Jus' do yo' work and he'll be square wid ya. I don't think he likes colored folks very much, but he figured out a long time ago that he kin get a lot mo' work done by treatin' people fair."

Zebediah followed along quietly as Pickens led him into a small unpainted shed. Pointing to some shelves against one wall, Pickens said, "You kin' put yo' stuff over there, Zeb, ain't nobody gonna bother it. This is where we eat our dinner and where we go if it gits to rainin' too hard. Do ya have anything to eat, Zeb?"

"A few potatoes is all," said Zeb.

"We share what we has," said Pickens. "We don't let nobody go hungry if we kin he'p it. A man ain't gonna last long on this job wid an empty belly, and we all has to depend on each other so nobody gits kilt."

"Men get killed doin' this work?" asked Zebediah guardedly.

"It's a sad thing, Zeb, but it happens mo' often than it prolly should," said Pickens with a sad, faraway look.

"How's that happen, Pickens?"

"Oh, different ways. A line can break and drop a load on a man. I seen men lose their footin' and git crushed between a boat and the wharf. I seen some fall in the water and drown 'cause they cain't swim. I even saw one man git snake bit and die. I'll do what I kin to keep ya safe, Zeb, and the other men will too, but ya gotta keep yo' eyes wide open ever minute." A very sober Zebediah followed Pickens out of the shed and to a place on the wharf where several men were waiting. All the assembled men greeted Pickens as they approached. "Mornin' to y'all," said Pickens. "This here is Zebediah, he gonna be workin' wid us today. He go by Zeb."

The men greeted Zebediah by nodding their heads and speaking quietly. Their faces all seemed to be asking Zebediah if he knew what he was getting himself into. The men were, to an individual, lean and muscular. Perkins spoke up. "I'd give ya everybody's name, but I ain't got time fo' that right now, Zeb. You gonna get met up with these men soon enough. Let's git to it, men."

Pickens led the crew onto the deck of a type of riverboat Zebediah had never seen. It had a large open-deck area, stacked high with wooden boxes of various sizes, all of them tied down with heavy nets of hemp fiber. The cabins, paddle wheel, and wheelhouse were all located at the stern end of the vessel. Sensing Zebediah's curiosity, Pickens said, "This be what they call a 'lighter,' Zeb. We're seein' mo' of 'em all the time. They don't carry any passengers, jus' freight. Some of 'em even goes out into the gulf a ways, and they unloads ships straight onto 'em, then they come back upriver to unload. This one here ain't got a roof over the cargo, but some of 'em does, and some of 'em now has cranes built right on the deck to speed up the loadin' and unloadin'."

Pickens led the way to the stack of boxes nearest the gangway. "We gonna start with this stack, men." Perkins spoke with quiet authority, and the men did not hesitate to follow his instructions. Three of the men went directly to work, unlashing the netting that secured the pile of boxes. As the netting fell away, two of the men scrambled to the top of the pile and began handing down crates to the men waiting below. One by one, the boxes came down and onto the shoulders of the waiting dock hands. Zebediah followed their lead and accepted his load in turn. As he shouldered the box, Zebediah's legs nearly buckled under the weight. The crate on his shoulders weighed at least a hundred pounds. He followed the other men unsteadily down the gangway. Back on the wharf, the men stacked their boxes on two-wheeled carts.

The men returned to the boat and continued hauling boxes onto the wharf until the two-wheeled carts were fully loaded. The men then tipped the carts back and began rolling them into the warehouse. Zebediah did as the others and joined the parade. Inside the dimly lit building, they were met by a tall gaunt white man with hollow eyes and a sallow complexion. The cadaverous man compared the numbers on the boxes to a list on a clipboard then directed the men to where to take their loads. The man's breath reeked of liquor and tobacco. There was a Colt revolver on his belt, and his clothing had not been washed in some time. The man's appearance frightened Zebediah even more than the man who hired him. Zebediah had little doubt that the skeletal man directing traffic in the warehouse would not hesitate to wreak violence on the workers.

Zebediah took his load to the designated spot in the warehouse and eased the two-wheeled truck from below the stack. Another crew of men began carefully stacking the boxes. Zebediah followed the other dock hands back to the wharf. The man ahead of him slowed his pace enough for Zebediah to walk beside him then turned and said quietly, "How'd you like the Spook?"

"That's his name?" whispered Zebediah incredulously.

"Naw, his real name's Leander Thibodeaux, but we calls him the Spook. Jus' not to his face or very loud." The other dock hand chuckled quietly. "He a crazy, mean ole' Cajun sumbitch. I ain't never seen him shoot nobody, but I ain't got a doubt that he would. My name's DeMond. Most folks calls me D."

Before Zebediah could introduce himself, they were back at the lighter and in line to receive a new load. Unloading for the second trip into the warehouse was no easier than the first. It was not until they had completely cleared the initial stack of crates that the task became any easier. With deck space now open, the men were able to bring the two-wheeled carts up the gangway and onto the boat itself. Though this made the job a bit easier, the pace of the work increased, and the men now had to lift the boxes up to the other men in the warehouse. The inside crew stacked boxes to the rafters.

By the time the large deep-throated steam whistle signaled midday, Zebediah was exhausted, and there was still a full afternoon ahead of him. The dock hands retired to the shack where Zebediah had earlier stored his bag. The men broke out baskets and large tobacco cans of food. Zebediah retrieved the last of the potatoes from his bag and bit into one. The men gathered around the rude table began speaking up.

"Hey, Zeb, pass me one of yo' spuds, and I'll swap ya a couple hard-boiled eggs fo' it."

"Yeah, Zeb, I'll take one of 'em too, and y'all kin have this chunk o' my wife's corn bread."

And so it went until the all the men had meals of roughly equal portions.

The men ate quickly and mostly in silence. A few offered up their names, but there was little in the way of conversation. All the men helped themselves to the bucket of water provided for their use. Once they were done eating, most of the men stretched out on the floor and were immediately asleep. They did not stir until the steam whistle blew again, announcing that the men had three minutes to return to work. The men stood, stretched, and drank more water. Zebediah followed their example. Though they could have all done with more food, water, and rest, the men were soon back at their labor. The crew had cleared half the lighter's deck during the morning, and they had been told to complete the unloading by day's end.

The morning had been hot, but the afternoon was hotter. The men's misery was increased by several small rain showers that drove the humidity even higher. On the afternoon's third trip into the warehouse, Zebediah stopped before Leander Thibodeaux for directions and made the mistake of looking directly at the warehouseman. Thibodeaux's hand went instantly to the grip of his Colt, and he growled into Zebediah's face, "WHAT THE HAIL YOU LOOKIN' AT, BOY?" The man's breath smelled like a chicken coop that had recently housed a moonshine still.

Thibodeaux's eyes bored into Zebediah, who lowered his head in fear. "Nothin', sir, I ain't lookin' at nothin'."

"You a lyin' sumbitch, boy!" came Thibodeaux's guttural growl. The warehouse man's empty eyes bored into Zebediah, and his gaunt frame was quaking with rage.

Thibodeaux's gaze left Zebediah too frightened to speak, and he could only look down at the floor. As the line of dock hands behind Zebediah grew, Thibodeaux at last spat out, "L-10, boy! now move yo' sorry ass out!"

Back on the wharf, the dock hand who called himself D said quietly, "Damn, Zeb, I's sorry. The Spook drinks his dinner, and it makes him even crazier and meaner. It ain't never a good idea to look him in the face, and ya fo' damn sure don't wanna do it when he's liquored up."

"I's gonna be sure and remember that," said Zebediah without humor.

Even though Zebediah was careful to never look directly at Leander Thibodeaux, the warehouseman continued to focus his wrath on Zebediah throughout the rest of the long afternoon. With every trip, Thibodeaux would spend several uncomfortable seconds glaring at Zebediah, as if daring him to speak. D whispered to Zebediah that such behavior was not unusual for Thibodeaux and that the foul-smelling old Cajun nearly always singled out someone to terrorize. "All ya kin do is hope he picks somebody else tomorrow, Zeb," said D.

The sun was hanging low in the western sky when the last stack of boxes was cleared from the deck. The men returned to the shed and retrieved their belongings then followed Pickens back to the whitewashed office. Turner was positioned at an open window, dispensing coins to each man as they exited the wharf. Zebediah noticed that most of the men received ninety cents in payment while Pickens pocketed nearly two dollars. Outside the gate, D fell in alongside Zebediah and asked, "You a travelin' man, Zeb?"

"Yeah, I am. I been on the bum fo' a while now. I'm startin' to git a li'l tired of it though, and If I could find a place to settle, I prolly would," said Zebediah.

"I hear ya," said D. "I jus' don't think Nawlins is the place though. Leastwise, not fo' me. I comes from up in Ohio, and it jus' gits too damn hot fo' me here in the summer."

The day had been so warm that Zebediah had largely forgotten that it was autumn, and he laughed. "You means it gits hotter than it was today?"

"Oh *hell* yes," laughed D. "Round about August, you'd do anything fo' a day like today. I tried it here one summer, and it damn near kilt me. It ain't too bad in the winter though. There's even some days around Christmas when it gits plumb chilly. I tough it out on the docks over the winter, then I looks to hire on as a stoker and head back upriver in spring. I has people in Ohio, and most years I'm able to git back and see 'em fo' a while in summer. I kin always pick up some farm work up there in summer. I's only been back in Nawlins fo' a week myself, that's why Pickens is still gittin' ten cents o' my money. When the leaves start turnin' in Ohio, I make my way back down here on a boat if I can. If I cain't get on a boat, then I hops on a freight."

Zebediah and D reentered the city, and as they walked along, D said, "The first thing y'all needs to take care of, Zeb, is gittin' yourself fixed up fo' tomorrow." D pointed down a side street and said, "See that store on the corner there, Zeb? There's a black man who runs it. It's the first place most of the dock men goes after work, and they get stocked up for the next day. Roberts, who run the store, will treat ya fair."

Zebediah followed D down the side street and into the store. D picked up canned goods and potatoes, and Zebediah did the same. Zebediah was struck by how much the store resembled the one he had visited in Parkersburg with Zeke and Mary so many miles ago. He was very impressed by the fact that this store was owned by a black man. After purchasing his food, Zebediah still had twenty-five cents remaining. D spoke up. "Hide it real good, Zeb. There's plenty o' folks who'd be glad to steal it from ya."

"Oh, I know," said Zebediah. "I's been on the bum fo' quite a while."

D appeared somewhat embarrassed at having made the suggestion and quickly added, "What I really meant to say was, Nawlins is worse than most places when it comes to thievery. Much worse. There's folks here who'd steal the teeth right outa' yo' mouth and try sellin' 'em back to ya." D chuckled at his own joke, but Zebediah knew his new companion was telling the truth. "Where you campin' at, Zeb?"

Zebediah did his best to describe last night's location. "It ain't far, and there was a decent bunch there las' night," said Zeb, "but I's sure you know how fast that kin change."

"Oh, I fo' damn sure do," said D, laughing quietly. "If'n you don't mind, Zeb, I'm gonna tag along. The place I been stayin' is further away, and I ain't never felt very safe there, the truth be told."

"It don't make me no never mind," said Zebediah. "It's back in the trees a ways and real peaceful. There's a pump in a man's field where ya kin draw water once it gits dark."

"That sounds good, Zeb."

The pair made their way along the tracks and out of the city. In the gathering dusk, Zebediah led the way down the twisting path into the woods. When they neared the campground, Zebediah again employed his instinctive caution. There were dangerous and frightening people among the traveling men, and if a man wanted to survive, he could never let his guard down. As they approached the clearing, Zebediah saw Deacon sitting by the fire where he had left him. He recognized some of the faces from the previous night, and there were some new comers as well. "Travelin' men comin' in," called Zebediah.

Deacon immediately spoke up as Zebediah and D emerged from the foliage, "Hey, Zeb, now where in the hell did you find D?"

"Hey, Deacon," said D as he advanced across the campground to shake Deacon's hand. "It's been awhile since the las' time I ran into y'all, Deacon. I jus' got back from Ohio a few days ago, and I'll be hangin' around fo' the winter."

"Was you able to git on a boat, or did ya have to ride the rails?" asked Deacon.

"I done some o' both," said D. "I worked on a boat as far as St. Lou, but the boat I was workin' turned around and headed back upriver. I couldn't git on another boat, so I hopped a few freights."

Being recognized by Deacon eased their entry into the group. Zebediah and D made their contributions to the stew pot, and since they contributed the most, they ate the most. After eating, the two dockworkers did not tarry long by the fire and soon retired to their blankets. When he was awakened by the predawn cacophony of birdsong, Zebediah would have sworn that he had only just closed his eyes. D and Zebediah opened cans of beef stew and ate them cold. They did not offer to share their breakfast with the other men, most of whom were still asleep. D seemed driven by a sense of urgency as they gathered their things and made away from the campground.

As they hiked along the rail line, Zebediah had to work at it to keep up with D. "You in some kinda' hurry, D?" asked Zebediah.

D turned to Zebediah, and the fear on his face was evident. "Zeb, I'll tell ya right now, there's at least one o' those men back there who's gonna be dead befo' long."

"Dead? How you know that?"

"I knows that 'cause I know the Deacon. He a crazy-assed ole' preacher and a stone-cold killer. Yo' lucky he didn't take a likin' to you. They say that ole' sumbitch kilt his whole family, wife, children, his folks, all of 'em," said D. "I always makes nice whenever I run into him, but I don't never hang around any longer than I has to. He's likely waitin' fo' one of these men, or maybe you, to git a couple dollars ahead, and then in the middle of the night, he'll git out his pig sticker. You suit yo'self, Zeb, but I'll be findin' a new place to camp tonight."

"Now that you tol' me about the Deacon, I reckon I'll do the same," said Zebediah gratefully.

"Campin' spots change, but I know of a couple that ain't much further away than this one," said D. "It don't really pay to stay too long in the same place anyway."

"Yeah, I know," said Zebediah. "Three days is a long time to be in one place."

Zebediah and D made their way back into the city and to the colored workers' entrance at the wharf. They stopped at the window, and Turner assured them of another day's employment. Once inside, they deposited their bags in the workers' shed. They took large drinks of water then joined the other men on the wharf. Pickens soon made his appearance, and once again, they were back to the brutal task of working the dock. This day found the men unloading cargo from the deep well of a barge. The men took turns working down inside the barge, handing boxes up to the wharf. It took over an hour of lifting boxes hand to hand before there was enough space cleared inside the barge for a second gangway to be lowered into the vessel itself. One by one, the men loaded their two-wheeled carts then pushed or pulled them up the incline and back down to the wharf.

Zebediah had desperately hoped Leander Thibodeaux would select a new target this day, but the old Cajun did not. Zebediah's every trip into the warehouse included several seconds of the foul-smelling man glaring down at him. D whispered to Zebediah, "Damn, Zeb, he don't usually pick on the same man two days runnin'."

"I guess I's jus' lucky," said Zebediah without humor.

Two trips later, as Zebediah was standing his cart up in front of Thibodeaux, the top box slipped from the stack and went crashing to the floor. Zebediah moved quickly to gather up the box and restack it on the cart. He had no more than put the box in place when Leander Thibodeaux viciously struck Zebediah across the face with the back of his hand. The tall, gaunt man had surprising strength, and the blow sent Zebediah sprawling backward on the floor. Zebediah had been in many fights during his time on the road, and he was instantly back on his feet and set to retaliate when he found himself looking down the barrel of Thibodeaux's Colt.

"G'won', boy! Try it! I'll splatter yer goddamn brains all over the floor and make yer friends mop it up and then dump yo' miserable ass in the river!" Thibodeaux spoke in a guttural growl; his eyes were blazing, but the hand holding the Colt was rock steady.

Zebediah froze. He looked into the barrel of the gun and then turned his eyes to the floor. Zebediah had little doubt he could make short work of Thibodeaux if it only involved fists, but the man was holding a gun. Slowly, using everything Aunt Mary and Uncle Zeke ever taught him, Zebediah brought himself under control and, at last, managed to say, "I's sorry, Mr. Thibodeaux. I didn't mean to do it, and it won't happen again."

"You dammed right on both counts, boy!" snarled Thibodeaux. "You's sorry as hell, and it ain't gonna happen again." Thibodeaux compared the numbers on Zebediah's boxes to his list and hissed, "B-9, now move the hell out."

Badly shaken, Zebediah pushed his cart to the designated section of the warehouse and began handing boxes up to a man from the warehouse crew. Zebediah was poised to hand up the second box when the man working on the stack dropped a clean handkerchief down to Zebediah and said quietly, "Take this, yo' bleedin'."

His emotions were running so high that, until the other man mentioned it, Zebediah was unaware of his split and bleeding lip. He gratefully accepted the handkerchief and held it to his lips. It was soon red with blood. He looked up at the man on the boxes and said, "I'm ruinin' yo' hanky."

"Don't worry about it," said the other man. "I'm Johnny. Jus' hold it tight against yo' cut, and it'll stop bleedin' pretty quick. Come on around the side of the stack where the Spook cain't see ya."

Zebediah did as the man suggested. A minute later, Zebediah carefully lifted the handkerchief away from his lip and looked up at Johnny. "Did it stop?"

The man on the stack looked at Zebediah's lip carefully and said, "Yup, I believe it did."

Zebediah started to hand the handkerchief back to Johnny, and the other man said, "Naw, jus' keep it. Wait around fo' me outside the gate after we knock off tonight," said Johnny quietly.

Zebediah put the handkerchief in his pocket and thanked Johnny. He looked carefully at Johnny and saw that the man on the stack of boxes was a good deal older than himself, broad shouldered, and heavily muscled.

"I'm Zeb."

"Yeah, I know. Fo' whatever the reason, that damned ole' spook's got it in fo' ya, and we should prolly talk, just not here and not now," said Johnny quietly.

Zebediah thanked Johnny again and, after handing up the remaining boxes, returned to the wharf. Fortunately for Zebediah, Leander Thibodeaux paid closer attention to traffic entering the warehouse than he did to the men returning to the dock. He had apparently not noticed the extra time Zebediah had taken. Emerging back into the sun, the angry faces of the other dockworkers told Zebediah that word of the incident had spread quickly. Although the men said nothing, their facial expressions and brief nods to Zebediah voiced their solidarity. All through the remainder of the afternoon, Zebediah was forced to endure Thibodeaux's taunts each time he returned with a load. In the back of his mind, Aunt Mary was cautioning against it, but Zebediah swore to himself that he would take revenge on the man if ever the opportunity presented itself, but for now at least, he had to accept the situation and keep himself under control. As if being struck by Thibodeaux hadn't been enough for one day, Zebediah had another unpleasant surprise waiting for him at the pay window. When he reached the window, instead of the expected ninety cents, Turner handed him fifty cents.

Before Zebediah could raise a question, Turner spoke, "That's what happens when you shoot yo' mouth off at the warehouse foreman and go to slackin' boy."

Zebediah paused for a moment and stared at the man in the pay window. Turner said, "Either take the money, boy, or don't bother showin' up tomorrow or ever."

"Yes, sir," said Zebediah. He nodded his head, lowered his eyes, and accepted the fifty cents. Outside the fence, Zebediah joined D and they made their way to Roberts' store. "How's the lip?" asked D.

"I'll live," said Zeb. "That sumbitch of a Spook ain't gonna live long if I ever git the chance to even the score though."

D lifted his head and, after glancing cautiously around, said, "It's okay to feel that way, Zeb, Lord knows you got the right, jus' be careful who you lets hear ya say it. The walls in this here town have ears."

"Yeah," said Zebediah, "you right." At that moment, Zebediah was physically and emotionally drained. He wanted only to eat, sleep, and be far away. "I'm thinkin' I prolly catch out tomorrow, D."

"You do what ya think ya has to, Zeb, but ya might want to stick it out a li'l longer and put a few dollars in yo' pocket befo' you go. There's lots o' travelin' men who head south in winter. Jobs ain't always easy to find, and bummin' can be pretty tough in winter. I's prolly jus' tellin' ya what ya already know," said D quietly.

"You is," said Zebediah with a wry smile, "but that don't mean I don't need to hear it. You're right, D, I ain't ready to catch out jus' yet."

As Zebediah and D neared the store, a voice called to them from behind. "Hey, Zeb! Y'all forgit about me?"

Zebediah turned around and saw the warehouseman Johnny a few paces behind them. Zebediah grinned sheepishly and answered, "Well, I guess I sorta' did."

Johnny smiled as Zebediah and D waited for him to catch up. "How much did Turner dock yer pay, Zeb?" asked Johnny.

"Forty cents," said Zebediah sullenly. "'Taint right."

"No, it sho' as hell ain't," said Johnny. Johnny turned to D and asked, "How you doin', young man? They call you D, don't they?"

"Yes, sir, I'm DeMond, I goes by D mostly. Oh, I's doin' okay, a li'l better than my man Zeb," said D, clapping Zebediah lightly on the shoulder.

"I'm Johnny Pike, D. Pleased to meet ya." Johnny withdrew some coins from his pocket, sorted through them, then held his hand out to Zebediah and said, "This is fo' you, Zeb," then dropped forty cents into Zebediah's hand.

"What's this?" asked Zebediah, his eyes wide with surprise.

"When a man gits beat on and docked pay through no fault of his own, the other men chips in what they can to he'p make up fo' his loss," said Johnny. "That damned old Spook's livin' on borrowed time, he jus' don't know it," said Johnny with quiet determination.

"I do rightly thank ya, Johnny," said Zebediah humbly.

"Ain't no need to thank me," said Johnny. "We he'p out each other when we can. Jus' keep in mind that you prolly be asked to chip in a nickel or a dime one day to he'p somebody else."

"Oh yes, sir, Johnny. I'll fo' sure he'p out if I can," said Zebediah gratefully.

Johnny turned to leave then turned back to the boys, paused a moment, then asked, "You boys on the bum?"

"Yeah," said D, "we is."

"We be lookin' fo' a new place to camp tonight," said Zebediah.

Johnny eyed the two boys carefully for a few seconds before speaking, "I's seen how you boys work, and y'all seem pretty square to me. I ain't never made this offer befo', but I has a shed that my wife and I has talked about rentin' out if the right person should come along. It ain't much to look at, but it has a floor and it'll keep the rain out. It's a damn sight better than sleepin' outside in winter. How does fifty cents a week sound to y'all?"

Zebediah and D looked at each other then back at Johnny. D said, "That sounds pretty good to me, Johnny."

"Yeah, it sho' does," added Zebediah.

"Well, you men go ahead on and git what ya need at the sto', and I'll wait here fo' ya," said Johnny.

The two young men quickly completed their purchases and rejoined Johnny, who then led them the few blocks to his house. The small unpainted dwelling stood on stilts a few feet above the ground. The house was unpretentious, neat, and tidy. As they neared the door, Johnny called out, "Clarice! I has some people you needs to meet."

A moment later, a stout woman appeared on the porch, drying her hands on her apron. "Who you go draggin' home now, Johnny Pike?" The woman spoke sternly, but her voice carried a certain good humor, and a moment after speaking, her face softened and she smiled down at the young men.

"This here is Zebediah, and this is D," said Johnny, pointing to each of the men in turn. "They been workin' on the docks, and I thinks they's good men. I tol' 'em we would rent the shed to 'em fo' fifty cents a week. Men, this here is my wife, Clarice."

"The hell you say, Johnny!" said Clarice sharply. Before the boys had a chance to speak, she looked directly at her husband and then back at the boys and said, "He'll rent it to y'all fo' thirty cents a week. What the hell's the matter wid you, Johnny?"

Johnny shrugged his shoulders and smiled helplessly then looked back at the boys and said with a laugh, "Well, you heard her, men, she the boss."

"Fifty cents a week sounds plenty fair to us, ma'am," said Zebediah.

"Yeah, it sho' do," added D.

Clarice eyed the boys carefully then said, "Okay. You go on and take a look at it, and if y'all willin' to pay fifty cents a week, then I guess you can, but speak up if ya think it's too much."

"Yes, ma'am," said the boys in one voice. They followed Johnny around the side of the house into a small backyard, mostly taken up by a vegetable garden. In the back corner of the lot stood an unpainted shed, approximately eight feet square.

"Like I said, it ain't much to look at, but it has a decent roof, a floor, and a window," said Johnny. "We keeps our gardenin' tools in there, but they all hangin' up and shouldn't git in yo' way too much. I'll look around and see if I kin come up with somethin' fo' ya to sit on. Shouldn't be too hard to find, there's always somebody lookin' to sell somethin'. Privy's right over there, you kin draw water at the back o' the house, and you kin use this old iron wheel fo' a cookin' fire, jus' be careful."

Zebediah and D looked at each other then back at Johnny. They could scarcely believe their good fortune, and Zebediah said, "Oh yes, sir, Johnny." This was the first semblance of a home Zebediah had known since the few days, a thousand bridges ago, he spent with Judah

Parsons. A warm feeling came over Zebediah as remembered the old bachelor. He wondered if Judah was still living, and he thought of how good the old man's corn bread, beans, and molasses would taste at the moment. As he mused over Judah, another thought crossed Zebediah's mind, and an idea stirred. When he found the time, he resolved to look for any work that might be had making shingles. Turning out shakes would be a whole lot easier way to make a living than unloading riverboats.

In the days that followed, Johnny procured an oil lamp along with a small table and two old kitchen chairs for the young men. The furniture was well used and none too sturdy, but it was still a welcome departure from sitting on the ground. Their household was rounded out by a few old dishes given to them by Mrs. Pike. Knowing they would have a roof over their heads at the end of the day made life on the docks a little more bearable for Zebediah and D. The young men procured a checkerboard, a deck of cards, and a cribbage board that helped fill their free time. Sunday afternoons would often find the boys and Johnny back at the river, fishing poles in hand. As winter approached, work on the docks began slowing down as river traffic slowed. Zebediah and D were now working no more than two or three days a week. They carefully managed their funds and always made sure Johnny and Clarice received their fifty cents every Friday. D told Zebediah that the slack activity in winter was made up for by the big surge of outbound freight when the ice went off the northern reaches of the river system.

On the days he didn't work the docks, Zebediah began seeking out carpenters that might be in need of someone who could make shakes. Several inquiries later, he found the man he was looking for. Joshua King was a carpenter and mason who maintained his own crew and did subcontracting for bigger builders. King told Zebediah that he would prefer not to hire him directly but would willingly pay seven cents each for good handmade shakes. This left Zebediah with a dilemma. Not being able to work directly for the builder meant he must purchase his own tools, and he was pretty sure he didn't have enough money for that. Zebediah began pricing the things he needed and was not surprised to find himself well short of what would be required. His life savings consisted of less than three dollars, and he still had to eat and pay rent.

He discussed the matter with D, whose finances were no better than his own. Unknown to Zebediah, D in turn discussed the matter with Johnny. As the trio made their way home from the docks a few days later, Johnny surprised Zebediah by asking, "So, Zeb, tell me about this shake-makin' business."

Zebediah shot D a questioning look, and D responded with a shrug of the shoulders and a sheepish grin. "Well, ain't much to tell, really. This old man taught me how to do it, back when I first went on the bum. I've worked at it here and there when I could, but I ain't got my own tools, and it ain't easy to hire on if you don't have yo' own gear."

"How much you think it gonna cost you to git set up?" asked Johnny.

"Near as I can tell, it's gonna be between ten and twelve dollars, dependin' on exactly what I was to buy," said Zebediah.

"And you say Josh King is willin' to pay seven cents apiece fo' 'em?" asked Johnny.

"That's what he tol' me," responded Zebediah.

"How many do you reckon ya kin make in a day, Zeb?"

Zebediah thought for a moment and responded, "Oh, I think I could easy make at least a hundred of 'em. More, if I worked as long a day as we do on the docks."

"Damn, Zeb, that be seven dollars a day!" said Johnny with surprise.

"Well, more like half that," said Zebediah. "You has to buy the lumber to make 'em from."

"That's still a lot mo' money than a man can make humpin' freight on the docks," said Johnny with quiet surprise, "and you kin stop and git a drink o' water whenever ya want to."

"That's true, Johnny," said Zebediah. "It's jus' a matter of comin' up wid the money to git started."

"Let me talk to Roberts," said Johnny. "Maybe we kin work somethin' out."

Johnny entered the store with the boys and sought out Roberts. The two older men shook hands and clapped each other on the shoulders. Johnny leaned forward and spoke earnestly with Roberts. The merchant turned and eyed Zebediah carefully for a moment before resuming his conversation with Johnny. After a little more talk, Johnny motioned for Zebediah to join them.

Zebediah did as he was asked, and when he reached the older men, Roberts extended his hand and said, "Pleased to meet ya, Zeb, I'm Al Roberts, but I expect you already know who I am," said Roberts with a smile.

"Yes, sir, Mr. Roberts, all the men who work on the docks know who you are."

"I see ya in here most every day," said Roberts. "I just never caught your name before Johnny talked to me." Roberts paused and eyed Zebediah carefully before speaking again. "Johnny here says you have a talent for makin' shingles, but you don't have the tools ya need to make a business of it. He tells me Josh King is willin' to buy what you make. That about right?"

"Yes, sir," said Zebediah.

"What would you need to get started, son?" asked Roberts.

Zebediah thought carefully then said, "First, I need to build a bench to work on, but that shouldn't take mo' than a few boards. Then I needs a yardstick, a cabinet saw, a draw knife, and a set of stones to keep the knife sharp."

"That's it?" asked Roberts, who appeared surprised that Zebediah's requirements were so few. "Hell, son, I'll give ya a yardstick." Roberts chuckled.

"Yes, sir, Mr. Roberts, that's all I be needin'," said Zebediah.

Roberts again eyed Zebediah calmly then said, "Johnny thinks you're a good man, Zeb, and if Johnny's willin' to vouch for ya, that's enough for me. Give me a day or so to git in touch with Josh King, and if he tells me he's willin' to buy yo' shingles, then I think I kin git you set up in business. I might not have just what you need on hand, but I kin git it in a couple days. Do you think you could pay me three dollars a week, Zeb?"

Again, Zebediah thought carefully before answering, "Yes, sir, Mr. Roberts, if Mr. King's willing to buy everything I make, then I believe I kin handle three dollars a week well enough."

"Then I think we have a deal," said Roberts. "Just let me talk to Josh, and I'll git back to you. If he says this is on the up and up, then we'll get the stuff you need ordered. Jus' so you understand, Zeb, those tools will belong to me until you gets 'em completely paid for," said Roberts. "That's jus' the way business works, son."

"Oh yes, sir, Mr. Roberts, that sounds fair to me," said Zebediah with a smile.

Roberts shook Zebediah's hand and said, "You'll probably be stoppin' in tomorrow after work anyway, but make sure to come by every day and check with me until I have the chance to talk to Josh."

With the help of Roberts and Johnny, Zebediah was able to establish himself in business, and in only a little over a month, he had repaid Roberts' investment in him. After establishing his business, Zebediah only worked the docks sporadically, when Josh King was between projects and the demand for his shingles fell. For the first time since leaving on the cattle drive, Zebediah knew a semblance of home and allowed himself to fall into a comfortable routine of work, rest, and a bit of fun. D was less fortunate. Leander Thibodeaux had somehow become aware of the friendship between the two young men, and in Zebediah's absence, the Spook turned his attention to D.

Chapter Nine

"D"

Zebediah opened his eyes to pitch darkness, occasionally punctuated by hellish flashes of green lightning. The wind continued to scream in his ears. The driving rain had not abated, and now the raging torrent that had been the gentle creek was within arm's reach. "Why not just wade in?" thought Zebediah. "It wouldn't take long. I wouldn't fight it. Then it would be over, and it wouldn't hurt no more." He mechanically broke off a few more kernels of corn and began to softly chew them until, mercifully, his tortured consciousness again faded away.

* * *

There was a spring in Zebediah's step as he pulled the handcart in the direction of the place he had come to think of as home. It was the first such place he had known since departing on the cattle drive many, many miles ago. He had recently purchased the handcart from Joshua King for three dollars, and the cart made the task of transporting his shingles much easier. King had concluded that the cart was no longer sturdy enough to bear the weight of lumber and bricks, but it served Zebediah's needs well. As Zebediah prepared to turn down Johnny's street, he saw, to his surprise, D approaching from the opposite direction. Zebediah waved his greeting. He should have realized immediately that something was wrong when D did not return the wave. Zebediah assumed incorrectly that D had simply not seen him.

D had been able to dimly make out Zebediah, but he was unable to lift his right arm, and D needed his left arm to steady himself against anything handy as he stumbled along. As D drew closer, Zebediah dropped the handles of the handcart and ran to his friend's side. D's right arm was hanging low at his side, and his face was a mass of bruises and blood. One eye was swollen completely shut, and the other was open but a slit. "Good God, D, what happened to ya?" cried Zebediah.

D struggled to speak but managed only to weakly murmur, "Spook." As D struggled to speak, fresh blood trickled from his mouth.

For a second that lasted an eternity, Zebediah stood frozen in horror, then finding his inner strength, he told D, "Don't try walkin' any further, D. Jus' hold on to this here fence while I run to git my cart." Zebediah raced to get his cart and then back to D, who was wavering unsteadily on his feet. He tipped the handles up until the back edge of the cart's bed rested on the ground. "C'mon, D, jus' lean against the cart, and I'll tip it down. You kin ride the rest o' the way home."

D was unsteady on his feet but managed to weakly comply with Zebediah's request. When Zebediah had D lying on the cart, he began transporting the injured man as quickly as he dared to the Pike's home. As he neared the front door, Zebediah began calling out at the top of his voice, "Miz' Pike, Miz' Pike, ya got to come quick! Miz' Pike! Miz' Pike!"

Clarice was at the sink, peeling potatoes, when she heard Zebediah calling. The panic in his voice caused her to drop what was in her hands and rush to the door. The instant she saw D lying battered and bloodied on the cart, she raced down the steps and up the street to meet them. "Oh, dear God, what happened, Zeb?" cried Clarice.

"I ain't real sure, Miz' Pike, I found him like this walkin' home," said Zebediah. His voice was thick, and his vision was distorted by tears. "All I heard him say was 'Spook,'" said Zebediah. "I think he's maybe talking about that damned ole' Cajun at the docks. Pardon my language, ma'am."

Clarice shot Zebediah a quick glance and said sharply, "Callin' Leander Thibodeaux a 'damned ole' Cajun is the nicest thing you could say about that miserable ole' sumbitch."

Zebediah was momentarily taken aback by the pious, churchgoing Clarice Pike's choice of words, but the moment passed quickly, and they turned their attention to D. When they reached the bottom of the steps, Clarice said, "Tip up the cart, Zeb, I'll he'p him to git stood up." Zebediah tipped the cart up, and with Mrs. Pike's assistance, D was able to regain his feet. "Pull the cart outa' the way now, Zeb, then help me wid D." Zebediah obeyed, then together, they began helping D climb the steps and into the Pike's home. "Let's git him laid down on the divan," said Mrs. Pike, her voice quaking with fear. "Here we go, easy does it now, D." As they helped lower D to the divan, the injured man gripped his right arm, uttered a guttural yowl, and winced in pain. A mixture of tears and fresh blood made its way down D's cheeks. The instant they had D lying down, Clarice hurried out of the room then returned seconds later with a pillow. Zebediah helped her gently place the pillow under D's head. "Zeb, would ya please go draw a kettle o' water and git it to heatin'," said Clarice.

"Yes, ma'am," said Zebediah. Since taking up residence in the shed, the two young men had become frequent Sunday dinner guests of the Pikes, and Zebediah was familiar with her kitchen. As the weeks passed, Zebediah and D had virtually been adopted by Clarice Pike, who seemed to have an especially soft spot for D. In addition to urging them to read their Bibles, Clarice Pike always made sure the boys had clean clothes and regular baths. Zebediah filled the large copper teakettle and touched a match to the gas ring. He was soon joined in the kitchen by Mrs. Pike, who filled an enameled washbasin with cold water from the tap.

As she turned to go back to the parlor, she said to Zebediah absently, "Warm water's better, but I has to git started cleanin' him up.

Zebediah rejoined Mrs. Pike in the parlor and looked on helplessly as his landlady began carefully dabbing the blood from D's face.

Without turning her head, she said, "Zeb, I need ya to fetch me a couple mo' clean washcloths."

Grateful for something to ease his sense of helplessness, Zebediah hurried to the kitchen cabinet where Mrs. Pike kept the clean towels. The teakettle had begun to whistle, and Zebediah turned off the gas ring and filled a pan half full of cold water from the tap. He returned to the parlor and set his things on the table. The pan of water Mrs. Pike had been using was now tinted red from D's blood, and Zebediah winced at the sight. He added hot water to the pan he brought from the kitchen then exchanged it for the pan of bloody water. He took the bloody washcloth from Mrs. Pike and handed her a clean one. So intent was Clarice Pike on her work, she accepted the new situation without comment and did not pause in her work.

Continuing to address D's battered and bloody face, she asked, "Zeb, do you know Samuels?"

"No, ma'am," said Zebediah.

"Kin you run and meet Johnny the second he gits off work and tell him we needs Samuels?" asked Clarice Pike.

"Yes'em," said Zebediah. "Is Samuels a doctor?"

"Chester Samuels is about as dumb as a mule, but he's the closest thing to a doctor we has in this ward. He's pretty good at settin' broken bones though. Run along now, Zeb, and be there waiting fo' Johnny when he come out the gate. He prolly already know about D, but be there anyway."

"Yes, ma'am," said Zebediah. He hurried out the front door and down the stairs. A crowd of curious neighbors had gathered in front of the Pike's home, and several voices called out questions as Zebediah hurried past. "D got hurt" was all Zebediah could manage to get out. His voice was thick, and Zebediah felt as if the words were coming from the soles of his feet. He turned his back to the crowd and hurried away in the direction of the docks. When Zebediah realized he was running, he slowed his pace. It would do no good to just stand around waiting in front of the gate. As Zebediah continued on his way, he looked up and saw Albert Roberts striding toward him.

The two men hurried to meet each other, and Roberts asked in a tight, angry voice, "What happened to D, Zeb? I heard he got beat up."

"D's hurt pretty bad, Mr. Roberts. Miz' Pike's tending to him as best she can. I don't know jus' what happened to him." Zebediah spoke in a voice choked with emotion, and his tears were again flowing freely. "Miz' Pike sent me to fetch Johnny when he git off work so he kin git the doctor."

"You go ahead and wait for Johnny, Zeb. I'll see to it that Samuels gits right over to the Pike's." Roberts did not wait for Zebediah's reply but turned away sharply and resumed his brisk march down the street.

As he numbly watched Roberts disappear down the street, Zebediah's legs suddenly felt as if he had been handed an enormous burden. Zebediah's heart was pounding heavily in his chest. He had not felt such emotion since that awful day when Mary collapsed before his eyes. The vision of Aunt Mary swam before his eyes. In Zebediah's mind, he had just bridled a mule and had begun his mad ride to fetch the Reverend Williams.

Zebediah made his way to the wharf and sought out a place where he could wait for Johnny. He did not have long to wait, for he had no more than settled himself when a stream of angry men began pouring out of the dockyard even though it was well ahead of quitting time. The men emerging from the wharf numbered far more than just the dock crew. The throng of men took no notice of Zebediah as he sat numbly watching them pass. Suddenly, a hand clasped him on the shoulder, startling Zebediah badly. He wheeled around, ready to fight, and saw Johnny standing before him.

"Damn, Zeb, I didn't mean to scare you like that. I should have said something, but I thought you might not hear me over the noise," said Johnny.

Such was the storm raging in Zebediah's mind that the noise being made by the throng of men passing before him had not registered. The men were speaking loudly among themselves, and many of them turned and hurled oaths back across the high wooden fence.

"C'mon, Zeb," said Johnny urgently, "we needs to git plumb away from the docks befo' the militia gits here."

"The militia?" asked Zebediah numbly.

"Sorta' like the army," said Johnny, "but mostly jus' a bunch o' damn killers. Leastwise, when it comes to black folks. Now, come along quick, Zeb, we needs to git outa' here."

There was real fear in Johnny's voice, and Zebediah wasted no time complying.

The two men hurried away from the wharf, alternating between running and walking briskly. They did not speak again until they were nearly back to the Pike's house, when Zebediah at last ventured to ask, "What happened, Johnny? Who hurt D?"

Johnny Pike seemed to regain a sense of himself and slowed his pace to a normal walk. "I'm still tryin' to put it all together, Zeb, but as near as I kin tell, D said or did somethin' that set the damned Spook off. The Spook hit D wid the back of his hand then took out that damn Colt and went to pistol whippin' and kickin' him. It didn't look like the ole' sumbitch was gonna stop, so some o' the dockmen pulled the ole' bastard off D, and that's when all hell broke loose. Turner came outa' the office and fired a twelve bore in the air. The men let the Spook go, and we's been in a standoff ever since. 'Bout two hundred black men agin' a dozen white men, but all the white men had guns." Johnny paused then looked at Zeb, paused a moment, then said, "Listen to me, runnin' on. How's D, Zeb? Did he make it home?"

Zebediah related the story of meeting D and carrying him home on the handcart. Johnny said, "Well, at least he had a little bit o' decent luck today. They shoved him out the gate, and we half expected to find him lyin' dead in the street." Johnny's normally soft voice now carried a mixture of anger, fear, and disgust.

As Zebediah and Johnny neared the Pike's home, the crowd gathered in front of the house saw them approaching and began moving en masse to meet them. The many voices blended into incoherence, and Johnny raised his hands for quiet. "Look, all I know fo' sho' is that D, one o' the young men who's been rentin' our shed, got beat up real bad," said Johnny, his voice breaking. "We're still tryin' to figure out jus' what started it. I do truly thank y'all for carin' about D, but right now we has to keep our wits about us and keep this business from gittin' outa' hand." The tremor in Johnny's voice betrayed his inner turmoil. "So, folks, the best thing y'all kin do for D right now is to go home and stay indoors. We all know what happened the las' time the militia came marchin' into the ward." Johnny stressed the word *all*.

The crowd murmured its acknowledgment and began slowly dispersing. Individual voices called out to please let them know if there was anything they could do to help. Johnny thanked them, then he and Zebediah made their way up the steps and into the parlor. When they entered the room, they found a slightly built gray-haired man shaping plaster around D's arm. D appeared to be sleeping. Clarice turned to Zebediah and Johnny as they entered the room. Her face was drawn, and her eyes were red. Before either of them could speak, Clarice said quietly, "It don't look good, Johnny."

Zebediah and Johnny stood over Samuels, watching as the doctor continued working on D's arm. The older man was so intent on his task, he did not appear to have noticed their arrival. "Doc thinks D may be busted up on the inside, Johnny," said Clarice weakly fighting back tears. "D passed out while Doc was settin' his arm, which is prolly a blessin' 'cuz he's in a lotta' pain, Johnny. A lotta' pain," she added for emphasis. "After Zeb ran to fetch you, D started spittin' up blood, and his color ain't a bit good."

Upon hearing Clarice's words, Zebediah saw that the front of his friend's shirt was stained with fresh blood, and D's skin had taken on a deathly pallor. His breathing was slow and labored. The doctor gently propped D's arm across a kitchen chair, then stood and spoke for the first time. "I think the arm set good, but his arm's probably the least of this young man's troubles," said Samuels, continuing to look down at his patient. The doctor turned to Johnny, nodded slightly, and said in a low voice, "Hey, Johnny." Samuels dipped his hands in a pan of clean water and began washing away the plaster. "I'm damned sorry I can't do more for him. The way he's been spitting up blood is a worry.

It, more than likely, means he's bleedin' on the inside, and that's never good. Don't let him lie flat, keep his head elevated above his heart. Keep checking his forehead, and if he gets to running a fever, then send for me right away. Right now I have a baby to birth, but I'll stop by later if there's a light on. If not, I'll take that as a good sign, and I'll be by in the morning." Samuels put on his hat and coat then closed his bag. "I'll show myself out, Clarice. You tend to this young man," said the doctor as he made his exit.

Clarice knelt beside D and bathed his forehead with a damp cloth. D gave no sign of having felt anything. Without looking up, Clarice said, "There's food in the kitchen, Johnny. The neighbors brought it over."

Johnny and Zebediah glanced at each other briefly then left the room. In the kitchen they found cold fried chicken, corn bread, and a pitcher of sweet tea. The two men sat down and began eating, each lost in his own thoughts and seemingly unaware of the other's presence. After eating in silence for a few minutes, Zebediah looked up to Johnny and asked in a pleading voice, "What we gonna do, Johnny?"

It was as if Johnny's eyes did not want to focus, and he did not respond immediately. Slowly, Johnny looked up at Zebediah and said in a distant voice, "I don't rightly know, Zeb, but I knows we gonna do somethin'. Right now, we has to worry about D."

"I know, Johnny, but it's jus' so hard to watch. I feel helpless as a baby."

"We all do, Zeb. I reckon you kin try prayin' if you've a mind to, but prayer never seemed to make much difference to me, one way or the other," said Johnny in a voice that did not appear directed at anyone in particular.

It flashed across Zebediah's mind that he had done little praying in quite some time. He saw Aunt Mary's face before him, and he felt the sting of guilt at the thought of having failed her. Still and all, Johnny had a point. So many black people, so many prayers, so many preachers, and yet their lives never seemed to get any better. A man like Leander Thibodeaux could still maim and murder without fear of consequence, while good men like D paid the price. It only took a moment thinking about the Spook, and Aunt Mary's guilt was pushed aside by hot anger. Zebediah's thoughts turned to the Deacon. Zebediah was near to asking Johnny if he knew of the Deacon, but he held his tongue. "We needs to wait and see what happens to D befo' we start thinkin' about murder," thought Zebediah.

Johnny, Clarice, and Zebediah took turns looking after D. A few minutes before midnight, there came a soft knock. Clarice tiptoed to the door and admitted the doctor.

"I didn't expect to see a light on, Clarice," said Samuels in a quiet voice. "It was a long, difficult birthin' process, but I'm pleased to say that mother and son are now doin' well." Turning his attention to D, Samuels asked, "Clarice, would you please turn the lamps up a bit. How's this young man doin'?"

"Bout the same, near as I kin tell," said Clarice. "His breathin' don't seem any easier, but I don't think it's got any worse either."

Samuels gently lifted D's eyelids, one at a time, and studied his patient's eyes. He applied his stethoscope to D's chest and listened carefully while moving it about. "He spit up any more blood?" asked the doctor.

"A little bit. Shortly after you lef', but he ain't done it for a while now," said Clarice.

Samuels held his hand to D's forehead and, after a minute, began gently probing the sides of D's neck. The doctor appeared lost in thought and did not speak for several seconds. He lifted D's shirt and studied his abdomen carefully then, tenderly, began probing D's midsection while keeping his eyes fixed on the injured man's face for any reaction. The doctor gave the cast a cursory inspection then stood up and straightened himself. He returned the stethoscope to his bag and said quietly, "I don't want to get your hopes up, but I'm encouraged by what I'm seein'. It could still go either way, and don't forget that, but he seems to be stable. He's quit spitting up blood, and there's no fever. His breathing is a worry, but his heartbeat's regular. I'll stop back in the morning. Good night, Clarice."

"Good night, Doc," said Clarice. When the doctor had gone, Clarice felt a weariness that went beyond words. She sat down on a chair for a few minutes and buried her face in her hands. Clarice felt like crying, but her tears were all spent. The tears in her eyes were now being replaced by the glowing coal of anger forming in her belly. The room was very quiet; the only sounds were the ticking of the mantle clock and D's labored breathing. Wearily, she rose and, after a long look at D, went to wake Johnny.

The Pikes exchanged few words as Clarice sank onto the bed and Johnny went to attend to D. After checking on the injured man, Johnny went into the kitchen and washed his face in cold water. Johnny Pike was not a drinking man, and that was something that made him a respected member of his community. As rarely as he touched liquor, Johnny would have paid good money at that moment for a shot of corn. He would have reached out to nearly anything that might help ease the pain of this terrible night. Johnny returned to the parlor and settled himself in a chair where he could observe D in the dim light. Periodically, he rose and checked D's forehead. Johnny was grateful that D did not appear to be failing. Time passed, and he may have dozed a moment or he may have been lost in thought, but regardless, he was startled alert when Zebediah touched his arm.

After a moment's confusion, Johnny whispered, "What's up, Zeb?"

"Nothin', Johnny, I jus' wanted you to know I was sittin' here. You kin go git some sleep if ya want, I'll sit wid D."

Johnny was now fully alert and said quietly, "Naw, I'll stay up wid ya, Zeb." Johnny glanced at the clock and said, "Let's go make some coffee. I'm pretty damn sure there ain't gonna be no work at the docks today anyway." After Johnny checked D's forehead again, they went to the kitchen, where Johnny filled the coffee pot with water and lit the gas ring. He added ground coffee to the water then sat down and waited for the coffee to brew. Johnny seemed focused on something very far away, and he remained in this state until he heard the water in the coffee pot beginning to bubble. Then, he rose and turned the gas off. After allowing the coffee grounds to settle, he filled mugs for each of them. Johnny sat down again and resumed gazing into space for several more minutes. Otherwise silent, Johnny occasionally drummed his fingers on the table as he slowly sipped his coffee. When his cup was empty, Johnny rose and began to pour more then decided against it. He replaced the pot on the gas ring and, with Zebediah in tow, returned to the parlor to check on D.

Johnny bent low over the injured man, first feeling the patient's forehead then holding his ear close to D's nose and listening to his breathing. A look of cautious relief crossed Johnny's face as he stood and faced Zebediah. "I think he's holdin' his own, Zeb," Johnny whispered. They returned to the kitchen, and Johnny refilled their mugs. They passed the rest of the night mostly in silence, each man in his own faraway place. The first blush of the predawn was showing itself on the kitchen window when Johnny turned to Zebediah and said in a quiet, steady voice, "Zeb, you ever hear of a man they call the Deacon? I've only ever heard of him, I ain't never met him. I've heard he stays mostly in the hobo camps."

Zebediah did not reply immediately, but his involuntary gasp answered Johnny's question. At last, Zebediah said, "I cain't say I really knows him, but I've met him."

Johnny nodded his head slightly, paused a moment, then asked, "You think you could find him, Zeb?"

"I could try," said Zebediah. "I know where some of the camps are, and it ain't hard to find travelin' men who knows how to find the others. I kin always go lookin' for the signs and hunt around too."

"Don't do that, Zeb," said Johnny quietly. "Not yet anyway. And, Zeb, don't mention my askin' this question to anybody, not even Clarice. Especially not Clarice."

The look on Johnny's face and his tone of voice informed Zebediah that he was being admitted into a great confidence. Zebediah nodded to Johnny and said with genuine humility, "Yes, sir, Johnny. I won't say nothin' to nobody. Jus' let me know if you want me to go lookin' fo' the Deacon or anything else I kin do."

Johnny gave Zebediah a slight nod and said, "I will, Zeb, jus' remember what I said."

Shortly after Johnny finished speaking, Clarice joined them in the kitchen. She squeezed Zebediah's shoulder as she passed then bent and kissed Johnny's forehead. "Mornin', y'all." Her voice was tired, but it had lost some of the previous day's quaver. "How's D doin'?" she asked.

"We checked on him a little while ago, and he was about the same," said Johnny. The three of them returned to the parlor, and Clarice bent over D, feeling his forehead and listening to his breathing.

After taking a long look at D's face, Clarice said, "I don't think he's any worse, and I guess that's somethin'. I hope it is anyway." She glanced at the clock and said, "I'm gonna git some breakfast cooked befo' the doctor gits here."

After they had eaten, Zebediah helped Clarice wash the breakfast dishes, grateful for any activity that would help fill the time. A little past seven, they heard a knock at the front door.

Clarice returned to the parlor and admitted the doctor. "Mornin', Clarice, how's the patient doing?" asked Samuels in a quiet voice as Clarice led him to D.

"No better, no worse, as near as I kin tell," said Clarice.

"He wake up at all last night?" asked the doctor.

"Not that I saw," said Clarice.

"Me neither," said Johnny. "Is that bad, Doc?"

"It ain't good," said Samuels wearily as he again applied his stethoscope to D's chest. "Not unusual for a person to pass out when having a broken bone set, but he's been passed out a long time. Too long."

"What's gonna happen, Doc?" asked Johnny.

"If he doesn't wake up and take some water pretty soon, his organs will start shutting down, and he's basically going to be dying of thirst," said Samuels. "I've read that some hospitals back east are giving unconscious patients fluids directly into their veins and having pretty good success with it. I'm afraid we're not going to see that happen in this ward soon enough to help this young man though," said the doctor sadly. "As a last resort, I can try putting a tube down his throat and giving him water that way, but if the tube goes into his lung, I could drown him." Samuels rummaged through his bag and found an eyedropper. "Wash this real good in hot soapy water, Clarice, then about every fifteen minutes, give him a dropper of water. With a little luck, he'll swallow it and not just cough it back out. Use a wet washcloth to keep his lips from drying out too bad, and keep an eye on his temperature." Samuels checked his watch and said, "I need to go check in on that baby boy and his mama and then get around and see about a dozen other patients. I'll stop back this evening. Sooner if I can."

After seeing the doctor out, Clarice wasted no time in complying with his instructions. After thoroughly washing the eyedropper, she filled it with cool water. Clarice gently opened D's lips and slowly squirted its contents into the unconscious man's mouth. To their relief, D did not cough the water back out, and a few minutes later, she repeated the process. Near mid-morning, D stirred softly and struggled to open the eye that was not swollen shut.

Managing the weakest of smiles, D said, "Hey, Mama."

Clarice said, "Oh, D, I'm not yo' mother, I'm Clarice. Mrs. Pike." A tear appeared in the corner of Clarice Pike's eyes.

D found Clarice Pike's words confusing and said, "Yo' not my ma? You sho' looks like my ma."

"Oh, honey, don't you worry 'bout that, you can fo' sure call me mama if you wants to," said Clarice, overwhelmed with emotion.

With Zebediah's help, they eased D into a sitting position, and he slowly took more water. When D signaled he had drunk enough for the moment, he looked at Zebediah and, grinning weakly, said, "Billy, what you all doin' here? You never leaves Ohio."

Zebediah responded immediately, "D, it's me, Zeb."

D did not appear to understand what Zebediah was saying but, after a moment's confusion, accepted the situation and said, "Right pleased to meet ya, Zeb." Turning his good eye to Clarice, he asked, "Do ya reckon I could have a li'l mo' water, Mama?"

Tears were now flowing freely down Clarice Pike's face as she said, "Sure, son, anything you need me to do." Everyone present knew D was not Clarice Pike's son, and everyone present knew it did not matter. Throughout the morning, D continued to gain strength. He took more water and was able to swallow a bit of thin oatmeal. Neighbors came and went, and one of them evidently informed the doctor of D's progress because a little past midday, Samuels knocked at the door.

As Johnny opened the door, the doctor said, "A little bird told me there was a bit of good news over at the Pike's house, Johnny."

"He's awake, Doc, and he's been takin' water and a li'l oat meal." Johnny had been mostly silent all through the morning and, when he spoke, was surprised by the rasp in his voice. "He don't seem to know anybody though. He thinks Clarice is his mama and Zeb's his brother."

"That's not the best thing that could happen, but it's not the worst either," said Samuels. "It's not unusual for a person who's had their head beat on to be confused when they wake up. The good news is, he woke up."

Zebediah and Clarice murmured their greetings to the doctor as he approached D. Samuels did not appear to notice either of them as the doctor turned his full attention to D. Samuels knelt on one knee before D and, after taking a close look at the injured man's eyes, asked, "How you feeling, young man?"

D found this question as confusing as all the others had been and said, "Well, I reckon I's had better days. My eyes don't seem to wanna work right, an' my arm and haid hurts to beat hell." The instant he uttered the word *hell*, D turned to Clarice and said in a childlike voice, "Pardon my language, Mama."

Choking back sobs, Clarice said, "Oh, don't you worry about that one bit, son."

"Thank you, mama. I's sorry I said it."

"D," said the doctor, "look here at my finger, and try to follow it with your eye when I move it back and forth." Samuels held up his index finger and moved it slowly left and right while keeping his own attention on D's face.

D did his best to comply with the doctor's request, but his focus lagged well behind the doctor's movement. The doctor listened to D's chest then carefully inspected the injured man's abdomen, probing gently. Samuels said nothing until after he stood and straightened himself. The doctor was only partially successful in hiding his concern. "He's awake and taking food and water, and that's no small thing," said Samuels, closing his bag. "Keep watching him close, and give him all the water he's willing to swallow. Clarice, if you could strip his clothes and bathe him then get him into a proper bed, that's likely to help too. Just remember to use a plenty of pillows, and keep his head elevated." The doctor finished gathering his things as he spoke and then turned to the door. "I'll be back this evening" was all Samuels said before making his exit.

Samuels was loath to tell either the Pikes or Zebediah what he really felt. He wanted to leave them with a modicum of hope, but as he knew only too well, hope could be a more dangerous commodity than despair. Samuels had seen many people with head injuries rally briefly before they expired. The next few hours would be crucial. His skills and tools were severely limited, and Samuels understood that reality better than anyone. He had done all he could, and he would continue to apply those skills he did possess, but Samuels knew D's fate was beyond his control. The doctor also knew that he dare not allow himself to become consumed by his inability to save D because doing so might well leave him unable to help anyone. Chester Samuels had apprenticed under a man even less educated than himself, and he had struggled all his life to live up to the title of doctor. He read every medical book and publication he could acquire. He bought every piece of equipment he could afford. After much pleading, he had been allowed to observe a full body dissection at the white medical school. In the end, he knew he lagged far behind the best medicine that could be had.

Throughout the day, D continued to rally. He took food and water, and his mind continued to clear. With Zebediah's help, Clarice was able to bathe D and get him dressed in clean long johns. They propped pillows under his head and got him comfortably settled in the Pike's bed. At least, half the time, D recognized that Clarice Pike was not his mother, and he no longer mistook Zebediah for his brother Billy. Samuels returned in late afternoon and, after another examination, pronounced himself reasonably happy with D's progress. Samuels hoped with all his heart that he was maintaining the proper line between caution and optimism. D was alive and building strength, but the doctor knew better than anyone just how fast these things could reverse themselves.

Hope and optimism continued to grow over the next three days. D managed to eat and keep down some solid food. His lungs were clearing, and his breathing had become less labored. D could now stand and walk short distances without assistance, and the swelling around his eyes was greatly reduced. A group of D's coworkers, led by Pickens, stopped by the house and presented the Pikes with the money they had collected to help defray the cost of D's care. Tensions on the docks had subsided enough to allow work to resume. Johnny and the men who called at the Pike home talked seriously and quietly late into the night.

The fourth day following D's beating was a Sunday, and Clarice felt secure enough about D's condition to leave the injured man in the care of Johnny and Zebediah while she attended services. The three men were sitting in the Pike's parlor, talking quietly and joking. D appeared fully aware of his surroundings and, other than his injuries, seemed much his old self. They spoke of Christmas, which was but two weeks away, and the feast Clarice would lay before them. As they chatted, D's good hand suddenly went to his temple. His face froze; his eyes went wide with fear. Then D's eyes rolled backward in their sockets, his body convulsed, and blood poured from his eye sockets, nose, and mouth. There was another convulsion, and D pitched forward off the divan and onto the floor. In but a moment, D passed to a place beyond all pain.

A simultaneous guttural wail, sound reduced to pure emotion, erupted from Johnny and Zebediah. They by turn begged, pleaded, prayed, and cursed the universe, but they knew D would not return. For what seemed an eternity, the two men knelt by D's body, paralyzed with despair, their muscular bodies convulsing in sobs. "No, no, no, dear God, no," was repeated by both men over and again. That was how Clarice found them. She was returning from services, and near home, when she heard the men wailing. A white-hot dagger of fear pierced her breast, and she ran the rest of the way. When Clarice saw D's body on the floor, she collapsed into Johnny's arms, and he held her tightly until, at long last, her uncontrollable sobs began to ease.

Perhaps one of the neighbors saw Clarice running to her home; perhaps someone heard the wailing from within the Pike's house. No one could have said with certainty, but very quickly, the entire neighborhood and then the ward knew what had happened. A respectful crowd gathered outside the Pike's front step. Clarice Pike's minister was the first to enter the house, followed shortly by Dr. Samuels. As the minister tried to offer comfort, Samuels did his best to offer an explanation. After examining D's body, Samuels left Clarice with her pastor. He took Johnny and Zebediah into the kitchen and said quietly, "I expect it was an aneurysm. A blood vessel was probably weakened by the beating, and it likely ballooned up then finally ruptured. Until doctors can learn how to operate inside a person's head, there isn't a damn thing that can be done about it." Samuels shook his head sadly; his voice was a mixture of regret and disgust. The doctor lowered his head a moment then turned and looked at Johnny, saying with quiet ferocity, "Not beating the hell out of that young man in the first place would have been mighty helpful though."

The doctor stepped back into the parlor and expressed his condolences to Clarice. He told her that he would personally call on Butler, the undertaker, on his way home. The doctor and the minister regarded each other warily for a moment, then Samuels nodded slightly in the pastor's direction and said simply, "Micah."

The pastor returned an equally terse nod and said, "Chester."

Later that evening, when a semblance of calm had returned to the Pike's home, Zebediah ventured to ask Johnny about the curious exchange between the pastor and the doctor. In spite of the enormous grief hanging over the house that evening, the question drew a small chuckle and a grin from Johnny, who shook his head and said, "Well, a few years ago, a fella' got busted up pretty bad on the docks, and when Doc got there to tend to him, he found Micah preachin' away, beggin' and pleadin' fo' the family to pray for the man's recovery. Well, Doc made the mistake of sayin' that he never yet saw prayers set a broken leg." Johnny laughed softly at the memory then shook his head again, looked at Zebediah wryly, and added, "Let's jus' say the preacher and the doctor ain't exactly been the best o' friends ever since."

The ensuing two days were not unlike those that followed Mary's passing. D was attended to, food was brought in by neighbors, and there was a great outpouring of love and compassion. Anyone with a connection to either the Pikes, D, or Zebediah did what they could to ease the pain of D's passing. In the days following the funeral, Zebediah returned to building shakes for Josh King, and though the construction trades were slow ahead of Christmas, Zebediah swore an oath to himself and to D's memory that come hell or high water, he would never return to the docks. Johnny, however, did return to the warehouse. He said things were tense but under control. All the workers were steering as clear of Leander Thibodeaux as their duties would allow. Thibodeaux himself appeared completely unmoved by the murder he had committed. Johnny, Clarice, and Zebediah sorted through D's belongings and found his mother's address in Ohio. Notifications were made, and D's things were duly sent to her.

Zebediah now spent lonely nights in the shed, playing solitaire in the glow of the kerosene lamp as the winter rains beat against the window. The little shed was no longer the home it had been, and Zebediah felt a loneliness he had not experienced since leaving the farm. D had become the nearest thing to family Zebediah had known since going on the bum. He had no real plan for the future, but he knew that come hell or high water, he would not be spending the summer in Nawlins. Without his friend, the pain was just too great, and although Johnny and Clarice went on being kind and considerate landlords, something seemed to have gone out of their lives as well. As the winter turned to spring, the warmer weather did much to improve the general mood in and around the Pike home. Zebediah helped Johnny and Clarice work up then plant their garden. With the passing of winter, traffic on the river rose steadily. Johnny now worked every day and was often too tired for fishing on Sunday. Zebediah made all the shakes he could, saved his money, and prepared to "catch out."

It was a mild spring evening, and Zebediah was sitting outdoors, leaning his back against the door of the shed. As he enjoyed the sunset, the Pike's back door opened, and Zebediah was surprised to see Albert Roberts accompanying Johnny. Zebediah automatically stood and waited respectfully for the older men to approach. Roberts extended his hand to Zebediah and said, "Evenin', Zeb, I hope we're not interrupting anything."

"Aw no, sir, Mr. Roberts, I'm just sittin' out, enjoyin' the evenin' for a bit befo' turnin' in," said Zebediah.

Roberts took a moment and inspected the bench Zebediah had constructed along the side of the shed. "So this is where you build your shingles, Zeb?" asked Roberts.

"Yes, sir," answered Zebediah. Zebediah did not think Albert Roberts had come to inspect his workbench and waited politely for the grocer to speak again.

"Josh King has a lot of good things to say about the quality of your work, Zeb. I made a good investment in you." The grocer paused a moment then looked directly at Zebediah and asked, "Do you s'pose we could step inside your house and chat a bit, Zeb?"

Zebediah found the request surprising but quickly agreed, saying, "Oh sure, Mr. Roberts. It ain't much to look at though."

ZEBEDIAH

Johnny and Roberts both laughed at Zeb's remark, and Roberts said, "Oh, don't worry about that, Zeb."

The three men stepped inside the shed, and Zebediah apologized. "I ain't got but two chairs, I'll sit on the floor."

"Oh no, no, Zeb, you sit. We'll stand. This won't take long," said Roberts.

Zebediah's curiosity was running wild, and he eyed the two men curiously as he seated himself before them.

Johnny spoke first. "Zeb, do you remember, sometime back, me asking you about the Deacon?"

When the shock of Johnny's question passed, Zebediah said quietly, "Yes, sir."

Roberts said, "I've heard from a few of the travelin' men in the store that he's around. Most likely living in one of the camps. Do you think you could scout around and try findin' him for us, Zeb?"

"I reckon I could," said Zebediah cautiously. "What do you all want me to tell him if I find him?"

"We don't need you to tell him anything directly, Zebediah," said Roberts, removing an envelope from his pocket. "What we would like is for you to find him and give him this."

"What's in it?" asked Zebediah.

Johnny looked at Zebediah intensely and said quietly, "Zeb, it's really fo' the best if you don't know what's in this envelope. Jus' find the Deacon if ya can and give it to him. The letter is fo' him alone. That's all you needs to know, and trust me here, Zeb, not knowin' is fo' yo' own good."

"Yes, sir," said Zebediah humbly. "When do ya want me to do this?"

"Soon, Zeb," said Roberts. "Tomorrow if ya can."

"Yes, sir," said Zebediah, "I'll try, but Mr. King is expecting me to deliver shingles tomorrow."

"Josh King knows what you'll be doing, Zeb, and you don't need to worry about it."

"Yes, sir."

"There's more, Zeb," said Johnny. "There's a steamer leavin' upriver as soon as they're loaded. Prolly in about three days' time. We need you to be on it. We have you a job lined up as a stoker. After you deliver the letter to the Deacon, get straight over to the store and let Mr. Roberts know. Your tools and your bag will be delivered to ya."

Zebediah was rocked by this turn of events but did not attempt to get any further explanation from the men. The urgency in their voices told him that his best course of action lay in following their instructions to the letter. "One last thing, Zeb," said Johnny. "Do not mention any of this to Clarice. I'll love that woman till my dyin' day, but she jus' cain't know about this, Zeb. There's several people whose lives are ridin' on keepin' this business as quiet as we can. Do ya understand what I'm sayin' here, Zeb?"

The quaver in Johnny's voice provided Zebediah with all the convincing he needed. "Yes, sir, Johnny, I understand. I won't say nothin' to her or anybody else. I'm damn sure gonna miss her though," said Zebediah with a thickening voice. "You too, Johnny."

Johnny clasped Zebediah on the shoulder and said, "And we'll miss you too Zeb. Mo' than you know son but Zeb, I'd rather be missin' ya than be mournin' fo' ya."

Roberts handed Zebediah the envelope and said with quiet intensity, "Zeb, there's nothing we can do to keep you from opening this once we're gone, but for your sake and ours and people unknown to you, don't do it."

Zebediah accepted the envelope from Roberts and said quietly, "Yes, sir, Mr. Roberts, I won't let you down."

"If we thought there was any chance of you letting us down, we wouldn't be havin' this conversation, Zeb," said Roberts evenly. "Before you go to sleep tonight, have everything packed and be ready to leave. If you can't find the Deacon tomorrow, then come back here as usual. But if you do find him, then head straight to the store and tell me, then I'll let you know then what to do next. Johnny here will see to it that your things are fetched over to you. If you can't find the Deacon before the steamer leaves, then we'll pull back and make another plan. Any questions, Zeb?"

Zebediah had nothing but questions. His mind was full to overflowing with questions, and yet he answered, "No, sir. Find the Deacon, give him the letter, git over to the store, and tell Mr. Roberts."

Albert Roberts shook Zebediah's hand and said evenly, "That's it, son. We'll get outa' your hair now, Zeb. Get packed up, and get some sleep. Could be a long day for ya tomorrow."

After the older men departed, Zebediah packed his bag, leaving out only those things he would need for the night. He filled Reverend Williams' old stone jug with water and, after applying a generous coat of oil to his tools, packed them into the cedar box he had built for the purpose. Zebediah's packing didn't take long. All the skills honed over his years of traveling were still there. He was, first and foremost, a man well schooled in the art of living and traveling light. Sleep came late and reluctantly to Zebediah that night. He knew his life was about to take a sharp turn, and he did not know in what direction that turn might lie.

Zebediah rose in the predawn and finished packing his few belongings. After washing his face at the garden tap, he made quietly away from the Pike's home for the last time. Zebediah was just beyond the edge of the city when the sun cleared the horizon. The seasons were changing, and it would soon be full on summer. As he swung along the tracks, burdened only by the water bottle, it all felt slightly odd after several months spent rooted to one spot. Odd and yet oddly familiar at the same time. Zebediah experienced anew the urge to be on the bum again and free.

The possibility, voiced by Albert Roberts, that Zebediah might spend a long day seeking out the Deacon did not come to be. It did not take long at all to find the man he was looking for. The first place Zebediah chose to look was the last place he had seen him. Exercising all the old cautions, he eased his way carefully through the woods in the direction of that first Nawlins campground. Nearing the edge of the clearing, he called out, "Travelin' man comin' in." There, sitting by the fire, as if expecting Zebediah's arrival, sat the Deacon, who did not appear the least surprised to see him.

"Mornin', Zeb," said the Deacon in a casual tone that suggested Zebediah had been away but a few hours. There was nothing outwardly threatening by either the man's tone or his words, and yet the exchange came near to unnerving Zebediah. "I kinda' had a feeling someone, prolly you, might be about ready to go lookin' me up, and so I moved in here a few days ago. I figured this would be the first place you'd look." The Deacon eyed Zebediah coolly and said, "Sit down, Zeb, and take a load off. Help yourself to the coffee if ya want to." There was a cold, dead nothingness in the Deacon's eyes and voice. Those things may well have always been there, but in Zebediah's limited contact with the man, he had been unaware of them before this minute. "You wouldn't happen to have somethin' fo' me, would ya, Zeb?" asked the Deacon dryly.

Zebediah felt as if his mind was now being controlled by the icy man sitting near the fire. Raw fear surged through every fiber of Zebediah's being, and it took all his strength to keep himself under control. At last, Zebediah managed what he hoped was an innocent smile and said as normally as he could, "Hey, Deacon, how you been keepin'?"

The Deacon's expression did not change, and he maintained his gaze on Zebediah, saying at last, "Oh, I'm fine as always, Zeb. How about yourself?" The utter lack of emotion in the Deacon's voice further eroded Zebediah's sense of well-being.

"You hear about D?" asked Zebediah.

"Yeah, I heard." There was an uncomfortable pause before the Deacon spoke again. "That's why I thought somebody might be lookin' me up." The Deacon paused again, continuing to eye Zebediah without emotion, then again asked, "You bring me somethin', Zebediah?"

Zebediah looked around cautiously. He spotted only three other men in the camp. They were all well back from the fire and appeared to be sleeping. Zebediah said nothing to the Deacon; he simply walked up to the man and, after another look around, withdrew the envelope from his overalls and handed over the letter. The Deacon accepted the letter without comment. He held the envelope by its end and gave Zebediah a sharp little wave with it before placing it in the inside pocket of his coat. "Like I said, coffee here if ya want some, Zeb."

"No thanks, Deacon, I think I'll jus' be goin' now."

Any effect Zebediah's words might have had on the Deacon did not reveal themselves on the man's face. "Well then, good day to you, Zebediah, and fare thee well in your travels."

Zebediah nodded slightly to the Deacon and said, "Good luck to you, Deacon."

The Deacon said nothing further; he merely continued eying Zebediah. When he could no longer endure the man's gaze, Zebediah turned on his heels and exited the camp as quickly as he dared, fighting desperately against the urge to run. Several yards into the trees, Zebediah veered suddenly off the trail and concealed himself behind a large oak. He waited there for several long, anxious minutes, listening for the footsteps of a pursuer. When he was satisfied that he was not being followed, Zebediah hurried on out of the woods and back to the rail line. The feeling that he was being followed did not leave him completely until days later, when the steamer he was aboard was many miles up the Mississippi. Later, Zebediah would wonder to himself if the sleeping men at the Deacon's camp were, in fact, sleeping.

* * *

In the dying moonlight of an early Sunday morning, a disheveled, foul-smelling man staggered along the top of a levee. A Colt revolver dangled from a holster on the man's hip. Leander Thibodeaux had been taken with the uneasy feeling that he was being followed since leaving the barroom a half hour earlier. Three times Thibodeaux had whipped around with the drawn Colt, demanding of the darkness that whoever was following him announce themselves. The darkness did not respond. Leander Thibodeaux's mind, addled by a lifetime of heavy alcohol consumption, was a web of fear and hate. In the middle of the levee, Thibodeaux stopped to relieve himself. He had been in need of doing so for some time but had held off until reaching this spot that afforded the best field of vision. When Thibodeaux was satisfied that he was alone, he unbuttoned his overalls and began to urinate.

A hand emerged from the darkness and savagely jerked Thibodeaux backward by the shirt collar, while a second hand drove an eight-inch pig sticker deeply and repeatedly into his back and gut. In less time than it takes to describe the event, Leander Thibodeaux lay dead and bleeding on the levee. The attacker disassembled the revolver, removed the cylinder from the frame, then emptied the cartridges on to the ground. The revolver's cylinder was pushed into Thibodeaux's mouth, then the frame of the Colt was used to hammer the cylinder deep into the dead man's throat. Before departing, the assailant sliced off Thibodeaux's genitals and left them lying across dead man's face. Leander Thibodeaux's attacker made no attempt to hide the body, for that would have defeated the purpose.

* * *

Six days before Leander Thibodeaux met his fate, on a riverboat bearing a cargo of yellow pine lumber, Zebediah and seven other men had steamed out of Nawlins, bound for St. Louis and points west, on the Missouri.

Chapter Ten

The Road to Keller

Zebediah stood alongside Lemon and watched as fire consumed the steamboat. Other members of the crew pulled themselves and each other from the water until all the boat's complement stood gathered on the wharf. It was a glorious, dead-calm summer day. The cloudless sky was a brilliant cobalt blue, and the only sound that met the ears of those assembled on the wharf was the roar of the flames steadily devouring the remnants of the steamer that had carried them north from New Orleans. Zebediah was one of the lucky ones in that little assembly. He had been in the crew quarters when the fire bell rang, and he alone had the presence of mind to grab his bag before fleeing the burning vessel. He had managed to save his bag but not his toolbox, and now, Zebediah's best means of earning a living was being destroyed in the inferno raging on the water.

As the crew watched the boat burn, the stout bearded captain appeared in the doorway of a warehouse building. The man paused a moment then began running toward the dock. When he reached the edge of the wharf, dumbstruck by what was unfolding in front of him, the captain paused again. After a long moment, he advanced again, though slowly and unsteadily. When he neared the men, they saw the horror on his face and the tears in his eyes. The spectacle unfolding before them rendered the captain mute. His jaw moved, and his mouth attempted to shape words, but no sound came forth. As if suddenly burdened with a massive weight, the captain's knees buckled, and he sank to the planking in a crouch. The captain buried his face in his hands, his body wracked with soundless convulsive sobs.

From start to finish, the burning of the steamer took less than twenty minutes. If every one of the eight-man crew had been asked to render an account of the fire's origin, there would have been eight different versions of the event offered up. The truth would never be known. The boat was lost and, with it, most of the crew's possessions. When at last the captain found his voice, he informed the crew in a breaking voice that the money to pay them had also just vanished into the river. The captain was also the boat's owner, and the crew felt as much sadness as anger toward the man because he too had just lost everything. As the boat burned, the bewildered crewmen were joined on the pier by several curious onlookers. There was no danger of the fire spreading ashore because, only moments after the alarm sounded, dockworkers raced to the burning boat and used axes to chop through the mooring lines. The current soon carried the burning vessel safely away from the wooden dock.

Once the burning hulk reached midstream, the remnants of the steamer were quickly broken apart by the current. Floating pieces of the boat quickly drifted downstream and out of sight. At the end of a half hour, there was nothing left to see. The captain and crew continued to idle uneasily on the wharf until, as if all the men received a silent signal, crewmen and onlookers alike began wandering off. Suddenly, a wave of fear rolled across Zebediah, and he felt very vulnerable. He alone among the survivors had managed to save his possessions, meager as they might be. Once again, his survival instincts came to the front, and Zebediah knew he might soon be seen as fair game by those who had just lost everything. Without good-byes, Zebediah put the strap of his bag over his shoulder and strode away from the dock as quickly as he dared, hyper-alert for the sound of footsteps approaching from behind. The road he followed bore west, and Zebediah did not look back until he had put over a mile between himself and the river.

Well beyond the town, Zebediah dropped down over a small hill and saw, off away from the road, a place he could hide. He was, for the moment at least, out of sight of anyone who might be following, and he seized the opportunity to dart off the road and sprint to the cover of a plum thicket some fifty yards distant. He took cover and made himself as comfortable as he could, then Zebediah settled down to wait. He opened his jug and drank the little water it contained. Zebediah was thirsty and the day was warm, but he knew his survival could well hang on his ability to endure the hardship and remain hidden for a day or longer. Although Zebediah had not seen anyone following him, the precaution of hiding was not unwarranted because, scarcely a half hour later, two of the other crewmen passed before him. Zebediah had been setting a rapid pace away from the river, but these two men were setting a faster one, and he knew that his precautions were justified.

Zebediah remained well hidden until after sunset. Under other circumstances, he would have traveled at night, as he often did. On this night, however, knowing that men with little to lose could be waiting to ambush him, Zebediah felt he could venture no farther than a half mile in search of water. He had observed the road all day and had heard nothing suspicious after the two men passed. Zebediah felt, with reasonable certainty, that the two men were not nearby. Leaving the seclusion of the plum thicket, he began exploring along the road, and for the second time that day, Zebediah was fortunate. No more than a quarter mile beyond his hiding place, he crossed over a small bridge. In the dying light, he inspected the ground carefully for footprints, and when he found no signs of anyone having left the road for the shelter of the bridge, Zebediah carefully made his way below. To his relief, Zebediah discovered that the creek bed was rocky and the water running clear. He took a tentative taste of the water, alert for the telltale signs of alkali, and found none. Zebediah waited a few minutes before risking another swallow, giving any poison lurking in the water a chance to show itself. Once his immediate thirst had been addressed, Zebediah gathered sticks he found lying along the creek and started a small fire. He took great care to keep the fire well banked, allowing as little light as possible to creep beyond the edges of the bridge.

Zebediah filled his battered coffee pot from the creek then placed it alongside the fire. No one he ever met could tell him why boiled water was safe to drink, but it was well understood to be true. When Zebediah heard the water begin to bubble, he removed the pot from the fire and sat it in the creek to cool. He banked the fire even more carefully, keeping only a few glowing embers alive. Once the water in the coffee pot had cooled sufficiently, he drank all of it. Then, Zebediah refilled the pot and kept repeating the process. By the time he was ready to be on the move again, Zebediah had drunk all the water he wanted, and his jug was full. Zebediah was very hungry, and although he was not overly fond of acorns as food, he knew they were edible and—in this case—plentiful, and he managed to take the edge off his hunger.

* * *

The time he spent hiding from his pursuers gave Zebediah ample opportunity to reflect on the trip away from Nawlins. After contacting the Deacon, Zebediah returned immediately to the city and proceeded directly to Roberts' store as he had been instructed. When the store owner saw Zebediah enter, the merchant said nothing, only arching his eyebrows in a questioning manner. Neither did Zebediah say anything aloud; he only responded with a slightly nodding yes. Roberts tipped his head in the direction of the back door and indicated that Zebediah should follow. He accompanied Roberts through the door and into the store's back room. Not until Roberts had closed the door behind them did the merchant ask quietly, "Get it all taken care of, Zeb?"

"Yes, sir."

"Follow me, Zeb." Roberts led Zebediah up a stairway to what was evidently the residence Roberts shared with his wife. "My missus is working downstairs, Zeb, and she'll stay there until after we have you moved. We just can't be too careful, and it's best she not even know who you are in case she might happen to say something by accident. Just make yourself comfortable, and we'll have you on your way by nightfall. There's plenty of food in the icebox. Jus' help yourself to whatever looks good."

Zebediah seated himself on the divan and spent the rest of the day relaxing, eating, leafing through newspapers, and dozing. Dusk had fallen when Albert Roberts returned to the apartment, accompanied by a powerfully built and very bald black man. "Zeb, this is Lemon. He's the mate on the steamer I told you about. You need to go with him now. He'll get you squared away on the boat."

Lemon stepped forward, extended his hand to Zebediah, and said quietly, "How do, Zeb. Albert says you've done some good work."

"Just tryin' to help out" was all Zebediah could manage.

"Okay, Zeb, on your way," said Roberts. "Johnny fetched your bag over earlier. It's waiting for you downstairs. He thought about coming up, but we talked it over and decided against it. He and Clarice sends you their best, Zeb. Good luck to ya, Zeb," said Roberts, extending his hand and clasping Zebediah on the shoulder. "And, Zebediah, never a word of this business to anyone."

The merchant's use of his full name reinforced the seriousness of the situation, and Zebediah answered with quiet humility, "Yes, sir, Mr. Roberts."

Under the cover of darkness, Zebediah was escorted through back alleys and down side streets to a wharf. Once aboard the steamboat, Zebediah was assigned a billet in the crew quarters. "It's real important that you to stay inside and out of sight until we're upriver and away from Nawlins," said Lemon. "You can pass through to anywhere on the boat without going outside though, and there's no real reason to go out on deck, so keeping out of sight shouldn't be a big deal. Just stay away from windows. I'll get you filled in on what your job's gonna be come mornin'," said Lemon. "Good night, Zeb. Go to sleep knowin' you done some good today."

The following afternoon, Zebediah and the other crewmen working under Lemon's direction stoked the firebox, got up steam, and prepared the boat for leaving. As the sun was setting, the boat's steam whistle signaled departure, the lines were cast off, and the big paddle wheel began slowly pulling the boat backward out to the middle of the river. In midstream, after aligning the vessel with the current, the captain gave the order, and the engineer reversed the paddle wheel's direction. The boat paused a moment, held in balance between the thrust of the paddle wheel and the current. Then, the paddle wheel gained the upper hand, and the boat moved forward and began beating its way against the Mississippi. Shoveling coal into the firebox was not a complicated business; it was hard but bearable work. In spite of the toil, riverboating proved to be the joy Judah Parsons and D said it was. The huge pistons kept the paddle wheel steadily turning, and the steamer kept pushing its way upriver. At one point during the journey, Lemon explained to Zebediah that the boat was capable of more speed, but unless there was a pressing need to be somewhere on time, going faster burned up a lot more coal than it was worth. Zebediah was in no hurry; he didn't care if the trip took six months. Hour after hour, all through the day and night, the vessel made its way northward. The pay was a dollar a day, collectable at the journey's end. The food was plain but ample. Zebediah was having one of the grandest times of his life. The trip upriver lasted a bit over three weeks, and it would remain a cherished memory for the rest of Zebediah's life.

* * *

Zebediah was jolted back to the present by the sound of approaching footsteps and agitated male voices. He could not be certain, but he thought the voices were those of the two men he had observed the day before. Zebediah could only hear bits and snatches of their conversation, but the two men seemed to be talking about him. Zebediah found this disturbing, but he was not about to risk taking a look to verify his suspicions. Zebediah prepared himself for a fight, but to his relief, the two men did not search below the bridge and continued quickly on their way back toward the river. Soon the two men were out of earshot, and Zebediah hoped they had given up the chase. A few hours later, with only the moonlight to guide him, Zebediah made his way out from below the bridge and back to the road. Twice that night, Zebediah was able to remove a few potatoes and carrots from the gardens he found growing near the road. Zebediah was always careful to leave no tracks and never take very much from any one garden. He hoped his small thefts would never be noticed.

As he continued westward and away from the river, the land became more arid and the trees fewer. The road he was following turned into a trail, then at last, in the midst of a vast sea of grass, it simply ended. With nothing better to do at the moment, Zebediah stretched out on the grass with his hands clasped behind his head and gazed at the clouds drifting overhead. He lay there for some time, gathering his thoughts, and considered his options. Zebediah had seen a few towns along the way but had always given them a wide berth. He had been living off the land and had little need of towns, but now, he had a decision to make. Perhaps he should turn eastward and bum his way to Ohio and try looking up D's people. Returning to Parkersburg and attempting to reestablish a life there also crossed his mind. Surely, the people around Parkersburg would remember him. That idea vanished quickly, and Zebediah brought himself up short, laughing inwardly when he realized, with some sadness, that he was not sure he could even find Parkersburg.

With no plan in mind, Zebediah decided to simply turn around and return the way he came. The following day, he saw a town in the distance and, after some consideration, decided that instead of going around it, he would proceed directly through it. When Zebediah arrived in the village, he found nothing unusual about the place. Everything in the little hamlet looked very new. The houses were small and unpretentious, with little grass and only a few small trees surrounding them. As Zebediah made his way down the dusty main street, he saw not a single black face, only a few curious and apprehensive white ones. Once he was across the town, Zebediah's inclination was to simply keep walking, but a sudden thought led him to the livery stable. He approached respectfully and knocked on the door of the adjoining smithy, where a blacksmith worked at his forge.

When the blacksmith finally heard Zebediah's knocking between the strikes of his hammer, he looked up and was more than a little surprised when he saw Zebediah standing in the doorway. The man paused a moment, gathered himself, then said, "Somethin' I can do for ya?"

Zebediah entered cautiously and asked respectfully, "Good afternoon, Mister. I was just wonderin' if you might have any work that needs doin'?"

"What kinda' work?" asked the blacksmith.

"Oh, paintin', muckin' out, cleanin' up, oilin' harness, anything like that," said Zebediah. "I grew up on a farm, and I know how to do all that sorta' thing."

The perplexity in the blacksmith's expression showed no signs of diminishing. Evidently, having a black man show up at his door, looking for work, was not an everyday occurrence. After another moment's consideration, the smith said, "Well, I reckon if you was to muck out those stalls and throw down some fresh straw, I'd pay ya two bits for yer time."

"That suits me fine," said Zebediah. "Where you want me to haul the old bedding out to?"

The blacksmith motioned for Zebediah to follow and led him to a pile of soiled straw behind the livery barn. The blacksmith said, "Start a new pile next to this one, and when you're done haulin' out, fork the old pile over on top of the new one. I leave it here for the folks who want it for their gardens." The blacksmith paused then looked at Zebediah quizzically and asked with a serious expression, "Do ya reckon I oughta be chargin' for it?"

The question confused Zebediah, and he did not know if he should laugh or try answering the man's question, so he simply returned the man's blank stare and said nothing.

The smith continued to give Zebediah a questioning look until, to Zebediah's relief, the man chuckled and said, "I'm just pullin' yer leg, son. There ain't no need to try and answer."

Much relieved by the smith's wry sense of humor, Zebediah proceeded to clean the stalls and lay down fresh bedding. When the job was complete, the blacksmith allowed Zebediah to refill his water jug at his pump then bade him a good day. Zebediah returned to the road with twenty-five cents in his pocket. This exchange established a pattern for the months that followed. Zebediah learned that, although there were few black faces in the west, livery stables often afforded a few hours' work. The jobs were always short-term, never lasting more than two days. Zebediah's needs were few, and the small amounts of money these jobs provided paid for those things he could not find along the way. This phase of Zebediah's sojourn continued throughout most of the following year until he was overtaken by a growing weariness. Zebediah's health had not yet begun to fail him, and he knew he was more fortunate than many traveling men were. Declining health brought about by constant exposure to the elements, poor food, and chronic injuries from riding the rails seemed to be the destiny of traveling men. Zebediah dreaded the approaching winter. He had neither the desire to spend another winter bumming in the north nor the energy to catch out for the south. Zebediah knew full well he had pressed his luck too long, and the time had come to leave the traveling life behind.

Three days later, Zebediah jumped down from a train when it slowed to a crawl prior to crossing a high trestle. He needed to visit a town soon, and the town he had seen in the distance was probably as good as any. Jumping from trains was something Zebediah rarely did at this stage of his long journey because a traveling man was never more than a broken bone away from disaster. He took the risk on this day because the train was moving very slowly, his supplies were nearly spent, and it was growing dark. It was never smart to enter a town after dark, and the stores would now be closed in any event. Zebediah surveyed the surrounding countryside. He inspected the abutment of the trestle and saw that the ground below fell away steeply, offering little in the way of shelter. The train was still in view, and Zebediah knew there would not be another following so close behind, and it was unlikely there would soon be a train from the other direction. Both the canyon and the river that had carved it were imposing obstacles, and Zebediah saw nothing in the way of shelter on his side of the trestle. Looking down at the river far below, he knew that attempting to cross it in darkness would be pure folly. He suddenly wished he had been blessed with the presence of mind to have waited until the train was across the trestle before departing the empty boxcar.

After assessing his options, Zebediah decided to attempt crossing the span via the narrow walkway running alongside the rails. After walking several paces onto the trestle, Zebediah felt his knees begin to shake, nausea began welling up, and everything around him began to go out of focus. He had never experienced vertigo and had no idea what was happening to him. In desperation, Zebediah dropped to his knees and, keeping his face close to the walkway, crawled slowly back to his starting point. Once off the bridge, Zebediah drank some water and tried to calm himself as he pondered his predicament. He did not understand the thing that had just happened to him, but when his head cleared a few minutes later, Zebediah decided to try crossing the trestle again. He judged the trestle to be more than a quarter mile in length, and it was simply too far to crawl. This time, he would bend low, keeping one hand on a rail and shielding his eyes with the other while looking at nothing but the walkway below his feet. Although his second attempt at crossing the canyon was successful, he felt weak and disoriented by the time he had his feet back on solid ground. Simply looking back at the span of the trestle made Zebediah's head spin.

When his system regained its equilibrium, Zebediah got to his feet and began following the tracks in the direction of the town that was now only a collection of lights on the horizon. There was very little light remaining when Zebediah came to a smaller bridge, of the type he had become so familiar with, and he quickly made his way below. Going under the bridge without exercising his usual precautions was risky, but his decision was forced by the growing cold and darkness. Once he was below the bridge and out of the wind, Zebediah struck a match and, to his relief, found nothing alarming. His luck was still holding. During the match's brief life, Zebediah visually mapped out the locations of the driftwood scattered along the stream bed and then quickly gathered pieces together after the match died. Within minutes he had a small fire burning. In keeping with his usual practice, Zebediah kept the fire very small, allowing as little light as possible to escape from the ravine while affording himself a bit of warmth.

Zebediah made his supper from the few dried biscuits he had left. Now, there would be nothing to eat until he could visit a store and replenish his supplies. It was autumn and nearer winter than summer. The food he could find in summer had long vanished. Zebediah did not know what kind of reception he would receive in the town ahead, and if he was forced to keep on traveling, it wouldn't be the first time. With that eventuality in mind, he used some of his time that night to replenish is supply of drinking water. In his years on the road, Zebediah had become so self-reliant that he rarely felt lonely. However, as this particular night wore on, Zebediah's deep weariness opened the floodgates of a loneliness the likes of which he had not experienced since D's passing. On this night, with coyotes howling in the distance and the wind playing a melancholy dirge in the leafless trees, Zebediah was driven to a place deep inside himself. This night, under this bridge, was the most like that very first night of his long journey. That awful long-ago day when he returned to the farm to find Zeke gone and himself homeless. And yet not even on that first night of his journey had Zebediah felt so alone. On that first night, he still had the proximity of familiar people and places to buoy his spirit, but here in this place, he had nothing but his own tortured soul.

All through that long strange night, Zebediah drifted in and out of a shallow sleep, and many ghosts came to call. Mayellen put in her first appearance in years, and Zebediah's mind was sent reeling. Aunt Mary, Zeke, Judah, Johnny, Clarice, the Reverend Drinkwalter, and others came to visit before the dawn arrived at last. D came and stayed the longest. So real was D's presence that all sense of time and place vanished from Zebediah's mind. The two young men sat by the fire late into the night, talking of old times, joking, and speaking of people they both loved and missed. D wondered aloud how his family in Ohio might be faring, as he had not been to see them in quite some time. Zebediah voiced similar feelings to D regarding Zeke, Judah, and Mayellen. "D, I ain't seen my mama since I was but barely old enough to use the privy by myself, and I cain't say I miss her, and I fo' damn sure don't want to see her, but I'd just kinda' like knowin' whatever become of her. Do ya know what I mean, D?" Zebediah paused as his mind snapped back to the present. Had he just asked that question aloud, or was it just part of this odd waking dream? The realities of that dark, cold night pushed Zebediah's visitors aside for the moment. He added a few sticks to the fire and pulled his blanket close around him, against the deepening cold.

When daylight came at last, it revealed a thick coat of frost covering everything in sight. For the moment at least, the tawny prairie had been rendered a brilliant white. The fire was out cold, but since he had neither food to cook nor coffee to brew, Zebediah decided against rebuilding it. The wind was calm, and he could keep warm enough with his blanket until the time came to visit the town. Keeping his blanket wrapped around him, Zebediah inspected the area below the bridge more carefully. In the daylight, he saw, to his alarm, footprints other than his own that had gone unnoticed in the firelight. Some of them were old and nearly obscured by weather; others, however, were much fresher. Zebediah found the presence of footprints puzzling because the creek below the bridge was little more than a trickle, and it likely only carried much water after a rain. It clearly wasn't a place where people came to go fishing. Additionally strange was the absence of any signs of traveling men. No symbols, no extinct campfires, no empty cans, no nothing that said this was a place used by men on the bum. Zebediah had marked this place in his mind as somewhere to which he might return if need be. The unknown footprints left him feeling so uneasy that he quickly dismissed that possibility.

Zebediah remained out of sight in the small ravine but moved over to its western slope, where he could sit in the sun. He remained there, wrapped in his blanket, until the last of the frost had burned off, and he judged that the stores in the town would likely be open. Zebediah shook the sand from his blanket then rolled it neatly before packing it in his bag. Life on the road had taught him that keeping his things neat and organized was time well spent. Zebediah eased his way up the incline and, as always, looked carefully in all directions before climbing out of the gully and beginning his walk into the town. The footprints under the bridge were weighing heavily on Zebediah's mind. As he walked along the rail line in the direction of the town, he had the uneasy feeling that he was being watched. Zebediah tended to trust his feelings, and more than a few times, trusting his feelings had steered him away from trouble. Still and all, Zebediah could think of no reason why anyone would be watching him on this vast, empty prairie.

A half-mile distant, hidden behind a patch of sumac, Clyde Goodwin watched as Zebediah made his way in the direction of Keller. The moment Goodwin had seen Zebediah's head rise out of the ravine, he swung off his horse and took cover. Goodwin hoped the stranger had not discovered any of his hiding places under the bridge. He had used the hidden pockets under the bridge to keep secret any number of things since first caching his father's weapons there years earlier. Now that he had established himself as a lawman, he could come and go freely to this and his other hiding places without arousing suspicion. Had he not spotted the man and had simply ridden in on him, Goodwin would have drawn the .44 and become the dutiful lawman. He might have arrested the traveler on some bogus charge, or he might have let him off with a verbal harangue after confiscating any valuables the unfortunate man was carrying. As it stood, Goodwin had been spared the need to do anything, which was always his preferred outcome. In any event, surprising a man always carried its own set of dangers. Once the traveler was out of sight, he would retrieve the bag of money from its hiding place and relocate it. If the money was missing, then the stranger had a bleak future. If the money was untouched, then no worries; it was a nice day for a ride.

The day was warming quickly, and by the time Zebediah reached the edge of Keller, he had removed his coat and packed it in his bag. The town he entered seemed both larger and more prosperous than the places Zebediah was accustomed to. Judging by the size of the trees, Zebediah suspected the town had been carved out of an existing grove of cottonwood, and the presence of large trees gave the community a more established feel. A number of masonry buildings lined the main street, and there were some substantial homes set back away from the business district. As he made his way to the store, he saw that the main street was paved with brick. Zebediah was surprised to see one of the automobiles, which were becoming ever more common, parked in front of the bank. Everywhere he looked, he saw construction, and it occurred to Zebediah that there might well be a market here for shingles. Missing were the boardwalks common to new towns. This town had concrete sidewalks that not only flanked the main street but extended down the side streets as well.

Zebediah paused in front of the general store before entering. The building had a brick facade instead of the usual wooden storefront. Zebediah was accustomed to ruder places and was finding this town a bit intimidating. Even in Nawlins, he had only rarely ventured outside the ward and had never become familiar with white-owned businesses. The sign hanging in the door said Open. Zebediah straightened himself and entered. The slightly built balding man behind the counter was clearly startled by Zebediah's sudden appearance in his place of business. Zebediah was not only a rare black face; his extended period of bumming had left him looking rather rough.

Charles Bonebright paused and considered reaching for the revolver he kept under the counter. A tense moment passed as the merchant evaluated the situation. When Bonebright detected no hostile intent in Zebediah, he recovered his composure enough to ask tentatively, "Can I help you?"

"I need to pick up a few things," said Zebediah, "flour, coffee, dried beans, molasses, dry biscuits, and some canned goods."

"Do you have the money to pay for them?" Bonebright asked uneasily. The merchant realized the moment he uttered the words how ridiculous they sounded.

Zebediah, however, was unfazed by the question and answered, "Yes, sir, I have money enough to buy the things I need."

Attempting to regain control of the situation, Bonebright said, "Well then, let's get you taken care of." Bonebright always needed money and was never one to turn away business. He was, however, secretly grateful for the early hour and the absence of other customers. "All my canned goods are along that wall. Flour comes in one-pound packages, or I can scoop up what you want from the barrel and weigh it out for you. Same with the dried beans."

"Thanks, Mister," said Zebediah. He crossed to the far wall and scanned the selection of canned goods then made his selections. After placing the items on the counter, Zebediah selected two packages each of flour and dried beans, then requested a pound of ground coffee.

Bonebright ground the coffee beans, totaled up Zebediah's purchases, then said in a tone that suggested doubt as to his customer's ability to meet the obligation, "That comes to a dollar and sixty-five cents."

Zebediah withdrew his coin purse and counted out the exact amount requested. The grocer seemed somewhat surprised by his customer's ability to do so. "Will you be needing a paper bag for your goods?" asked Bonebright.

Zebediah responded, "No, thank you, sir, I'll just pack it all inside my bag. Thank you, Mister. Good day to you."

"Good day to you, young man," said Bonebright, who continued to be taken aback by Zebediah's visit.

Returning outside, Zebediah continued walking in his earlier direction of travel. When he reached the edge of town, he paused a moment, looked around, then returned the way he came. The town had a certain appeal, and Zebediah decided it was worth more attention. He always kept his expectations low when dealing with white merchants, and although the man he had just dealt with did not seem overly happy to find him in his store, neither did the man react with hostility. The merchant had conducted the transaction in a civil manner, and it was a consideration. Zebediah had experienced many less-than-civil transactions during his years on the road. Some of them much less than civil. The town, whose name he did not yet know, was by no means a city, but it was more substantial than the usual cluster of shabby buildings huddled along a rail line. The winds of progress were definitely in the air here, and Zebediah wondered if the town might grow into a place where he could carve out a little home for himself and bring his journey to an end at last.

He walked the length of the main street again, this time paying more attention to the businesses along the way. Zebediah found the variety of stores encouraging. Not that he would ever have need of a milliner's shop, but it was something one simply did not see in smaller villages. When he neared the far edge of town, Zebediah spotted the livery stable, sitting a block back from the main street, and made his way to it. As he approached, he saw carpenters working on an addition to the building. What they were building appeared identical to an existing wing extending from the other side of the barn. The building, with its extensions, had an unconventional but not-unpleasing look for a livery. The large center section was a classic gambrel-roofed barn while the wings extending from its flanks had conventional pitched roofs that sloped toward and away from the street. From the completed wing of the building, he heard the ring of a blacksmith's hammer.

Zebediah walked up to the open door of the smithy and knocked politely. From the doorway, Zebediah saw the largest man he had ever seen working at the forge. Blacksmiths tended to be large, muscular men, but this man was exceptional. He swung the five-pound hammer as effortlessly as an ordinary man might manage a soup spoon. The blacksmith had his back to the door, and when he gave no sign of being able to hear Zebediah's repeated knocking, Zebediah entered the shop. Giving himself all the space he could, Zebediah worked his way around to the back side of the forge and into the blacksmith's field of vision.

When the blacksmith saw Zebediah, he paused in midswing, clearly startled. The big man took a half step backward with the hammer poised above his shoulder, and for a terrifying moment, Zebediah feared the blacksmith was going to throw the hammer at him. The huge man quickly regained his composure and boomed, "GOOD GOD, YA SCARED THE HELL OUTA' ME!" To Zebediah's immense relief, the man's words were accompanied by a deep, rolling belly laugh. The smith shook his head as if trying to rid himself of the shock he had just experienced then asked in a pleasant voice, "What can I do for ya?"

"I was just wonderin' if you might have any work you need doing," said Zebediah. "I grew up on a farm, and I know how to tend to horses and mules. I can oil and mend harness, muck out, clean up, all that sorta' thing that goes on around a livery barn."

"Can ya work on automobiles?" asked the blacksmith, cocking his head slightly.

The question surprised Zebediah, and he lowered his eyes slightly and answered, "Naw, sir, I ain't never learnt how to work on automobiles."

The blacksmith shrugged his shoulders and said with a wry smile, "I just thought I'd ask. I don't know how to work on the damn things either. I can't say I'm exactly crazy about automobiles, but I know they're the coming thing, and I might as well get used to the idea. That's what the new addition's gonna be for. My boy's off learnin' how to work on 'em. That's gonna be his side of the business when he thinks he's ready to run it." The blacksmith brought himself back to the moment and said, "But to answer your question, I got more of the kinda' work you're talkin' about than I can shake a stick at. The smithy keeps me so damn busy, there just ain't enough hours in the day to get it all done." The blacksmith paused and eyed Zebediah carefully, taking stock of his visitor. It was another uncomfortable moment for

Zebediah, but he was relieved when the blacksmith said, "Okay, son, I'll give ya a try. When can ya start?"

Zebediah smiled and said, "Well, sir, I can start right now or anytime you want."

The big man laughed warmly and said, "Well then, I want ya to start now." The blacksmith extended his hand and said, "I'm Karl Emmett."

For the second time in his life, Zebediah shook hands with a white man and said, "I'm Zebediah, Mr. Emmett. Most everybody calls me Zeb." So huge was the blacksmith's hand, Zebediah's mind involuntarily flashed back to when, as a young boy, he had first shaken hands with his uncle Zeke. "I'm real sorry about scarin' ya, Mr. Emmett," said Zebediah.

Upon hearing Zebediah's apology, the big ruddy-faced blacksmith tipped his head back and laughed. "Oh hell, son, don't worry about that. If I had a lick of sense, I'd always work facing the door and that wouldn't happen. As it is, it's a rare day when somebody doesn't scare the hell outa' me at least once!" When the blacksmith's laughter subsided, he asked Zebediah to follow, and when they reached the barn, Emmett began pointing out the things that needed doing. "As you can see Zeb, I'm a long way from being caught up around the livery. Keeping up with the chores was a damn sight easier before my boy went off to learn about automobiles. Straw and hay are up in the mow of course, and I boarded up this stall and made a little granary out of it." Stepping out the back door, Karl Emmett continued, "I pile the old straw out back, and once a week, a gent who boards his horses and wagons here hauls it off for me." The blacksmith showed Zebediah where the wheelbarrow, shovels, rakes, and pitchforks were kept and said, "Find a peg to hang your bag on, and I'll leave you to it, Zeb."

The work before him was straightforward, and Zebediah approached it methodically. He used a pitchfork and a scoop shovel to muck out the stalls. Once he had a stall cleared, he employed a wet push broom with stiff bristles to wash down the sides and the floor of the unoccupied stall. Once a stall had been completely cleaned, he hauled down fresh straw from the mow. When all the unoccupied stalls had been cleaned, Zebediah returned to the smithy and told Karl Emmett. The blacksmith came into the barn and moved horses and mules from the stalls they had been occupying to freshly cleaned ones. The numbers were not even, and some of the animals would have to wait their turn until the recently vacated stalls had received their cleaning.

"You say you've spent time tending to animals, Zebediah?" asked the blacksmith.

"Yes, sir," said Zebediah, "from the time I was jus' a little boy on my aunt and uncle's farm."

Again, Emmett eyed Zebediah, taking stock of his new employee, then said, "Well then, you should know to be careful around livestock. Especially draft horses. Go ahead and move the next one yourself, and we'll see how you do. Why don't you just move them one at a time as you get a stall cleaned, that tends to keep 'em calmed down. What you're showing me so far looks real good, Zeb. Keep it up." There was nothing that especially stood out in the blacksmith's tone, but there was something about the combination of the man's demeanor and sheer physical presence that inspired a desire in Zebediah to do the best job possible. "I'll leave you to it. You know where to find me if you need me."

Buoyed by the confidence the blacksmith had shown him, Zebediah responded, "Yes, sir, Mr. Emmett, one at a time, and I'll be real careful movin' animals." With a renewed sense of purpose, Zebediah returned to his work. Late that afternoon, as he was cleaning the last stall, a man rolled up to the back door of the livery in a heavy freight wagon drawn by four huge horses. The teamster climbed down from the wagon. The man unhitched one of the Belgians then led it into the dimly lit barn and into an empty stall.

Zebediah heard the man mutter to himself, "Well, I'll be damned. Looks like Karl finally found time to do some cleanin' up." The freighter spoke in the deepest voice Zebediah had ever heard. After removing the horse's harness and pouring out a measure of oats, the man was returning outside to collect the next horse when he spotted Zebediah working in the empty stall. Clearly startled, the tall man asked sharply, "And just who the hell are you? Does Karl know you're in his barn?"

"Yes, sir, Mister. I've been working for Mr. Emmett today, mucking out and such," said Zebediah in a defensive voice.

Before the freighter could speak again, Karl Emmett appeared from the blacksmith shop and called out, "Now Harley, don't be scarin' my help." The blacksmith laughed as he spoke, and the freighter was put at ease.

The teamster smiled slightly and chuckled as he said to the blacksmith, "Well Karl, I didn't know ya had anybody workin' for ya. In fact, I didn't know you could get anybody to work for ya."

The blacksmith ignored the freighter's remark and said, "Harley Childers, meet Zebediah. Zeb here wandered in this morning looking for work, and I took him up on it. He's done a pretty fair job of it too, wouldn't you say, Harley? Not that you'd know a decent barn if ya saw one."

"Your barn didn't have but one way to go, Karl, and it does look a damn sight better than it did," said the freighter.

"You're just lucky I'm willing to have you as a customer," said the blacksmith.

"You're just lucky there ain't another livery in town," growled the freighter.

"Zeb," said the blacksmith, pointing to where tools hung along the wall, "why don't ya grab a curry comb from over there and brush down Harley's horses as he brings 'em in. Just be extra careful. His horses are all about half-wild, mean as hell, and can't be trusted."

"Don't listen to him son, my horses is gentle as lambs. It's just the poor grade of feed they get here that makes 'em jumpy." The freighter looked at Zebediah and said earnestly, "You need to know that Karl here can only spot the difference between a horse and a mule about half the time."

"Your horses would still be jumpy if I spread molasses on their oats and kissed 'em good night," said the blacksmith.

"I'd pay good money to watch you kiss a horse good night, Karl."

The two men continued to go back and forth in a similar vein as a very confused Zebediah entered the stall and began carefully brushing down the big horse. The huge draft horse proved to be very gentle and receptive to being curried, giving Zebediah no reason to be afraid. It would not be until sometime later that Zebediah would come to realize the blacksmith and the freighter were the best of friends but seemed determined to never utter a kind word to each other.

In less than an hour, all four of Harley Childers' horses were bedded down, fed, and curried. While Zebediah worked, the two men retired to the blacksmith's small office and began a card game. When they reappeared, the freighter departed, and Karl Emmett returned to the barn to inspect Zebediah's work. "You did a real good job today, Zeb. Do you think you can do as well every day?"

"Yes, sir, Mr. Emmett. I always tries to do the best job I can," said Zebediah sincerely.

"Well then, come back tomorrow. I never seem to run out of work on this side of the business." Emmett turned to leave then paused and looked back at Zebediah, asking, "Where ya stayin', son?"

"I don't have anywhere special," said Zebediah. "I'll prolly go find me a place to camp out along the tracks somewhere."

"Oh hell and tarnation," said the blacksmith, "I ain't about to turn anybody out in the cold when I have a haymow to offer. I slept in many a haymow back in my younger days, and they ain't the worst place you could be on a cold night. By the way, does four dollars a week and your dinner sound fair for a startin' wage? My missus always brings my dinner over to the shop, and when she sees you, she won't let you go hungry."

So stunned was Zebediah, he could barely bring himself to speak. At last he managed to stammer, "Oh, that sounds real good, Mr. Emmett."

"Well, four dollars a week and your dinner it is then," said the blacksmith. "Keep doin' as well as you did today, and I'll do better by ya."

From the top of his head to the tips of his toes, Zebediah was both numb and tingling. In the space of a day, he had gone from homeless vagabond to having a job and a roof over his head, even if it was only a barn roof. As Karl Emmett was bidding him good night, Zebediah ventured to ask, "Mr. Emmett, what's the name of this town?"

"Keller," said the blacksmith. "I used to know why they named the place Keller, but I'm dammed if I can remember. I'll ask my wife. She likely knows."

Chapter Eleven

Life in Keller

Zebediah was finishing up his chores for the day and beginning to think of fixing himself some supper when Karl Emmett appeared in the barn. Zebediah was at the end of his second week in the employ of the blacksmith, and his chores had settled into a routine. "Say, Zeb," said the blacksmith, "why don't you take a couple minutes and come with me. I'd like to show ya somethin'."

"Yes, sir, Mr. Emmett."

The blacksmith led the way up the stairs to the haymow and then to a locked door located midway down the large mow. Karl Emmett withdrew a key from his pocket and opened the padlock. The blacksmith stepped inside the door, motioning for Zebediah to follow. Once inside, Karl Emmett struck a match and lit a kerosene lantern. "You're lookin' at what I thought was a good idea, Zeb. When I built the smithy, I had the carpenters connect the attic above the shop to the haymow. I thought I'd be able to use this space for storage. Well, it turned out to be so damned unhandy that I never really made much use of it. I'm thinkin' of havin' the carpenters frame up a room for ya there at the end. I can have 'em hang a ceiling from the rafters, and there should still be enough room to stand up and walk around. There's a window there in the gable end, so you won't feel like you're livin' in a dungeon. If we bunker in some straw along the sides and throw some over the ceiling, it should be pretty cozy when winter sets in. I'll have 'em cut a hole in the floor and put a grate over it so the heat from the shop will find its way up here. What do ya think?"

Zebediah was too stunned to speak. At last he managed to stammer, "Really, Mr. Emmett?"

The blacksmith laughed and said, "Zeb, I think you're just too damn used to livin' rough. All I'm offerin' you is an eight-by-twelve room over a blacksmith shop. It ain't hardly a palace."

"Sounds like a palace to me, Mr. Emmett. Sounds like a palace to me," Zebediah repeated humbly, his voice trailing off to a whisper.

Karl Emmett laughed and said, "Truth be told, Zeb, my missus has taken a liking to you, and she's been givin' me seven kinds of hell for makin' you sleep in the haymow."

"I ain't minded livin' in the haymow a bit, Mr. Emmett," said Zebediah sincerely.

"I know ya ain't, Zeb. I knew after the first day you wasn't a complainer. But, Mrs. Emmett is determined that I do better by you, she's the boss, and that's what I aim to do." The blacksmith paused a moment, looked Zebediah in the eye, and said, "It's a sad thing to say, Zeb, but it ain't likely that anybody in this town would rent a room to a colored man. So I'm just gonna build you one. I'm hopin' you'll stick with me here, Zeb. You're doing a good job with the barn, I need the help, and I'm glad to have ya workin' for me."

"I'm glad to be here, Mr. Emmett. Real glad," said Zebediah quietly. Karl Emmett was proving to be as kind as he was big.

"I kinda' figured you'd be all right with the idea." The blacksmith chuckled. "But I wanted to run it by you first. I'll have the carpenters get to it first thing tomorrow. Shouldn't take 'em more than a day or so to get it done."

"Thank you, Mr. Emmett. Thank you very much."

"Oh road apples, Zebediah, it ain't nothin' really." Karl Emmett paused then looked directly at Zebediah and said with mock seriousness, "Besides, Zeb, you'll still have to put up with the smell of Harley Childers' horses, and that ain't nothin' to celebrate."

Zebediah could not help but laugh at having been included in the absurd, comic feud carried on between the freighter and the blacksmith.

As the blacksmith predicted, the carpenters were quickly done with the project. Even before they began building his room, Zebediah had received his share of curious looks from the carpenters as they worked on the addition for the blacksmith's son. When they discovered the room's purpose, a few of them began grumbling aloud. On more than one occasion, Zebediah overheard the men make remarks regarding the blacksmith's hiring practices. None of the workmen, however, voiced those questions to Karl Emmett directly. It occurred to Zebediah that his employer's good nature might be due, in part, to the fact that no sane man would even think of confronting the huge blacksmith. If Emmett heard any of the carpenter's grumblings, he paid them no mind.

Harley Childers was a reticent man who rarely had many words for anyone but the blacksmith and his landlady, Emily Kellogg. However, as time went by, Childers began displaying a certain openness toward Zebediah, often asking comic questions regarding the blacksmith's behavior. Zebediah resisted the urge to laugh openly, not wanting to put himself in a difficult position. Without intending to, Zebediah had become something of a foil for the two men, with each man using him to needle the other. To Zebediah's surprise, Childers began supplementing his pay by fifty cents a week. "I just want ya to know, Zeb, that the care you're giving my horses matters to me," said Childers.

Zebediah protested, saying, "Mr. Emmett is paying me real good, Mr. Harley, and taking care of your horses is just part of my job."

Childers would book no protest, telling Zebediah, "Look, son, I don't care what that old tightwad Karl Emmett is payin' ya. I'm a businessman too, and I know it don't hurt none to let people know they're doing a good job."

"Thank you, Mr. Harley."

"Think nothin' of it, Zebediah."

Zebediah did think something of it though. He thought a great deal of it. The fifty cents a week Harley Childers had begun adding to his pay just because he had done a good job meant nearly as much to him as the consideration Karl Emmett had shown him. Later that night, alone in the room that now contained a bed and a few other pieces of old furniture, Zebediah thought long and hard about his current situation and swore an oath to himself and to the memory of everyone he ever loved that he would do nothing that might put his new life in jeopardy.

A few blocks away, Theresa Bender sat alone in the parsonage and looked up at the mantle clock. She wondered why Richard was running so late. As he settled into his life as a pastor in Keller, the Reverend Bender had an ever-increasing number of pastoral calls to make. Theresa was well aware of what a minister's life involved and did not view it as an unusual development. Still and all, it did seem rather odd to her that so many of Richard's calls were during the evening hours. The first few weeks of her marriage to Richard had been a dream, almost too wonderful to be real. Richard had been a dutiful and passionate husband, ever ready with some little compliment meant to brighten her day. As the weeks turned to months, and after her father made Richard a full pastor, he had begun easing away. Theresa was trying desperately to believe this was a purely natural process brought about by the increasing demands of her husband's position. What she wanted to believe, however, was very different from the thing that had taken up residence in a dark recess of her mind.

Theresa Bender worked hard at not allowing her nagging fear to show. Richard, however, always seemed to sense when his wife's feelings were nearing the surface, and for a few days at least, he became again the attentive, romantic man she had married. Once Theresa had been shown the appropriate attention, he would begin inching away again. The Benders were nearing their first anniversary, and Theresa fully expected that she would have become pregnant by this time. That she had not, puzzled her less than did her own ambivalence to the idea of having a family. Was it because she had never known her own mother, or was it some defect in her character that left her with a certain sense of relief at being unable to conceive? Theresa had always loved children, but at the same time, she was finding the idea of being childless strangely liberating.

When the prospect of having a family began looking less likely, Theresa threw herself into the role of pastor's wife. She organized the woman's Bible study, took over as choir director, oversaw the cleaning of the church, and began giving piano lessons. Within a few weeks, her schedule was nearly as full as her husband's. Theresa no longer found it quite so odd that a certain space had developed between Richard and herself. Given their busy lives and the maturing nature of their relationship, it all seemed perfectly normal. She did not find it overly strange when Richard, professing a difficulty sleeping, began spending most nights in a separate bedroom. Though she missed his presence, she did not see any reason to be alarmed, as his work load was growing ever heavier, and he clearly needed his rest.

Theresa was greatly pleased when one of the deacons, Charles Bonebright, expressed his gratitude to both Richard and herself, regarding his wife Emma's greatly improved church attendance. Theresa was well schooled in the petty politics that can drag down a congregation and strongly resisted gossip. Even so, it was not possible to miss overhearing the comments made by members of the women's group regarding Mrs. Bonebright. Though Theresa never asked any questions regarding the issue, she reached the conclusion that Emma Bonebright had not endeared herself either to the congregation or to the town as a whole. The merchant's wife, it seemed, considered herself rather more sophisticated and worldly than the other women of the community. There was even talk that she would not allow her young daughters to attend the local school, preferring instead to take them east for what she considered a "proper" education.

Emma Bonebright did not mix well with the other women in the study group, but she appeared determined to establish a place for herself in the congregation. After having developed a reputation for spotty church attendance, Mrs. Bonebright now only rarely missed a Sunday morning service and frequently attended the Wednesday evening prayer meeting as well. Emma's greatest degree of acceptance came when she began hosting the women's group in her home. Other ladies expressed their admiration at her ability to get the reverend himself to drop by and lead them in study through at least part of the lesson. Though Emma Bonebright would never be fully accepted, she had at least shifted the group's opinion of her from rather hostile to neutral. Gaining the group's acceptance was never Emma Bonebright's objective in any event.

Standing in a darkened ally, Luther Boggs watched as several of Keller's most prominent citizens entered Bonebright's store one at a time. He saw the lights burning in the second-story apartment, and Boggs knew full well that the Bonebright family had not lived there in some time. Luther Boggs knew something was afoot, and he had strong suspicions as to its nature. "It's gotta be that bastard Corker and his damn saloon," thought Boggs angrily. "He'll get what he wants. Conniving bastards like Corker always get what they want. This bunch of fine, upstanding hypocrites will sell out to him sure enough."

Inside the Bonebright apartment, Cyrus Hitchcock stood, thereby calling the informal meeting to order. The banker moved to the middle of the small parlor and began addressing the others in attendance. "Gentlemen, I've been in contact with people I know at the capital, and they tell me Corker has been making overtures to the governor's office concerning his acquisition of a liquor license in Keller. I don't think we can hold him off much longer and manage to keep this matter out of the courts. The thing that must be born in mind is, if we wind up in court, it's going to start getting expensive."

A murmur went through the room, and Charles Bonebright asked tentatively, "What do you think our best course of action is going to be now, Cyrus? We seem to be running out of options."

"I think I may have hit upon a solution, albeit an imperfect one," said the banker. "Through an intermediary, I've made it clear to Corker that even with the governor's help, we can still keep him tied up in court for at least a year and possibly longer." Hitchcock paused, letting his last remark sink in before continuing. "Mr. Corker is a tough adversary, gentlemen, which is something I'm sure you're all aware of. He is, however, a businessman and a pragmatic one. I hope, gentlemen, that you will not take offense at my having negotiated secretly with the man on our behalf. It isn't that I desire to keep things from any of you. It's just that my position allows me better access to certain people, not to mention that this is a matter that must be handled with the utmost discretion."

The banker paused again, allowing the assembly to absorb what he had just said. Horace Schmalle broke the heavy silence. "I think that, given the circumstances Cyrus, you have our support. Are you prepared to share with us, at this time, the solution you have in mind?"

"Yes, I am, Horace," said the banker, "and that is why I've called this meeting. I wanted to have my ducks in a row, so to speak, before broaching my plan to the group." The banker shifted his gaze one by one to every person in the room before continuing. "Bankers love numbers, gentlemen. Numbers are what we do best. I did some calculations and came up with an estimate of what a year in court would cost Corker and added that sum to the money he would likely have to spread around the capital to get what he wants. What I propose to do, gentlemen, is make him a slightly better offer."

There was an audible gasp in the room, and after a long pause, Horace Schmalle asked cautiously, "Are you suggesting bribery, Cyrus?"

Cyrus Hitchcock betrayed no emotion upon hearing the word *bribery* but merely directed his gaze upon his fellow councilman and said evenly, "I suppose there are those who might view it as such, Horace. However, I prefer to think of it as a rather straightforward business transaction, one where all the parties come out ahead. Value for value."

Another heavy silence ensued before Bonebright asked tentatively, "What's going to happen now, Cyrus?"

"Very little really, Charles, provided we all agree on this course of action," answered the banker. "If we agree to move forward, then the matter requires no further discussion. In fact, the less discussion there is, the better for all of us. If you gentlemen find your bank statements acceptable at the end of the month, then we simply vote on the matter at the next council meeting, and we need never speak of the matter again." The banker looked from face to face, being deliberately slow, allowing his words to take full effect. "I know you gentlemen are all curious about figures, and I will not say anything regarding that subject aloud in this meeting. That is for your own safety as well as mine. Trust me sirs, none of you will ever gain so much through so little effort."

Charles Bonebright's insides began to quiver with excitement. Could this possibly mean he would be able to rid himself of the illegal liquor business and manage to keep his house and business at the same time? Thoughts danced wildly through his mind. In his excitement, he asked himself, "Perhaps I should discuss the matter with Reverend Bender. Perhaps not. What if it cost me my position as a deacon?" Charles Bonebright considered the reverend to be a righteous man, and he feared Bender might react very badly to his having accepted a bribe that allowed a saloon to be built in Keller. Emma certainly had to know, but then again, although she seemed vaguely aware of his illicit activities, she never asked a single question. "Maybe it's best to follow Cyrus' advice and discuss it with no one," thought Bonebright.

Cyrus Hitchcock cleared his throat and asked, "Are we of one mind here, gentlemen? If you have reservations, now is the time to voice them." No one in the room said a word. There was another long pause, then the banker turned to each of them individually. Every man nodded yes, giving his silent assent to the plan.

Luther Boggs, hidden deep in the shadows, saw the light go out in the Bonebright apartment. He watched as the councilmen and other prominent citizens departed. "Who do you think you're fooling, you miserable pack of hypocrites?" thought Boggs bitterly. Boggs noted each and every person in attendance and saw to his satisfaction that neither Harley Childers nor Karl Emmett were among the prominent citizens leaving the meeting. "Probably the only two honest businessmen in this whole miserable excuse for a town," thought the angry little man.

Boggs wasn't the only one who observed the people leave the meeting. Clyde Goodwin did so as well, but he wasn't watching from the shadows. Far from concealing himself, Goodwin stood leaning against a streetlight pole, in full view of those departing. Goodwin didn't know the exact nature of what had transpired above Bonebright's store but then, he didn't need to know the details. It had been obvious to him from the time Corker made his proposal that the councilors, and probably a few other leading citizens, were going to be bribed. No, he didn't need to know the details; all he needed was for those attending the meeting to know that he knew. It was part of Goodwin's predatory instinct to understand that the implied threat was almost always more effective than the overt threat. He wouldn't even have to ask for a share in the loot. They would give it up voluntarily once he casually mentioned the meetings to them. He would mention the meetings to everyone but the banker. Clyde Goodwin was not one to pick a fight when he was over matched. Cyrus Hitchcock had resources Goodwin could only dream of.

As the autumn turned to winter, Zebediah was ever more grateful for the kindness Karl Emmett had shown him. The blacksmith always shoveled some extra coal in the stove before departing for the day, and the warmth drifted up to Zebediah's room. When Mrs. Emmett learned that Zebediah could read, she began supplying him with old books, magazines, and newspapers for his entertainment. Zebediah bought a deck of cards from Bonebright and played many games of solitaire. In short order, Zebediah could scarcely imagine himself living rough again, especially in the winter. When Christmas drew near, he wrote and mailed a letter to Johnny and Clarice Pike, but he never received a reply. He did not know their actual street address and could only hope the letter would find its way into their hands. The kindness the Emmett's had shown him could only go so far toward warding off Zebediah's loneliness, however. He missed the Pikes, Uncle Zeke, Judah, and many others, but mostly, he missed D, the one person he knew for certain that he would never see again.

The mere impossibility of seeing D in person did not prevent his friend from visiting on long winter nights. Their conversations were not unlike the one they held that very last night Zebediah spent under a bridge. Sadly, no matter how enjoyable a visit from D might be, Zebediah was always jolted back to the present. The comfort of his room, pleasant as it was, at times only added to his sense of isolation. Zebediah sometimes found himself at such moments with tears in his eyes. Only in the depths of these late-night bouts of isolation, with no one to share his thoughts, did Zebediah question the hand he had been dealt in life. He was not inclined to self-pity and, with the exception of these lonely hours, considered himself far better off than many of the traveling men he had known. Men who, after but a few years spent on the bum, had not even a pauper's grave to mark the passing of their lives.

Zebediah's spirits rose again with the coming of green grass, and D's visits became less frequent. With the arrival of spring, Zebediah found himself working so much that he rarely had time for anything but sleep in his room. Karl Emmett was besieged on all sides by farmers needing plows sharpened, horses shod, and other repair work associated with the planting season. When the blacksmith was busiest, he occasionally called upon Zebediah to help out around the smithy, and Zebediah did whatever he could to assist the blacksmith.

As the mad rush of planting began to ease, Zebediah's life took another unexpected turn. After first consulting with Karl Emmett, Harley Childers began employing Zebediah to assist with some of his heavier lifting. Construction had begun on a new hotel and saloon, and it seemed every arriving train brought materials that needed hauling from the depot to the construction site. To Zebediah's surprise, the blacksmith did not reduce his wages for the time he spent working for Childers. "You're still getting all your work done at the livery, Zeb, and if it was worth four dollars then, it's worth four dollars now," said Emmett. What Zebediah did not know was that, between his two employers, he had become one of the most highly paid working men in Keller.

Had Zebediah's modest prosperity become known to certain members of the community, it would have certainly resulted in angry resentment. Harley Childers foresaw that possibility and told Zebediah in quiet confidence, "You know, Zeb, you're doing pretty well fer yourself, but it wouldn't be a good idea for you to do anything flashy with your money. Buy simple stuff that ya need, like good boots and work clothes. Save your money, Zeb, a man gits old before he knows what hit him. You don't need any of the lazy riffraff around Keller causin' trouble for ya." Though Zebediah continued to find himself in the middle of the constant needling that went on between the blacksmith and the freighter, he knew that when either of the men spoke to him seriously, they were offering advice worth listening to. Zebediah followed Childers' recommendation and avoided buying anything that would draw attention to himself. Bit by bit, he acquired a good pair of boots, a warm winter coat, and a decent set of work clothes.

One of the more curious aspects of Zebediah's job with with the freighter came on the first Monday of the month, when the grocer Bonebright, in addition to his regular shipment of goods, received at least a full wagonload of sugar and sometimes more. Zebediah had no idea that a store could sell so much sugar. It seemed additionally odd to him that the sugar was never unloaded into the back room of the store with Bonebright's other merchandise but instead into a storage building across the alley. Harley Childers knew the truth, but the freighter never said a word about the sugar shipments to Zebediah. Childers only expressed his appreciation of having a back younger and stronger than his own to help with the loading and unloading. Helping Harley Childers move a wagonload of sugar earned Zebediah an additional fifty cents a month.

Charles Bonebright retired the mortgage on his home and had been eagerly looking forward to being out of the illegal-whiskey business. That small dream had a short life. To his horror, Bonebright soon discovered that the coming of Corker's saloon had done nothing to curb the demand for illegal whiskey. If anything, the loosening of the town's liquor laws had actually increased the demand for moonshine, and the grocer now found himself selling more sugar than ever. How long would it be before someone noticed and began asking questions? Bonebright had once allowed himself to dream of being free of the moonshiners, but now he found himself being squeezed in a circular game orchestrated by Clyde Goodwin. Bonebright cursed himself for not having grasped the situation sooner, when it might have been possible to extricate himself. After becoming sheriff, Goodwin quickly identified every moonshiner in the area. The new sheriff found accepting payment from the moonshiners to be vastly more profitable than putting them out of business. All it took was the sheriff's implied threat of revenue agents to keep the grocer and the whiskey makers in the game. Bonebright felt trapped as never before, and now Emma was again speaking of taking the girls east. The merchant's own whiskey consumption had risen steadily over the past months, although he had at least replaced the moonshine with Corker's more genteel product.

Charles Bonebright had chosen to retire his burdensome mortgage while other prominent citizens bought automobiles and put additions on their homes. Cyrus Hitchcock and his wife would later spend an entire summer touring Europe, leading many who had been the recipients of John Corker's money to conclude that the banker's share of the payoff must have been a good deal larger than their own. They may have thought it, but they never discussed it among themselves, and they certainly never broached the subject with the banker. None of this activity passed unnoticed by Luther Boggs, who continued to stew and eye the conspirators angrily at every opportunity. The little man understood the situation completely, and just as completely, Clyde Goodwin understood the threat Luther Boggs posed to the equilibrium of the community. If he was left with no other option, Goodwin would take matters into his own hands and deal with Boggs personally. The angry little pest simply could not be bought off or frightened into silence. While taking the matter into his own hands was an option he might have to exercise, who, Goodwin wondered, would be willing to pay the most to have that particular problem go away?

Richard Bender sat in his handsome office, allowing himself to bask in the glow of his achievement. He had become the leader of a substantial and growing congregation without believing a word of what he preached. His was not the only church in Keller, but it was, by far, the largest and the one to which most of the prominent citizens belonged. He had a decent income and lived in a large comfortable home that he did not have to pay for. Thoughts of his extended family laboring on their farms in all weather were never far from his mind, and those thoughts always made him smile. Most of all, he had the thing he desired most, the attention of women and the time to return that attention. Women had always been attracted to him, and Bender sometimes found "the game" almost too easy. His marriage to Theresa had worked out much as he had planned it. She was the appropriate compliment to that side of himself he presented to the public. Actually caring about his wife had never been part of the plan however, and his inability to completely rid himself of his lingering feelings for Theresa troubled him slightly.

The reverend's feelings for his wife were not, however, troubling enough to keep him away from the hunt, and it was the hunt that Richard Bender lived for. That the Reverend Bender did not hunt animals and did not even posses a weapon made him no less a hunter. Since his youth, Richard Bender had divided women into three categories: The first group were those who would never stray. The second was made up of those looking to him for something more than a tryst. The third group consisted of those willing to compromise their virtue for the sheer joy of the moment. The first group Bender dismissed out of hand and presented himself to them as the very soul of piety. To the second group, he extended just enough encouragement that they might continue to dream while not becoming his enemies.

The third group was the smallest of the three but large enough. It was to this group that Bender devoted his attention. He was available for "spiritual counseling" at all hours, usually conducted in his office in the church, behind securely locked doors.

After arriving at his post in Keller, it had taken Bender less than a month to identify Emma Bonebright as belonging to the third category. It was Mrs. Bonebright, however, who had become the unsettling fly in the ointment of his grand plan. She was something that he had not anticipated, and the situation was growing increasingly complicated for the reverend. Bender was no longer sure which of them was the hunter and which of them the hunted. He was so taken by Emma Bonebright that he eased away from the other members of the third category to the extent he could. The grocer's wife was a woman he had never expected to meet in a place like Keller. She was beautiful, poised, educated, and possessed of a passion Bender had never experienced. Richard Bender could not imagine finding more in any one person. How, he often wondered, did she ever come to marry a man as mild as Charles Bonebright?

Just as Luther Boggs kept his eye on the councilmen, ever alert to their malfeasance, he also began to sense there something was amiss where the preacher Bender was concerned. Nighttime often found Boggs stationed in the shadows, where he could observe the door to the church office. It did not take him long to realize that an inordinate number of the people calling at the reverend's office were women, and Emma Bonebright was his most frequent visitor. Boggs's temples throbbed at the hypocrisy of it all. "There's a whole hell of a lot more sinning going on in that damnable church than there is prayin'. That ridiculous ass Bonebright is nothing but a dammed cuckold," he fumed. It was during one of his nighttime observations that Luther Boggs hit upon an idea. Heretofore, he had been what some in Keller called "the village atheist," openly scorning religion and everything associated with it. Boggs voiced his opinions to anyone willing to listen and, occasionally, to those who weren't. It all seemed so breathtakingly simple to him now. Luther Boggs decided that he would begin attending church.

The following Sunday morning found Luther Boggs dressed in his best and sitting in the front pew as near the pulpit as he could get. When Bender took his position to speak, Boggs' eyes began boring into him with all the venomous intensity he could muster. To Boggs' enormous disappointment, his presence did not appear to make any impression on Bender whatsoever. The effect his ploy had on the deacons however, exceeded Boggs' hopes. Charles Bonebright visibly blanched when he saw Boggs sitting in the front pew, and Horace Schmalle's face became a noticeable shade more pale. Back and forth between the deacons and the pastor went the angry eyes of Luther Boggs. Emma Bonebright had only a passing awareness of Boggs from having seen him in the store. She could not, however, avoid noticing the effect the man's presence had on her husband.

Cyrus Hitchcock sat in a prominent position near the front of the church. He too was startled by the appearance of Luther Boggs but was far too experienced in life to betray any emotion. Although Hitchcock possessed no more faith than did either Bender or Boggs, the banker fully understood how much appearances meant in a small town. The business generated by his church attendance left him well compensated for the time he spent sitting in a pew. Hitchcock knew something about Luther Boggs that few, if any, of the other citizens of Keller knew. Though he chose to live a very simple lifestyle, Luther Boggs was a man of considerable means. He probably wasn't as rich as the banker, but he certainly had enough money to cause real trouble should he ever decide to do so. Hitchcock knew of the substantial sum Boggs had on deposit in his own bank and was reasonably certain that the strange little man had money in several other banks as well. On more than one occasion, Hitchcock gave serious consideration to facilitating a permanent end to the problem of Luther Boggs.

At the conclusion of the service, the Reverend Bender led the deacons in a procession down the aisle as his wife played the piano and the choir sang the recessional. Outside the church door, the pastor and the deacons formed a receiving line, with Bender at its head. Together, they greeted the congregation as they exited, thanking them for attending and wishing blessings upon them for the coming week. Having seated himself in the front row, Boggs was one of the last people to appear before Bender and the deacons. When his turn came, he made an exaggerated display of introducing himself to the pastor. Reverend Bender did not know who Luther Boggs was and appeared to find the exchange perplexing. When Boggs reached Charles Bonebright, he lifted his hat and said grandly, "A very good morning to you, Charles. A lovely day, and lovely service, wasn't it?"

Bonebright found Boggs so unnerving that he feared for a terrifying moment that he might actually lose control of his bladder. For a few terrible seconds, Bonebright struggled to answer Boggs, but the words would not come. Boggs gave Bonebright a wide smile then turned his attention to Horace Schmalle, producing a similar effect on the owner of the newspaper.

Cyrus Hitchcock was not a member of the receiving line, but ever alert to the possibility of new business, he always took time to mingle with the congregation at the conclusion of services. He had, thus far, successfully avoided being appointed a deacon, not wanting to give up any more time to the church than strictly necessary. When Hitchcock saw Luther Boggs approaching, he displayed no alarm. He merely extended his hand and said warmly, "Well, Luther, what a nice surprise to see you here. It's always a wonderful thing when a man sees the light at last."

"Oh, indeed, Cyrus," said Boggs with the faintest trace of sarcasm. "I've well and truly seen the light, and a grand thing it is too." There were very few men in the town of Keller outside of the city council who would dare address the banker by his first name and in a familiar tone. In spite of this, no one in attendance that morning picked up on the fact that Luther Boggs had just done so with impunity and had drawn no rebuke from the banker. "Good day to you, Cyrus, I'll be looking forward to seeing you here again next Sunday."

Hitchcock raised his walking stick and gave Boggs a small salute with its silver knob, smiled, and said, "And a very good day to you as well, Luther. Everyone is welcome here in God's house."

The banker betrayed no emotion as he watched Boggs depart and soon turned his attention back to the other members of the congregation. There may have been no visible signs, but Cyrus Hitchcock scorned nothing the way he scorned a man who could not be bought, and his thoughts regarding Boggs were another matter entirely. "You've done yourself no good this morning, Luther. I know people who know people who know people who can turn your life to pure hell or bring it to a quick end."

Chapter Twelve

The Crucible

During his second winter in Keller, Zebediah spent much of January doing work nearly as difficult as laboring on the docks of New Orleans. Although work around the livery and smithy was typically slow during the coldest part of winter, Zebediah found himself spending long days in the employ of Harley Childers cutting ice on area ponds. "The colder the better" was the rule of thumb for ice harvesting, and the frigid conditions made the work all the more arduous. A cubic foot of ice, as Zebediah soon discovered, weighs over sixty pounds, and most of the blocks they cut weighed a hundred pounds or more. Together, the freighter and Zebediah sawed out blocks of ice then used long tongs to extract them with from the water. Once the blocks were clear of the water, they were loaded in Childers' heavy wagon. When the wagon was filled, they threw the buffalo robe over their knees and hauled the ice back to Keller. The task of storing the blocks in the ice houses was equally hard work. They stacked the heavy blocks, keeping a thick layer of sawdust between the blocks on all sides. Bonebright's ice house involved the most work, as it was large and sat a full story below ground.

Childers explained to Zebediah that he had always done the ice cutting on his own, but as he was growing older, he appreciated Zebediah's help greatly. "Freighting always falls off in winter, and I suppose I could turn the ice business over to somebody else and just spend my days playing cribbage and drinking coffee with Emily Kellogg, but I need to keep busy. It's got to be cold enough for me to worry about the horses before I stay indoors." Childers paused a moment then added with a sly chuckle, "At least you're learnin' where the fishin' holes are, Zeb."

"It's been plenty cold enough for me, Mr. Harley." Zebediah laughed. "The best winter I ever had was down in Nawlins, at least as far as the cold goes."

"Why didn't ya go back?" asked Childers.

"It's a long way to travel, and not all my memories of Nawlins are good ones," said Zebediah, sensing that he had perhaps said too much. Zebediah had always been reluctant to reveal too much of himself to his employers, preferring instead to do good work and avoid situations that might prove awkward. There was something about Harley Childers' quiet honesty, however, that moved Zebediah to relate the story of his winter in New Orleans. Zebediah's voice was growing thick with emotion as he completed telling Childers the story of D's murder. Zebediah did not tell Childers about how he had been asked to seek out the Deacon or how he made his departure from New Orleans.

Harley Childers listened quietly as Zebediah told his story then, after several seconds, said in his deep, rumbling voice, "That's a hell of a thing, Zebediah. A hell of a thing." For several minutes, the only sounds were the crunch of the wagon wheels on snow and the plodding of the horses. Neither man spoke until at last Childers said, "Zeb, I hope we never see anything like that happen in Keller." After another long pause, the freighter cocked his head toward Zebediah and said with a wry smile, "Zeb, if you can manage to overlook Karl Emmett's bad habits, we're glad to have ya here."

Childers' words had their desired effect, and the somber mood on the wagon seat lifted considerably. "Oh, I get along with Mr. Emmett jus' fine, Mr. Harley. Him and his missus have been real good to me."

"Even though the man cheats at cribbage?" growled Childers, eying Zebediah suspiciously. As usual, when he found himself caught in the middle of his endlessly jesting employers, Zebediah did not know if he should laugh or not, so he merely smiled sheepishly at Childers. At last the freighter chuckled and said, "Don't be tellin' Karl I said that, Zebediah. One of these days, he might take me serious, then I'd have to find somebody else to play cards with."

The ice harvesting lasted most of January. Though the cold weather was holding, the season ended when the ice houses were full. The new hotel and saloon purchased a full week's worth of their ice cutting efforts, leading Childers to remark, "This has been the best winter for ice I ever had. I keep hearin' stories about mechanical machines they have nowadays that can make ice any time of year. I'd kinda' hate to see it, though. It would sure take a bite out of my wintertime earnin's."

As winter was turning to spring that year, Charles Bonebright sat alone in his study, attempting, with little success, to read a newspaper. He looked out at the darkness beyond the window, lost in thought as the gaslight softly hissed above his head. There had already been two visits to the wall safe on this evening, and he was contemplating a third. daughters were in bed and Emma was visiting the Reverend Bender for spiritual counseling yet again. In the darkest recess of his mind, Bonebright was beginning to understand that spiritual counseling was not the thing his wife was seeking from the Richard Bender. He may have known it at some level, but he could not bring himself to truly think about it, and he certainly couldn't bring himself to speak to Emma about it. Bonebright had felt trapped for a long time but never like this. He was being squeezed in the iron grip of the sheriff and the moonshiners, and now his wife was rapidly slipping away from him. As he had done when he failed to spot Clyde Goodwin's game in time, Bonebright again cursed himself. "How could I have been so stupid?" he asked himself again and again. The deeper Bonebright descended into the morass of his mind, the more desperate his thoughts became.

"This could all be over in a minute," Bonebright thought sadly as his eyes began tearing. "If I was just man enough to walk out to the back yard and pull the trigger, none of this would matter anymore. The girls are young and they would soon get over it. It would for damn sure visit a punishment on Emma," he thought bitterly. Simply thinking of his wife sent new waves of shame, guilt, and anger cursing through Bonebright. "It would serve her right," thought Bonebright, allowing himself to wallow ever deeper in self-pity. "It's obvious that she doesn't care about me anymore . . . if she ever did. Why in hell did the woman ever marry me in the first place? Don't her vows mean anything to her? Doesn't she care about our daughters and our position in the community?" For several long, agonizing seconds, the violent and angry thoughts racing through Charles Bonebright's mind brought him near to paralysis. Thoughts that he could never have imagined himself having but a few short months ago. "Maybe I should clean out my bank account, buy a case of whiskey, and just head on out of town." Bonebright paused a moment, smiling slightly and laughing inwardly, as he allowed himself to dream of the freedom his last idea conjured up. "I could leave on a sugar night and just keep on going. By morning, I'd be long gone."

Bonebright rose from his chair and made his way to the wall safe. As he was dialing the combination and anticipating a hard pull on the whiskey bottle, the idea of leaving that he had quickly dismissed a moment earlier came back to him in a flash of clarity. Bonebright paused then slowly replaced the books that concealed the safe. He returned to his chair and, for the first time in a long while, found himself thinking clearly. Running away might be seen as cowardly but not surely as bad as taking one's own life. Then again, if he was going to leave and never return, or kill himself for that matter, why the hell worry about what anyone thought of him? Bonebright quickly realized that he couldn't just walk into the bank and withdraw all his money. Hitchcock simply wouldn't let him have it. "Cyrus is a cagey bastard," thought Bonebright with a mixture of respect and disgust. "He would immediately call the mortgage on the store, and then he'd have me. No," thought Bonebright, "leaving town is something that might actually work, but only if it's been properly planned out. People can think whatever the hell they want about me once I'm gone."

Charles Bonebright was lying in bed, feigning sleep, when his wife joined him. He did nothing to let her know he was aware of her presence. That night, for the first time in many weeks, Bonebright managed to sleep soundly. He rose in the morning, refreshed and with a sense of purpose. His only fear was that his wife might detect his improved mood and begin questioning him. Bonebright resolved to keep his emotions firmly in check. Later that morning, when he was safely in his office, the grocer began auditing his own books in an effort to determine just how much he could skim from his bank deposits without arousing the attention of Cyrus Hitchcock. He would start small, a dollar here and a dollar there. As time went by, he would gradually increase what he withheld from his deposits, and by cutting back on his own spending, Bonebright calculated that in no more than a year, he could be ready to leave. While a year might seem a long time to wait, he did not want to make his departure with inadequate funds. No, he would need sufficient money to live for at least six months. If it took a year to embezzle that much money from himself, then so be it. Charles Bonebright was now a man with a goal, and if he had failed to devote enough thought to other decisions in his life, he would not make that mistake this time. There was an end to his torment waiting in the distance, and knowing the end was achievable would sustain him in the months to come.

Luther Boggs was not a man to second-guess himself, but he was now in a quandary. He had grown weary of attending church, and the effect he had once exerted on Bonebright and the others had diminished considerably. "The bastards are just laughing at me under their breath now," thought Boggs bitterly. If he simply quit attending church, it would be an admission of defeat on his part, and that would only result in more laughter. If there was going to be any ridicule handed out, Luther Boggs had no intention of being on the receiving end of it. He searched his brain, trying to come up with a new tactic that might expose the hypocrisy of the town's leading citizens and settle a few scores along the way. Boggs briefly flirted with the idea of opening a second newspaper in Keller, one that he would fund entirely with his own money without having to placate the sensibilities of advertisers. "A free press! Ha! What a dammed joke!" fumed Boggs. "That sniveling weasel Horace Schmalle won't print a dammed thing that might cost him ten cents' worth of advertising."

He found the idea of opening a newspaper intriguing but, after considering the idea for a few minutes, decided against actually doing it. Boggs quickly realized he would be unable to do all the work himself, and he found the idea of having to hire someone too abhorrent to contemplate. He thought about taking a trip somewhere and getting away from Keller and its problems for a while, but he had no real desire to travel. Then, it occurred to him that if he did go visit a larger city, perhaps the capital, he could make arrangements with a printer. Once he had a printer lined up, he could send them what he wanted to have printed up, and they could ship back the handbills he would then distribute. "I can afford that, and it might actually work," thought Boggs. "That bastard Goodwin would figure it out soon enough though, and I wouldn't put it past the son of a bitch to just drag me off somewhere and shoot me in the head." Luther Boggs did not scare easily but, he knew that Clyde Goodwin didn't scare at all.

Of all the people Luther Boggs despised, Clyde Goodwin was near the top of his list. For the most part, Boggs understood people very well, but he could never quite mange to understand Goodwin. Some part of the man just seemed to be missing. Mostly, Boggs could not understand how the people of Keller could elect then keep reelecting a sheriff who was such an obvious criminal himself. "These sanctimonious hypocrite bastards just don't seem to care about the graft," muttered Boggs. "As long as the top dogs are getting their share of the loot, then everything's fine and dandy, but let some poor man's kid pull a prank on one of them, and these sons of bitches are ready to cart him straight off to the penitentiary. Clyde Goodwin will be right there to do their dirty work for them. Let that bastard Cyrus Hitchcock steal a satchel full of money from some poor farmer, and Goodwin will be there to run the farmer out of the county. When all these sorry fools dress up and parade around for each other on Sunday morning, Clyde Goodwin will be right there, keeping an eye on things." Boggs felt his temples begin to throb, and his chest was pounding as thoughts of Keller's hypocrisy flooded his mind.

When Zebediah was in his second year in Keller, Theresa Bender was entering the third year of her marriage. It was a marriage that was leaving her feeling increasingly isolated and confused. Richard rarely shared her bed these days, and she was missing that aspect of her marriage terribly. As she again sat alone in the parsonage, awaiting his return, Theresa found herself in the throes of emotions that left her filled with confusion and guilt. Was it wrong for a married woman to want her husband at home and in their bed? Richard was at his office for yet another counseling session with a congregant. These sessions had occurred no more that twice a month in the beginning of their time in Keller, but now he was holding as many as three a week. In her heart of hearts, she suspected the truth of the matter but could not bring herself to face it.

Even though some citizens might think it unseemly for a pastor's wife to be seen walking unescorted on the darkened sidewalks of Keller, Theresa felt absolutely compelled to get outside and walk. So great was her anxiety that she simply could not remain sitting still. She stepped out on to the front porch and, seeing no reason to lock the door, descended to the sidewalk. Theresa sat off with no destination in mind, mere movement being her pressing need. A half block from her home, she decided that a walk around the block would be sufficient. However, when she returned to her door, she found that she had no desire to return inside. She paused a moment in front of her house, drinking in the sounds of a summer evening. After a moment's consideration, she crossed the street with the intention of walking around that block as well. The church stood on the block across the street. It occurred to her that being seen walking in the vicinity of the church, alone at night, might look doubly strange to any congregant witnessing it. Had Theresa Bender been in a less emotional frame of mind, she would have certainly thought better of it. As it was, she could not have cared less how anything looked or what anyone thought.

Theresa crossed the street and turned to her left, setting a course away from the church. As she continued to walk, she felt some of the tension began to ease. She rounded one corner then another and was walking on the back side of the church when Luther Boggs saw her approaching in the distance. In the dim light, Boggs was uncertain who the approaching person was other than the person was wearing a dress. Not wanting to give a fright, Boggs stepped out of the shadows and onto the sidewalk. began walking in her direction, reasonably sure that the woman walking toward him had not seen him emerge from his hiding place. Luther set a jaunty pace, hoping that the impending meeting would seem entirely normal. As the woman drew closer, Boggs' heart skipped a beat when he realized it was Theresa Bender. Boggs thought quickly and approached Theresa with the air of a man simply out to enjoy his evening constitutional. When they drew near, Boggs stopped, tipped his hat, and said, "A very good evening to you, ma'am. It's Mrs. Bender I think."

Theresa recognized Boggs and found his voice so friendly that she felt no alarm. "Good evening, sir. Yes, I'm Theresa Bender. I believe you're Mr. Boggs, aren't you?"

"Yes, indeed, ma'am. Luther Boggs at your service. A truly lovely evening to be out for a walk, isn't it, ma'am?" It suddenly occurred to Boggs that if he could engage Mrs. Bender in conversation for a few minutes, he might possibly spare her the pain of observing Emma Bonebright leaving her husband's office.

"Oh, it's a very lovely evening, Mr. Boggs. I found it much too nice to stay cooped up inside," said Theresa.

Boggs paused thoughtfully then asked, "If I might be so bold as to ask, ma'am, now that you've lived here in Keller for a bit, how are you liking our little community?" The contempt Luther Boggs felt for hypocrites and fools was equaled by his compassion for their victims.

Boggs definitely felt Theresa Bender was an innocent victim of her husband's hypocrisy.

Theresa was momentarily taken aback by Boggs' question but responded a moment later, "We have found Keller to be a very welcoming community, Mr. Boggs, and we are feeling very much at home here." Her words were not an accurate reflection of her inner turmoil. Had she been truthful, Theresa Bender would have told Boggs that at that moment, she would prefer to be almost anywhere but Keller.

"Oh, it pleases me greatly to hear that," said Boggs warmly. "My own late father was one of the early settlers hereabouts, and he had much to do with getting the town platted, organized, and on the map, so to speak. It would please him, to no end, to hear that a newcomer was finding the town he helped start to their liking."

"I take it that your father was one of the early homesteaders, Mr. Boggs?"

"Homesteading was but one of the things my father did after emigrating from Ireland," said Boggs. "In addition to his farming, he dabbled in a number of businesses over his lifetime, with a good deal more success than failure. Mostly, he was fortunate enough to have picked up a number of building lots for a song that later turned out to be highly desired properties. That was the thing that afforded me an education at Harvard College."

"Oh my goodness, Mr. Boggs," said Theresa with surprise and laughing warmly, "I certainly did not expect to encounter a Harvard man on my stroll this evening. I too attended school in Boston, and I've had occasion to meet a number of Harvard students."

"Well, ma'am, you know what they say about Harvard men, don't you?" asked Boggs mischievously.

Theresa had been totally disarmed by Luther Boggs' charm and responded with a smile, "I'm afraid you have me at a disadvantage, Mr. Boggs."

"Well, ma'am," said Boggs, pausing for effect, "You can always tell a Harvard man, but you can't tell him much." Boggs laughed with genuine self-deprecating humor, and Theresa Bender laughed along with him. "I won't be taking up any more of your time, ma'am," said Boggs graciously, tipping his hat again. "I'll be off now. A very good evening to you, missus," said Boggs. As Boggs walked away, he desperately hoped he had bought enough time to spare Theresa Bender from heartbreak.

Theresa's spirits had been lifted considerably by her conversation with Luther Boggs. In this improved state of mind, she wondered why such a pleasant little man seemed to have such a disturbing effect on so many others in the congregation. "I guess it's just one more of the many things I do not understand about the human condition," she thought as she continued past the church. Theresa was softly humming to herself when she saw the light from her husband's office door as it opened. Then, she saw Emma Bonebright emerge and turn back to face her husband. It was very dark, but the light from the open door was sufficient to see the looks on both their faces. In an instant, Theresa understood everything. In the space of one horrifying second, she understood her husband down to the last detail. How long she stood in that spot, frozen by her anguish, she could not have said. It was not until well after Mrs. Bonebright departed and her husband returned inside his office that Theresa found the strength to move.

She next found herself in her bedroom, unable to recall a single detail of the walk home. Theresa Bender's nervous system was a raging electrical storm, and she felt as if she was only lightly tethered to reality, dangling above the abyss of blind panic. At that awful, wrenching moment, Theresa desperately wished she had her father there to guide her. She wished, just as desperately, that she had someone, anyone, to turn to, but she had no such person in Keller. Never in all her long, lonely childhood had she felt so alone. Using every ounce of her strength, she fought back against the panic. When at last her nerves had calmed sufficiently, she reached the decision to spend the night in the hotel. She would telegraph her father in the morning and leave Keller on the first available train. Theresa retrieved her small travel bag from the top shelf of her closet and quickly began packing the things she would need for the night. As she was buckling the case closed, her husband entered the room.

"Theresa? What on earth are you doing?" asked Richard, alarmed by what he saw.

Theresa stared at her husband blankly and struggled to speak, but the words refused to come.

"Are you going somewhere, Theresa? Whatever is the matter?"

When Theresa found her voice at last, the words came in a raging torrent. "I know what you've been doing, Richard!" she hissed. "I saw Emma Bonebright leaving your office! You made love to her! I know you did! You've been cheating on me since the beginning, haven't you, Richard? It's all been a lie, hasn't it? Just one horrible lie on top of another. 've made a fool of me Richard and now my father will ruin you!" cried Theresa, in a voice that was not her own. Her body was quaking in rage, her eyes were red, and tears were flowing freely.

Richard Bender did not think that his mild wife was capable of such rage and, thinking quickly, tried in vain to calm her. "Theresa, it isn't what you think."

"Liar!" screamed Theresa all the louder. "You're a filthy liar, Richard! I'm leaving this house, I'm leaving you, and you're going to answer for what you've done!" Theresa's eyes were wild; she was gasping for breath and convulsing with rage.

Bender advanced toward his wife and made an effort to place his hands on her shoulders, "Theresa, darling, you're making a terrible mistake here. Please try to calm down so we can talk about this."

"Stay away from me! Don't touch me!" she screamed, jumping back away from her husband.

"My dear, we have to talk about this," pleaded Bender, sensing for the first time that this was a problem that would not be easily resolved.

"I am not your dear, and I was never your dear! You are a liar and a bastard!" screamed Theresa louder than ever.

"Please calm down, Theresa, the whole town is going to hear you!" said Bender sharply.

"I damned well hope they do hear me!" she screamed. "I'm going to make sure everyone in this miserable town knows what you've been up to with your whore, Richard!" Theresa spoke with a ferocity she would have thought impossible only a few hours earlier. She gathered up her bag and attempted to walk around her husband, who refused to let her pass. Theresa backed away slightly and said in a more even voice, "Have you not one shred of decency left, Richard? Let me pass."

"Think about what you're doing to me, Theresa."

"Doing to you?" she asked incredulously. "Doing to you, Richard? You go whoring and you dare ask what I'm doing to you?" She paused, her reddened eyes boring into Bender, then said, "Let me pass, Richard."

Richard Bender was not easily moved to panic, but he knew his whole life was now hanging in the balance of what happened next, and it filled him with cold dread. "Theresa, I beg of you, please reconsider. Try and be sensible. You've not even given me a chance to explain myself. It isn't what you think."

"And now you're going to tell me what I think, Richard?" she asked venomously.

"You've jumped to a conclusion, Theresa. A false conclusion. Everything can be explained," said Bender.

Theresa's inner strength began to assert itself, and with remarkable calmness under the circumstances, she said, "Oh yes, Richard. You always have an explanation, don't you? I've no doubt you could explain everything, and I'm equally certain there would not be a word of truth in it. I am not the fool you evidently think I am, Richard. Our marriage is over, now step aside and let me pass."

"I can't allow that," said Bender in a cold, hard voice.

She had been angry, but now the cold, empty look in her husband's eyes began to frighten Theresa. She took another step toward the door, and again, he blocked her path. "Richard, please let me pass," she said, her voice weakening.

"We will talk about this or not, but one way or another, you are not leaving this house tonight," said Bender with icy finality.

"You would raise your hand to me?" asked Theresa incredulously.

Bender eyed his wife intensely for several seconds before saying coldly, "If that's what it will take, Theresa. It's entirely up to you."

They stood with their eyes locked for a long, frightening moment until Theresa said weakly, "You are a deceitful man, Richard, but I do not think you are so evil that you would harm me. Now step aside, and let me pass." Even as she uttered the words, her rage was spent and she felt her strength deserting her. She made one more feeble attempt to step past her husband, and as she did so, Bender grabbed her by the upper arms and threw her violently back across the room. The edge of the bed caught her at the waist, causing her body to bend painfully backward. Theresa fell to the floor beside the bed, dazed and in pain. She was staring up at her husband in bewilderment as he brought a heavy lamp crashing down over her head. In an instant, Theresa Bender felt no more.

Bender was perspiring and breathing heavily, stunned to immobility by the thing he had just done. He had allowed himself to lose control, and he had lost it completely. His sudden, violent outburst was not the thing he planned. When Theresa made her last attempt to leave, visions of Emma Bonebright flashed before his eyes, and Richard Bender's reason deserted him. He simply could not allow his meek little mouse of a wife to destroy him. The stark reality of what lay before him left no doubt in Bender's mind that he had just acted very foolishly. Though he had acted foolishly, Richard Bender was no fool. Quickly, by sheer force of will, he regained control of his emotions and his mind. When the panic subsided, Bender realized there existed a narrow window of time to formulate a plan and that the rest of his life depended on how well that plan could be executed. In less than a minute, all his emotion vanished, and Bender again became the cold, calculating person he was.

He looked closely at his wife's lifeless body and saw that although she had bled from the scalp, the blood had not reached the floor. He removed his jacket and then stripped to the waist. Bender jerked back the coverlet then carefully picked up Theresa's body and positioned it on the bed. He gathered up the broken shards of the murder weapon and scattered them alongside his wife's head then placed the broken lamp where it looked as if it had naturally fallen. Lastly, he began systematically tearing his wife's clothing with his bare hands. He took special care, tearing her undergarments, then partially removed them. Next, he unpacked Theresa's traveling case and returned her things to their proper places. After storing the travel bag in the closet, Bender stood back and gave every detail of the room a careful inspection. When he was satisfied with what he saw, he went into the bathroom and carefully washed his hands and face, making sure that no trace of blood or other incriminating evidence clung to his hands.

After washing, Bender put the dampened towel in the laundry hamper beneath other soiled linen, then he hung a clean, dry towel near the sink. He redressed, being careful to be correct in his appearance. He wanted to look like a respectable minister who had come home from the church to find his wife murdered. Bender made one more inspection of the murder scene and then inspected the rest of the house, making sure the back door was unlocked. No more than twenty minutes elapsed between Theresa's murder and the moment Richard Bender embarked on what he knew had to be the best performance of his life. He stood in the front parlor, focused his mind, and steeled himself for what he had to do next. When he was ready, Bender charged across the room, nearly knocking the front door off its hinges as he burst through to the outside. He ran down the street in the direction of Main Street, yelling, *"Murder! Murder!* There has been a murder at my house!" Bender screamed out the words, filling his voice with anguish. Everything he ever learned about delivering a sermon was brought to bear as he ran in the direction of the sheriff's office. His performance began working as he had hoped. All along the street, lights began coming on. People began emerging from their houses and calling out to Bender, asking what had happened.

"It's my wife," cried Bender in the most pleading tone of voice he could manage. "She's been murdered in our bed."

As if a massive electric shock had been delivered to the town of Keller, people began swarming out of their homes, and Bender soon met Clyde Goodwin coming on the run from the opposite direction. Goodwin had been making his rounds and came quickly when he heard the commotion from two blocks away. A mass of people quickly formed around Bender, and Goodwin had to elbow his way through to him.

Struggling for quiet, Goodwin fired his pistol in the air, shocking the crowd to silence. Goodwin then demanded of Bender, "Now, what the hell's going on, Reverend?"

Calling on all his talents, Bender began executing the second part of his plan. Doing everything in his power to make his voice as distraught as possible, Bender said in a breaking voice, "It's my wife, Sheriff! My wife has been murdered, and I saw that colored man, Zebediah, running from my house!"

"You saw Karl Emmett's hired man running from your house?" asked Goodwin calmly.

"He's the only colored man in Keller," said Bender.

Goodwin turned his attention to the crowd and said loudly, "All right! All you people go home!" When the crowd failed to immediately disperse, Goodwin again drew his weapon and, holding it for all to see, yelled, "I said, GO HOME, NOW!" The sheriff's sharp words and the display of the .44 moved the mob to silence, and they began backing slowly away. Goodwin turned to Bender and said, "Come on, Reverend, I need to see what happened."

Bender led Goodwin back to the parsonage. Even though the sheriff had ordered the crowd to disperse, a number of people began following them at a distance. entered the parsonage and Bender led Goodwin up to the bedroom where Theresa's body lay. Goodwin ordered Bender to wait outside the door while he entered alone and began to inspect the room. Goodwin studied the crime scene, Bender came as close as he ever did to actually praying. The irony of praying that his dreadful crime not be exposed was not lost on the reverend.

Goodwin spent several minutes studying the crime scene then asked Bender, "Is this how you found her? Did you move anything?"

"I touched her face, that was all" said Bender, "Then I ran to find you."

Goodwin eyed Bender as if he didn't quite believe the story then asked, "Where were you when this happened?"

"I was in my office at the church," said Bender.

"Can anybody confirm that?" asked Goodwin suspiciously.

"Yes. Emma Bonebright was visiting me for spiritual counseling." Bender had not wanted to bring Emma into the situation if he could avoid it, but if his survival depended on it, then it had to be done.

A look of derision flashed briefly across the sheriff's face before he asked, "She can testify to this?"

"Yes."

"You say you saw that colored man who works for Karl Emmett running from your house? How'd you happen to see that?"

Bender fervently hoped his acting abilities would yet save the day because he rightfully felt that the sheriff was not quite believing his story. Bender's pulse was pounding in his ears as he said, "I returned home from the church, and when I realized that I had forgotten my house key, I rang the bell that Theresa might come and let me in. A moment later I heard the back door slam and when I went around to check, I saw that colored man running away."

Before the sheriff could ask any additional questions they were joined in the room by the town's physician, Dr. Witherspoon. "Sheriff Goodwin, Reverend Bender, I came as soon as I heard," said the doctor, moving to where Theresa Bender's body lie. The doctor held his fingers to Theresa's neck then placed his stethoscope to her chest. After a moment, the doctor shook his head sadly and said, "She's gone, I'm afraid. My condolences, Reverend Bender."

"Any idea how long, Doc?" asked Goodwin.

The doctor carefully felt Theresa's skin and, after a moment, said, "Not long. No more than a half hour."

Bender struggled to suppress his growing panic, hoping against hope that he could maintain the appropriate outward appearance. He wanted to be the grief-stricken husband while desperately hoping that Clyde Goodwin did not inspect the time line of events too carefully. He needn't have worried. Goodwin had no more concern for Theresa Bender than he had for anyone else. If her husband wanted to blame the colored man, then that would just make his job easier.

Goodwin turned to the doctor and said, "Doc, I'm going to leave you in charge here. Get your coroner's report to me when you can." Turning back to Bender, he said, "Reverend, I need you to come down to the office with me so I can get your statement written up."

When Bender and Goodwin emerged from the parsonage, they were greeted by a large crowd, gathered in front of the house. Goodwin's hand went to the grip of his revolver. He lifted his left arm and, pointing at the crowed, called out sharply, "I told you people to disperse, *and I meant it!* This crime is going to be lawfully investigated and I'm not going to tolerate a mob!" The ferocity of Goodwin's words quieted the crowd, but they did not move.

A young man cradling a shotgun in his arms edged his way to the front of the crowd, postured aggressively before the sheriff, and asked belligerently, "You gonna tell us what the hell is going on here, Sheriff, or do we need to figure it out for ourselves?"

In an instant, Clyde Goodwin was down the steps of the parsonage with his weapon drawn. Using his free hand, he snatched the shotgun away from the young man, threw it to the ground, and placed the muzzle of the deadly .44 directly against his antagonist's forehead. Then, as calmly as he might ask a fellow diner to pass the sugar, Goodwin asked, "Any more questions, Billy? Come on, boy, speak up! Cat got yer tongue?"

"No, sir," said the boy in a weak and trembling voice, "No more questions."

"That's good, Billy. That's real good. Now, turn around and put yer hands behind your back. You're under arrest." As Goodwin handcuffed the young man, an angry murmur began rising from the crowd that had been stunned to silence by the sheriff's swift action. Completely unfazed, Goodwin placed his hand back on the grip of his revolver, turned to the mob, and said, "If anyone else shows me a weapon, I'll return fire in a heartbeat." Goodwin paused, allowing his words to sink in, then said with cold determination, "This the only warning you're gonna get, people! Now, GO HOME!" barked Goodwin loudly. There was not an individual in the crowd who did not take Clyde Goodwin's threat to shoot seriously.

Ever so slowly, the crowd in front of the parsonage began dispersing. Goodwin, Bender, and the prisoner did not move until everyone was well away from the house. "Come along, Billy, I'm thinkin' your pa's gonna be real proud of you before the night's over," said Goodwin, giving the prisoner a rude shove in the direction of downtown. Goodwin suspected correctly that the boy's father would easily part with a hundred dollars to keep his son out of prison. "Would you mind carrying the boy's shotgun for me, Reverend?" asked Goodwin. "I need to keep my hands free. Break open the breach and unload it first."

Bender broke open the shotgun and ejected the shells. It was the first time he had held a firearm in his hands since leaving the farm for the seminary. The thing felt odd and alien in his hands. In spite of now having committed two murders, Bender did not consider himself to be a violent man. The trio walked to the sheriff's office in silence, with Goodwin periodically turning around to scan the street for followers. inside the sheriff's office, Goodwin locked the front door behind them then escorted the now-very-penitent young man to a cell in the back room. When Goodwin returned to the front office, he found Bender sitting in a chair across from his desk. Goodwin seated himself and, after removing his hat, turned his attention to Bender, eying him coolly.

The ensuing pause lasted a very long time for Richard Bender. last, Goodwin said in a skeptical tone, "I have to tell you Reverend, I'm having a little trouble believin' your story. It just don't seem to add up. I've never seen that boy Zebediah do anything but work his tail off since he came to Keller. He's never caused any trouble for anybody, and believe me, Reverend, I kept my eye on him for a long time after he showed up in town."

Bender's insides went stone cold, and he knew, beyond a doubt, that he must play his cards with extreme caution. "I've told you the truth, Sheriff. I give you my word as a man of the cloth."

Goodwin snickered derisively and said, "That's rich, preacher man." Goodwin leaned back in his chair, crossing his arms in front of him. Another uncomfortable silence ensued as the sheriff's eyes bored into Bender. The minister's heart was pounding by the time Goodwin said, "You've got some brass, I'll hand you that. There's plenty of people in this town willin' to buy what you're sellin', preacher man, but I ain't one of 'em."

Richard Bender had never felt the kind of fear he felt at this moment. Visions of a hangman's noose danced before his eyes as he struggle to gain control of the conversation. Playing the last cards he held, Bender said aggressively, "I am a man of God, sir!" Bender felt that he was losing the game as he struggled to gain control of the conversation and bluster his way out of the predicament.

Goodwin paused then gave another derisive snort before responding, "Yeah, Reverend, me too." The look on Bender's face told Goodwin that he had just won the exchange, and now was the moment to press his advantage home. Goodwin waited before saying another word, letting the fear dominate Bender's mind. The only sound in the room was the pendulum clock on the wall above the sheriff's head and the hiss of the gaslight. When he felt the moment was right, Goodwin asked quietly, "Just how bad do you want me to believe that colored man killed your wife, Reverend?" Goodwin spoke in a tone calculated to give Bender a modicum of hope.

"I expect you to believe it because it's the truth," said Bender, defensively.

Goodwin displayed no emotion as he continued to stare directly into Bender's eyes. Finally, the sheriff smiled slightly and said, "Well Reverend, if that's your story then I've got to get a telegram sent off yet tonight to the attorney general's office at the capital. They'll have some men here by tomorrow that have a whole lot more experience investigating murders than I do. Nothin' gets past 'em, from what I hear." Goodwin's words were delivered flatly and without emotion, but they cut straight through what remained of Bender's poise nonetheless.

"Is there nothing we can do?" asked Bender weakly.

Again Goodwin paused then said calmly, "Oh, there's always things we can do preacher man but you're running out of options and by tomorrow afternoon, your options are gonna be plumb gone." Bender sputtered, but before he could respond, Goodwin raised his hand to silence him and continued, "I had you pegged as a player two days after you showed up here, preacher man. You might be able to get Emma Bonebright into your bed, but you ain't a poker player." Goodwin gave his words some time to sink in then said, "This is what I'm thinkin', preacher man . . . I'm thinkin' that you, bein' what you are, have probably been skimming a little off your collections right along. I'm right, ain't I?"

The sheriff was right. Goodwin had Bender completely trapped, and Bender was now fighting a losing battle against panic. He was bigger and probably stronger than the sheriff. Could he overpower him and make a run for it? After seeing how Goodwin handled himself at the parsonage, Bender considered that to be a dicey proposition at best. Bender fought to keep control of his mind and his emotions. At last he said, "And if that's right, what of it?"

"How much do you have stashed away preacher man?" asked Goodwin in a cold, hard voice.

Bender hung his head and after a moment, sighed heavily and said, "Nearly five hundred dollars. Mostly coins and dollar bills."

Goodwin's eyes continued to bore into Bender until he laughed out loud and said, "Like I said preacher man, you ain't a poker player and now ain't the time to start learnin'. I'm thinkin' you probably have at least twice that amount, and that, preacher man, is what having me go arrest that boy Zebediah is gonna cost you. A thousand dollars sounds like a reasonable price to avoid hanging, don't ya think, preacher man?"

Goodwin uttered the words *preacher man* in a mocking and sarcastic tone. "You've got a half hour before I send the telegram" was all Goodwin said.

Bender knew he was beaten and said no more. He rose and left to retrieve the locked box hidden in his office. When Bender was a block away from his office, he heard the church bell begin ringing wildly, and then he saw a glow coming from the direction of Karl Emmett's livery. Then the words *"Fire! Fire! The livery's on fire!"* rang through the streets of Keller.

After Goodwin, Bender, and the prisoner Billy left the parsonage, the doctor had been joined at the crime scene by the undertaker, Bradshaw. As the two men were preparing to remove Theresa's Bender's body, the doctor told the undertaker, in confidence, that Bender claimed to have seen Karl Emmett's hired man, Zebediah, running from the house. While Bradshaw's discretion could be relied on, his assistant's could not, and the doctor's remarks were overheard from outside the bedroom. By the time Theresa's body had been moved to the funeral parlor, the story of Zebediah's flight from the parsonage had reached nearly every available ear in Keller.

While Goodwin questioned Bender at the sheriff's office, the mob he had so bravely faced down quickly reformed upon hearing of the accusations against Zebediah. The mob that Goodwin had been able to silence earlier quickly grew into something beyond the sheriff's control. As the swarm of people began moving in the direction of the livery, torches appeared, and a loud roar rose from dozens of people enraged by the murder of the pastor's wife. Karl Emmett was roused by the sounds of the approaching mob and came out of his house, clad only in his night shirt, demanding an explanation. The mob paid the blacksmith no attention and rushed on past him. Someone broke through the door of the smithy, and men began pouring inside, searching for the route up to Zebediah's room. A moment after, Zebediah was awakened by the sounds of his door bursting open, and another moment later, he was set upon and pummeled by a mass of men. The dreadful beating they administered mercifully caused

Zebediah to lose consciousness almost immediately. At some point during the melee, the smithy was set afire.

When he regained consciousness, Zebediah found himself in a jail cell, bandaged and bloody. What he would never learn was that it was only through the heroic efforts of his two employers that he lived to see another sunrise. Harley Childers was playing cribbage with Emily Kellogg when he heard the commotion. There was something about the sounds that led the freighter to grab his ten gauge before rushing to investigate. When Childers saw the mob in front of the smithy, he discharged both barrels of the shotgun into the air. Not taking his eyes from the mob, Childers reloaded in seconds then leveled the weapon at the crowd. The deafening roar of the big shotgun was enough to stop the mob long enough for Karl Emmett to wade into the crowd. The blacksmith's huge arms and fists cut a swath through the people as he made his way to where the rioters had dragged Zebediah's unconscious body. Childers and Emmett were soon joined in the middle of the mob by Clyde Goodwin, who had been trailing Bender in the event the reverend attempted to flee. The mob was now looking into the barrels of Goodwin's .44 and Childers' double-barreled ten gauge as the two men stood back-to-back. An uneasy peace ensued, and then the flames began spreading from the smithy to the barn.

As the flames grew, Childers handed the shotgun over to Karl Emmett then, risking his life, raced into the burning barn. Childers knew that once the flames spread to the haymow, the whole structure would erupt in seconds. The freighter groped his way through the dark barn, freeing horses and mules from certain death, managing to get out the back door only seconds before the entire structure was engulfed. The lynch mob, Zebediah's battered body, and horses mad with fear, were all illuminated by the inferno that had been Karl Emmett's livery stable. This hellish scene would scar the town of Keller for a generation. From the shadows, a block away, Richard Bender watched as the livery stable blazed, and smiled. He bore Karl Emmett no ill will, but this turn of events had just saved him a thousand dollars. For all practical purposes, the town of Keller had already convicted

Zebediah, and now, there would be no need to pay off Clyde Goodwin. Bender had little doubt that the sheriff would likely try to extract revenge at some point, but that possibility had now been deferred to a later day.

Slowly, ever so slowly, the mob began moving back and away from the fire. After returning the shotgun to Childers, Karl Emmett could only hold his wife's hand and stare mutely at the flaming rubble that had been his business. Harley Childers kept his attention focused on the lingering crowd, his shotgun cocked and leveled until at last, only the Emmett's, Childers, Sheriff Goodwin, and Zebediah remained at the scene. Childers handed the ten gauge back to the blacksmith and began searching through the rubble for a board they might use as a litter to carry Zebediah. When he found one that would serve the purpose, he helped Emmett ease the still unconscious Zebediah on to the wide board, and together, they began carrying him to the sheriff's office. None of the men said a word during the walk to the jail. They all knew Zebediah was innocent, and all three men knew how things were going to play out. Emmett and Childers carried Zebediah on through to the cell block then lowered him to the floor.

"I'm gonna go find the doc," said the freighter, turning for the door.

"That would be a waste of time, Mr. Childers," said Clyde Goodwin coldly.

Harley Childers turned back to the sheriff abruptly, stared at Goodwin incredulously, then asked, "You aim to just leave him lyin' there?"

"I don't see any reason to waste the county's money on a man that's gonna hang in a few days anyway," said Goodwin with indifference.

"You know damn well Zebediah didn't kill anybody, Sheriff," growled Childers.

"Do I?" asked Goodwin archly. "The victim's husband made a sworn statement, testifying that this man lying here killed his wife."

"I'll pay for Zebediah's treatment, and his lawyer too," responded Childers roughly.

"Ain't no lawyer within a hundred miles that's gonna defend this colored man against a charge of murdering a white woman," said Goodwin evenly. "A preacher's wife no less." Goodwin spoke with cold finality.

Childers paused then said, "There ain't no reason to let him lie there and suffer. I'm getting the doctor."

Goodwin rested his hand on the grip of the .44, and he said in a malevolent tone, "That would be a real big mistake on your part, Mr. Childers. You two men did your parts, now go on home."

Childers and Emmett stared at each other mutely for a moment then left the sheriff's office and began walking back to the smoldering ruins of the livery stable. Midway to their destination, Childers broke away, saying, "Karl, I'm going for the doctor. You go be with your missus. Goodwin tries stoppin' me, I'll shoot the son of a bitch!" Childers spoke with bitter determination.

Karl Emmett was in a state of shock from the events of the dreadful night but, when he heard Childers's words, the blacksmith drew himself back to the moment and said with remarkable calmness, "Don't do it, Harley. Goodwin's a killer. You ain't. Go tell Doc Witherspoon Harley but, stay away from Goodwin. There ain't no good that can come from it." Karl Emmett spoke in the exhausted tone of a man who had already lost too much. "If Goodwin won't let the doc treat Zeb, then word will get around soon enough, and that will be the end of Goodwin's days in Keller. I'm damn scared that Zeb's fate is plumb out of our hands, Harley."

Childers paused, amazed by his friend's ability to think reasonably in the face of the still-unfolding tragedy. He eyed the blacksmith for a few seconds, nodded slightly, then said, "You're right, Karl. After I find the doc, I'll head back over to the livery, and we'll see what we can do about the horses." Childers and Emmett looked up and saw Mrs. Emmett approaching. Childers waited for her to arrive before going to seek the doctor. "Molly, I'm just so damn sorry," was all the freighter could manage, his voice breaking.

"You saved Zebediah's life, Harley, at least for now," said Molly Emmett sadly. "We can rebuild the barn, Harley. It's Zebediah I'm worried about."

"Me too, Molly. Me too" was all Childers could manage to get out before abruptly turning away from the Emmett's and going in search of the doctor. The freighter located Dr. Witherspoon at the funeral parlor, where he expected he would be. After telling the doctor to send his bill to him, and what to expect from Goodwin, Childers excused himself and returned the smoldering remains of the livery. He found Karl and Molly Emmett standing there, holding hands and staring silently at the wreckage, she resting her head on her husband's shoulder. Childers approached his friend, laid a hand on the blacksmith's shoulder, and said kindly, "Karl, there ain't nothin' you can do tonight, why don't you go on home and try and get a little rest. I know my horses will come to me when I call 'em. My wagons are safe, and I've got spare ropes and halters in the boxes on both of 'em."

As if slowly waking from a dream, Karl Emmett turned to Childers and said mildly, "All right, Harley. If that's what you think best."

"I do, Karl. I do," said the freighter. As Mrs. Emmett began leading her husband in the direction of their home, the big blacksmith appeared to be sleepwalking, and the sight of his friend in such a state filled Childers with a terrible anger. It took all his willpower to resist returning to the sheriff's office and putting an end to Clyde Goodwin. He stood, watching silently, until the Emmett's were inside their home. As Childers turned to go in search of his horses, he was startled to see Emily Kellogg striding briskly, nearly running, in his direction.

She came quickly up to Childers and threw her arms around him and embraced him tightly, sobbing deeply and unable to speak. When at last Emily broke away, she said in a trembling voice, "Oh lord, Harley, I've never been so damn scared." She struggled to say more, but the words would not come. She buried her face in his chest and again embraced Childers with all her strength. This time he returned her embrace. They held each other for a long while until at last she drew back and said, "Let's get your horses rounded up, Harley."

After finding and haltering his horses, Childers, with Emily Kellogg's assistance, secured them until more permanent arrangements could be made. Together they walked back to the boarding house, her arms wrapped around one of his. After they entered the kitchen, Childers said, "Good night, Emily, thanks a lot for your help," and turned to go up to his room.

"Stop right where you are, Harley Childers," she said sharply.

Startled by her words and tone of voice, the freighter turned to his landlady, waiting for an explanation.

"Harley Childers, you have got to be the most thickheaded mule of a man I have ever known." Emily Kellogg's words were sharp but not angry.

After the momentous events of the evening, his landlady's words only added to the freighter's bewilderment. He could think of nothing other than standing there, staring blankly at her before finally managing to mumble, "Emily I don't—"

"I damn well *know* you don't Harley!" she said in exasperation. She paused, staring intently at the confused freighter, then laughed softly, smiled, and said in a kinder tone, "Harley, I've been waiting for you to propose to me for years, and I'm tired of waiting, so I'm asking you."

For a long, confusing moment, Childers found himself unable to speak then finally stammered, "You mean you want to git married?"

Emily Kellogg put her arms around Childers neck, kissed him solidly, and said, "I'll take that as a yes, Harley." She looked into his eyes then took him by the hand and said, "I'm moving you to a new room, starting tonight, Harley." Seeing the shock on Childers' face, she placed her hand on his cheek then looked at him and said in a very serious tone, "Harley, we're grown-ups, and we don't need anybody's permission. I can't be alone tonight, Harley. Neither one of us should be. After what happened tonight, I give less than a damn what anybody in the town of Keller thinks of me."

Chapter Thirteen

Resolution

Dawn broke reluctantly over the town of Keller. Low-hanging clouds were scudding across the dark sky, driven by a wind too strong and too cold for summer. The weather was a perfect reflection of the town's mood. Bonebright opened the store an hour late and, fearing the worst, Cyrus Hitchcock did not open the bank at all that day. All through Keller, neighbors resisted looking at one another. No one in Keller wanted to be reminded of any role they might have played in the dreadful events of the previous night. As the day wore on, Corker's saloon was the only business that saw a steady stream of customers. The drinkers were subdued and seemed to be seeking refuge from the twin tragedies, out beyond the barroom doors. In the jail, Zebediah lay on his bunk. His head was throbbing; his thoughts were random and incoherent. Zebediah's eyes were nearly swollen shut, and he could not see clearly. Goodwin had reluctantly allowed the doctor to treat Zebediah only after Witherspoon made it clear to the sheriff that there would be serious repercussions if he was not allowed in to see the prisoner. The doctor cleaned, stitched, and bandaged the worst of his wounds then determined, to his amazement, that Zebediah had suffered no broken bones from the beating.

No one living in Keller at that time would ever forget the murder of Theresa Bender and the burning of the livery stable. The most remarkable thing about the day that followed, however, was just how little actually happened. Deep gloom, made more intense by the weather, pervaded the community, and most citizens spent the day deep inside their own thoughts. Luther Boggs brooded in the book-lined study of his house, fuming, tormented by the thought that he might have done something to prevent the events of the previous evening. Emma Bonebright was distant and withdrawn and refused to speak to her husband at all that day. Richard Bender rose early and went to visit his wife's body at the funeral parlor, appearing for all the world to be the grief-stricken husband. Bender wired the dreadful news to his father-in-law, and after a rapid exchange of telegrams, it was decided that Theresa's body would be returned to the seminary for burial in the college cemetery.

With the exception of the saloon, few people were seen in the stores of Keller that day. Merchants had brief, guarded conversations with one another. News of the murder and fire spread quickly, and reporters began arriving with the first train. The newsmen found few people willing to speak of the previous night's events, and those that did speak to the reporters gave them little beyond the bare facts of the matter. The entire community was paralyzed by a combination of anger, sorrow, and guilt. It was their shared feelings that would cement the memories of the twin tragedies.

Luther Boggs did not leave his house during that long, dark day. He brooded on the injustice of everything that had happened. "Why Karl Emmett of all people?" he thought bitterly. "As decent and honest a man as I ever met. And the preacher's wife? What in the hell did she ever do to anyone?" When his cleaning lady came for her weekly visit, Boggs pleaded illness and politely asked her to come another time. Boggs had slept little, and he spent much of the day pacing back and forth, his hands clasped behind his back. At last, he decided upon a desperate course of action. What, after all, did he really have to lose? What, if anything, was his own life actually worth in the vast scheme of things? Was he a man of genuine principle, or was he simply the empty little windbag so many people in Keller thought he was? "If these hypocritical bastards will go along with hanging an innocent man, then the least I can do is risk my life trying to stop it," Boggs resolved firmly.

Boggs had his own small stable behind his house and did not make use of the livery. Therefore, his mare and buggy were untouched by the calamity. Boggs managed to get a little sleep late in the afternoon and evening then, shortly before midnight, he went out to the stable and harnessed his horse, daring only to light a small candle. When the harnessing was complete, Boggs blew out the candle and left the horse and buggy waiting inside the stable with the doors closed. Returning to his house, he took his father's solid oak shillelagh down from its place above the mantel. He put a large pair of pliers in his pocket. After easing out the back door, he quietly walked the short distance over to Main Street. Keeping well hidden, Boggs observed the sheriff's office from across the street. He saw Goodwin, apparently asleep, with his feet on the desk and his arms folded across his chest. Goodwin had, as part of his job, the use of a small apartment above the office but had apparently chosen to sleep downstairs because of the prisoner being held in the first-floor jail. "Good. Good," thought Boggs. "Just what I hoped he would be doing."

Listening carefully and taking great care not to be seen, Boggs made his way down the alley behind city hall. From his prowling, he knew the master gas valve controlling the town's streetlights was located on the back wall of the building. Boggs dearly hoped he would have enough strength to turn the valve. He had no real idea how long it would take the streetlights to burn up the gas in the lines, but he hoped it would allow him at least a half minute so that he could take up a position in a tiny alcove at the front of the sheriff's office. Boggs groped about in the darkness, not daring to risk striking a match. When he finally located the gas valve, he kept one hand on the knob then removed the pliers from his pocket. He carefully fitted the jaws of the pliers around the knob then, to his enormous relief, found that the valve turned easily. Boggs returned the pliers to his pocket then hurried to a dark spot alongside city hall, where he could wait until the lights began to fail. He had hoped it would take at least a half minute for the lights to go out, but instead, it took an agonizing five minutes for the gaslights to begin flickering. Boggs waited with rising anxiety until the last light was sputtering out then darted across the street and crouched inside the tiny alcove outside the sheriff's door. The instant the light died, Boggs reached out with the heavy end of the shillelagh and solidly slapped the front of the building with it, hoping the noise would be enough to rouse the sleeping sheriff. Then he waited.

For the first time in his life, Boggs saw his small stature as an advantage. The space he was hiding in was much too small to conceal a normal-sized man, and Boggs was betting his life that the sheriff would not think to look in his direction. As Luther had anticipated, Goodwin did not immediately take the bait. Boggs waited, focusing all his energy on the shillelagh. Boggs knew that he had but one chance to lay the sheriff low. If the blow he intended to deliver missed its target and failed to solidly connect even by a little, then this folly would likely cost him his life.

Slowly, Clyde Goodwin emerged from the sheriff's office, weapon drawn. First his head and then his body. Goodwin struggled to see in the dim light. What had he heard? He saw nothing broken. Why were the streetlights out? A problem at the gas works? It did not occur to the sheriff that the lights had been deliberately extinguished. Seeing nothing alarming, Goodwin stepped out to the middle of the sidewalk and surveyed the street, still gripping the deadly .44 in his right hand. From his crouching position, Boggs sprang, bringing the heavy knob end of the shillelagh crashing down on Goodwin's skull. The sheriff collapsed instantly. Boggs picked up the revolver and put it in his pocket then began dragging the sheriff back inside the office. Goodwin was not a large man, but it took all of Boggs' strength to drag the inert body back inside. Step by difficult step, he dragged Goodwin's body into the back, only stopping when the sheriff was in an empty cell. Boggs returned to the outer office and turned the gaslight down to where it was barely alive. He went back to the cell block then closed the door to the outer office and lit a lamp. Boggs unloaded the revolver and hid it under the mattress in an empty cell. Perspiring and breathing heavily, he removed the key ring from the sheriff's belt and, spotting an opportunity, decided to go ahead and handcuff the sheriff to the cell door for good measure. Working frantically, Boggs found the right key at last and opened Zebediah's cell. He roused the prisoner and urged him to his feet.

Boggs extinguished the light as they left the cell block. In his battered condition, Zebediah never got a clear view of the man who was helping him escape. Zebediah, in fact, did not know he was being helped to escape. In his current condition, he was capable of little more than obeying the voice urging him forward. With his strength flagging, Boggs struggled to keep the injured man upright and moving. Boggs felt naked and exposed while helping Zebediah across the street, but after what seemed an eternity, they reached the stable. Lifting with all his might, Boggs helped Zebediah up and into the buggy then, he led the mare outside and closed the barn door behind him. Driving as quietly as he could, Boggs stayed off Main Street, where his horse's shod hooves would echo off the bricks, and made for the edge of Keller through backstreets. Once beyond the town, he drove the mare as fast as he dared in the darkness. Boggs kept all his senses peeled for the sound of horses or automobiles that might be approaching from behind, but his luck was holding. On into the night he drove, and when the clouds began to break, allowing a bit of moonlight, Boggs goaded the mare into a gallop where he dared. An hour out of Keller, Boggs threw the sheriff's key ring into the darkness.

At last, Boggs halted the buggy then lit a match and looked at his watch. If he turned back now, he might just possibly have the horse and buggy back in the barn before sunrise. Boggs dismounted and walked around to the other side of the buggy. He took Zebediah by the hands and helped him down to the ground. "I've bought you a good ten or twelve-mile head start, son," said Boggs, his voice thick with emotion. "Now, you need to go on as best you can then hide yourself real good before the sun comes up."

Zebediah struggled to speak but could not. The combination of his badly swollen eyes and the faint light allowed him no clear picture of the man who had come to his aid. At last Zebediah managed a raspy "Thank you, Mister."

"No need for thanks, son." Boggs put his hands on Zebediah's shoulders and began guiding him from behind. He escorted Zebediah several paces down the road, then pointing to the distance, Boggs said, "You need to keep going that way, son. Just keep on going. Get as far as you can before sunrise, then find a place to hide. If you hear horses or automobiles coming, then get as far from the road as you can, as fast as you can. Get yourself to a rail line somewhere and catch a freight train plumb out of these parts," urged Boggs. "I've got to go now, son. Maybe I can still save my own skin, not that my skin matters very much. Good luck to you. Now get moving!"

Zebediah stood, watching silently, as Boggs turned his horse and buggy around and then vanish into the darkness. Zebediah began doing as his rescuer had urged him. He walked slowly but with determination. It hurt to walk. Everything hurt, but he had known pain before. One more step, then another and yet another. Zebediah began bargaining with himself, "I'll do ten more steps then give myself a rest." So it continued, one painful step followed by another. When the sky began to lighten, Zebediah had added another three miles to what Luther Boggs had staked him to, and he knew he must seek shelter.

As Boggs drove back to Keller, the skies continued to clear, and he settled the mare into a brisk trot. "She should be able to hold this pace all the way home," he thought. "She's going to be one hell of a sore girl tomorrow though. I just hope she doesn't go full-on lame before we see the barn. If she gets me home safe, she'll get a double ration of oats, and I'll rub down every muscle she has with liniment." Boggs viewed the improved viability as something of a mixed blessing. While it was allowing him to travel faster and safer, it would be doing the same for the sheriff's posse that would surely be coming in pursuit of the prisoner. As Boggs drew closer to Keller, his anxiety grew into a molten ball of lead in his stomach. He was near, very near, to having pulled it off. If his luck could only hold a little longer.

Luther Boggs closed his barn door behind him as the first predawn light was appearing in the eastern sky. He unhitched the horse and poured out oats as the mare drank heavily from the trough. Boggs dried his horse thoroughly while she ate then left her covered with a blanket before departing. Had he been seen? He could only assume that he had. It would be foolish for him to think otherwise, and it would only be a matter of time before they came for him. Then it struck him that there was, perhaps, some advantage in being thought of as an eccentric. There was nothing unusual about him being seen out and about, with or without his horse, at odd hours. "Maybe someone saw me and they just thought it was me being an old coot," he mused. Boggs smiled inwardly at the prospect but stopped well short of actually believing it. Luther Boggs was physically and mentally spent. The night's exertion, coupled with his lack of sleep, was weighing on him heavily, but he had more to do before he rested. After carefully washing away any trace of Goodwin's blood remaining on the shillelagh, he returned it to its place above the mantle. Boggs then slipped back outside and walked over to Main Street, where he could venture a peek at the sheriff's office. What he saw amazed him. He saw nothing. There was no activity at the sheriff's office whatsoever. "Oh my god," said Boggs slowly and incredulously under his breath, "I may have done it."

Emily Kellogg discovered Clyde Goodwin handcuffed and semiconscious when she arrived with the prisoner's breakfast at 7:00 a.m. Unable to open the cell door, Emily ran in search of help and the doctor. She stuck her head into Bonebright's store long enough to call out to the grocer that the sheriff had been attacked. This piece of news flew down Main Street at the speed of the wind, and by the time Mrs. Kellogg returned with Witherspoon, there were a number of men in the sheriff's office, none of whom immediately realized that the prisoner had escaped. They could not find the key ring, and it took over an hour for the rescuers to get the cell door open and Goodwin free of the handcuffs. Dr. Witherspoon got Goodwin into a sitting position, and the sheriff was struggling to speak. There was blood on the floor and on Goodwin's clothing. After Witherspoon's initial examination, Goodwin was carried to the doctor's office, where he could be treated more effectively. The doctor cleaned Goodwin's scalp thoroughly, sutured the laceration, and bandaged the wound. Through it all, Goodwin rambled incoherently. The doctor and the others in attendance made nothing of his repeatedly calling out, "Dooley, you son of a bitch!"

Addressing no one in particular, Dr. Witherspoon said, "I don't know who Dooley is, but I don't think the sheriff likes him much. He's clearly suffering from a concussion, and I'm pretty sure he has a skull fracture. If I had one of those new x-ray machines, I could tell for sure."

"Is he going to be all right?" asked Bonebright.

"That's a good question," said the doctor. "It could go either way. It's normal for a person to be confused and disoriented after a bad head injury. We need to keep him awake and watch him. I'll have a better idea as to the prognosis in a few hours."

By mid morning, Goodwin had begun to rally, and by noon, the sheriff was determined to leave and go in pursuit of the escaped prisoner. Witherspoon tried, without success, to dissuade his patient, but Goodwin was resolved to go in search of Zebediah. It was clear to everyone in the room that Goodwin was not thinking clearly, but no one was bold enough to attempt physically restraining the sheriff. In spite of his inability to think clearly, Goodwin had sufficient presence of mind to realize that he would need at least two search parties, as they had no idea as to the prisoner's direction of travel. It was mid afternoon before the two groups could be organized and deputized, but before they could depart, the weather intervened. A massive storm, the likes of which had never been seen in the area, rolled across the prairies and the town of Keller. Torrential rain driven by fierce winds made travel impossible. While the deputized citizens of Keller waited for the weather to clear, Zebediah drew his knees to his chest and huddled beneath the bridge where he had taken refuge.

The huge storm would periodically lift only to see another front come racing in behind the last one and deliver another barrage of wind, rain, and lightning. By the time the horses and automobiles were away from Keller, a full day had elapsed, and no one expected to find Zebediah alive, if at all. The enormous amount of rain had wiped out all traces of his trail. Goodwin attempted to employ a citizen's coonhounds in the search, but not even their hypersensitive noses could pick up any scent. It was determined that one party would head generally eastward while the other would go west, along the rail line. Both parties would ride in ever-widening circles to the north and south of the tracks. If either party picked up the trail, they were to wait while one of their members went to get the rest of the searchers. The zeal of the search parties ebbed steadily as the day wore on. Given time to reflect, few of the searchers believed Zebediah was responsible for the murder of Theresa Bender. The mood of the search parties had shifted from blood lust to wanting to capture Zebediah alive and ensure he received a fair trial. If the sense of urgency was lifting among the searchers, bringing Zebediah to justice had grown into a psychotic obsession for Clyde Goodwin.

In Goodwin's confused state, Zebediah was not only the killer of Theresa Bender; he was also the person responsible for the brutal pain in his head. Goodwin cared little about Theresa Bender or who might have killed her, but he cared a great deal about the person who had cracked his skull, and in his mind, that person could only be Zebediah. He would find him and he would take his revenge. He would either kill him or bring him in, whichever proved to be the easiest, and he was leaning toward killing him. Goodwin's mind was not completely addled; in a moment of clarity, he suddenly remembered the first time he had seen Zebediah as he emerged from beneath the railroad bridge on that frosty morning. "That's where the son of a bitch will be hiding! He's beat up too bad to get very far, and he's in no shape to hop a freight train either!" thought the sheriff triumphantly. This revelation left Goodwin about as near to happiness as he ever came. He gave orders to all the members of the search parties to pay special attention to bridges, and if they found the escapee, they were to wait for him and not attempt to capture him themselves.

It was just after daybreak on the second morning of the search when word reached Clyde Goodwin that Zebediah had been spotted—asleep, unconscious, or possibly dead—under a bridge, just as the sheriff had predicted. Spurring his horse, Goodwin rode full tilt in the direction of Zebediah's hiding place, with other members of the search party struggling to keep up. If Zebediah was cornered, what, they all wondered, was the rush? Spending over twenty-four hours in the saddle had not helped the pain in Clyde Goodwin's head. The pain had become an intense, blinding thing that would have driven an ordinary man to his bed. Goodwin now knew beyond doubt that only by killing Zebediah could he make the pain go away.

Goodwin raced up to where a group of searchers had gathered. The men were waiting quietly, looking down into the ravine where Zebediah lay in the sand, below the bridge. The sheriff vaulted off his heavily lathered horse, snatching a rifle from its scabbard as he leapt. Goodwin had in his hands not the Winchester carbine but the .440-caliber Henry. The sheriff rushed to the edge of the ravine and studied Zebediah carefully. "He's breathing," said the sheriff. Goodwin chambered a round and, before anyone could stop him, took aim and fired into the planking above Zebediah's head. The roar of the Henry and the splintering wood roused Zebediah from his stupor. In spite of his weakened condition, Zebediah was instantly on his feet. The swelling around his eyes had eased enough that he could clearly see the sheriff's rifle leveled at him.

"Don't move a muscle," bellowed Goodwin, his voice reduced to a raspy howl. All the brutal pain in Goodwin's head was now being channeled down the barrel of the rifle he had pointed at Zebediah's chest.

Zebediah paused, balanced on the edge of a precipice, then in an instant, he decided to dive into the water. He managed a half step in the direction of the swollen stream, then the Henry spoke again and Zebediah felt no more.

Zebediah got to his feet and dusted off his overalls. Uncle Zeke put his hand on Zebediah's shoulder and said, "C'mon along, Zeb, milkin's done, time to git washed up for supper." Zebediah thought it odd, but not unpleasant, to find that he was a small boy again. As they carried the milk to the screen porch for separating, Zeke said mischievously, "Aunt Mary's got a li'l surprise waitin' for ya, Zeb."

"A surprise?" asked Zebediah eagerly. "What is it?"

Zeke laughed and said, "Well now, if I was to tell ya, then it wouldn't be a surprise, would it?"

Zebediah smiled up at his uncle, laughed, and said, "You s'pose we could walk a li'l faster, Uncle Zeke?"

"Well, we could, but we don't want to spill the milk, so we better take it easy," teased his uncle, who began walking even slower.

The normally short walk in from the barn now seemed very long to Zebediah as his anticipation built. When they reached the door at last, he was greeted there by Aunt Mary, who scooped him up in her arms, squeezed him tightly, and said excitedly, "Zeb, I need you to come in here and see somethin'." After kissing his cheek, she put him down then led Zebediah by the hand into the kitchen. There, gathered around the table, sat Johnny and Clarice Pike, Harley Childers, Judah Parsons, Karl Emmett, and D. "Can you believe it, Zeb? All these friends o' yours dropped by for supper! They all said this was the perfect day for it."

The heavy bullet caught Zebediah squarely in the chest and sent him flying violently backward. For a moment, Zebediah stood, propped against the bridge abutment, his swollen eyes wide open. Then he pitched forward onto the sand and did not move again. Goodwin immediately levered another round into the Henry and made ready to fire again when one of the searchers bravely grabbed the barrel of the rifle and pointed it skyward. "Good God, Sheriff, he's dead!" cried the man. Had Goodwin not been in his own weakened and confused condition, such an action might well have cost the man his life. Instead, Goodwin could only manage to stare vacantly at the man holding on to the barrel of the rifle.

The standoff continued for several tense seconds, then Goodwin relaxed and said, "Okay, some of you men get down there and carry him up." No one moved, then Goodwin said loudly, "You heard me, now get down there and get him!"

The man holding the barrel of the Henry was a well-respected rancher named Dawkins. Dawkins continued to keep the barrel of the Henry firmly pointed skyward but used his free hand to remove his deputy's badge then drop it at Goodwin's feet. One by one, all the men in the search party followed suit and tossed their badges to the ground as well. Dawkins, then proceeded to jerk the rifle away from Goodwin while another man relieved the sheriff of his sidearm. "We signed up to help catch an escaped prisoner, Goodwin, we didn't sign up to commit murder," said Dawkins angrily.

"Do you sons of bitches think you're gonna arrest me?" asked Goodwin belligerently.

"Only if you force us to, Sheriff," said Dawkins.

Trying to regain control of the situation, Goodwin said venomously, "You men need to get down there and get that body carried up. Now!"

Again, no one moved. By stepping forward when he did, Dawkins became the leader of the posse without intending to. At last Dawkins said, "Sheriff, that man would have come up on his own, but you chose to shoot him. If you want him up out of that gully, then you do it yourself. I've got chores waitin' at home, and these other men do too. I'll let the undertaker know."

One member of the search party removed the Winchester from Goodwin's saddle, and having collected all the sheriff's weapons, the men then mounted their horses and cranked their automobiles to life. They rode and drove slowly away while Goodwin screamed curses after them. The sheriff watched until all the searchers were out of sight then set about the task of removing Zebediah's body from the ravine. Goodwin's reason had completely deserted him. The pain did not end with Zebediah's death and confusion and pain were piled layer upon layer in the sheriff's tormented mind. He looked up from the ravine, and there, across the bridge, stood his father. Dooley was leaning against the railing with his arms folded across his chest, laughing at him. Clyde Goodwin drew the .44 and leveled it at his father, but it refused to fire no matter how many times he pulled the trigger. Dooley then slapped his knee and laughed all the louder, finally calling out, "What you gonna do now? You dumb son of a bitch!"

Goodwin ran across the bridge and struck Dooley full in the face with all his strength. The pain in his head was temporarily displaced by a white-hot river running from his hand to his shoulder. For several terrible, pain-filled seconds, the world around Clyde Goodwin flashed white to red and back again until at last, he came near enough to reality to realize he had struck the iron framework of the bridge. Clyde looked around wildly then spotted his father standing some distance away, watching, bent over with laughter at his son's agony. Dooley stopped laughing then shook his head with disgust and said, "You always was a dumb son of a bitch, Clyde." His father then turned away and vanished slowly into the trees behind him. The world around Clyde Goodwin began to spin faster and faster until he was no longer able to stand. He collapsed into a sitting position, leaning against the framework of the bridge. Dusk was approaching by the time Goodwin regained enough of himself to get back to his feet again.

Goodwin walked to the edge of the ravine, where he could see Zebediah's body. He thought for a moment then caught his horse and led it to the far side of the bridge. Goodwin threw his coiled rope down near the body then worked his way down to Zebediah. He tied one end of the rope around Zebediah's feet then climbed back out of the gully with the rope. Goodwin looped the rope around his saddle horn and began pulling Zebediah's body by the feet up out of the rocky ravine. A sane and rational man would have ridden to Keller and returned with the undertaker and a wagon, but Clyde Goodwin was far from either. Once he had Zebediah's battered corpse back to the road, he shortened up on the rope and began dragging the body in the direction of Keller. He didn't go far. Even in the fading light, the sight of the battered corpse being dragged along the roadway was too much, even for Clyde Goodwin. Abandoning his plan, Goodwin pulled the corpse off the road and back near the creek. Then, he began gathering wood from along the ravine.

When the news of Zebediah's death reached Karl Emmett and Harley Childers, they immediately set about building a coffin, using boards salvaged from the wreckage of the livery stable. It didn't take long for the two men to complete the plain wooden box intended for their friend. When the coffin was finished, they loaded it into the back of one of Childers' wagons, and they set off to find Zebediah. What they discovered a few hours later horrified them. The two men saw the flames from a distance, and when they drove up to investigate, they found Clyde Goodwin sitting next to the fire, gazing impassively into the flames. Within the flames, they could just make out the outline of what remained of Zebediah. Goodwin looked up at the two men, stared at them vacantly for a moment, and said, "I thought burnin' that boy might get the pain to stop, but it ain't workin'." Then he turned his attention back to the fire, scarcely aware of their presence.

Childers hurried back to the wagon and reached under the seat for the ten gauge, but before he could return, Karl Emmett settled the matter. Goodwin stood and began snickering at the blacksmith, saying, "Yer colored boy ain't havin' a real good day, Emmett." Goodwin paused a moment then began to laugh loudly, directly into the face of Karl Emmett. The laughter was short lived. The blacksmith's mighty right hand, fueled by all that had happened, drove deep into Goodwin's midsection, followed an instant later by a crushing uppercut that nearly separated Goodwin's head from his body.

Childers ran back to the fire, struck dumb by what he had just witnessed. When Goodwin did not move, Childers bent down and felt for a pulse. He then looked up at the blacksmith and said, "I think you killed him, Karl."

"I don't relish killin', Harley, but if ever a man deserved it, it was him," said Karl Emmett, outwardly unfazed by what he had just done.

Neither man spoke for a long time as they looked at the dying fire and then back to where Goodwin lay. At last Childers asked, "What do you think we should do, Karl?"

"Do ya think Zebediah would mind having company, Harley?" asked the blacksmith.

"Company?" asked Childers.

"Well, we built a good-sized coffin, and what's left of Zeb ain't gonna take up much room. It would save us digging two graves."

Childers thought about the blacksmith's idea a moment then said thoughtfully, "I'm pretty sure Zeb's beyond caring if he has company or not, and it would save a lot of digging." Childers paused then deadpanned, "You always was one to shirk hard work Karl."

Karl Emmett sighed and said mildly, "I wasn't always a shirker, Harley. I think it comes from associating with a man who spends his days sittin' on a wagon seat, starin' at horses' butts." Emmett paused then looked directly at Childers and continued. "It's taken a toll on me, Harley." An outsider would have been baffled or even shocked by the exchange between the blacksmith and the freighter. Had Zebediah overheard them, he would have known the healing had begun.

Childers and Emmett loaded Goodwin's body in the coffin first then scattered what remained of the fire. Working by the light of a candle lantern, they carefully shoveled Zebediah's charred remains in on top of Goodwin. Neither man enjoyed the task. Each man reminded the other that Zebediah was beyond caring and that the man they knew had ceased to be, the moment Goodwin's rifle bullet tore through his chest. The two friends supported each other through the awful task until they were satisfied that no part of Zebediah remained on the ground. They nailed the lid of the coffin shut and loaded the box onto the wagon. Before they left the scene, they caught Goodwin's horse and tied it to the back of the wagon. Childers drove his team down the road for some distance, then turned out on to the prairie. They had no destination in mind; they simply knew they would recognize the proper place when they came to it.

They ambled slowly across the prairie in the moonlight until they crested a ridge and saw the high bridge outside Keller, ghostly in the distance. Childers halted the wagon and looked over to the blacksmith. Emmett nodded his head in approval and said, "Zeb always seemed to have a thing about bridges, Harley."

The two men dismounted. Childers unsaddled Goodwin's horse then gave it a hard whack with his quirt, sending the horse racing across the prairie. They walked around for a few minutes, then Childers jammed his spade into the earth and looked at Emmett, asking silently if this was the place. Emmett again nodded his agreement. They unloaded the coffin and marked out the area that would be the grave then sat the coffin aside. They worked together at first, and as the grave got deeper, they took turns. When they were satisfied with the depth, Emmett spoke for the first time since the digging began. "Harley, how in the hell are we going to get the coffin down there without just dropping it?"

"I'm way ahead of you, Karl. As usual," rumbled Childers. The freighter went to the toolbox on the side of the freight wagon and returned with two heavy iron stakes. "There ain't always something available to tie up to, so you have to be prepared," said the freighter as he began driving the stakes into the ground alongside the grave. Childers tied one end of a stout rope to each stake then stretched the ropes across the grave. Childers unhitched the single tree from the wagon then maneuvered the horses to where they were, facing away from the grave, then he secured the middle of the rope to the single tree. Childers walked the horses forward until the ropes across the grave were taut.

"You're a damn sight smarter than I ever gave you credit for, Harley," said the blacksmith with a touch of admiration.

"There's something to be said for spending time staring at horses' butts, Karl."

Together, they carefully sat the coffin on top of the ropes then stepped back. Childers gently coaxed his horses backward, allowing the coffin to be lowered smoothly into the grave. When the coffin was resting on the bottom, they untied the ropes from the stakes, and the horses easily pulled the ropes free. Before filling in the grave, Goodwin's saddle and all of the sheriff's gear were thrown down on top of the coffin. The vast prairie was being bathed in a glorious sunrise as they added the last shovel of dirt to the grave. Tired and emotionally drained, the two men leaned on their shovels and spent a long time, looking at the mound of earth. At last Emmett asked, "Do you think we should say a few words, Harley?"

Childers growled, "I don't know what the hell for, Karl. If there's a hereafter, then I don't need to tell anybody that a good man came their way." The freighter paused a moment then went back to the wagon, returning with a bottle of whiskey and two tin cups. He poured out a generous measure for each of them. The two men lifted their cups to the grave then, tossed the whiskey back. Having committed Zebediah to the earth, Childers and Emmett remounted the wagon and began the return to Keller. They were in no hurry, and Childers set a roundabout course that took them well away from the town before he turned back toward Keller. The added distance gave them time to finish the whiskey and wash some of the awful night away, if only for a while. They did not want to be seen coming from the grave site. The location of Zebediah's final resting place would be something they would take to their own graves.

After receiving the word late in the day, the undertaker decided to wait until daylight to go in search of Zebediah's remains. When Bradshaw and two assistants reached the bridge at mid morning the following day, they found neither Zebediah nor any sign of Clyde Goodwin. They wrote the pile of ashes off to a lightning strike. Bradshaw duly reported this information to the authorities in Keller. Those men who had been at the scene of Zebediah's shooting agreed that not returning Clyde Goodwin to Keller had been a mistake on their part, given the sheriff's state of mind. In time it came to be generally held that Goodwin had probably just ridden off. They thought that, perhaps, the still-rising water had carried Zebediah's body away. Though few people ever dared criticize the sheriff directly when he was alive and in Keller, his sudden absence was like a burden being lifted from the shoulders of the community. It was the first piece of modestly good news the town of Keller had heard in what seemed a long time. Like his father before him, Clyde Goodwin's departure from the world would not be seriously investigated.

A coroner's jury was duly called and sworn. No one serving on that jury wanted the proceedings to last a minute longer than absolutely necessary. The town of Keller had seen enough, and they wanted only to put the matter behind them. The proceedings lasted less than two hours. The jury's decision read:

> "A colored man, known as Zebediah, last name, if any, unknown, is hereby deemed to have been responsible for the murder, and possible rape, of Mrs. Theresa Bender. Said colored man, Zebediah, then did forcibly escape from jail, inflicting serious bodily harm to the, then-serving, sheriff, Clyde Goodwin, during his escape. Sheriff Goodwin, a sworn officer of the law, was subsequently left without option when he killed the colored man Zebediah as he attempted to avoid arrest. This jury also finds it likely that the body of the escapee, Zebediah, was washed away by flood waters before it could be recovered."

The members of the jury knew there were many unanswered questions, but none of them had even the slightest desire to find those answers.

Jim Dawkins, the rancher who had bravely stood up to Goodwin at the scene of the shooting, reluctantly agreed to fill the position of sheriff until a permanent replacement could be found. Unlike his predecessor, Dawkins would not be bought off by the moonshiners, and to the great relief of Charles Bonebright and John Corker, the illegal-whiskey business soon collapsed. Dawkins proved to be the solid, reliable man that is the bedrock of any community. For the rest of his life, he would be called upon to fill a series of local political offices, including two terms in the state legislature.

Emma Bonebright and her daughters left Keller a few weeks after the murder of Theresa Bender, never to return. A year later, she filed for divorce, and her husband did not contest the action. Charles Bonebright sold his home and moved back to the apartment above the grocery. He used the money from the sale of his house to retire the mortgage on his store and, for the first time in his life, achieved a degree of financial independence. Even after paying Emma substantial amounts of alimony, he had money left over. Sadly, the freedom he had craved for so long did not translate into happiness for the grocer. As time passed, Bonebright began to see his failed marriage and the loss of his family as living proof of his overall failure as a human being. Bonebright began drinking ever more heavily, and within two years, he found himself back in debt to Cyrus Hitchcock. Four years to the day after the murder of Theresa Bender, Charles Bonebright died from acute alcohol poisoning.

To those who knew Karl Emmett only through their business dealings, little about the blacksmith seemed to have changed. He was as pleasant and amiable as ever. Harley Childers and others who knew him well, understood that something important had passed out of the blacksmith. After the fire, Emmett made a feeble attempt to rebuild, but his heart wasn't in it. The town of Keller had poisoned itself in the mind of Karl Emmett for all time. A year after the fire, the Emmett's sold their property and moved to a town a hundred miles from Keller. They had insurance money from the fire, the proceeds from the sale of their property, and the money they had carefully saved over the years. The Emmett's kept a big garden, and Karl would occasionally do work for other blacksmiths during their peak seasons, always turning down their offers of full-time employment. Throughout the rest of his life, Karl Emmett would receive unsigned letters from Keller. The letters would express sorrow and often contained money. Some letters contained only a dollar, while others had five—and ten-dollar bills enclosed. Karl's first response was to give the money away, but his wife said no. "If people want to say they're sorry, Karl, then the least you can do is spend their money," said Molly Emmett.

A month after the twin tragedies, Harley Childers and Emily Kellogg were married by the justice of the peace, attended by Karl and Molly Emmett. Shaking his friend's hand and clapping him on the shoulder, the blacksmith said, "Well, Harley, it's about time you made it legal. Folks was startin' to talk."

For once, the freighter found himself without a response and could only laugh at his friend's remark. Mrs. Childers, however, spoke up immediately. She punched the blacksmith on the shoulder playfully and said, "Let the bastards talk, Karl, just let 'em talk."

Though they married late in life, it was to be a happy marriage, enduring until the freighter's death nearly twenty years later. Following their marriage, Harley Childers was only too willing to let his new wife take over his finances. Keeping books had never been anything he cared much about. He earned money, he put it in the bank, he spent what he needed to keep his business running, and his personal needs were few. Emily was sorting through Harley's tangled records when she looked up and across the table to her husband and said, "Harley, are you even dimly aware that you're a rich man?"

"Rich?" asked Childers. "What do you mean *rich*?"

"I mean rich, as in having enough money that you only work if you want to. Or in your case, too mule-headed to know any better," said his wife, laughing. "If I'd had any idea you had this kind of money, I'd have doubled your rent a long time ago."

"Now, don't be saying bad things about mules, Emily. I earned a lot of that money with mules I'll have you know, and besides, I'm living here for free now." Childers chuckled.

"Yes and no, Harley," she said archly and with a smile as she held up her hand and displayed her wedding band. "Yes and no."

Emily laid out his finances to him, and along with her own property, she made it clear to him that they had no further need to work. It proved to be an easy sell. He was tired of the heavy lifting, tired of being out in the weather, and was ready for a change. They sold the boarding house along with all of Harley's horses, mules, and freight wagons. Then, they too moved away from Keller, settling near Karl and Molly Emmett. Mr. and Mrs. Childers were not reckless spenders by any means, but they thoroughly enjoyed their money in the years that followed, traveling all around the country and once to Europe.

Zebediah's death had a devastating effect on Luther Boggs. His initial happiness at having effected Zebediah's escape was soon replaced by enormous guilt at having possibly facilitated Zebediah's murder at the hands of Clyde Goodwin. The events went back and forth in his mind, and there were days when he could nearly convince himself that he had given Zebediah his only chance, even if it failed. Then, he would come back to thinking that he should have used his considerable financial resources to pay for Zebediah's defense while making sure the matter of Theresa Bender's murder was properly investigated. But then again, events of that terrible time were moving too fast. There was never enough time to mount a defense. Boggs would never be able to free himself completely from the torment. He was not finished with the town of Keller, however. Boggs had one more blow to deliver. Eight years after the murder, the country found itself in the midst of a widespread financial panic. When he judged the crises to be at its worst, Boggs suddenly withdrew all his money from Hitchcock's bank, sending it into receivership.

Richard Bender departed Keller two days after murdering his wife. He escorted Theresa's body back to the seminary and played the role of the grieving spouse with great success. He tearfully asked his father-in-law for reassignment, saying it would simply be too difficult for him to continue on in Keller. The bishop promptly granted his request. Bender returned to Keller only long enough to vacate the parsonage, retrieve his lock-box, and tidy up his affairs. The bishop assigned Bender to a large church in the city near the seminary. The position to which he was assigned was as an assistant pastor but, it was seen as an excellent position and held the promise of advancement. The position as an assistant was expected to last from three to five years, at which time the presiding pastor was to retire. Bender was, however, made pastor less than two years into his assignment, when the man he was serving under died unexpectedly, in his sleep. The church did not allow its ministers to marry divorced women but, when Emma Bonebright became a widow, she soon married Richard Bender. Bender was next promoted to the position of rector of the seminary chapel and, ten years later, elected bishop of the synod.

Made in the USA
Lexington, KY
30 October 2013